Previio in the Luna

Spokane Words, Book 1

"Lost Soul" Raychelle Carter often escapes her uninspiring home life in Santa Monica, California, to check in at a virtual bar. The Last Chance Saloon visitors are encouraged to confess secrets and plot lies. Stories are written and read, but communication between guests is not possible… in theory.

Coerced by her overbearing mother into a loveless engagement, and helped by her friend Sofie to dump (P)Rick, Raychelle shares her misery online. Moving forward, she relies on guidance from Luna, the resident virtual astrologer, and becomes increasingly intrigued with tales posted by the "Haunted Man."

Raychelle encounters that moniker again while at a Las Vegas conference, which leads her into a dubious encounter with an enigmatic musical stranger. He takes her on a twisted journey leading her into his dark past, and to a crossroads where reality and cyber space converge.

A Twisted Tale from Luna's Attic

Twice Dead

A Twisted Tale from Luna's Attic

Twice Dead

Cheryl Cocroft

cherylcocroft@gmail.com

A Twisted Tale from Luna's Attic
Twice Dead

Volume Two in the Luna's Attic series

©2019 Cheryl Cocroft

All rights reserved. No portion of this book may be reproduced in any form without permission from the publisher, except as permitted by U.S. copyright law.

Spokane Tales Publications
Cave Creek, AZ
cherylcocroft@gmail.com

ISBN: 9781698550466 (paperback)
Library of Congress Control Number: 2019916029

Book Shepherd: Ann Narcisian Videan, ANVidean.com

Cover art/design: Consuelo Parra
www.facebook.com/C.PBookCoverdesigns
Model Mirish.DeviantArt
Background: Ashensorrow.DeviantArt

Dedication

For Taylar, Raychelle, and Harley.
It's about time you three got together,
your reunion is long overdue.

Table of Contents

1.	Missing You	1
2.	Unwelcome Guest	15
3.	Trick or Treat	27
4.	Raw Honey	39
5.	Café Noir	51
6.	Black Bears	63
7.	Who Are You?	71
8.	Don't Look Back	79
9.	Bubble Bath	89
10.	Blind Panic	99
11.	Hibiscus, Darling	109
12.	That Hat Thing	119
13.	Petals & Pearls	129
14.	Razor Cut	141
15.	Totally Wrecked	147
16.	Identity Crisis	157
17.	Road to Nowhere	165
18.	Wiped Out	177
19.	No Accident	185
20.	Passport Control	197
21.	Evidently Not	205
22.	Dead Roses	213
23.	She Is Me	219
24.	China Sea	229
25.	So Long, Raychelle	237
26.	Raychelle's Reflection	249
27.	Mystery Tour	257
28.	Dead End	269
29.	Halloween Ball	277
30.	Las Vegas, Baby	287
	Acknowledgments	297
	About the Author	299

1. Missing You

Steely Dan blasts out from the radio on the kitchen windowsill and, even though I can't sing, it doesn't stop me from joining in and mangling the words to "Do It Again." With no one around to hear the tuneless racket, apart from Butch, my cat, I perform with wild abandon while he continues to sleep. A strategically placed limb pins his ears forward and covers his eyes, ensuring neither sight nor sound will disturb his slumber.

Just like the lyrics, I find myself back in Vegas—reminiscing about Kaleb—with a handle in my hand. It's a knife handle, though, not a one-armed bandit. Carried away by the music, I wave the blade around and slash the air. I carve out fantastical shapes and find the pepper mill is an excellent substitute for maracas.

The song ends and I return to the kitchen counter and the task at hand. I'm preparing a Thai green curry for Kaleb, and with it comes a subliminal message meant to impress. By creating his favorite meal, I intend to increase my appeal, and stimulate more than just his appetite for food. So, this dish must look, smell, and taste divine; nothing less than perfection will suffice.

The telephone rings. With Kaleb at the forefront of my thoughts I dash down the hallway and snatch the phone. "Hi, Raych, here… Hello… Hello." A baby cries in the background, and the line goes dead. I replace the receiver and wait a moment. Wrong number, I conclude—probably a stressed-out mom punching the wrong button.

Back in the kitchen, with the ingredients laid out before me, I set to work.

Happily slicing through bamboo shoots, I realize my usual tense expression has been replaced with a placid smile. A rush of excitement floods my body as I examine the cause. The apparition of Kaleb standing on my front doorstep yesterday evening was both shocking and thrilling.

After several weeks of no contact, I'd convinced myself I'd irrevocably screwed things up between us and would never see him again. Desperate to lure him back, I had consulted *Love Magic, Potions & Spells*, and cast a spell to conjure my heart's desire.

As if by magic, Kaleb materialized from nowhere and casually strolled back into my life. Like a talented sorceress, my deepest wish was granted, and I was rewarded with the ultimate prize.

His miraculous appearance almost had me believing I possessed supernatural magical abilities, and I'd like to attribute his return to my skill at practicing the ancient art of "love magic," but as usual he's one step ahead of me and readily confessed to playing me at my own game. I should know better than to assume anything he does is spontaneous or innocent.

Of course, he's forgiven, and now he's back, I'm determined to go the extra mile and do all I can to keep him enthralled. Later on, when he's finished eating his delicious meal, I will pour him some whiskey, and serve myself up for dessert.

Luckily, I have all the time in the world to prepare this feast. Since quitting my job a few weeks ago, my time's my own. So earlier this afternoon, I leisurely scoured the Asian Emporium on Wilshire and hunted down the freshest items: a plump-breasted organic chicken, aromatic basil I sampled before buying, and cute baby eggplants. Afterwards, I dropped by the seafood market for prawns straight off the fishing boats. Examining them now, they feel plump and juicy.

Kaleb's due home about seven, so there's no rush. He's currently working on his band's latest album *Lost Vegas Rocks* at a recording studio in West Hollywood. He's the creative force behind Torment Loves Company, but his heart's no longer in it since longtime friend and bandmate Jake MacClintock died from an accidental heroin overdose. The tragedy occurred two months ago but Carl, the group's manager, wants the remaining band members, Kaleb and Ryder, back in the studio.

He told Kaleb, "A rock 'n' roll death is great for sales… We need to roll with it, guys, and reap the rewards."

Carl's quick to dismiss the incident and move on, having already forgotten how Kaleb was wrongly accused and arrested for controlled substance homicide.

A voice from the radio reminds me, "You are listening to Ocean Rock, Santa Monica's number one station." Through the patio doors, the distant pier invites me to stroll out along the boardwalk and stand defiantly over the Pacific Ocean. "Here's a teaser from Torment Loves Company's latest album. Remember, you heard it here first. "Hooker's Eyes," for all you green-eyed girls out there… this is exclusively for you."

The DJ's words cause a tantalizing shiver. On the chopping board, the chicken is centered and ready for dissection. Butch raises his head, sniffs the air, but for once sleep takes priority over food. Kaleb's seductive voice travels across the airwaves and hits me head on.

"She looks at me with dark green eyes.
Love and longing, she gently sighs.
She's scared and wary, no surprise.
Hints of lust and wild desires.
She's got Hooker's eyes,
The deepest green you've ever seen,
A green so deep it's evergreen.

I'm the reason she hates the dark.
The reason she avoids the park.
She sees the woods, but she can't see me.
I'm the tree she cannot see.
I'm the shadow and the big dark cloud,
The wolf who tracks her through the crowd.
She looks behind, but she can't see me.

She sees the forest but not the tree.
Eyes so green like a forest fir.
Fur and skin make me think of her.
Her cautious stare and her awkward stance,

She's unsure about our wild romance.
She's got Hooker's eyes.
The deepest green you've ever seen.
A green so deep it's evergreen.

The sea-glass glint of a lover's glance.
The steps and moves of our courting dance.
Her eyes are green as drowning dreams.
Oceans and rivers, and forest streams.
She's got Hooker's eyes
The deepest green you've ever seen.
A green so deep it's evergreen."

Poised with a ten-inch steel knife, hovering over the chicken's fleshy breast, the DJ asks, "I wonder who Kaleb Hausser had in mind, when he wrote this little ditty?"

I pause and recall Kaleb's words from last night as we lay in bed. "Staring into your eyes is like being lost in the forest."

Smug as hell and with a tight smile, I continue with my culinary preparations.

I stab the knife into the chicken's breastbone and hack through cartilage and bone, all the while thinking about these past few months and the crazy chain of events that led me to Kaleb. From our first online encounter at The Last Chance Saloon—a virtual bar—to last night, and him assuming the role as my personal bodyguard. After hearing how'd I'd been assaulted in this house by my ex-boss, he decided he was moving in, and I offered absolutely no resistance whatsoever.

I dare to think about the future—our future—and my mind races away. It's still early days, but Kaleb makes me feel like the one. I must keep myself in check, though, and not get carried away. Although, deep down, I know it's already too late for restraint, I'm a long way down the river and on the brink of being washed out to sea.

Fantasizing about Kaleb is a welcome distraction from the mounting stockpile of worries stacking up behind me, which threaten to bury me under the crush. Instead of losing myself in a dreamy future, I should prioritize, and focus on the actual tasks directly ahead, but I don't know where to start. No longer pining for Kaleb reduces the stress, but I'm anxious about the future, everything is so unsettled.

During the past year, every aspect of my life has been turned upside down. Where? When? How did it unravel? I guess it started with an ending. The ending of my pretend relationship with then boyfriend, Rick, followed by a series of unfortunate events. My promising new job turned out to be a contract with a sexual predator, culminating in a serious assault. My father died from cancer, and three months later my mother succumbed to a fatal car accident.

Just thinking about these past events stirs up a storm of raw emotion. I look at the kitchen clock and decide five-twenty is not too early for a drink. It's at times like this, I miss stopping by The Last Chance Saloon. Normally, I'd grab a glass of wine and log in on their website, but the bar is closed. The barroom doors have been boarded up and a sign nailed across the planks reads *"Gone Away."*

The virtual bar was hailed as an outpost for the lost and lonely, a hideaway for the disillusioned and desperate... for people like me. A place where I could pour my heart out and offload my worries. I adopted the moniker "Lost Soul," as using my real name, Raychelle, was not permitted. At the same time, Kaleb was masquerading as the "Haunted Man," and divulging heart-wrenching tales about his traumatic childhood.

"Talking" to Absinthe, the gay, green-clad bartender became a welcome escape, and it was there where I confessed my "Boyfriend Rick" problem online, and described the farce that ensued when I dumped him. My mad antics caught Kaleb's attention, and he orchestrated a carefully engineered strategy to track me down. That fact, I only became fully aware of last night, when he explained how The Last Chance Saloon was his brainchild. A place conjured from his wild imagination and convincingly brought to life by bandmate Ryder's technical expertise. I also learned that Luna, the virtual bar's resident astrologer, whose predictions I religiously followed, was another of Kaleb's personas. He confessed to being the lunatic in Luna's Attic and to stringing me along.

He cyber-stalked me. Creepy, I know, but who cares... I'm in love with my creeper.

I raise my glass. "Cheers to that." And I knock back the contents.

Bob Seger's "Night Moves," prompts me to crank the radio a few notches and shimmy around the kitchen.

I belt out "night moves," and hack at the air like some crazed killer whilst remembering a few night moves I performed with Kaleb last night. "Night moves!"

Butch releases an ear, opens an eye and gives me a judgmental look. I return to the chopping board and continue slicing shallots. With everything chopped and diced, I blend the ingredients with fish sauce and let them simmer in coconut milk and lemongrass. To increase the heat and satisfy Kaleb's palate, I add extra young, green chilies.

I set the table and check the time. I consider pouring another glass of wine to calm my nerves. *Like mother, like daughter*. Comparing myself to her is enough to dissuade me.

Taking a shower and deciding what I will wear this evening occupies the time. I ponder Kaleb's parting words from this morning.

"I'll be back by seven, this evening," he said, when he left. "If there's a change of plan I'll call."

Although drowsy and not fully awake, I was sure that's what he said. Not wanting to rush him the moment he steps through the door, I decide we'll eat at seven-thirty.

Seven o'clock comes and goes—LA traffic I tell myself. Eight, an accident—a delay while they remove the body, do what's required for insurance purposes, and throw down sand to absorb any vehicular and bodily fluids prior to reopening the highway.

The kitchen smoke detector emits a piercing scream and cuts through my spiraling despair. I rush to save our dinner and, without thinking, reach inside the oven to rescue the red Le Creuset dish. Simultaneously, I yelp and my hands recoil—I should've worn oven mitts. Blisters bud on my fingertips. *Run your hands under cold water.* But I'm shocked and fixed to the spot, torn between removing the casserole and attending to my burns. Food takes priority and I snatch the tea towel.

His special meal now sits atop the stove. After sweating for hours inside the cast iron pot, the curry is blackened and congealed, and bonded to the enameled surface. The fluffy coconut rice is dry and crusty.

Reaching inside the fridge, I grab the oaked Chardonnay. The cold bottle soothes my fingertips, and the contents dull my angst. With half the bottle gone, my tears relent, but mounting anxiety encourages me to down the rest. Reality blurs, but one bottle's not enough to knock me out.

Nine requires a greater stretch of imagination, so I torture myself and imagine the worst. By ten I finally get it—he's in a bar, drunk with no conscience. Eleven—he's picked up some girl and taken her back to his hotel. Midnight—I'm back at the earlier crash scene and there's been a fatality. It's him, and the sand is blotting up his blood. I picture his long, beautiful, lean limbs snapped and broken, and contorted into unnatural positions. His golden shaggy hair sponges the blood trickling from his ear and mouth, and his piercing grey eyes stare vacantly up to the stars, into infinity. Was *I* his last thought? Did he conjure my face and say, "I love you?"

I rock back and forth, worry weighs heavy on my chest, and shallow breaths cannot sustain me. I take an almighty gasp, my throat constricts, my face contorts, and the tears I've been struggling to contain erupt in wailing, hopeless, helpless sobs.

With no known next of kin, his stone-cold body now lies inside a refrigerator, unidentified and unclaimed. Something terrible has happened, there can be no other explanation.

I think of my mother's recent car accident and know first-hand how suddenly tragedy can strike. She died not far from here and was inebriated at the time—at nine twenty-three in the morning—as the free local paper likes to frequently remind the whole neighborhood. My father's death from prostate cancer, three months prior, was less shocking, but losing both parents within the space of a year has left me vulnerable and isolated, and expecting the worst. Even though I wasn't particularly close to either of them, it reassured me knowing someone else was in the house.

Upstairs in my bedroom, last night's sweaty sheets, crowned with yesterday's dirty clothes, lie bundled on the floor. I undress for bed, grab Kaleb's T-shirt from the pile, and slip the grubby garment over my head.

I lie in bed, positioned exactly as he left me this morning, and press a scrunched up fistful of his T-shirt against my nose. Once again, I trawl my memory and reexamine his early-bird departure. Did I hear him correctly? Was there a hint of doubt in his voice? Were his words sincere?

He rose before the sun and snuck out of bed so as not to wake me. Knowing he was leaving made me wish he was staying. I had listened intently to the noises dampened by the bathroom door. He peed and I wondered if he'd flush. He did. Next came the hiss of a quick shower, and a quiet pause while he toweled himself dry. Running water, a gargle and spit confirmed his teeth were clean.

He crept back into the bedroom and infused the space with my frangipani shower gel. Through sly eyes I witnessed him tip the contents of his bag onto the bedroom floor. Clothes fell with a muffled tumble, and his knees cracked as he crouched to rummage through his wardrobe. Even with only meagre daylight, he couldn't go wrong. All he needed were jeans and a shirt. I heard the pull and stretch of fabric against his skin, the zip of his fly and the slap of leather and clunk of a buckle as he secured his belt.

When he approached—not wanting to be caught spying—I pressed my eyelids tight. His giveaway tell-tale knees signaled his proximity, and his minty breath indicated his mouth was close to mine. Anticipating his kiss, I puckered my lips. He didn't disappoint and his enthusiasm demonstrated his reluctance to leave. It definitely was *not* a goodbye-kiss. Then he whispered, "I'll be back by seven this evening. If there's a change of plan I'll call."

I'm *certain* that's what he said.

My ears had twitched when his truck fired up. I ran a finger across my lips, still tingling from his kiss, and traced my smile. Tonight, my lips contort into a miserable downward arc and I swipe away my tears.

I stare into the darkness and will his headlights to illuminate the hallway until my heavy swollen eyelids close. All night, I cling to his T-shirt and faint hope, waiting for his call to fracture the silence, for his excuses to shatter my illusions, for his words to break my fragile heart. Every so often, I raise the phone's receiver to my ear and check the connection. As dawn shows herself, I reach for the phone and listen to the dial tone. My heart breaks a little more. My pillow is damp with tears.

The shock of hot water on my skin momentarily scalds my worries, but soaping my body reminds me how much I crave his touch.

Sitting on the bed wrapped in a towel, I stare at a magazine and his hurriedly scribbled contact details, but can't bring myself to call. What if a woman answers?

Downstairs, dizzy with tiredness, I bump around the kitchen, and the strong coffee I've brewed launches me into orbit.

Nine o'clock the phone rings, causing palpitations and momentary paralysis. "Hello," I whisper into the mouthpiece.

"Good morning, my dear," says Doreen Tracey, my elderly neighbor. "I've left my pineapples in your car."

A stray bag of yesterday's shopping lurks behind my car seat, but clenched teeth prevent me from responding.

"Raychelle, are you okay, my dear?" Silence. "Whatever's the matter? ... I'm popping 'round."

Over a cup of tea, I tell Mrs. Tracey, "Kaleb's disappeared. I think he's dead."

"Why *ever* do you think that, my dear?"

"He said he'd be back by seven."

"Morning or evening?"

"Yesterday evening."

"Don't jump the gun. He's probably absorbed in something and lost track of time. These creative types can be quite obsessive..."

"He said he'd phone."

Mrs. Tracey pats my hand. "That's men for you, my dear. One-track minds—they're easily distracted."

By more attractive women.

"He's not like that," I say, hoping to convince myself.

Mrs. Tracey sighs and offers a sympathetic smile. "Let's put the local news on, my dear. With his recent notoriety, they'll be on him like vultures if he's involved in a spot of bother."

There's nothing on the news, not a peep, which is probably a good thing.

"Have you tried phoning him?" asks Mrs. Tracey. My hesitation prompts her to say. "Well go on, my dear, go and get his number."

With furrowed brow, she watches me punch the numbers. Pressing the buttons with blistered fingers adds insult to injury. "Unavailable," I whisper.

Mrs. Tracey stays with me all morning, making tea and distracting me with trivial conversation. At midday, she squeezes my arm and says, "I'm nipping next door to make us a bite to eat, my dear. Follow me when you're ready."

"What if he calls?" I ask, but she turns a deaf ear.

I'm out of my mind with worry. We sit in Mrs. Tracey's bay window eating egg and tomato sandwiches, and drinking copious amounts of tea. A man pulls up in a black Jeep and parks in my driveway. We both freeze, sandwiches poised mid-air. He exits his vehicle and assesses the property. Our man wrinkles his face like there's a bad smell, pushes his shades to the bridge of his nose, and peers skywards to the upstairs windows. He's wearing dark jeans and a black hoodie with *"Counting Crows"* emblazoned on his chest. He holds a note and checks the details before walking up to the house. He raises a hand to his brow, as if saluting, and peers in through Mom's lounge window.

Mrs. Tracey taps my forearm and whispers, "He looks a right shifty beggar."

We stare intently as he sidles over to ring the bell and hammer on the door. He doesn't call out for me and, anyway, he's not the type of man I'd want to answer the door to. He walks across the lawn and takes the shortest route possible, through a flowerbed, to my mailbox.

"Bloody cheek," says Mrs. Tracey.

We can't see what he's doing, there's a bush in the way. He retraces his route through the garden, snaps off a rose, sniffs the bloom, and discards it. Mrs. Tracey stands and bangs on the window pane. She opens the window, flicks her gnarly index finger at him, and shouts, "Sling yer 'ook."

He pans around and fixes Mrs. Tracey with mirrored lenses. He smirks and slowly raises his middle finger.

"Well, I never," says Mrs. Tracey.

He strolls over to his Jeep, climbs in and does a speedy reversing maneuver out of the driveway and into the road.

"What was all that about?" I ask.

"I don't know, but if he comes back I'm calling the police. Cheeky bloody so-and-so."

We know when he turned up, but we speculate about who, what, and why. He might be interested in buying the property, but I've told, Barbara, my Realtor, "No more visitors without prior warning."

There's no way I'm spending another night alone in that house. Recently, Mrs. Tracey's spare room has become my second home.

Back home, I pack my overnight bag. Kaleb's clothes litter the bedroom floor, and imply he'll be back. Stepping over them and taking a closer look, I conclude they're just a bunch of old clothes, no value, and no great loss. He has no reason to return, and no need to face me with awkward excuses. Deflated, I sit on the edge of my bed and cast my eyes across the mess. A glance at the bedside table reveals Kaleb's fang pendant. When we made love last night he removed the necklace—it was getting in the way. Tears of real hope well up. He might abandon me, but not his precious talisman.

I reach across, pinch the chain between my fingers, and hold the tooth aloft. "Where are you?" The fang slowly spins, but offers no divine direction. Resting the tooth in my palm, I precisely coil the chain around the enamel surface and create a protective barrier. I press my hands together and kiss my knuckle. "Please come home. I love you."

Inspired to keep his treasure safe, I fasten the clasp around my neck and stroke the tactile tooth.

On my way out, I can't resist one last check of the phone messages.

Barbara's voice asks, "How about this weekend for an open house event?"

An emphatic, "No!" escapes my lips.

Best friend, Sofie, asks, "Where are you? Call me! Better still, get your ass over here. My wedding shoes have arrived from Paris and they're *stunningly* fabulous."

I also have a dental appointment—tomorrow—how could I forget? I bare my teeth and inspect them in the hall mirror. My eye catches Kaleb's necklace resting against my heart and my fingers travel instantly to the hard enamel fetish, an automatic reaction I've seen Kaleb perform so many times. Green and pink eyes stare back at me—an attractive color combination for roses, but not so much for eyes.

I'm curious to know what the mysterious man in black was up to, so I leave the front door ajar and jog down the driveway to investigate what, if anything, he deposited inside the mailbox. A raven perched atop the box greets me with a raucous warning.

I flick my hand and shoo it away. "Move it, birdie, or else my cat will eat you."

Talons scratch metal and wings swoosh as the bird takes flight. Opening the flap, I discover a parcel wrapped inside a Barnes & Noble carrier bag. Power of suggestion makes me believe it's two large paperbacks. I head back indoors and further examine the package. Closer inspection reveals a thick brown envelope, the size of a hefty brick with *"Leb"* scrawled across it. It takes a moment before I make the leap to Kaleb.

My tingling fingers refuse to open the mystery item, so I hide it in the cupboard under the stairs, behind Butch's cat basket, and pretend it doesn't exist. I don't know for sure if the shady caller delivered the package, but the likelihood is high.

The cupboard's awkward latch frustrates me. "Bloody thing."

The violent sound of shattering glass shocks me.

I gasp and jump and momentarily freeze.

My heart pounds like a jack-hammer. My eyes hone in on the bay tree by the front door and focus on a specific leaf, when really I should be seeking out the baseball bat hidden behind it in the corner. My mouth is dry. I envision the menacing man from earlier, assuming the property is empty, and breaking in. My ears strain to detect any follow-up noises.

A squawking bird.

After several long minutes, hand on chest, baseball bat in the other, I nudge open the door leading into Pops' study.

A large raven with beady black eyes stares me in the face. The evil harbinger lowers its beak and points at a large jagged stone between its feet. The bird throws its head back, crows with laughter and bounces across the rug. A breeze blows through the shattered pane and the curtains flap. My eyes flit between the bird and the broken window as my brain processes this bizarre scene.

Butch appears, delivers the hiss of death, and lunges at the feathery intruder. The dark augur releases a demented cackle and exits the room the same way it entered, through the shattered window.

I drop the wooden bat and grab Butch, concerned he'll cut his paws on broken glass and land me with another expensive vet bill. He wrestles in my arms and makes it clear the fight with this cocky bird is not yet over. Holding him at arm's-length, like a bomb about to explode, I carry him into the hallway, deposit him on the floor and open the front door. He races outside, hackles raised, ready to confront and kill the enemy.

Palm pressed against my forehead, I take a deep breath and assess the practical measures required to fix this mess. First, I phone Mrs. Tracey and explain my delay. Next, I contact the glazier and agree to await their arrival in two hours, time.

Meanwhile, I gather up the larger shards of glass and place them in the pink plastic bucket from under the kitchen sink. In my hand, I weigh and assess the sharp, shiny stone left behind by the bird, and admire the tactile quality. I decide to keep and repurpose the curious souvenir, and place the newly discovered paperweight on Pops' desk. The vacuum cleaner sucks up the smaller splinters of glass, and anticipating the mess the glazier will make, I leave the Dyson parked and ready in the corner of the room.

At least this minor drama has distracted me from worrying about Kaleb for several hours.

Missing You

2. Unwelcome Guest

Butch jumps onto the bed and pokes my mouth with his paw. Having digested his early morning feathery appetizer, he's ready for the main course, a serving of Kitty Delight. Following a night of disturbing dreams, I open my eyes and discover my dreamcatcher is absent. Tossing the comforter aside, I realize I'm in Mrs. Tracey's guest room.

Kaleb's missing. Jolted by this realization, I climb out of bed and slip my feet into my flip-flops. I stand by the bedroom door, left ajar when Butch squeezed through, and listen for signs that Mrs. Tracey is up and about. She's a self-confessed night-owl, late to bed and late to rise, so it's no surprise to hear steady snoring coming from behind her firmly closed bedroom door.

I creep into her lounge and peer at my empty driveway. There's no sign of Kaleb's black truck. Butch dances around my ankles, surely thinking, *This won't get the cat fed. Get your priorities right, lady.*

"You're right," I say. Going next door to my house, too, will allow me to check the phone messages. I take my spare set of keys hanging from a hook in Mrs. Tracey's kitchen and, still dressed in my sleep-shorts and T-shirt, I walk through our rear gardens.

Key inserted in the lock, I appeal to a higher power, "Please, let there be a message." I'm torn between going straight to the phone and feeding Butch, but his glare says it all. *Don't even think about it, lady.*

"What would you like? Rabbit or duck? Bugs Bunny or Donald Duck?"

Butch stands on his hind legs, front paws resting on the countertop. *Just get on with it.*

I empty the contents in a bowl and drizzle the gravy over the meat. Unimpressed by the long wait for breakfast, Butch springs up onto the work surface and plunges his head into the dish. His voracious eating shunts the bowl along the draining board, and in all likelihood it will land in the sink before he finishes.

The pull of the answering machine and potential news lures me down the hallway. My heart flickers in time with the rapid red-flashing message indicator. I take a deep breath, press one-one for messages, and exhale. An android voice informs me. "You have three new messages."

"Hi, girlfriend, Sofie here. See you midday. I'm in love with my shoes. I think I love them more than Paolo."

Message two. Five seconds of nothing. My heart sinks.

Message three. "Hello, Raychelle, this is Pearly Whites. This is a courtesy reminder. At ten-thirty today, you have a forty-minute dental appointment scheduled with Selina the hygienist. We look forward to seeing you."

Butch's dish crashes into the sink. I turn as he jumps down from the counter and watch his furry butt disappear through the cat-door.

Arms folded across my chest, I gaze tight-lipped into the hall mirror and witness the tears well-up, until my image becomes a blur.

At least I have distractions to occupy me today: forty minutes of pain with Selina the sadist, and an afternoon and possibly dinner with Sofie. I shouldn't be so negative about seeing my best-and-only-friend, but she'll know instantly something is wrong and I'm not in the mood for explaining. She's understandably all bubbly and up-beat about her wedding, and I'm withering under a burgeoning storm cloud, knowing I'm about to get drenched in a downburst of worries.

The phone rings and makes me jump. I look down and check the number on the recorder's display screen, but it's not Kaleb.

"Hey, Raych, long time no see."

Stunned, I reach for the banister and plant myself on the second stair. I fight the urge to cover my ears. Instead, I listen, not wanting to hear.

"Rick, here, in case you haven't guessed. Thought I'd check in and see how you're doing." There's a pause, like he might be waiting to see if I pick up. *No. Chance.*

This is the first time I've heard from Rick since we split up last year. Neither of us were serious, but both sets of parents thought otherwise. They thought we were the perfect match and had begun making wedding plans.

"Richard and Raychelle—even your names fit so beautifully together." So thought my deluded mother. Driven by desperation, I discovered I had a spine and brought all that nonsense to an abrupt halt. Unfortunately, Jolene was unavailable that particular weekend, she was tied up taking someone else's man, so I enacted my own dumb plan to dump my fiancé. I flirted outrageously with Rick's dad, and staged a stumble in impossibly high stilettos allowing him to land on my chest. Our tumble triggered the garden light sensors and led the party guests to believe we were embroiled in some sleazy affair. So, with Dick on my chest, I got Rick off my back—mission accomplished. I thought I'd put that embarrassing saga behind me, but hearing Rick's voice brings the episode back into clear focus.

"Look, as you know I'm no good at small talk. I wanted to let you know I've got a kid now, Ricky Junior. I got married as well a few months back… you're the accountant, do the math." He chuckles, amused by his own wit.

I resemble a goldfish taking in oxygen, mouth opening and closing, eyes wide-open.

"I heard about your mom and dad. Well, actually, Mom pointed it out to me in the local freebie. Sorry about that. Who would've guessed your mom was an *alkie*, she was always so uptight."

I shake my head from side to side.

"Stop me rambling. Look, d'you fancy hooking up sometime soon? We could go for a drink. Or I could come over to yours? You probably get lonely in that big old house." I grip the banister and hold on tight for stability. A baby squawks in the background. Yesterday's crying baby?

"Shit, that's Ricky Junior the third waking up for his feed. Look I gotta go, his mom's coming." This is so wrong on so many levels. "See you soon." I press my hand against my stomach. This is really messed up. "I'll email you."

I lunge for the message machine and stab my finger at the "Delete" button, but in my distressed state I accidently hit "Replay." I endure another listening to make sure I heard right the first time.

ೞ ♈ ಜ

Selina doesn't disappoint. She scrapes my teeth and gouges my gums, and tells me I'm doing a great job. God knows what she must do to those with poor dental hygiene standards. Surviving the ordeal lifts my mood slightly and, for Sofie's benefit, spurs me on to behave in a positive manner. We won't talk about me, about: leaving my job, being assaulted by my ex-boss, selling my house, and being in love with a dubious rocker who's gone missing. I'll make sure the conversation is entirely about her, about the wedding. Luckily, the topics seem endless: dress, shoes, make-up, cake, caterers, menu, photographer, Paolo, his family—that should keep her going for several hours.

I pull through the Ventura's main entrance into the holding area where visitors meet with a second set of gates and are screened before proceeding farther. Sensors in the ground trigger their security system and, if your license plate isn't preapproved in their database, you must wait for manual intervention from inside the house. I've driven through these gates hundreds of times so I wait a moment for the tall ornate ironwork to swing open.

Along the gravel driveway leading up to the Tuscan-style villa, stone urns planted with spikey, burgundy cordylines and trailing ferns line the route. Classical statues hide between tall Italian cypress trees, and by the grand front entrance, an ornate circular fountain creates an obstacle to navigate. Atop the water feature, a group of carved stone cherubs each hold a cornucopia, and continually pour water into their scallop-rimmed basin. Below them a circle of big-lipped scaly fish spew even more water into the larger pool.

Scrunching along the gravel, past the fountain and on towards the parking area at the front, I recall the time Fabian, Sofie's twin, poured laundry detergent and red food coloring into the water feature. Rivers of frothy blood flowed down the Ventura's driveway and created a convincing scene for a Gothic horror movie.

I scan the parked cars: Sofie's Audi, Mrs. Ventura's Lexus, and Ken Hunter's black BMW.

I slam the brakes. "What the hell...?" I think my head and heart are going to explode.

Ken Hunter is my former boss. Last month, following a year of intense sexual harassment, I impetuously quit my job because of him, forsaking any chance of a decent reference, and have potentially ruined my accounting career before it's even started.

In the week following my resignation, he turned up on my doorstep, and armed with some spurious excuse he conned his way into my home and viciously assaulted me. The house is now on the market—not due to the attack, although that alone would be reason enough. A four-bedroom house is simply too big for a twenty-two-year-old, single person like me, and the monthly bills are ridiculous.

I'm about to circle the fountain and drive away, but Sofie appears at the front door, holding a silvery-grey shoe in each hand and twirling each by their heel. I grip the steering wheel so hard I have to forcefully tell myself to return her wave. I proceed slowly to the parking space beside Ken's car. As the license plate comes into focus, I laugh out loud. JAH 001. I thought it was KAH 007. Clearly, I should have visited the optician this morning, rather than the dentist.

I exit my car laughing.

"What's so funny, girlfriend?"

"You, waving those shoes around."

I run up the stone steps and we pop our lips and perform dramatic Hollywood air kisses.

"Aren't these the most exquisite shoes ever?" Sofie asks.

"Until the next pair come along."

We laugh and enter the house. Calm and curious after my big fright. "Whose car is that, I don't recognize it?"

"One of Mom's clients from the *exclusive* Pine Canyon residences. Mom's just finished a three-hundred grand remodel of their living area, and now they're discussing plans for the kitchen."

"Wow, some folk sure have a lot of spare cash."

Abrianna Ventura, runs a high-end interior design company—Italianesque Interiors—her logo inspired by two composite architectural columns. Her work has been featured in several glossy magazines and she's well known in the LA area.

"What do you want to drink? Sauvignon Blanc is open, or do you want coffee?"

It's a little early for alcohol, but it sure is welcome. "Wine, please."

"Thought so, I've already got you a glass."

We saunter into the Summer Room, an annex, built from stone and reclaimed timber, with a tiled floor. The roof trusses are completely exposed and the walls are predominantly stone with occasional plastered frescoes of fruit spilling from classic urns. The structure is completely open along one side, and the roof is supported by Abrianna Ventura's trademark columns. Concealed sliding doors can be drawn across during inclement weather, but for most of the year the room remains open.

Sofie places her shoes in full view on a table close by. "I can't stop looking at them. I'm so in love. When I'm at the altar, I shall marry my shoes along with Paolo."

We take our usual spot on two lounge chairs overlooking the pool and, through the trees, a view of the Pacific Ocean provides a perfect backdrop. Sofie pours me a glass of white wine. We raise our glasses and Sofie delivers a toast. "To life-long friends and fabulous shoes." We chink glasses and drink. "Help yourself," she says and points at the olives, cured meats, and artichoke hearts.

Settling back in our seats our eyes rest on the shoes—hand embroidered shot silk with Tahitian grey pearls. The heel, a four-inch twisted metal vine. The slipper, the palest grey silk, embroidered with leaves and embellished with flowers and tiny pearls, and the ankle strap, a chain of pearls. I know how much they cost, and my instinct would be to never wear them, wrap them in tissue paper, and keep them safe in their box out of harms' way.

Voices in the background indicate Mrs. Ventura is showing her client around and presenting her with several design options. "This is the Summer Room, but obviously we use this versatile space nearly all year round."

"I recognize those columns," her client says.

Mrs. Ventura laughs. "Oh Jan, you're so observant. Yes, those are my signature composite columns."

"So elegant and timeless. Did you design them, Abrianna?"

Sofie rolls her eyes, raises her eyebrows, and whispers so only I can hear. "No, the fucking Romans designed them, like two-thousand years ago, dopey cow."

We both sputter with laughter.

"Oh, Sofie, there you are," says her mother. "Let me introduce you to my wonderful client."

Mrs. Ventura walks in front of our loungers, closely followed by her wonderful client. All eyes are on Sofie.

"Sofie, this Janine Hunter."

The blood rushes away from my head and I feel a little faint.

"Hello, Sofie," says Ken Hunter's wife. "How lovely to meet you at last."

"Lovely to meet you too, Janine," Sofie says, as she shakes the woman's hand. Sofie, half-heartedly moves to stand up.

"There's no need to get up," Janine says. She looks at Mrs. Ventura, then back to Sofie. "Your mother keeps me fully informed about all your meticulous wedding preparations. What a gorgeous house and beautiful gardens. It's absolutely stunning, like something out of the movies… better than the movies."

Janine shuts up abruptly, probably realizing she's going too far. Her eyes flit to me… the quiet motionless girl on the lounger adjacent to Sofie.

Abrianna waves her hand towards me, about to introduce me. "This is…"

Janine Hunter issues a stammering nervous laugh. "Raychelle Carter."

"Oh! You two know each other," Mrs. Ventura exclaims.

Completely dumbstruck, I nod. Sofie must recognize my panic. She reaches over and grabs my hand. "Raych and I have been *besties* ever since preschool."

Mrs. Ventura asks Janine. "So, how do you two know each other?"

I let Janine Hunter explain. "My husband, Kenneth, very kindly employs Raychelle at his prestigious company."

"What a small world it is," Sofie's mother concludes. "Let's move on, Jan, and leave the girls to it. We've got quite a few decisions to make, today."

"Oh my god," Sofie says. "I don't believe it. *She* is your boss's wife. That is *so* funny."

I swallow a large mouthful of wine. Sofie doesn't know I've walked out on my job, and it appears neither does Janine Hunter, unless she's not letting on. A fresh flush of panic runs through me. Mrs. Hunter's probably wondering why I'm sat on a lounger, drinking wine on a Friday afternoon when I should be in the office helping her husband earn the funds to pay for her fancy new kitchen.

"So, she's the wife of the lecherous old guy who wants to knob you." Sofie tips her head back and laughs, uproariously. "How come you're off work today, anyway?"

The lie readily slips off my tongue. "Time owing for a weekend conference I attended."

"They treat you nice at that place."

"Yes."

After discussing the shoes once more, conversation reverts back to the wedding. Sofie wanders off to the kitchen for more olives and any other nonfat snacks she can lay her hands on. While she's gone, I worry about Kaleb and try to keep a lid on my urge to rush home and check the phone messages. Remembering the call from Rick induces a flash of dread. Why did he call? Who am I kidding, I know exactly why he called. Why can't everyone just leave me alone? Why hasn't Kaleb, called? Maybe he has. Maybe his truck's in the driveway.

Just as I'm thinking of excuses to leave, Sofie reappears with a tray, bearing a salad and an array of nibbles. "More wine?" she asks.

"Better not, I'm driving."

"You can stay."

"Work tomorrow."

"It's Saturday!"

"Preparatory spreadsheets for a new client."

I hate telling all these lies. I hate lying to Sofie.

I pop a large olive into my mouth. "Hey," Sofie says, "I've been meaning to tell you, but didn't want to say it over the phone."

Oh god, what now?

I look at her with inquisitive eyes. "Bad news?"

"Not really, but you know Rick…"

"Yes, I know Rick."

"Well, I thought I should tell you, so it doesn't come as a shock, but he got married like four months ago, and now he's got a kid. A mini-me—predictably called Ricky Junior."

"Thanks for letting me know."

"You don't seem surprised."

I shrug. "Well, it was to be expected."

"Do you ever hear from him?"

"No."

Munching celery and crunching cucumber halts our conversation. Abrianna and Janine approach, their laughter and clicking heels provide fair warning.

"Sofie," Mrs. Ventura says. "Janine is leaving now and just wanted to say goodbye."

"Lovely to meet you, Sofie," says Janine. "I shall see you soon." She looks at me and nods.

"Goodbye," I mutter.

Once they're out of earshot, Sofie mimics Mrs. Hunter's squeaky voice. "I shall see you soon. Not if I see you first, lady." We both snort. "Who the fuck does she think she is?"

Abrianna strides over and finds us laughing uncontrollably.

"I hope you two girls haven't drank too much."

"No, Mamma. Never."

"She's a lovely woman, Janine Hunter."

"If you say so, Mamma."

"I've invited her and her husband Kenneth to your wedding-evening soiree. They're already acquainted with several of our other guests. Kenneth Hunter's reputation precedes him. I look forward to meeting him. He'll be a rewarding contact."

My body feels leaden. This cannot be happening. Mrs. Ventura has just invited a potential rapist to her daughter's wedding celebration. I don't want him here, not only for my own justifiable reasons, but I don't want him tarnishing Sofie's special day.

How can I stop this? I can't suddenly come clean about all that has passed. By keeping quiet about Ken's harassment, I've enabled him to carry on unchecked. Who would believe me, anyway? Like Mrs. Ventura stated, his reputation precedes him. Who would give credence to a flakey, mediocre, junior accountant like me? I'd be accused of bearing grudges; annoyed I'd been overlooked for promotion; the victim of an unrequited crush; a sad lonely individual, unhinged by the sudden loss of both parents.

I know exactly where I stand. How am I going to get out of this predicament?

"Whatever," Sofie says. "What's it got to do with me anyway, you're paying?"

"I can't believe we've not come across the Hunters' before... even Raychelle knows them. We mix in the same social circles and they know the lawyer who works for your father's property investment company. It really is a small world."

Abrianna wanders off.

"Any more cucum-*bear*?" Sofie asks, delicately holding a thin slice between her fingers.

I shake my head. I feel physically sick. I manage another hour of small talk and make my excuses. "I'd better get going. I've got an early start tomorrow."

"Well it was great to see you, sweetie. Don't be a stranger. I know you're coming to stay with me a few days before the wedding, but in the meantime, give me a call if you're free.

I sit in my car and put my hands over my face. Why, oh why, is this happening to me? Give me a break.

Back home, I park my car in Mrs. Tracey's garage to keep it hidden from view. Before entering her house, I slip inside my own place to check for messages on the answer machine—nothing important. Emails are a longshot, but I fire-up my computer and scan the list. Rick's name stands out, a name I've not seen on my screen for almost a year, and there's an attachment. I open the email, but there's no message, just a JPEG file.

My mouse hovers over the attached photo. Shall I or shan't I open it.

I open it.

A photo of Rick sitting in a Lay-Z-Boy recliner inside his parents' house. On his knee is his newborn son. I'm momentarily, stunned, and unsure what to make of this odd communication. Should I respond? Maybe he sent it accidentally, a blanket email sent erroneously to all his email contacts, instead of selecting the correct individual.

After pondering the right thing to do, I send a simple message. *"Cute baby. Looks like his dad!"* Polite, innocuous, and proof I've moved on.

Unwelcome Guest

3. Trick or Treat

It's Wednesday, six days since Kaleb's disappearance, and I'm writing my shopping list and pretending everything is normal. I take a deep breath, release a heartfelt sigh, and struggle to ignore the burning worry that steals my waking hours and haunts my dreams. Santa Ana winds blow down from the mountains, whistle through the canyons, and jangle my nerves. The front door rattles—*El Diablo's* determined to get in.

Above nature's din, another distinctive sound sets my heart racing even faster—Kaleb's truck pulls into the driveway. A phantom hand grips my throat and holds me in a stranglehold of fear. Blood drums inside my ears. Suddenly, I'm dizzy and shaking, overwhelmed by a barrage of conflicting emotions, all wrestling for dominance.

"Act cool and wait for the doorbell," I tell myself. He can't know my desperation, I don't want to scare him away. But, he's taking too long to ring the bell. I envision him writing a farewell note, delivering his excuses and driving away. I reach the door as Big Ben chimes. Pulling it open reveals a horror show.

"Trick or treat?" he asks.

I gasp and collapse to my knees.

"It's not as bad as it looks," he says, "better than it was a few days ago."

Winded and crouching on all fours, I catch my breath and look up. His left arm's strapped across his body. Grazed knuckles peek over the bandages. Motionless fat fingers rest like a claw against his chest. Blood still seeps and dries from fragile wounds, and defines his fingernails.

He steps across the threshold wearing a grey-plastic medical boot and closes the door.

"I'm sorry, I can't help you up," he says. "Bending's difficult—it hurts. Cracked ribs."

He hobbles into Pops' study using a metal cane. Still unsteady, I haul myself up and follow. He flops onto the sofa and I take a seat, opposite, in the leather wing-back chair. He grimaces and places a hand on his ribcage. I stare at his hideous face, searching for the man I know and love hiding behind this grotesque mask.

He's got two black eyes, the white of one entirely red, and the other's crusty and swollen shut. Neat stitches trace the contour of his eyebrow, his cheek resembles a purple baseball, and a split lip and broken tooth completes his convincingly scary Halloween character.

Remembering my manners, I ask, "Can I get you something? Is there anything you want?"

"Take off your clothes."

I'm stunned by his stark request. My head spins. Images of my ex-boss, Ken Hunter, making a similar demand in the room across the hallway makes me weep, but still he stares, awaiting my reaction. He's not joking. He provides no words of encouragement. No smile. No explanation. He offers no apology. He's not forcing me to do anything, and he's so incapacitated he can't.

I could say, "No," and leave the room, or laugh at his odd remark, but I don't. He's testing my limits, my unquestioning devotion, and must realize how much this pains me.

I take a deep breath, clench my jaw, and tug at the studs on my denim shirt.

Pop, pop, pop.

Slowly, I remove my clothes. There's nothing sensual in my actions. Expressionless, he watches my distress as I undress. I stand before him, my skin prickling and raw. I've never felt so naked. I'm exposing more than flesh. I want to crawl into his lap, but seeing his injuries deadens the impulse. My eyes drop to the floor.

"You wear it well. It suits you."

I look up, unsure what he's referring to.

"Fang's tooth sits beautifully between your breasts."

Fire and ice inhabit my body. My face burns, my feet are frozen. He fidgets on the sofa. "I need help with my pants."

Struggling against a force-field of invisible resistance, I move towards him. I lift his T-shirt and discover a gauze dressing taped across his abdomen. Bristly hairs sprout through shaved patches of skin. My tears land on his belly as I unhitch his belt buckle.

"Who dressed you this morning?"

His face crinkles, he raises his buttocks and I tug his shorts. "Careful," he says, ignoring my question.

"The plastic boot's in the way."

"Take it off. It's overkill. It's only a broken toe."

I unfasten the Velcro straps and cast the boot aside. He raises his butt again and I ease his shorts down. *He was wearing jeans the morning he left.*

I kneel between his parted legs and take him in my mouth. When I'm finished, I wipe the back of my hand across my lips. I hope he's satisfied, and look to his eyes for approval. I find him weeping.

"Did I hurt you?"

He shakes his head. "No, my love."

I rest my head against his thigh, and he strokes my hair while I listen to his gurgling guts. He sounds hungry.

"Can I get you something to eat?"

"Strong coffee would be good. The stuff they serve in the hospital's as weak as piss."

I reach for my denim shirt and wrap it tightly around my body.

My head's swimming. I hang onto the kitchen counter and steady myself while I wait on the coffee. *If he's been in a road accident, how come the truck's unscathed?*

From the kitchen, I carry the coffee jug and mugs on a tray, and set them down on Pops' desk. I place his drink beside him and focus on his swollen fingers. "Can you grip the handle, okay?"

"I'll manage."

I cocoon myself inside the scratchy tartan throw and sit in the wing-back chair. Across the room we regard each other, both guessing what the other is thinking. I'm not asking and he's not telling. We're mapping out the blueprint for our relationship—this is how it will be.

It's hard to look at him. Occasional tears leak out. I let them dry. With difficulty, he rolls a cigarette, but lights up with ease, still able to perform his slick one-handed stunt with his Zippo lighter. I lean forward and position the Versace ashtray within arm's reach.

The carriage clock on the mantelpiece chimes, an indicator of time moving on.

"It's Wednesday. I'm taking Mrs. Tracey to the supermarket," I remind him. I gather my clothes and wander upstairs to shower.

ঙ ♈ ଔ

The phone rings in the hallway. I rush downstairs and answer.

"I saw his truck in the driveway," says Mrs. Tracey. "Is everything okay, my dear?"

"Great, thank you," I say, lying through my teeth.

"So, where's he been?"

"Yes, everything's fine." I comb my fingers through wet hair and ease the tangles.

"Is he in earshot? Is that why you can't talk?"

"Sounds about right." I shake my head and loosen my mane.

"We can cancel if you'd rather?"

I gather my wild tresses and twist them into a ponytail. "I'll see you at two."

I must keep them apart, I don't want Mrs. Tracey to see Kaleb. She'll ask the questions I can't, and I don't want his answers meeting with her disapproval. I don't want to risk losing either of them.

"It's probably best if you wait in here," I say to Kaleb. "Is there anything you need before I disappear?"

The left side of his mouth twitches. I'm unsure if it's a sneer or a pathetic attempt to smile.

There's a knock at the kitchen door, and my head's in a cupboard checking inventory.

"Come in," I say, faking a cheerful tone.

"Lord Almighty! Good God in heaven! What the bloody hell have you been up to now?" asks Mrs. Tracey.

My head jerks away from the tuna and peanut butter. A ghoulish zombie, an extra from a horror flick stands in the kitchen doorway. I thought Kaleb understood the necessity to remain hidden until he's reasonably presentable.

"You look like you've been in the bloody wars," says Mrs. Tracey. "What's this all about?" Before Kaleb answers, she says, "I'll wager a bet and hazard a guess, it's either money, or a good hiding."

"Money," he says and adds, "Not mine."

Mrs. Tracey plants her red patent leather handbag on the table. "You've got some explaining to do, young man." She plops down heavy in the chair and the wood groans in response. Kaleb takes the seat opposite, and winces as he tentatively settles in place. Her chest swells in apparent anger and, with piercing eyes and pursed lips, she waves an arthritic finger at him—her lurid nail color matching her purse.

"No cock and bull from you, sonny boy. I want the full story, start to finish, no feelings spared."

Superfluous to their conversation, I prop myself against the counter, ready to witness the exchange. Kaleb sinks into the chair, sweeps his hair back, and looks Mrs. Tracey in the eye. With his hand strapped across his chest in the pledge position, Kaleb confesses. "Last Thursday we finished early at the studio, so I hung out with Carl at a bar and had a few."

Mrs. Tracey leans forward. "Carl?"

"My manager."

"Go on." She leans back.

"He likes gambling. Some guys…"

She leans forward. "Some guys?"

"Hudson, the local crack dealer, comes over and offers his condolences. Says he's sorry to hear about Jake my dead bandmate—he was a regular customer when we were in town. Anyway, Hudson invites us to join him at poker. I finish my drink, slap Carl on the back and say, 'Adios amigo.' Carl grabs my arm and says, 'Hey, pussy, I thought she wasn't expecting you back 'til seven?' Carl wanted me for protection."

"And, why would that be?" asks Mrs. Tracey, tapping impatient fingers on the table.

Kaleb massages the stubble on his chin and contemplates his answer.

I fight the urge to cover my ears and close my eyes—hear no evil, see no evil. There's no chance of me uttering a word to anyone. I reach inside my shirt, wrap my fingers around Fang's tooth, the same way Kaleb used to, and hold on for strength and reassurance.

Kaleb repositions himself and winces. He raises his chin, and calmly places his right hand on the table.

"Carl knows I don't shy away from trouble, and we both knew it was brewing. You see, Carl was fond of a crack whore this guy owned, but she smoked more than she earned. She was found floating under the dock a few weeks back with a bullet in her head. Carl wanted this guy's money, wanted to hurt him a bit. We drove to the port. I had a bad feeling about the location and told Carl we should bail, but he was pumped... said he wanted to nail the bastard. We ended up inside this boarded-up café with Hudson and his three henchmen: Mr. Ugly, Mr. Crazy, and The Goon. Carl played for high stakes while I sat out, drank beer, and read a book. I sized up The Goon on lookout duty, clocked our surroundings and waited for it to kick off, as I knew it would. You see, Carl has this nasty unsportsmanlike habit of card counting. He can't help himself, he's an evil genius with unresolved childhood issues."

Mrs. Tracey's eyes open wide. Her heavily-penciled eyebrows shoot skywards and stay there a moment. "I can see how that might lead to trouble."

Kaleb's fingers lightly tap the tabletop and bounce around to an unknown tune. "Carl's winning... a lot, and Hudson's a poor loser. Hostility crackles in the air. I put my book down and roll a cigarette. The moment I light up, Mr. Crazy yells, 'No smoking!' Probably worried about their crack factory exploding. Not wanting to spark an international incident I stub it out. Then Mr. Crazy leaps up, empties the table into Carl's lap and pulls out a gun. Carl follows suit."

There's a pause in conversation. Kaleb's fingers continue to dance across an imaginary keyboard. Butch appears through the cat flap and jumps onto his chair. He raises a back leg and tackles the fastidious business of cleaning his backside. He looks up suddenly, and his eyes challenge my curiosity. *What you lookin' at?*

Mrs. Tracey slaps the table to draw our attention. "Come on, let's hear the rest."

"You don't need graphic details, but there was a fight. A bad one."

"How bad?"

"Bullets fired, knives drawn. Two dead."

Mrs. Tracey purses her scarlet lips.

I make it to the pink powder room just in time to lose my lunch. Mrs. Tracey raises her voice. "Are you okay in there, my dear?"

"Fine," I say, my response a deep echo from inside the toilet pan.

"And, were you responsible for either of the casualties?" Mrs. Tracey asks Kaleb.

"Hard to say. One… maybe. The other, definitely not."

"And what about the other two?"

"They were moaning when we left."

"I bet they bloody were. But, how stupid leaving two live ones behind."

"It's okay, after Carl dumped me at the hospital he went back and finished the job."

"Well, thank God for small mercies. And is this incident common knowledge?"

"On the street they know Hudson's missing. Another gang is claiming credit for his disappearance… it elevates their ranking."

"Did you give Raychelle a thought while all this was going on?"

"I did what I had to."

There's a pause in conversation. The only sound is my embarrassing dry retching. I reach for the lever ready to flush again, and the handle slips from my fingers as Mrs. Tracey asks Kaleb, "Do you love her?"

A loud cascade of water replenishes the toilet bowl and drowns his words in Lysol blue.

"Are you hiding anything?" Mrs. Tracey asks him.

I'm the one guilty of concealing. I rinse my face and exit the bathroom. Reaching into the cupboard under the stairs I retrieve the hidden carrier bag. Back in the kitchen, I drop the bundle onto the table in front of Kaleb.

"This is for you."

He ignores it.

"Aren't you going to open it?" asks Mrs. Tracey.

"I know what's in it."

"We don't," says Mrs. Tracey. "Open the bloody thing."

Awkwardly, he unwraps the package and removes wads of hundred dollar bills. "Twenty-five grand," Kaleb states. "We agreed a ten percent cut. Carl's a man of his word. He must've dropped it off with your note."

"What note?" I whisper.

"I didn't want to worry you, so I asked Carl to let you know I'd been waylaid."

"There was no note."

"He promised me he'd leave you a message," Kaleb says. "My eyes were swollen shut, my phone was dead, and I couldn't charge it."

Kaleb peers inside the plastic bag, dips his hand in, and peels away a slip of static paper. He offers me the handwritten scrap.

"Hi, Honey, I'm a friend of Leb's. He had a wee accident at the studio—tripped over some cables. He's in the hospital getting fixed. Sends his love."

Mrs. Tracey points a finger at Kaleb. "I want you to promise me there'll be no more funny business. I'm not as young as I was. I can't be doing with sleepless nights and police knocking on the door in the early hours. No more, do you hear me, no more shenanigans?"

"Yes, Doreen."

"Give me your word."

"Promises extracted under duress don't count. And, if I'm honest, I lie when it suits me. It's a survival thing. In my world, self-preservation by far outweighs integrity. The past can be revealed in the present, but the future keeps its own counsel."

"Smart arse," says Mrs. Tracey.

I suspect Kaleb's smirking but, given the swelling, it's debatable. Mrs. Tracey knows she's hit a brick wall. She turns to me.

"Do you still fancy a trip to the shops, my dear? I could do with a strong cuppa and a fancy cupcake with extra sprinkles."

I disappear upstairs and tidy myself up. When I return, Mrs. Tracey's advising Kaleb.

"Put cold tea bags on your eyes, they always worked wonders for my Frankie. The best thing for removing blood from clothes is a bit of your own spit, but I expect there's rather a lot… and not all yours. Soak your jeans in cold salty water."

"How much salt?"

"Half a cup in a bucket should do the trick."

I pick up the Barnes and Noble bag, expecting to find it empty. "Kaleb, there's more."

"What is it?" Loathe to dip my hand in, I pass him the bag. He retrieves a dog-eared bundle of documents tied with tatty ribbon and a small opaque baggie—the type commonly used for drugs. He rips open the self-seal bag with his teeth, and tips the contents onto the table. I anticipate pills rolling across the surface but, instead, a pair of gold and diamond earrings reveal their worth in direct sunlight.

"D'you want them?" Kaleb asks.

I shake my head and decline.

"I'll have them," says Mrs. Tracey. "I could do with some new studs." She releases the gold clasp on her handbag and the jaws open wide, ready to consume the jewels. Kaleb tosses the expensive morsels into the hungry maw, and the shiny metallic lips close with a satisfied click.

"So, where did they come from?" asks Mrs. Tracey. Kaleb studies the papers in his hand. "I said, *where* did they come from, and what's that you're reading?"

"Carl's bounty from a few weeks back, from a gambling encounter he had with a cowboy from Phoenix. I was acting security guard and this is my share of the proceeds—I believe the earrings belonged to the dude's wife."

"And, what did your *friend* get out of it?"

"A night with the bronco's daughter."

"Ooh, you keep some bloody *charming* company, young man."

Kaleb snorts, but offers no defense.

With eyes fixed on the bundle of grubby papers, Mrs. Tracey asks, "And what are those?"

"A mining claim… Redfield Mine, Weeping Creek, Arizona."

"And what the bloody hell are you going to do with that?"

Kaleb taps the documents, side-on against the table.

"No. Idea."

In unison, we turn our heads towards the kitchen window, to the yowling and squawking outside. Butch has surreptitiously left his comfy chair and is now engaged in all-out combat with a large raven, possibly the same bird that crashed through the window in Pops' study last week. I rush to the window and rap on the glass to no avail.

"Come on," Mrs. Tracey says to me as she elevates herself, "Let's get going."

Kaleb grabs my wrist, and presses two, hundred-dollar bills into my palm. "For the shopping. And, Doreen's extra sprinkles—they don't come cheap. Could you get me some raw honey and natural Greek yogurt?"

༄ ༄ ༄

We sit in my car, I look ahead, but can't speak. Mrs. Tracey squeezes my hand.

"It'll be okay, my dear. Don't dwell on it, these things happen. There's no point wishing it never happened, and there's no point wasting your energy on regrets. He had no choice, just be thankful he came home in one piece. Take my advice, though, don't ask smarty pants questions if you already know the answer—some things are best left unsaid. He's a good lad underneath it all, and he loves you, which goes a long way in my book."

Through tear-filled eyes I turn to Mrs. Tracey, and she delivers more advice. "Don't waste your life waiting for Mr. Right to come along, my dear, Mr. Wrong is always *much* more exciting."

She reaches into her bag and hands me a Kleenex. "I must get some more tissues," she reminds herself. "I've been getting through them like nobody's business."

༄ ༄ ༄

On returning from the shops, I draw breath before entering the house. I find Kaleb back in Pops' study, where I wish he'd stayed.

He's lying on the sofa, his injured leg rests on the footstool. Head back, mouth open, his snoring follows a steady rhythm. Pain medication—whiskey—has made him drowsy. I kneel before him while he dozes to study his poor face, but he'll always be beautiful to me. He has perfect bones. I want to cover him in kisses, but it's difficult knowing where to plant them, where they won't cause more pain. I smell coffee, tobacco, and whiskey on his breath, and still I want to kiss him. Three tiny stitches hold his fat lip together—a torn scab and a weeping wound—and still I want to kiss him. I lean forward, hover close, and let his jagged stitches scratch my lip. His tongue investigates the intrusion, but he doesn't wake. In this tranquil moment he's all mine, and all is well.

Alerted by his sixth sense, his head jerks up. I back off. Through one eye, he follows my retreat, and watches me sink into Pops' leather armchair. Earlier, in the kitchen, he confessed more than he ever needed to. He had opened a door leading into another dark chamber, and forced me inside to view his latest collection of morbid secrets. Expressionless, we stare at each other.

In turn, I study each of his injuries and imagine the associated pain. Emotion twists my gut and gets the better of me—tears emerge.

Someone has hurt the person I love the most. I hate the hoodlums who did this to him. How can a man beat another man so badly? Realization hits—four men are dead and he may have killed one of them.

Kaleb rolls his head and squints to pull me into focus. My face crumples and I look away.

"Are you still up for a bit of TLC?" he asks. "Do you still want to take your clothes off and kneel for me?"

Meeting his eyes, my fingers instinctively go to the buttons on my shirt.

He sheds a tear. We must be weeping for the same reason, but I'm too afraid to ask.

ഌ ϒ ଔ

For dinner, I make simple pasta and open a bottle of red wine. Neil Young cures the painful silence and sings of sadness floating in the air. Side-by-side on the sofa we gulp the Merlot, but slowly chew our rigatoni. Neither of us have much of an appetite for food, but the wine soon disappears. Kaleb hooks his "good" arm around my neck and draws me in. His forearm dangles midair before my face. Dead man's fingers poke out from the bandage and emit a sterile antiseptic tang.

Kaleb accompanies Neil and sings "Down by the River," where he shot his baby, and I wonder if I'll meet with a similar fate. As Neil hits the high notes, Kaleb's deep voice makes the words sound inevitable. He bends his elbow and his corpse-like hand caresses my cheek. I twist my neck to kiss his rough index finger—his trigger finger.

I'm physically and emotionally wrung out, I want to go to bed and keep willing Kaleb to suggest going upstairs, but he doesn't. I stand, hoping he'll take the hint. He reaches out and clamps his hand around my wrist.

"I can't manage the stairs, I'll sleep here if you don't mind. Lying next to you would be sheer torture, imagining what I want to do to you, if only I could."

His good eye flits across my face and studies my expression. *What am I getting into?* He draws my trembling hand to his mouth and scratches my skin with his scabby lips. "Goodnight. Sleep well, my love."

But, I don't sleep well, *at all*. I pick my way through each anxiety and worry each one to death—four men have died and he may've killed one of them. What if he gets caught? I'll be his alibi. What if the gang comes after him? We need to leave… immediately. Tomorrow, I'll make plans.

A car drives by. I anticipate the police breaking down the door, or worse still, angry cartel members seeking revenge and spraying the house with bullets. My heart bangs so intensely I'm convinced the bed is throbbing. The only way to get some sleep is to believe Mrs. Tracey and convince myself he had no choice, and *this* is the best possible outcome.

The clock reads *"3:12 a.m."* I sneak downstairs to reassure myself his presence is not the result of my vivid imagination. I find him fast asleep on the sofa, snoring again, a symptom of his fat lip and swollen face. After all that's transpired, I'm amazed he's able to sleep. He looks grotesque. I only stay a moment.

4. Raw Honey

Kaleb's awake, but he's hardly moved since I looked in on him last night. Determined to ignore the grim truth, I greet him with a smile and a cheery, "Good morning," and ask, "What would you like for breakfast?"

"Same as yesterday," he replies. "Coffee and a blowjob… not necessarily in that order."

After breakfast, I'm unsure what to do, and want to ask, "What next?" But, we exist in a fragile here-and-now, and I don't want to break it. Kaleb's engrossed in one of Pops' true crime books. With his bloodshot eye, he catches me staring.

"You don't need to wait on me. Forget I'm here." I deflect his rejection and bite my lip. "Aren't there things you need to be getting on with?" he asks.

I acknowledge his dismissal and nod. He's right, there are plenty of chores to attend to, if only I were motivated. Last weekend, while he was missing, there was meant to be an open house event, but I cancelled. Without specifying who, I told Barbara there'd been another death in the family, because his absence felt like bereavement. Now he's back, I must focus on house clearing.

After cleaning the breakfast mess from the work surfaces, I half-heartedly open and close kitchen cupboards, unsure where to begin. Mindful, I need to retain a few basic essentials, I contemplate each item and ask myself, *keep or chuck?* Indecision frustrates me. I consider ditching everything and starting afresh. Or, maybe I should put it all in storage. I want to scream.

Kaleb shuffles across the kitchen. "Don't mind me," he says. "You carry on."

So, in a random act of busyness, I take a wineglass, wrap it in paper and place it in the charity box. Ironically, it's an item I frequently use and should definitely keep.

The kettle boils. Kaleb reaches into a cupboard for a pan, into another for salt, and takes a wooden spoon from the utensil drawer, navigating his way around like he lives here. He empties the boiling water into the pan, adds a generous measure of salt, and stirs with the spoon until the crystals dissolve. He carries the pan to the study, slopping water onto the wooden floor as he goes. He doesn't ask for and I don't offer assistance. I'm curious, but focus instead on rearranging the contents of the dishwasher. Moments later he's back, he's in the pantry and in the fridge. He balances Greek yogurt, honey, and teaspoons on his bad arm. I can't believe he's still hungry after such a big breakfast. He grabs the roll of paper towels as an afterthought, wedges it under his chin, and hobbles back to his room before slamming the door.

Uninspired by the kitchen cupboards, I switch my attention to the garden. I grab a plastic bag for dead heads, rummage in the shed for gardening gloves, and don a baseball cap. Dressed in my disguise, I position myself against the wall and sneak a peek inside Pops' study. Kaleb's soaking his fingers in the pan. Dipping and inspecting. With difficulty he removes his T-shirt, raises his arms at right angles to his body, and slowly rotates his limbs to better examine the defense wounds crisscrossing his forearms. He stands, drops his shorts, and steps out of them. Cautiously, he stretches each leg, wincing and steeling as he assesses pain levels and mobility. Despite his injuries, he moves with intent, never hesitating. The camouflage of bruises disguising his body do not detract from his natural beauty—his sculpted torso, broad straight shoulders, and long limbs perfectly defined by taught muscle.

He squeezes his dick, it hardens. My cheeks burn, I want to rush indoors and offer my services. I want him so bad.

His tongue cautiously investigates a sore on his arm. With animal instinct he licks the wounds he can reach, rasping and cleaning the flesh. He swills his mouth with whiskey, forces the alcohol between his teeth, and swallows. Retaking his seat, he empties a paper bag of prescription pills and ointments onto the table, and examines each label before sweeping the whole lot aside and into the trash can. He opens the honey, takes a spoonful, and trickles long golden threads over his cuts, shunning conventional medicine in favor of more unorthodox remedies. He daubs the graze on his thigh, massages the sticky substance into his skin, and licks his fingers.

He leans back, slides his butt forward and rests his chin on his breastbone. With his thumbnail, he flicks the tape securing the dressing across his stomach. He grimaces and with one violent rip, tears the bandage away. I'm too scared for the big reveal—I want to see, but can't bear to look. I press my back against the bricks and catch my breath. Not wanting to miss a thing, I breathe deep and twist back into position, but the curtain's fallen across the window—not fallen, someone's released it. I'm frozen by fear of discovery.

To avoid an embarrassing encounter in the kitchen, I stay outside for longer than I intended, pottering amongst the flowerbeds, until harsh sun and thirst force me indoors. Despite the gloves, my hands are grubby, but I dare not use the downstairs bathroom. It's his domain now, so I wash my hands in the kitchen sink.

From behind he says, "I never suspected you were such an avid gardener."

"I'm not." My face burns. I catch his smirking reflection in the window. I turn and scurry past him. His words follow me upstairs and into my bathroom. "You've caught the sun."

Feeling fresh and composed after my shower, I enter Pops' study and tell Kaleb, "I'm taking Mrs. Tracey to the hospital this afternoon. She has a follow-up appointment with her knee-replacement surgeon."

"Good luck," he says. "Could you get me some whiskey while you're out? A couple of bottles... you know what I like."

He follows me into the kitchen, lifts the lid on his personal ATM, and reaches inside. The bread bin's performing double duty, storing two types of dough—wholegrain and hard cash. He removes the Barnes and Noble bag, fishes inside, and hands me a bunch of hundreds. I resist the urge to count the bills and, without a word, stuff them into my jeans.

His finger grazes my cheek. "Keep the change," he says. "Buy yourself something nice. You deserve something nice, my love."

"I have you."

"Don't make me laugh, it hurts."

We don't speak about what happened. My head's full of questions, but what's the point in asking? I already know the answers. I still want to ask, because I want him to prove me wrong. He reads my mind, and presses his finger against my lips. I supply an automatic kiss.

"You know better than to ask," he says.

My silence pleases him, but I can't contain myself. "Does it prey on your mind?"

He knows what I'm referring to. "No," he says, "but you do. Let me show you what I'm actually thinking about."

I must look curious, because he reverses me into the kitchen counter and fumbles with my bra. Unfortunately, his injuries and my imminent departure prevent us from doing anything too adventurous.

༄ ♈ ༄

We've been gone three hours and, as I pull into Mrs. Tracey's driveway, Kaleb's waiting, sitting on her front steps, legs apart and smoking.

"He's keen," says Mrs. Tracey. "Missing you already. That's a good sign, my dear."

He doesn't look happy.

He pinches the end of his cigarette and stashes the roll-up in his shirt pocket—saving it for later. With the aid of Pops' walking cane—he prefers the knotty wood to the metal hospital issue—he hauls himself up and takes the shortest route possible to meet us, through the dahlias.

He opens the passenger door and takes Mrs. Tracey's handbag.

"Am I being mugged?" she asks. He doesn't laugh, just hoists her out of the car. "Thank you, dear," she says.

He nods.

Something's wrong.

"Everything okay?" I ask. Don't ask questions if you know the answer.

Kaleb grips Mrs. Tracey's elbow and ushers us indoors. Mrs. Tracey decides we need a cup of tea before anything is said and puts the kettle on.

Minutes later she trundles into the lounge with a fully loaded tea trolley. "Come on, spill the beans."

Kaleb sits next to me on the sofa and takes my hand. "*He* came round while you were out."

My blood runs cold. Kaleb must be referring to *He,* who cannot be named—Ken Hunter—my ex-boss, who attacked me in my home a few weeks back. I've not thought about Ken Hunter much these past few days. Kaleb's shocking reappearance has completely eclipsed worrying about Ken Hunter's invitation to Sofie's wedding.

Mrs. Tracey lifts the teapot lid, dips a teaspoon in, and stirs the witch's cauldron. "I smell trouble brewing." She replaces the lid with a clank and situates the knitted tea cozy.

I haven't told Mrs. Tracey either, about the Hunters' wedding invite, because I haven't decided what I'm going to do yet. I may want to unwittingly use her as an excuse when the time comes. "*I'm so sorry, Sofie, but I can't be with you on your special day. Mrs. Tracey's been attacked/fallen/rushed to hospital. She's dying and has no one else. I must stay with her. I hope you understand.*"

Kaleb continues, "I answered the door with a wrench in my hand, and he asked who I was. I knew immediately who he was, I recognized his motor. I told him I was the handyman, fixing a few things while the lady of the house was away. He was a little disconcerted by my appearance, and suggested I didn't look too handy."

"Ooh, I don't like where this is going," says Mrs. Tracey.

"It's okay, Doreen," Kaleb reassures, "There's no immediate rush to dig up the flowerbeds. Sure, I want to kill the bastard, but I let him walk this time." Kaleb's grip tightens.

"So, he invites himself in, says he's an old friend of the family, a close friend of your father's—that he's your godfather."

"What!" I snatch my hand away and rub my temples. "The man's deluded."

Kaleb continues. "He looks around, checks I'm not robbing the place. I stand back and let him prattle on about how much he cares for you and his need to keep a special eye on you. I was interested to see what he'd do, so I gave him rope—enough to hang himself.

"He asked when you'd be back, so I said 'I'm just the odd job man, we're not on personal terms.' Then he says, 'Do you mind if I go upstairs?' I said, 'I do, because I don't know you, and Miss Carter's left me in charge and, if anything isn't right, my ass is on the line.' So, he makes a point of stuffing a wad of notes in my shirt pocket and goes upstairs. I drag my ass up after him and ask him what he's looking for. He smirks and shakes his head. He looks in your mom's room then heads for yours, and I say, 'I wouldn't go in there if I was you—the plumbing's fucked.' He looks uncomfortable at this point, keeps eyeing the wrench in my twitching hand. 'You should leave,' I say. 'Maybe you should call Miss Carter and check when she's home.'

"Outside, he clocks my truck and says, 'I see you're from out-of-state. California's a long way to come for odd jobs.' I say nothing. 'Are you a close friend?' he asks. So, I tell him, 'No, I'm not. But my brother is—he's shagging her, but I get to fix the blocked drains. Doesn't seem fair does it?' He looks winded, like I punched him. Then he asks 'How long has she been involved with your brother?' 'A while now, it might be serious. Hey, I shouldn't gossip. What do I know?' He looks at me long and hard. I can tell he's not happy."

Kaleb pauses, and lifts the thoughtfully provided, big handled mug to his lips. He slurps, and I experience a rush of pleasure as my mother's ghost says, *"How uncouth."*

Tea trickles from the corner of Kaleb's swollen lips. He gingerly drags the back of his hand over his mouth and continues. "Hunter bangs on, says he's worried about you, says you've been unwell. He taps his head, implying you're mad. So, I ask, 'What... She's crazy?' And, he says, 'It runs in the family. Did you ever meet her mother?' He asks when I'll be done, so I reel off a list of stuff and tell him at least another week. He asks where I'm staying, and I say, 'Right here.'

"As he's leaving, he says, 'Don't tell her I called, it'll spoil the surprise.' Then he asks if I've had any dealings with the old busybody who lives next door?"

"Bloody charming," says Mrs. Tracey.

"You just missed him, he left twenty minutes ago. He's dangerous, he needs fixing." Kaleb casts his eyes towards the window.

Mrs. Tracey waves a crooked finger at Kaleb. "Don't even think about it, sonny boy."

Kaleb turns to me. "Raych, I don't want you to ever be alone in the house. If I'm not around you must stay with Doreen."

☙ ♈ ❧

For dinner, I prepare beef stroganoff with wild rice. It's one of my specialty dishes—the tender steak will melt in our mouths. Kaleb stands by the stove and rests his chin on my shoulder. "That's a very sexy meal you're cooking up."

The moment we sit, Big Ben chimes in the hallway. "Are you expecting guests?" Kaleb asks.

I shake my head. "No."

"I'll get it." After Ken Hunter's earlier visit, Kaleb grabs the baseball bat lurking by the bay tree in the hallway, and conceals it behind his leg before opening the door.

"You've got a fuckin' nerve showing up here," Kaleb says.

"And, you look totally fucking ugly." I strain to recognize the voice.

"What the fuck are you doing here?"

"Thought I'd drop by and visit my sick friend."

"You're the only sick bastard around here," Kaleb says.

"Thought you might fancy a game of cards."

A strange man, carrying a bottle of wine in one hand and a box inside a large, brown paper bag in the other, follows Kaleb into the kitchen. My stomach lurches. I recognize him as the guy wearing the Counting Crows hoodie, who gave Mrs. Tracey the finger. He sees our steaming dinner laid out on the table.

"How opportune," Carl says. "Any going spare or are we sharing?" he asks Kaleb.

"I'll get you a plate," Kaleb replies. On his way to the cupboard, Kaleb notices the front door's still open. "Fucking hell, Carl, can't you even close the fucking door behind you?"

Kaleb limps along the hallway. Carl tosses the brown bag onto the sofa in the family room, walks over to the kitchen table and bangs down a bottle of red. "So you're the fucking accountant—the accountant he is fucking. Make yourself useful, honey, get me a corkscrew."

Although, stunned by his crude remark and rude demand, I follow orders and root through the utensil drawer. While my back was turned, Carl's taken one of Mom's ornamental candles from the family room. He places it in the center of the table.

"Let's set the night on fire," he says, and sniggers as he lights the candle.

Kaleb and I eat in silence, but Carl makes loud chomping noises, like a bulldog with sinus issues working on a bowl of chow. "This is fucking good stuff," he says to Kaleb. "You've landed on your feet with this one, Leb. A good cook as well as a good fuck, and pretty loaded, too, I would guess."

Kaleb looks at me and carries on eating. Carl fills his glass and belches. I've lost my appetite.

Carl shovels a loaded forkful of rice into his mouth. Grains fly out as he speaks. "Ryder's fucked off to Phoenix. Sentimental bastard wants to get a new tattoo to commemorate his good buddy, Jake." Kaleb nods. "He wants that guy from Apache Junction who did Jake's tat, to do the same one across his heart."

"Cool," Kaleb says.

Carl scrapes every last grain from his dish. "Fucking pansy."

Kaleb toys with his wine. Expressionless, he looks my way. Tension grips my scalp, I clasp my hands and bite my lip. Kaleb chugs the Malbec. Carl, follows suit.

"What's for dessert?" Carl asks, as he rubs his stomach and belches again. I clear the plates away. "Got any brandy?" he asks.

They stand and Kaleb pokes Carl's back with his cane. The prodding herds him towards Pops' study. "In there," Kaleb orders.

The door closes.

I stand at the kitchen sink shaking, and rinse the plates before placing them in the dishwasher. Reality and fantasy are diverging. I'm in too deep and I'm not sure I want to get out. I bend over to load another plate and vocalize what I've come to realize, "I'm way out of my depth."

A hand grips my butt and the plate clatters as it drops into the rack.

"I'm a strong swimmer," Kaleb assures.

He holds a glass against the ice dispenser, fills it, and returns to the study. Am I meant to feel reassured? Because, I don't. And, I didn't even notice him creep up behind me. Even though he's barefoot, I can't believe I was so distracted by dirty dishes I never heard him. I turn off the running faucet. I really must pay closer attention to my surroundings, especially knowing Ken Hunter's still on the prowl.

I'm uncomfortable in my own home, I'm tired, and I want to go to bed. Instead, I retire to the family room with a book, nervous about putting the TV on in case I disturb them—or, if I'm honest, in case I miss something. Furthermore, I want to witness Carl leave—alone.

My eyes wander from the page and I stare at the box inside the carrier bag. This must be something for Kaleb, because, if Carl's been shopping for himself he'd would've left the item in his car. My imagination goes wild and my chest grows tight. What's inside the box? More money? A gun... to be disposed of? Two guns, supplied courtesy of Carl, for our own protection?

I take a deep breath and put my book down. I sidle closer to the bag. Consumed with guilt, I take hold of a handle and shudder at the loud crinkly-crackly noise of stiff brown paper. The study door opens. I leap up and forward, away from the mystery box.

Carl uses the pink powder room in the hallway without closing the door. Standing in the middle of the family room, frozen with fear of apprehension, I listen to Carl relieve himself. I don't hear him raise the toilet seat, nor does he flush or wash his hands. I envision the sanitary wipes kept under the kitchen sink, and first thing tomorrow, I will wipe all the door handles.

Carl returns to the study without noticing me, and I resume reading.

Hours later, a groaning door and mumbling voices wake me. They emerge from Pops' study preceded by a cloud of cannabis smoke.

Carl says, "I'll call you with a time."

"Fuck you," mutters Kaleb.

Carl yells, "Thanks for dinner, honey!"

The front door slams and I'm relieved to hear Carl's Jeep pull away. His box sits feet away, and I'm now convinced it must be something for Kaleb. I wait for him to appear with an explanation, but he goes back into the study and closes the door. Scared, I sit stone still and listen. Nothing.

I wake up sweating and dazed. Kaleb must've covered me with the throw. The box has gone. I'm tempted to stay here, but force myself up and tiptoe through the house. I hesitate by the closed study door, unsure whether to knock and wish Kaleb goodnight. His snoring deters me.

"Goodnight," I whisper. "I love you."

I wake during the night with a shocking realization—below me on Pops' Chesterfield, sleeps a killer. I throw back the cover, step outside my bedroom, and stare through the banisters at the closed study door. The man I love rests beyond the threshold. Why does it feel like he's a million miles away?

ෂ 'Y' ඥ

My possessions appear as sad grey objects in the gloomy light, and I know it's way too early to be awake. Eager to escape the shadow of pending doom, I cast the comforter aside and step into the shower. Tense fingers apply frangipani shower gel. I vigorously massage my muscles, and dig hard into my bones to dissipate the anxiety coursing through my veins. Loofah in hand, I scour my skin until it smarts, in the vain hope I can scrub my memory clean by punishing my body.

Although dressed and ready to leave my room, I hesitate, it's still too early to go downstairs, so I sit on the edge of my bed and listen. I detect Kaleb shuffling around below, and the beep-beep from the coffee machine is a clear signal I may now leave my room. The aroma of Arabica beans accompanies my descent and draws me to their source. Anticipating the first and best cup of the day fills me with fresh hope, and excites and calms me in equal measure.

Kaleb's in the kitchen, propped against the counter by the coffee machine with his head in a book, *California Gold Rush 1848*. He notices me and his face creases. I assume he's pleased to see me but, through the swelling and stitches, his expression is difficult to read. He limps over, draws my head to his chest, and kisses my hair. He needs a shower.

A flashback to last night prompts me to reach under the sink and locate the sanitizing wipes. Without Kaleb noticing, I move from doorknob to handle and wipe anything else Carl may have touched.

Carrying our coffee and his bowl of oatmeal, loaded with bananas, dates, peanut butter and honey, I follow Kaleb into Pop's study. Since commandeering the space, it's become his own private den, and he's rearranged the furniture to better suit his needs. Nothing is where I expect to find it.

"You can put it here," he says, pointing at the curio table.

I nudge aside the flint stone left behind by the crazy housebreaking raven, and place the tray.

Kaleb reaches for the jagged stone. A toss and a catch. "Can I have this?"

I shrug. "Sure... You know what it is, right?"

"Yeah, you said... Used for breaking and entering." He rolls the stone over in his palm. "You know what else this is?"

"Tell me."

He strokes the stone. "It's a tool. A small axe produced by flint knapping."

Looking closely at the object, the uniform carving is clear.

On Pops' desk, the old maps of Redfield Mine and Weeping Creek lie flat, anchored down with a stapler, a paperweight, a small flashlight, and a box of paperclips. "After The Gold Rush" plays in the background, and Neil Young's lyrics make as much sense as my life. I peer outside, half expecting to see the glint of spaceships flying past the sun, but instead a raven sweeps by. I glance at Kaleb to confirm he's not an apparition. His presence is so incongruous amongst these surroundings. This scene would never exist if my parents were alive, they would never allow him in the house. He catches me staring and smirks as best he can.

"I know,' he says. "I want you just as bad." I blush. He licks his upper lip.

"Come," he says.

Like an eager bitch desperate for her master's affection, I stand, and go towards him.

"I want to touch you," he says.

I let him run his murderous hands over my body. Hands that make love, hands that make music, hands that kill. I see the box has been removed from the brown paper bag. *"Wolverine."* I know better than to assume a new pair of shoes.

"What's in the box?"

Kaleb's face twists. His bloody eye stares into mine.

"Lift the lid and find out."

I hesitate and swallow. Reaching forward, I remove the lid.

"Toe protection," Kaleb says.

Taken aback, I drag the box towards me and read the label to hide my surprise. "Dark brown, steel-toe, work boot. Size 12." I lift one up. "They're really nice."

"When you've done admiring my footwear, can you check something on your computer?"

"Sure." I put the boot back in the box and take a seat in Pops' executive chair.

"See if you can find any info on Redfield Mine, and where precisely Weeping Creek is located."

Outside, the raven's rapid quorking jars me like mocking laughter. I power up my laptop and type the information into the search engine. "I can't find anything about Redfield Mine, but Weeping Creek lies forty miles northeast of Phoenix in the Sonoran desert foothills. It was settled in 1849, originally part of the Territory of New Mexico, has a population of three thousand and, according to the website, many of the original buildings still survive."

"Any photos?"

I click on images, open a few, and turn my computer screen towards Kaleb, so he can see.

"Hmm," Kaleb says, with meaning.

5. Café Noir

I sleep with my bedroom door ajar, forever hopeful Kaleb will break his resolve to stay on the sofa and succumb to temptation. I stare into the darkness and anticipate his clumsy footsteps on the stairs until I fall asleep.

Last night, I woke at two-thirty and heard him padding around downstairs. He opened the fridge—the weak light illuminated the hall ceiling. Minutes later, he went outside. I leapt out of bed and over to my window, where I hid amongst the curtain's folds and spied on his movements. The orange glow of a cigarette pinpointed his location, and traced a burning trail as he strolled across the lawn. Head down, he patrolled the flowerbeds, then bent awkwardly to touch the grass. Clearly tempted by its lush appeal, he lowered himself gingerly, laid on his back, and stared at the stars. He reached into his pocket, removed his tobacco, balanced it on his chest and rolled another cigarette. He brought the roll-up to his lips and kissed his fingers, and the lighter's flame momentarily illuminated his face as he inhaled the tobacco. He removed the cigarette in a slow steady sweep, and the burning tip etched a perfect arc through the darkness as it traveled from lip to hip.

Earlier today, with gritted teeth and much hissing, Kaleb unwound the gauze and removed the bandages from his hand. Afterwards he joked, "I might never play again."

Slowly he flexed his fingers with a grimace.

"What about physio?" I asked.

He had raised the whiskey bottle. "I find this works best."

Tonight, he's out there again, propped against a tree, guitar in hand, gently plucking strings. I crouch by my open window. He strums and I strain to hear his song.

> I'm sitting here thinking and killing time,
> Messing with words and creating a rhyme,
> Strumming some chords,
> And picking my words.
> I'm stalking my prey,
> Noting his route along the way.
> The Devil he's hiding in the details
> With his diabolic plans, he seldom fails.
> He knows your haunts and he knows your path.
> Not long now, 'til you face his wrath.
> He weighs his options as he plans your fate,
> He makes his choice and picks a date.
> Your days are numbered, one to ten.
> The countdown starts, let's begin.

He stops. He's muttering to himself, probably irritated and frustrated by his stiff and uncooperative fingers. Maybe he's mumbling to Butch, but he sounds annoyed. Boldly, I peer from behind the curtain and observe him holding a phone in one hand and chopping the air with the other. Determined to keep the noise down, he conducts a controlled argument and yells quietly through clenched teeth, but there's no mistaking his angry tone.

By the time he comes indoors, I'm back in bed and undercover. Minutes later, the kettle boils. The twist of a lid and the chink of a teaspoon against china indicates Nescafé—he hates instant coffee—but won't risk waking me with the beeping coffee machine.

Footsteps in the hallway send my pulse racing. I anticipate him mounting the stairs and climbing in bed beside me. I wriggle across the mattress to make room, but he fails to appear.

I don't hear the front door open and close, but a signature breeze stirs the wind chime hanging from my light fixture. Maybe he's bored with the back garden, and fancies a change of scenery, or maybe he's going somewhere. In a panic, I tear the comforter away and dash across my bedroom floor. I streak along the landing and enter Pops' bedroom. From the window, I observe the specter of his dark truck rolling quietly down the driveway before turning right into Oak Tree Place. The vehicle freewheels another twenty yards before he engages the ignition and turns the headlights on.

I conjure my worst fear and imagine him being summoned by a needy lover. I can't believe he'd sneak away and leave me in the middle of the night, especially after warning me to never be alone in the house. Exhausted, I doze off and experience nightmares of floors falling away, staircases tipping backwards, of never-ending corridors and doors leading nowhere. In the miserable predawn light, I lie awake. I dare not go downstairs for fear of what I might, or might not, find.

The first hint of daylight is excuse enough to get up and investigate. I don't know if Kaleb's back or not. I sneak along the landing and enter Pops' bedroom. The sight of his truck parked in the driveway creates a lump in my throat.

As I shower, I examine my new hairy body, and I'm still not convinced. Kaleb confessed to ditching my razors, telling me he associates hair with love, but assures me he's not into guys. I leave my tresses to dry naturally, spray the air with Coco Channel and pass through the cloud. After carefully selecting my clothes—a gossamer bra, a thin white cotton blouse, and cut-off denim shorts—I take my time getting dressed.

It's early, but sunrays in the hall make it okay to venture downstairs. The door to Pops' study is closed. Resting against it is another dead bird—Butch's repeated expression of gratitude to Kaleb for returning his beloved toy, Mr. Ratty.

Entering the kitchen, I'm greeted by a dozen doughnuts smiling at me from the countertop. I smile back. Kaleb knows I love the caramel fingers, and the lemon ones, too, with their shaved zesty icing. What I love more is he's not hiding the fact he disappeared in the middle of the night. I don't expect he went out explicitly to buy doughnuts for me, but I choose to believe this explanation.

I put the coffee machine on with the *expresso* wish of rousing him with beeps and aromatic beans. Through the kitchen window I watch Butch throw himself against a tree. He clamps himself to the trunk in an overbearing hug, and practices his scaling technique. I laugh to myself.

"You look and smell delicious," Kaleb says.

I jump. "Uh! You scared me. But, thank you."

"I was talking to the coffee and doughnuts."

I was so distracted by Butch's antics I failed to notice Kaleb's approaching reflection. *I must be more vigilant.*

From behind, he wraps me in his arms and rests his chin on my shoulder. "Fantastic view."

"Down to the ocean?"

"Down your blouse. And, I like this blouse because, if I pull this tie, everything falls apart, and I can get to you pretty quickly in an emergency situation. I'm having one in my pants right now."

We lie carefully entangled on the sofa in the family room. Kaleb reaches for the remote. The morning news reports a suspicious fire at a disused café in the Port of Los Angeles. Roads are cordoned off while fire investigators examine the scene. Aerial shots from earlier show billowing smoke turn from black to gray as firefighters get the blaze under control. A submerged car has been discovered under the dock. Police divers are searching the water.

Kaleb's glued to the screen.

Authorities are unsure if the two incidents are related. The smell of smoke in my nostrils is real, and I think Kaleb probably knows the answer… because he was there. I bite my lip, but, of course, I don't ask.

A *"Breaking News"* announcement flashes across the screen. The on-scene reporter announces, "We have just learned that several bodies have been discovered inside the burned-out remains of this building."

Kaleb reaches for the handset and switches over to The Weather Channel.

෩ ⋎ ෬

I'm in the kitchen, curled up in Butch's chair with my hands stuffed inside my sweatshirt. The enormity of Kaleb's latest exploits disturbs me far more than it bothers him. It makes fretting over Sofie's wedding a welcome distraction. The happy day is weeks away and I'm quaking inside, my nerves far worse than any bride's. Removing my hands from the warm pouch, I observe their tremulous shaking. A bad case of the D.T.s, except I've not been drinking. I'm a shattered mess, inert with anxiety, and tortured by my own selfish actions. Unable to summon enough energy to reach for another comforting doughnut, I inspect the cat hair stuck to my sleeve and brood some more.

The mere thought of the upcoming nuptials makes me recoil and glow with a flush of hot remorse. I scratch my itchy skin and revisit my selfish reasons for refusing Sofie's request to be her bridesmaid, now made worse by the possibility of Ken Hunter showing his face. I raise my chin and draw breath—a last gasp before I drown in guilt.

For three months, the jewel-embossed wedding invitation has stood against the toaster, taunting me. The swirling gold calligraphy is an unwelcome reminder of an event I'm anxious to avoid, but duty-bound to attend. Sofie's been planning this day for five years, although she's only been dating Paolo for two.

After the wedding, Paolo's whisking her off to Venice for a fairytale honeymoon, then onto the beautiful Tuscan countryside where they'll continue their charmed lives as newlyweds. They'll spend a year in Lucca with Paolo's family, and Sofie confided she plans to start her own brood, as soon as possible.

Understandably, Sofie's wildly excited, but I'm incredibly sad and unable to share in her happiness. I'll miss her dreadfully. I focus on my loss. For me, her departure represents another bereavement. Things will never be the same again.

The real reason for my refusal surfaces. Selfish thoughts turn to self-loathing, and keep me from entering into the celebratory spirit of her wedding.

Last year, Sofie handed me her guest list and asked, "Is anyone missing?"

I playfully replied, "Me."

She laughed. "The bridesmaids aren't on there, silly."

I stuttered my pathetic excuse. "I'm sorry, I can't do it. Pops' death has left me traumatized."

Luckily, Sofie was too stunned to question my reasoning. More recently, she asked if I'd reconsider her request.

I looked down and clasped my hands. "Everyone knows me as the daughter of the drunk driver. I'm too ashamed to stand up in public."

Which is partly true. I used my parents' demise—Pops succumbing to cancer, followed shortly by Mom's death by DUI—as an acceptable excuse. The truth, however, is several prominent guests on Sofie's list were present at the Martyn's party, where I made a spectacle of myself in my bid to get rid of boyfriend Rick and humiliated all concerned. Now, to cap it all, I have to deal with coming face-to-face with the man who tried to rape me.

Last year, my own close shave with marriage caused me to act out a harebrained scheme and put an end my mother's notion of a "Beckham" wedding. Trapped inside a loveless relationship with Rick, and with my mother determined to force me to the altar, I enlisted Sofie's help. Together we devised a foolproof plan.

Dressed like a hooker, I flirted outrageously with Rick's father and used him as a prop. In front of a crowd of guests, I contrived a scene leading the audience to believe I was involved in an illicit affair with my fiancé's father. Initially, the drama was deemed a great success; Rick was history and my mother's plans, thwarted.

However, my performance was so convincing, Ricks' father bragged to his golf buddies about my interest in older men, and I was wrongly labeled a sugar baby. My father, who belonged to the club, unwittingly boasted about how his recently graduated and brilliant daughter was struggling to find employment. Ken Hunter, a member of their clique, listened with interest. He came knocking at my door, and offered me a position at his acclaimed accounting practice, Hunter, Gomez & Smith. Naively, I accepted, only to find myself in the clutches of a sexual predator. Once his motives became apparent, though, it was too late, I'd signed the contract. He's been pursuing me ever since, and his recent visit leads me to believe he's still not finished with me. This underlying fear leaves me terrified of being attacked again inside my own home.

I never imagined I'd still be suffering the consequences of my foolish actions so long after the event.

On top of this, my career's in tatters. Sofie's still in the dark, completely unaware that I've left my job, and oblivious to how serious the situation with creepy Ken Hunter has become. I hinted about Ken's persistent demands, but never enlightened her about his sordid agenda—I was too ashamed. Sofie misinterpreted his attention.

"Fantastic," she said. "He notices you—it's your irresistible mix of brains and beauty. You should play him, but make sure you get a promotion out of it before you bin him."

There's no way I'll tell Sofie about the most recent assault—the attempted rape—it would ruin her excitement in the run-up to the wedding, especially now that her mother has invited the Hunters' to the evening soiree. I've caused enough trouble already.

I've still not told Kaleb about Ken Hunter being invited to Sofie's wedding. I can't find the words and, anyway, I'm going to come up with a viable excuse to avoid going altogether, so there's no point even mentioning the issue. I've still not fully explained to Kaleb what triggered Hunter's initial interest in me. Kaleb obviously read my online confession at The Last Chance Saloon about ridding myself of my intended, but I've not told him how my performance led to employment at Hunter, Gomez & Smith, and into the hands of a violent predator. Ken's image drifts before me, quickly replaced by Kaleb's face, and I realize the accusation could be levelled at both. I gasp and shake my head eager to remove this preposterous comparison from my mind, but the disturbing parallels refuse to disappear.

Ken Hunter lured me to his company and offered me employment after hearing fictitious tales about my preference for older men. At the same time, and without my knowledge, Kaleb was stalking and baiting me online each time I visited his website. Believing The Last Chance Saloon was somewhere I could anonymously let off steam, I freely poured out my heart. For weeks and months, Kaleb toyed with me and had me stupidly believing Luna was predicting my future. All the time, it was him behind the scenes, contriving scenes and pulling my strings.

Both Kaleb and Ken had designs on me, desired my body, and manipulated me for their own amusement. Kaleb used flattery and guile, and my own gullibility. Ken was just cold and violent, with no regard for me whatsoever.

For months, I fought off Ken Hunter's unwanted advances and made it clear I had nothing to offer apart from my accounting skills. He felt I should reward him, though, with a show of sexual gratitude in appreciation for my job. He threatened to fire me but, in the end, I finally had enough and stormed out of the office with no thought for how my rash action might affect my career.

Meantime, I was being further enticed into Kaleb's dark world on The Last Chance Saloon website. By cleverly using Luna, the fictitious astrologer, he groomed me and lured me to Las Vegas through a lonely hearts advertisement. For weeks he played around with me, refusing to admit he was the Haunted Man whose harrowing stories I'd read online. Meeting Kaleb's family though, left me in no doubt, he was one and the same.

The way Kaleb manipulates me so easily, perturbs me, but I'm in love, and I'm irrational and willing to forgive him almost anything. I admit I'm more than a tiny bit scared of the man I love and fear in equal measure. Kaleb's overwhelming, overpowering, and overbearing. He magnifies my inadequacy. I'm too mentally, physically, and emotionally weak for this man. He's expansive. He's uncharted land, a vast wilderness, impenetrable in places and stunningly beautiful in others. I'm a patch of desolate desert road shooting off into the distance, falling off the edge of the world, and disappearing into nothing.

I want the world to go away, but it won't. I hug my knees to my chest, but find no comfort. I'm trapped inside a continuum I created, and I want it to end, but I can't ignore that Kaleb's tangled up inside this twisted chain of fate.

Weighing my secrets against Kaleb's deadly catalogue, they pale into insignificance. His crimes are far worse than mine but, unlike me, he suffers no regrets.

My eyes land back on the wedding invitation. Avoiding the event altogether is not an option. I must attend, but I wish for a monumental excuse—something outside of my control—summer flu, alien abduction, or a significant tear along the San Andreas Fault.

Kaleb staggers across the hallway and disappears into the pink powder room. Not wanting him to catch me moping, I anticipate his needs, leap from the chair, reach for the coffee pot, and set about making a fresh brew.

He enters the kitchen and flops into the chair I've just vacated.

"That flowery bathroom makes me constipated," he says. "Unlike Butch, I'm uncomfortable shitting in a flowerbed. I can't let go with all those fucking pink roses everywhere."

He lifts his T-shirt, examines his belly, and strokes the dressing covering the stab wound. "Won't be too long before I'm back upstairs—where I belong."

"I'll put some more towels in there," I say, nodding at the bathroom door. "In case you want a shower."

"Do I stink?" I blush. "I stink," he says, smirking crookedly. "Raych, it's okay. You can tell me I smell like a dirty old dog. I won't be offended."

I present him with fresh coffee.

"What you up to?" he asks.

"Nothing much. I don't know where to start."

"I'll give you a hand," he says. "I'll tackle the garage and workshop. But, first I'm going to fix the toaster."

A promise he made earlier. This morning, I incinerated a bagel in the oven, set off the smoke alarm, and stank the house up with charred bread.

He clatters around in the garage searching for the necessary tools. I sink back into Butch's battered chair, coffee in hand, and procrastinate. I reflect on Kaleb's presence and convince myself it's only a matter of time before he'll leave. He'll wait until he's well enough, make an excuse—*"You're too good for me,"* meaning I'm dull and boring—then abandon me.

He reappears in the doorway holding a bunch of screwdrivers, and underscores my concerns. He takes control, he fixes things—that's what he does. He's beautiful, even his cuts and bruises look sexy.

"Fix *me*," I whisper. My eyes hold their tears, but his form blurs as he approaches. He responds to my distress and ditches the tools on the floor. He kneels awkwardly and cradles my head against his chest. "I'm sorry," I say.

"What are you sorry for?"

"For being like this, for being so miserable."

"Hey, come on, you're perfect. You're exactly what I ordered. 'Haunted Man seeks Lost Soul to share a lifetime of torment and misery.' You're more than perfect."

I manage a contorted smile. "I'm scared of losing you."

"Not much chance of that. I'm big and ugly, and can't move too fast at the moment, so I'm pretty easy to find."

"I don't understand why you want to be with me. I keep expecting you to leave, and it makes me incredibly sad."

"I'm not going anywhere, without you, my love." He brushes my hair aside, and tucks a strand behind my ear. "You're just a bit depressed. Remember, you and your cat put a spell on me and I showed up on a blue moon—love magic is powerful stuff. There's no easy way to get rid of me. There's no chapter on undoing the magic… I checked. Besides, Doreen thinks I'm perfect, just what you need."

"I'm pathetic."

"True, but it's okay—your parents died, you lost your job, you're selling your house, you nearly got raped, your best friend's deserting you, and you've got this dodgy dude in your life who's a magnet for death and disaster. It's a lot of shit to deal with all at once, so you have my permission to wallow in self-pity for a little while longer.

"I'm going to fix this toaster, and then I'm going to make a peanut butter, banana, and bacon sandwich. How does that grab you?"

I nod. "Sounds interesting… but isn't that what killed Elvis?"

"There're worse ways to die, believe me."

The voice of experience. I picture the remains of four charred bodies in a derelict café. Toast.

Kaleb seizes Sofie's wedding invitation, propped against the toaster, and reads aloud, "Mr. & Mrs. Terrance Ventura request the pleasure of Miss Raychelle Carter and Guest at the wedding of their beloved daughter, Signora Sofie Francesca Ventura, to Signore Paolo Raphael Ravenna."

I told Sofie I didn't have a guest to bring along, but she's forever hopeful I'll find one. She was sorry to hear things hadn't worked out with the weird lumberjack, but I doubt even she can imagine just how weird he is. I haven't told her the full story because I can't face the inevitable scrutiny. If she discovers his true identity she'll interrogate me for hours, and force me to confess all my covert liaisons.

"So, Miss Raychelle Carter, who's your guest?"

"I don't have one."

"You could ask me?"

"You?" I stutter, hardly able to speak as images of Kaleb confronting Ken Hunter crowd my mind. "You'd go to a wedding with me?"

"Why not? If you want me to."

My mind goes blank. The possibility of Kaleb inviting himself to Sofie's wedding is an unforeseen development, and I don't have a forthcoming excuse. "I didn't ask, because I didn't think you'd be interested."

"So, ask me."

"Will you please be my guest at Sofie's wedding? I'd love you to come." I cannot believe these words have left my mouth. What have I done?

"My pleasure, I love to come anytime, anywhere with you." He limps over and brushes his finger against my flushed cheek.

"There'll be plenty of food and drink, won't there?"

"Yes, it'll be an extravagant affair. You might need a new outfit."

Immediately, I'm nervous. My stomach cartwheels. I've only ever seen him in faded jeans, well-worn shirts, and sand-blasted leather boots.

"I've got a hat,' he says, referring to his beat-up khaki cowboy hat he's fond of wearing. "I could stick a feather in it."

Suddenly, his injuries take on new intensity. The fading cabbage-rose bruises adorning his body burst into full bloom—a blue, purple and yellow floral display. He stares at me with bloodshot eyes, and I notice the stark contrast between his shaved eyebrow and its bushy neighbor. Will the eyebrow grow back, and will the stitches be gone in time for the wedding?

Will Ken Hunter recognize the beat-up handyman, who's been repairing my house? Will he wonder why I'm now dating the handyman, and not his brother? All these lies and secrets are getting out of control. *Oh, what a tangled web we weave when first we practice to deceive.*

I regret asking.

"What?" he asks.

"Nothing." I imagine him smiling for photos, proudly displaying his missing tooth, but maybe I'm worrying unnecessarily, he rarely smiles. He smirks when he's happy, and sneers when he's not. I picture him grabbing Ken Hunter by the throat and smacking him in the face. I imagine the wedding descending into chaos and fingers pointing at me. "Her, again!" my accusers will say.

It's crystal clear—I cannot attend Sofie's wedding. I must do something drastic to avoid the event. My stomach aches—I massage the knot. "This wedding's making me ill."

"There's no need to get upset," Kaleb says. "It's not you getting married."

I wouldn't be upset if I was marrying you. Overwhelming love and desire for him brings a surge of emotion. My sad eyes betray me, again. He reaches out.

"Raych, come and dance with me."

"There's no music."

"I'll make some. It's what I do." I take his hand, and he pulls me close. "Let go, my love. You know you want to."

"I'm scared of falling." I tense a little more. Resistance is evident in my muscles, and his fingers knead my body.

"I'll catch you, my love. Together, we'll crash through the flames into the heart of the fire."

Tears flow. Cupid's arrow is lodged deep inside my heart. Any attempt to dislodge the barbed dart will result in instant death. I surrender, and admit his name is seared across my heart. I step off the precipice and let myself believe he loves me. We dance close around the kitchen, moving in slow circles. Kaleb softly sings, "I want you, and I know you want me, too."

I'm flying, soaring high, but I don't know how to land.

ಶ ♈ ಜ

The evening news updates us on this morning's fire. Four charred bodies have been recovered from the scene; all adult, gender unknown. The medical examiner will conduct extensive tests to determine identity. A strong lead on one victim may provide clues towards identifying the others. Speculation points to drug related, gang violence.

If I were into gambling, I'd bet the Jack of Hearts lying beside me knows the answer.

6. Black Bears

Butch wants his chair back... now, and is doing his utmost to unseat Kaleb. Claws extend, pierce denim, and puncture flesh.

"Okay, okay, you little furry fucker." Kaleb grips Butch's paw, and gently but firmly removes the talons from his thigh. "I'm moving as fast as I can."

Butch, unimpressed by Kaleb's slow reaction, emits a menacing guttural growl, followed by the hiss of death—a final warning. Butch's small cat brain has forgotten Kaleb's the person responsible for reuniting him with dear Mr. Ratty.

Kaleb struggles to raise himself from the sagging chair. "I'm off to the garage to escape your rabid cat. I shall return locked and loaded."

I can't help smiling. "Thanks for volunteering to sort the tools, I haven't a clue what most of them are for."

Kaleb heaves himself up. "No problem."

"Take whatever you want."

Without chance to rephrase my offer, his rough hands are up my shirt.

"Never one to refuse such an enticing invitation."

Mindful of his injuries, I wrestle him away, and point at the door leading into the garage. "Away. Now! Or, I'll set my cat on you."

Butch pads around in circles on the still-warm cushion and bats Kaleb's book to the floor. I retrieve *Panning for Gold in The Golden State*. Kaleb's exploring the rich seam of gold mining books he's discovered in Pops' study.

Amongst Pops' many interests, tinkering with the camper van and basic DIY were his favorites and, over the years, he acquired tools for every task imaginable. I'm just thankful Kaleb has the expertise and inclination to sort through them. Also requiring disposal are Pops' Lexus; and Mom's Audi which, on close inspection, displays remarkably little damage considering its role in a fatal accident. The windshield and paintwork are all intact; the only visible evidence is a smashed taillight and a grazed bumper where the truck clipped Mom's car and sent her into a death spin.

Taking pride of place inside the massive garage and hogging all the space, is the whale of a camper van, sitting idly between the two cars, jacked up and floating on air like a magic bus. Pops worried the tires might suffer under the vehicle's stationary weight, but was unconcerned about me—forced to park in the driveway. Why Pops insisted on keeping the large redundant vehicle, I don't know. And, whenever I suggested selling the thing he'd parrot Mom and come out with some poetic nonsense. "The van holds such happy memories of all the wonderful places we've visited." Now they're gone, I want rid of their vehicles, and their clutter. And, as for the fond memories… they elude me.

Kaleb's impressed with the camper. "It's very retro, with better facilities than my cabin."

"Have it, if you can start it," I tell him, "but I'm not riding shotgun." After serious consideration he decides keeping the van is impractical, and I should go ahead and list it.

♋ ♈ ♋

Over the past few days, and after several trips across town to specialist car-part suppliers, the engine runs, smoothly. Yesterday, Kaleb replaced the brakes and took the vehicle for a test drive. Satisfied it's roadworthy, and while the van's in a stripped-down state, prudence has him replacing all things rubber. Pipes may have perished, so the plumbing receives an overhaul, including the sink, the toilet, and shower cubicle.

Soft furnishings are laid out on a tarpaulin on the kitchen floor ready for me to launder. The curtains should survive the delicate cycle, and the cushions are getting steam cleaned—I dread to think what might be living in them. Kaleb's enjoying his task of fixing the vehicles and sorting the tools, and I wish his enthusiasm would infect me. I'm listless, and make slow progress clearing cupboards and closets. I want the house sold and the satisfaction of hearing the front door slam behind me—one last time.

Kaleb finds me in the laundry room, washing and sorting towels, ready for donation to the animal shelter. He presents me with a small pair of scarlet Converse All Stars and a Maine Black Bears sweatshirt.

"Remember these?" he asks.

"Should I?"

"They were jammed behind a panel under the seating area, next to the water pipes."

He sets them on the dryer. I hold the sweatshirt up and examine the logo. The snarling black bear with red tongue and blue lettering isn't something I'm familiar with.

"They're boys' clothes," I conclude. "Mom would never let me wear these." I inspect the basketball shoes. "Not mine."

"Maybe they belonged to a friend of yours?"

"I have one friend, and I assure you, Sofie would not be seen dead in this get-up. Besides, she never came camping with us."

Instinctively, I loosen the laces and yank the sides of the shoe apart. The tongue falls forward, and scrawled in an uneven childish hand is the owner's name. The shoe belongs to *"TaY C."*

"It's your name."

"I'm Ray C, not Tay C."

"Mmm, very *racy*," he says, and squeezes my butt. "Maybe you had crap handwriting back then. Maybe it's worn off."

"They're *definitely* not mine, and why would I support a team from Maine?"

"Don't know, but you love bears, maybe the logo attracted you."

"There's nothing cute about this sweatshirt—it's not exactly the Care Bears. Maybe they belonged to the van's previous owner."

I leave the shoes on top of the dryer along with the bags of clothes ready for drop-off at the recycling bin. Kaleb returns to the garage, cranks the radio and accompanies Kurt Cobain. "Come as you are," they implore, as I focus on the shoes with a second look.

After lunch, Kaleb resumes work on the camper and I venture upstairs, intent on clearing the closets. Sorting through Mom's and

Pops' clothes is easy enough, the only decision required is—recycle; charity; or wash first, then charity. All month, this simple task has been my primary goal, but a low boredom threshold diverts my attention to more stimulating, time-wasting distractions. Pops' Sudoku puzzle books lure me away. I'm currently working through the *very difficult* section, and pleased with my progress.

Sitting in the room where Pops died, I take the Sudoku book from his nightstand, and let my eyes wander aimlessly around as I compute the different number combinations. Mindlessly, I focus on his slippers still neatly tucked under the armchair, and worn so often they've taken on his feet's form. I remove them from their hiding place and contemplate throwing them away, but I'm not ready yet. Staring at the slippers evokes Pops' ghost—his voice, his laugh, his presence. As reality slowly trickles back, I lift my gaze from the floor and I'm surprised to find his slippers empty. For a moment, I forgot he was dead.

My mind turns to the Converse All Stars downstairs—whose feet walked in those shoes? I visualize the red canvas with the frayed, grubby-grey laces poking through metal eyelets. Instinctively, I look at my toes to examine their scuffed noses, but I'm wearing flip-flops. I raise my head to see who's standing in their favorite red shoes, and find a young, sad-faced me. A violent shiver jolts my body and my shoulders buck as someone walks across my grave. I tuck Pops' slippers back under the chair, and leave the room and the ghosts, behind.

Entering Mom's boudoir, I'm met by the lingering scent of roses and the echo of her voice. *"What are you doing in here?"*

"Go away," I say. But she won't, she's on my shoulder, and follows me into her closet. *"You're not allowed in here."*

"Too bad."

I take stock of the contents, and wonder at the thousands of dollars spent lining this small dark windowless room—the barely worn shoes still in their original boxes, the evening gowns encased in clear plastic, and suits hung with delicately embroidered lavender bags. All from another time, and most of which I never saw her wear. Sorting through this vast array is too daunting. I switch the light off and focus my attention on her bathroom.

There're so many toiletries, she must've spent a fortune over the years. Anti-aging, youth serum, day cream, night cream—none of them worked. It's all going in the trash, but I can't discard anything without first reading the product label—another sad attempt at getting to know my mother.

The bathroom cupboard yields a vast collection of cleaning products, along with several empty vodka bottles stashed behind a pack of twenty-four, velvet-texture, rose-embossed toilet tissue. It's the same cheap brand of vodka she had in her car the day she died.

I discover a jewelry box I never knew existed, full of dainty gold trinkets. I've no idea if they're valuable or sentimental, whether they're junk or heirlooms. I put the box aside. I'll examine the contents later, with Kaleb.

Still unable to muster any enthusiasm to tackle the closet, I move into the bedroom. Hidden in her nightstand are two very overdue library books and more empty vodka bottles. Also, the Bohemian crystal tumbler missing from the set downstairs. I pour the half-empty bottle of flat tonic water into the sink. When did Mom start drinking? Was it a reaction to Pops' death, or has she been hiding her secret for years? I never really knew her. All my life, I'd been living with a stranger. So much went unsaid and, now she's gone, there are so many unanswered questions.

From downstairs, Kaleb announces, "Won't be long, I'm off to pick up some parts for the van."

So much for never being alone in the house. I guess a brief errand doesn't count.

Once he's finished, Kaleb will advertise the camper online and in a few specialist publications, along with a photograph and brief description. The mileage is relatively low for a vintage vehicle, so he anticipates selling it for a good price to someone with a taste for nostalgia.

The phone rings. I move to the doorway and prick up my ears. Is Ken Hunter watching the house? Has he just seen Kaleb leave? Is he checking to see if I'm home?

The message recorder invites the caller to leave their name and number. A long drawn out beep follows.

"Hi, Raych. Me again, Rick. I don't know if you got my message the other day... maybe you're away? Anyway, about hooking up, my wife's at her sister's for a few days, so the coast is clear. You've got my number."

I grip the doorknob. *I've definitely got your number, Rick.*

He was never this interested when we were dating. Why is he calling me now? I don't think I need ask. I sit on Mom's bed and fantasize about running away—with Kaleb—and leaving all my problems behind.

The doorbell rings and interrupts my daydream, a sound guaranteed to send my heart racing. The caller's persistent. I peer out from behind lace curtains and see a lilac delivery van advertising Flo's Flowers.

I open the door and accept the pretty bouquet. The arrangement is a little formal for Kaleb's tastes, but understandable if he ordered them over the phone. I take the flowers to the kitchen, dismantle the trimmings and randomly place the blooms in a large jug of water.

The moment Kaleb steps through the door, I pounce, and drag him into the study. When I'm finished, he zips his fly and smirks at me.

"You're quite the expert. With a talent like yours, you could make a fortune. Who taught you?"

Shyly, I admit, "Fabian… Sofie's twin."

"I thought he was gay?"

"Exactly."

"If I ever meet Fabian, remind me to thank him. And, what did I do to deserve such a heartfelt homecoming?"

"You know."

"I don't know."

"You do, stop teasing. They're beautiful, thank you."

"You're beautiful, and thank you, but I still don't know what you think I've done. Tell me, please, because your show of gratitude was much appreciated."

"The flowers."

"What flowers?"

"You can be so infuriating sometimes."

"I don't know anything about any flowers."

I take his hand and lead him into the kitchen. I gesture towards my artistic arrangement. "See."

"Flowers."

"Thank you."

"They're not from me, but if this is what it takes to get a blowjob every time I walk through the door, I'm on it."

The flowers aren't from him. He's not joking. He's as I perplexed as I am. I put my hand to my mouth to stop myself speaking out loud. What if they're from Rick? The phone call and the flowers in quick succession—a coincidence? The unimaginative arrangement is exactly the type of trite expression Rick would make, at the same time applauding himself for acting suave.

"Did they come with a message?" Kaleb asks.

I read the florist's card. "No."

"Phone them."

I do, but first Kaleb concocts a story for me.

"I received a beautiful bouquet this afternoon. I think they're from my aunt or uncle and I want to thank them. The problem is, they got divorced recently and they hate each other, and I'm loathe to cause more trouble by thanking the wrong person. Could you possibly tell me who they're from, please?"

I nod at Kaleb and wait while the florist consults her records. I'm now convinced they're from Rick.

"They're from your uncle," she says. "Mr. Kenneth Hunter."

"Thank you," I whisper.

ಸಾ ᛫ ಇ

I can't sleep, and the weather's not helping. Why is Ken Hunter sending me flowers? Is this his crass apology? A loud crack of thunder sets my heart banging. Incessant lightning illuminates my room with violent silver light. I envision trickles of water swelling into floods and creating waterfalls in the canyons. I picture brown mud covering roads, forcing its way into homes, and making escape impossible for those stranded.

I imagine I'm drowning. A man grabs my hair and yanks my head above water. I'm safe, it's Kaleb, but he morphs into Ken Hunter. I scream. A Scooby-Doo crack of thunder rips through the sky and splits a tree. I scream again, and dive under the comforter.

Someone tugs the bedcover. I scream yet again.

"What's with all the screaming?" Kaleb asks. He slips in beside me and removes my T-shirt—his T-shirt. "This thing stinks." He snuggles up. "No interfering with me, my ribs are aching."

7. Who Are You?

The phone wakes me. I push through layers of consciousness and force my eyelids open. I turn my head and find Kaleb gone. My fingers explore the cool sheet—he's been gone awhile.

"Hey, are you awake?" he yells from downstairs.

I am now.

"I think so."

He plays the phone message and I strain to hear Barbara's orders—she's organizing an open house event for the coming weekend. She tactfully reminds me, "You might want to pack the doll collection away. Potential buyers might find the display a little excessive, or possibly a little off-putting. I'd hate for your family heirlooms to get damaged."

I picture a bonfire on the back lawn, the air thick with toxic smoke and acrid fumes, from melting plastic and real human hair.

"You should also consider removing the lacy curtains to allow natural sunlight to *flood* the rooms." *Flood*, prompts a vivid flashback to last night's nightmare, featuring Ken Hunter. She further explains, "The buyer needs to project their own personality onto a beautifully presented neutral canvas.

"Remove the cat bowls, the litter tray, the pet toys, the cat food from the fridge, the fur, the dead bird from the garage roof, and *the cat*." She has it in for Butch. "People have allergies," she says to justify her hatred. She makes several more suggestions, and finishes by saying, "I'll email the list. I don't expect you'll remember all my recommendations."

I'm unsure whether to be offended, or grateful she's taking such keen interest in selling my property.

"Are you hearing this?" Kaleb asks. "Barbara says your house is a horror show, she wants your cat dead, and we need to get this fucking mess cleared up by the weekend."

Not quite what Barbara said, but he captures the essence.

Over breakfast, I tell Kaleb, "I can't face Mom's lounge."

He leaves the table for a moment, and returns with Pops' Courvoisier. "Drink this."

I pull a face. "Cognac?"

"Fortification, before entering the creepy doll sanctuary."

The brandy soon has me giggling about the task ahead. Kaleb leads the way. We wander around Mom's lounge, and assess the situation. Kaleb seizes Beulah by the hair and dangles the scary life-size representation of a five-year-old girl in the air.

He confesses, "When I set eyes on it, I blurted out to Barbara, 'What the fuck is that?' She ignored me, said I could make an offer on the furniture."

It *is* funny, but the alcohol makes his recollection mildly hysterical.

Kaleb lies back on the chintz sofa, legs parted with his hands behind his head. "What do you think?" he asks. "Do flowery fabrics suit me?"

"You look good anywhere."

"You poor girl."

I kiss Kaleb's scabby lips and inhale his intoxicating brandy-breath. Suddenly, I picture Ken Hunter sitting there moments before he attacked me, and I go from amusement to distress in a nanosecond—from silly to sober.

Kaleb leads me from the room and into his den in Pops' study. He smothers me in hugs and kisses, and reassures me with his words. An hour later, I'm restored, and Kaleb leaves me to pore through the yards of literature lining the walls. On his way out of the door, he turns back. "Leave the maps and gold rush books. I'll sort them later."

The study is less scary than the doll depository, but equally as daunting. Assembling more cardboard boxes is a useful delaying tactic. Kaleb's already started a box of "keepers," and I'll fill it with anything he might find interesting. All other publications are destined for the second-hand bookstore.

The books are in no discernable order. How Pops ever found anything amongst this random assortment remains a mystery—maybe he enjoyed the hunt. I pull books of no interest whatsoever: military aircraft, steam trains, and great battles, but wonder if Kaleb might like them, so I leave them on the floor—pending. True crime is a popular topic: serial killers, crimes of passion, missing persons, and even stories about children discovered years later as adults. These all end up in Kaleb's camp—he relishes factual accounts, but has no time for horror stories.

With confidence, I place foreign language dictionaries and encyclopedias in the charity box—the Internet has rendered them obsolete. The top shelf surrenders: Lautrec, Gauguin, *Nude Photography, Techniques for Life Drawing,* and a comprehensive collection of Alberto Vargas illustrations—nothing too explicit. Kaleb confessed he'd discovered a porn stash in the cupboard above the mini-fridge in the garage, but reassured me, "I had a good look and there's nothing to worry about."

After my initial cull, I move onto natural wonders, atlases, travel guides and nature. Every publication becomes a distraction, and indecision has me moving the books from one box to another until I give up.

A short daydream ensues before I attack the novels. Don't judge a book by its cover—but I do. If the title or cover illustration doesn't grab me it goes directly into the charity box. If there's any hint of war, violence or suffering, without hesitation, I drop it in the charity box. Mom's collection of historical romances come to mind. They won't need sorting—I know exactly where they'll be going… recycling. I reach an impasse, I need Kaleb's decisive input, but he's busy working on the vehicles. Frustrated by my inability to perform this simple task, I scan the room for something less taxing. The filing cabinet represents a challenge, but clearing the desk and its six small draws is achievable.

I remove the "Treaty of Guadalupe Hidalgo 1848" from Pops' upholstered leather swivel chair, take a seat, and rest my feet on the large lock-box stowed under the footwell. The old metal munitions container protects our family's important documents, such as title deeds and insurance policies. Pops instructed me to save the box if ever there was a fire but, failing that, he felt sure the sturdy container could withstand the flames and preserve the paperwork. I assumed this precaution was a reaction to our San Diego experience, when the fire destroyed my first home and almost everything we owned. More than once I offered to scan the documents, but Pops said, "It's not worth the bother, we'd be extremely unlucky if lightning struck twice."

I've been meaning to check the contents for a while, in case I've overlooked any shares or savings, or items relating to my parents' estate. I drag the heavy munitions box from its dark hiding place, out into the open, and wonder if any trace of TNT still exists. I take the key from the slim, partially hidden, drawer in the center of Pop's desk, and prop myself against the sofa. Kaleb's clutter litters the room, and his irreverent use of once-deemed precious objects makes me smile. Old newspapers and T-shirts are stuffed down the Chesterfield, cigarette butts sit in the "display only" Versace ashtray, and his tobacco stash resides in the Czechoslovakian crystal fruit bowl. If only Mom could see it now.

Still smiling, I insert the key into the padlock and open the box. I pull out bundles of folded documents and brown envelopes, and scatter them across the rug into ordered piles according to subject matter: share certificates, old insurance documents, vehicle title deeds, and the house title deed, which I put aside in case it's needed for proof of ownership. I also create a pile for random items requiring closer scrutiny. One such item is a plain brown envelope inside another identical, but larger envelope. The double packaging both amuses and reminds me of the children's game—pass-the-parcel. But, the document contained within, hits me like a bullet to the frontal lobe. It causes severe mental and physical paralysis. The topic is difficult to categorize, and I don't have a pile for such incendiary information.

I'm reeling, unable to comprehend what I'm reading. I've discovered a stray hand grenade and inadvertently pulled its pin. Blood drains from my head and pools in my stomach. I scan the details on my death certificate. White paper and black words confirm—Raychelle Sarah Carter's date of birth and date of death. Died June 16th, 1986. Cause of death—"accidental drowning." Additional

Coroner's note—"body recovered from pool after indeterminate length of time." Place of death: "15036 Coronado Trail, San Diego, State of California."

The letters swim around on the page. I shut down and slump to the floor.

At some point, Kaleb rouses me with his foot. "Hey, sleepy drawers, are you napping on the job?"

I'm unsure how long I've been lying here. "Are you pissed? Have you been at your dad's brandy?"

I groan, unable to respond.

"Hey, are you okay?" He sounds concerned. My mouth opens, but words don't come. "Did you fall?"

Kaleb kneels and grips my shoulders. He hauls me upright and props me against the sofa. "You're not well are you? I'll get you some water."

By the time he returns, I'm coming to. He crouches, holds the glass to my lips and tips my head forward. I take a sip of water and struggle to breathe.

"You okay? You look deathly pale."

After a few more sips I say, "I've had a shock."

"Electrocuted?" He scans the immediate vicinity, searching for exposed wires. "What did you touch?"

A high-voltage charge has ripped through me, but it's not electricity. I locate the certificate and point. "Read that."

"Fuck! This is too fucking weird."

As I digest what I've read, the enormity of the situation burns a slow path along every fibrous nerve in my body, and I shake uncontrollably. Kaleb envelopes my quaking body. He presses his palm against my cheek and turns my face to his, "It's going to be okay, Raych. It'll be okay, there'll be some logical explanation... but I can't think what it is right now."

This cannot be happening. My eyes dart frantically around, desperately seeking an answer. There must've been a mistake. How could they issue a death certificate, when I'm indisputably alive?

"Where did you find it, Raych?"

"In Pops' box with all the other important papers."

Who Are You?

"There must be a good reason for this. Maybe they faked your death and claimed the life insurance? Maybe you're adopted? Maybe you had a twin who died? Maybe..."

Whatever the answer, it isn't immediately obvious.

My stomach ties itself in a thousand knots, my head pounds, and breathing becomes difficult—I've forgotten how to breathe. I count to regulate my oxygen inflow, but the moment my eyes rest on *that* piece of paper I stop breathing again. If I'm not Raychelle, who the hell am I? Can it be, I *am* someone else?

Standing by the window, Kaleb holds the certificate against the light. The clearly visible watermark proves it's genuine. I part my knees and vomit on the rug. Kaleb leaves the room, and returns with a wet towel and another glass of water. My head lolls around on my shoulders like a small boat at the mercy of unpredictable waves. He wipes my face with the towel and holds me. The room's spinning. I twist in his arms and lie down. He retrieves a cushion from the sofa and gently lifts my head to position the pillow. Without a word, he lies behind me, and holds my hair away from my mouth.

Kaleb rests his hand on my hip and anchors me to the ground. We lie there for a while. I'm alert but, at the same time, incredibly tired. Periodically, I open my eyes to check whether the room's stopped turning. Satisfied it's come to a complete rest, I watch shadows lengthen in the hallway, slowly at first before quickly stretching out. I follow dust motes in the golden light and watch them intensify as dusk encroaches, until they fade into the gloom.

I hear a paw connect with plastic, followed by a swish and the steady rhythmic tap of claws against wood as Butch comes to investigate what's happened to his catering crew. His little furry head cautiously appears around the door, and he looks surprised to find my eyes on a level with his. His pupils dilate, he knows something's awry. His nose pulls his wide eyes towards the vomit. I look at him. I look at the puke. He looks at me. I murmur, "Yes, I know it wasn't you, it was me."

The world's stopped spinning, the tumultuous seas have ceased their churning and I find myself adrift, bobbing around in calm shallow water. I cautiously move into a sitting position. Still lightheaded, I attempt to stand. Kaleb steadies me as I rise, and I'm thankful for his unquestioning silence. Swaying gently from side to side, he holds my head against his chest and kisses my hair. I'm reassured by his strong steady heartbeat and the familiar smell of sweat, tobacco, and oily car engines.

Butch pokes my legs, his stomach has no respect for anything. Everything and nothing has changed. I'm still in Pops' study, Butch still needs his dinner, Kaleb's still here, it's still Monday, but I'm *dead* according to the County of San Diego. Kaleb seats me on the sofa. "I'll feed Butch. Don't go anywhere."

He returns with the pink bucket, a towel and a scrubbing brush, and I'm frozen in place.

Crouching awkwardly, and to my embarrassment, he scours the rug and removes the puke. Job done he asks, "Do you want to get cleaned up?" I nod.

He guides me from the study and ushers me up the stairs to my bedroom. "Will you be okay if I leave you?"

My mind twists his innocent words into a devastating statement. I grab his lacerated arms, and dig my fingers in with no regard for his injuries. Sobbing hysterically I plead with him, "Don't leave me. Please, don't leave me."

"Hey, I only meant leave you so you could take a shower, while I finish cleaning up downstairs. I won't ever leave you."

Kaleb, once again, suppresses my shaking body and cocoons me in his arms. I don't want to be alone. In life, normally the one person you do know intimately is yourself. I panic. I can't remember who I really am. I must have amnesia. I don't know what reality is anymore. A crazy notion takes hold—I'm an alien inhabiting the host's body. I'm hysterical. Mental confusion turns into a physical struggle. I grapple with Kaleb.

He clamps my arms. "Raych, get a fucking grip."

He undresses me, removes his clothes also, and manhandles me into the shower. The spray is real and reaffirming, but my eyes won't open, they refuse to look at things differently.

"Face the wall," he orders. With my palms pressed against tile I brace myself while he washes my hair. He runs his soapy hands over my body, concentrating on some areas more than others. I wish I was sane enough to enjoy his touch. He shuts the faucet off and wraps me in a towel. He hands me my toothbrush and squirts a dollop of toothpaste on the bristles. My brain forces my body into shutdown. I crave sleep, I'm incredibly tired.

Wrapped in damp towels we make it to the bed. I curl into a fetal position. Kaleb stuffs my teddy bear against my chest and holds me from behind—covering me, protecting me, overwhelming me. The safety of being held in his arms is the only thing in the world that makes any sense.

8. Don't Look Back

Hours later, my eyes spring open, expecting zombies to emerge from the darkness, come to claim me as one of their own.

"Are you awake?" I whisper.

"Yeah."

I turn to Kaleb for refuge. I want him to transport me far away from this shocking new reality. I kiss him. "I've missed you."

"It won't be long now, my love. I'm almost healed, then you'll be sorry."

"I can't wait any longer I want you now. I need to escape... immediately. Take me back to the night at your cabin when we first made love."

We're both frustrated. He kneads my hip. I need his dick. Until now, his injuries have resulted in his self-imposed exile and prevented us from attempting anything too ambitious. In clumsy eagerness, I reach for his arm and knock the wound left by a grazing bullet. He winces. My fingers search for his face, but press too hard against his fractured cheekbone. His body tenses. I kick his broken toe. He knocks me back.

"There's only one way this is going to work," he says. He straddles me and reaches for the bedside lamp. The light comes on and he slides his hand under my pillow expecting to find the scarf he once wore, which I keep hidden. Predictably, he does. "It's purely for safety reasons," he explains. "I'm going about this slowly so neither of us gets hurt."

He binds my wrist, raises my arm, and nuzzles my armpit before threading the scarf through the branches of the headboard. He secures my other wrist. Our eyes lock as he looms over me.

"When I'm finished with you, you won't give a fuck who you are."

He lowers his head and licks my nipples, encouraging them with his teeth. His tongue traces a slow cool path to my neck. His lips come dangerously close to mine. He pulls back to regard my craving body. He takes me to the edge and leaves me dangling. His nose plows my hair away from my ear. His lips graze my lobe and his close words click inside my ear. "I'll torment your flesh and penetrate you slowly until you surrender. Then I'm going to fuck you so hard, for as long as it takes to steal your heart and make you mine."

His tongue and lips begin their journey of rediscovery, exploring every inch of my body and drive me insane. "I'm coming for you," he murmurs.

I'm already pleading, "Fuck me, now."

"You're in no position to make demands. Beg if you want, but I'm taking my time and I've only just begun."

"I want you now."

"I know what you want but, first, let me tell you what *I* want."

Without hesitation I surrender to his demands. Right now, I don't care who I am. I'd sell my soul to the devil if I could stay here forever. This is the only validation I need or want. He travels my body: around me, on me, in me, through me. Wherever he's led me I'm lost.

After suffering minutes of exquisite torture, I order him, "Stick your tongue out."

"No," he says. "It's rude."

"Show me your tongue," I demand.

He smirks and reveals he can lick the tip of his nose. "Satisfied?" he asks.

"More than," I reply.

෩ ϒ ଔ

Agitated and drowsy, I convince myself Butch is sleeping on my chest, but the weight of my discovery rests like a rock on my heart.

Who would think a sheet of paper could weigh so heavily. The deadly silence is deafening.

Kaleb's steely arm, like lifesaving flotsam, keeps me afloat in a merciless ocean. I cling on for dear life, kiss his biceps, and give thanks. The house timbers emit a loud crack. A jolt of terror sears through my body and alarms me into full consciousness. I swear my ears move, tensing muscles that fell dormant generations ago. Kaleb's arms tighten their hold, and his fingers fall like gentle rain across my face.

He tucks my hair behind my ear and whispers, "I'm starving. D'you fancy cheese on toast?"

After skipping dinner due to my earlier episode downstairs and our bedtime antics, I'm famished. I'm amazed Kaleb's lasted so long without sustenance.

I sit at the kitchen table and watch Kaleb multitask—he munches a gherkin while making grilled cheese sandwiches and sorting the coffee. I look towards Pops' study. Who would've guessed this house was harboring such dark secrets. For years, I've been sharing my space with highly explosive information hidden in plain sight. The munitions box served its purpose well—kept the TNT safe.

Casting my mind back, my life becomes a kaleidoscope of images, a forever changing landscape where nothing is quite what it seems. I examine my parents' often odd behavior: their isolation, fear of authority, and refusing my passport request. Several years ago, Sofie's family offered to take me skiing in Italy. Mom freaked out and became hysterical.

There's too much to consider, too much to process, and too much to misinterpret when you examine everything with suspicion. I want facts and evidence, not an index of possibilities and speculation. If I'm not Raychelle Sarah Carter, who am I? I don't remember being someone else. Kaleb bangs a plate down in front of me and interrupts my retrospection.

"What d'you want with it? Onions, mustard, pickle?"

"Caramelized onions please. In the fridge next to the ketchup."

Our eyes meet across the table as we lift our coffee mugs. He guesses where my mind is. "So, how old were you when you died?"

"Five years and two days according to the death certificate."

"How old were you when you moved here?"

"Five and a bit."

"Do you think they might've faked your death, got the insurance money then bought this place?"

"No. Mom and Pops were good people. They always did the right thing, paid their bills on time, and Pops was fanatical about completing his tax returns. They weren't the type to commit grand larceny. They were honest, respectable, ordinary people."

"With an extraordinary secret?"

"Maybe."

Kaleb wanders towards Pops' study and returns, clutching the death certificate. "It says you drowned at Coronado Trail, San Diego. Does the address sound familiar?"

Coronado Trail. Coronado Trail. I slowly shake my head from side to side. "No."

"Do you remember anything about your first home?"

I gaze into space and attempt to access my memory files, but there's been an office break-in, and everything's been turned upside down and strewn across the floor. "Not really."

"Tell me about your childhood?"

"There's not much to tell... just a few disjointed little girl memories of simple everyday events... nothing unusual."

"When did you say you moved here?"

Memories of us living in the camper van in the driveway spring to mind. At the time I was disturbed and confused as to why we couldn't inhabit the house. I guess we had no furniture. I distinctly remember Mom being excited and declaring, "The beds have arrived."

"September eighty-six, after our house in San Diego was destroyed by fire."

"Do you remember the actual fire?"

I turn my head towards imaginary flames and can almost feel the heat scorching my skin. "I think I remember the flames and, at the time, Mom claimed I was suffering with shock and confusion... the effects of smoke inhalation."

"Convenient." Kaleb seizes my left wrist, which makes me flinch. Anxiety flushes through my body. "And, what about this?" He scrutinizes my palm with the intensity of a wild gypsy fortune teller.

We study the unusual pink gouge on the heel of my palm. "Mom said it was a birth mark. A 'strawberry mark' she called it."

"It's not a birth mark though, is it? A birthmark is a discoloration, not an indentation? Did you get this in the fire?" He takes a closer look. "Doesn't look like a burn."

We stare at the evidence with expectation and patiently wait for my hand to speak. I'm physically marked, but have no recollection of the incident.

"Do you remember anything about your childhood before you lived in Santa Monica? The slightest thing might offer a clue."

"I don't."

"Okay, what's your first memory of your mom and dad?"

"A vacation in a forest in the camper van. I lost my teddy bear and Mom wouldn't let me look for him. I haven't forgiven her, I loved that bear."

"What did it look like?"

"Golden fur, hard limbs that moved, and glassy eyes. And, when I poked his belly, he growled."

"Sounds a lot like me. Do I remind you of your first love?"

Suddenly, I'm shy and blushing, but he might be right. He smirks. "Call me Bear if you want, but not Teddy."

I try it out for size, "Bear." It suits him—he's some type of animal, and Bear sounds nicer than Wolf.

Back on track he asks. "Where were you?"

"I don't know... in some woods."

"What about any other vacations: a beach, Disneyland, snow?"

"I remember playing in snow with two older boys. One threw a snowball... it hit me in the face. I cried. But, maybe I imagined it, because we never went anywhere cold."

"Memory is a peculiar thing. Sometimes fact becomes fiction, and fiction becomes fact. Don't turn memories into truth unless you're certain of the facts. This house could hold more clues. Question everything you find, and pay attention to your instincts."

We move to the sofa in the family room. TV fills the void. Kaleb nods off, hunger was keeping him awake, but I can't rest. My brain's in overdrive, swamped by jumbled images from the past. Given what I've unearthed, hindsight forces me to look sideways at my life and view events from a different perspective. Wide-eyed, I stare at the overhead fan. I attach new meaning to my parents' often odd and erratic behavior. Instances of their strange and unusual reactions gives me gooseflesh.

My scalp prickles as I recall the times I wished I was someone else, and how I convinced myself they'd brought the wrong baby home from the hospital. As a child, I often discussed the topic with Sofie, and she assured me all kids question their parentage, especially when they're misunderstood. Looking at Sofie, there's no doubt who her parents are. Her family share eyes, noses, hair color, even mannerisms. When I bring my own small family into focus, my physiological traits appear unattributable to either parent. Adrenalin courses through my veins, keeping me awake and focused on the spinning fan.

Deep in sleep, Kaleb's hold relaxes. I disentangle myself from his arms and slip away without waking him. Impatient for answers, I enter Pops' study. The need for truth far outweighs the fear of discovering further shocking information. I crouch and my knees land on the damp patch where Kaleb sponged the rug. With shoulders hunched, and the urgency of an intruder pushed for time, I sift through the documents scattered before me, but they yield no more clues.

I don't belong here, I never have. This house is not my home. It's where I live, but nothing more. I grab the family portrait displayed on Pops' desk and struggle to find a family resemblance. I consider families other than Sofie's and mentally summon their facial features. Alec and Alan, twins from my schooldays, provide momentary comfort—you'd never guess they were related. Alec, with his dark curly hair, stands six inches taller than his blond straight-haired brother. But, they're probably not adopted—Alec looks a bit like his dad and Alan's the image of his mom.

Kaleb's knees crack as he crouches beside me. He takes the photo from my hand and, without prompting, says, "There is no family likeness."

We type the San Diego street address into Google Earth and view the property from every angle, but nothing looks familiar.

"We should pay a visit," Kaleb says. "Explore the neighborhood."

"Sounds crazy."

"Why? You know I'm right."

Twice Dead

This conundrum requires a cold logical approach, emotion must not cloud the facts. Evidence must be examined and evaluated, there's no room for assumption or conjecture. I was five once, a hopeless witness to my own demise, and oblivious to my own death. My memory is unreliable. I can't even recall what I was doing this time last week.

"Raych, do you have photos from when you were a kid?"

"There are albums documenting our time here, but nothing earlier. Mom said our early memories were destroyed in the fire, along with my favorite toys."

We spend hours poring over photos from yesteryear, but find nothing of any consequence. It becomes apparent the images are only ever of me, Mom, or Pops. The only exception is the odd photo of me with Sofie. It's testament to the reclusive existence our family practiced. The photos are either taken in the back garden or on our summer vacation, usually in remote wooded areas, without another living soul in sight. Pops was insistent about avoiding strangers in his photos, making us appear to be the last of our kind on planet Earth.

ಎ ♈ ಐ

Wednesday afternoon means only one thing—taking Mrs. Tracey to the supermarket. Pink puffy eyes stare back at me from the mirror, but I'm unconcerned about Mrs. Tracey's reaction. Besides, if I do break down, I have several legitimate reasons—other than the truth—to explain my tears.

"Shall I take her, instead?" Kaleb offers.

But the trip presents an opportunity to raise questions regarding my past, and ask if she recalls any unusual conversations with my mother.

Before leaving the house, I use Mom's cosmetic concealers, but they don't hide much. With a deep breath and adopted smile, I knock on Mrs. Tracey's door.

Cheerfully, I announce, "Only me," but I'm fooling no one.

"You've been crying again, my dear," says Mrs. Tracey. I nod. "Is *laddo* behaving himself?"

"It's not Kaleb."

"Glad to hear it. Hopefully, he's learned his lesson."

I take a seat at the kitchen table and Mrs. Tracey slides a cup of tea towards me. She toys with her pearls and gazes at the garden. "His brooding passion reminds me of my Frankie. He'd go to the ends of the Earth for me. He wouldn't lie down and die for me, but he'd sure as hell kill anyone who dared to lay a finger on me. At least he'll keep you safe. I expect you'll be following your friend Sofie down the aisle, very soon."

I'm sure there's comfort in her words... somewhere. I slurp my tea.

"Anniversaries are always the worst," she says.

I glance at her wall calendar and rack my brain.

"Days like this, you're bound to feel a bit raw, my dear."

Realization hits hard, and brings a fresh flood of tears.

Mrs. Tracey shunts a box of tissues in my direction. "Grief mellows with time," she says. "One day, you'll look back with a fond smile."

Mrs. Tracey's got her dates mixed up. She thinks it's the anniversary of Pops' death, but that's next month. I'm not crying for Pops now, I'm worried Mrs. Tracey might have dementia, and concerned about who will look after her. Aware that elderly folk receive no mercy when it comes to confusing facts, I blame her misjudgment on my distressed state. I don't want to correct her either, because she'll want to know why I'm so upset.

"More tea, my dear?"

I drag my knuckles over sore, stinging eyes. "I'm not sure a trip to the supermarket is such a good idea. I look dreadful."

"It's just what you need, my dear. You can't stay cooped up in the house forever. Engaging with the real world will do you the power of good. Keep your sunglasses on, though."

Another cup of tea restores my composure. "Mrs. Tracey, did Mom ever say anything about the fire at our house in San Diego?"

"You're going back a bit. What's prompted this?"

"I found some old photos of the house and thought I might revisit the scene... see if I remember anything."

"The trouble is, my dear, things never look the same when you return. It's more about what's in your heart rather than what you see with your eyes. I always tell myself, 'Don't look back; stay focused on the road ahead.' Otherwise life can pass you by."

"I know, but I'm curious. Did Mom ever mention San Diego?"

"Let me see." Mrs. Tracey taps her chin and gazes at the ceiling. "You moved here the year after Frankie died. She'd often pop in for a cuppa and a chat, but then there was the little incident."

"What incident?"

"I don't expect you remember."

"What happened?"

"You're upset enough."

"Please, tell me?"

Mrs. Tracey hesitates and assesses my fragility.

"I felt bad at the time. See Jessica's picture over there, with our poodle Trixie." I gaze at the familiar image of Mrs. Tracey's late daughter. "You pointed at her and said, 'She's very pretty, can I be her friend?' You asked if she lived here, and I told you, 'She used to, but she lives in heaven with the angels now.' Anyway, I had a few tears and when your mother came back in the room I had to explain myself. Your mother became quite distraught when she discovered my Jessica had died so young. She overreacted and made a big fuss about you upsetting me. I said it wasn't a problem, but she scolded you and said you shouldn't pry into other people's business. Then she whisked you off home, and I didn't see her so often after that. I felt awful."

"I'm sorry."

"Oh, there's no need for apologies. What you said was very sweet, and I'm sure Jessica would've loved being your friend."

"You're very kind, Mrs. Tracey. Mom was always telling me not to ask questions. 'Questions are for the classroom,' she used to say. It's too late now, and I have lots of questions. Did she ever say what caused the fire or why we moved here?" I raise my cup to hide my face.

"Not really. She said you lost everything and were starting afresh. She was especially worried about you, though, said you'd become withdrawn and confused—she blamed it on smoke inhalation. But, you're perfectly fine now, aren't you, my dear—no long-lasting effects, thank God."

"I guess so."

Don't Look Back

9. Bubble Bath

Barbara's organized another open house event, so we're up early removing all traces of habitation from the dwelling. Barbara's still optimistic Mr. Morgan will reappear and make an offer—"He seemed *very* interested." A few weeks back, Kaleb posed as Lucas Morgan, fooled Barbara with his lies, and tricked his way into my home so he could snoop around. Now look at him, he's moved in and become a central fixture in my life.

Kaleb's keen to avoid an awkward meeting with Barbara, so he's departed well before her scheduled arrival time.

I hardly slept last night. Images of Kaleb incidentally killing others as he fought for his life kept me awake. In the background, Carl greedily raked up bloody hundred dollar bills from an upturned card table and stuffed the tainted cash into bulging pockets.

Kaleb's tried hard to persuade me to accompany him to the studio, but his argument, "Carl's okay when you get to know him," falls on deaf ears.

Carl is *not* okay, not on any level, whatsoever. Four men are dead because of him, and Kaleb was almost the fifth. I'll never forgive Carl. In fact, I hate Carl a little more every time his name is mentioned. He is the rudest, most arrogant egotistical individual I've ever encountered. Knowing Carl willfully put Kaleb in harms' way makes me wish Carl was number five.

I also blame Carl for making me lie to Kaleb. Earlier, I told him I was meeting Sofie at the mall, but I'm not. Originally, I planned to spend the day with Sofie, but I can't. She'll instantly realize I'm hiding something, but Kaleb doesn't know me so well.

Earlier, he commented, "You're a little edgy."

Maybe I'm not so good at hiding my deceit, after all.

"Just nervous about selling the house," I replied. "What if no one likes it?"

"Someone will."

Even now, with Barbara's imminent arrival, being alone in the house makes me nervous. The high-pitched alarm in my pocket and the pepper spray sitting amongst the condiments are my only defenses. My eyes flit to the knife block.

As I continue to "stage" the house, I concentrate on breathing to counter my anxiety, and count to regulate the flow. In: one, two, three. Hold: *Barbara will be here soon.* Out: one, two, three, four.

∞ ♈ ☙

A vehicle screeches into the driveway and my pulse reacts. I'm out of time. In a last frantic attempt at tidying, I stuff my and Kaleb's clothes under the comforter. Car doors open and slam. I rush into Pops' bedroom and look outside to witness Barbara daintily tapping the Open House sign into the front lawn with a flowery decorated hammer. Moments later, Big Ben chimes. I rush downstairs and swipe open the door.

"Good morning, Raychelle," says Barbara. "I have high expectations for today." She raises her nose, flares her nostrils, and inhales. "I sense an offer in the air."

She lifts her hand and brandishes the checklist, ready to inspect my accomplishments. "Let's get started."

I look at her. I know she's talking to me, but her words don't translate.

"Are you okay, Raychelle? If you don't mind me saying, you look a little pallid. Selling a house—your home—can be an awfully stressful and emotional experience. Letting go of physical reminders is difficult, but treasured memories always remain in one's heart and mind."

Her words echo my mother's musings, and I want to slap her—hard.

"Thank you," I say. "Would you like some coffee?"

"Are you sure you're okay?"

Barbara leads with her list, and I trail behind as she assesses and ticks each completed task. She's delighted Butch, plus accoutrements, have been banished.

"Is the cat door locked?" she asks, with unblinking *innocent* eyes. I nod. "Allergies," she says with a tight smile.

Denying Butch access to his home feels heartless, even though I suspect he's curled up and fast asleep on Mrs. Tracey's spare bed.

Entering Mom's lounge, Barbara's perturbed to find I've failed to address the doll situation but, overall, she's reasonably satisfied with the first-floor transformation.

Upstairs she examines the bedrooms, smoothing covers and flicking curtains as she goes. She removes a microfiber cloth from a pouch in her handbag and wipes away microscopic dust coating a mirror. Toilet seats are raised and lowered, and faucets tested. On exiting each bathroom she removes air freshener from her bag of tricks and turns to squirt the room's interior.

My bedroom's last up for inspection. She walks over to the window and shakes the curtains—harsh sunlight emphasizes billowing dust. She slaps my bed expecting the bulge under the comforter to disappear, but the mass of clothes is unforgiving. She pulls back the cover to investigate, and pinches Kaleb's Seahawks baseball cap between her fingers, like it's diseased. Detective Inspector Barbara looks at me, but says nothing.

"I didn't have time to put everything away," I say in my defense.

"You've been very busy."

"A friend helped me."

If only she knew just how much blood, sweat, tears, and vomit has been spilled here this week.

ಸ ୯ ଔ

I drive to a deserted private beach and on this windy day, find shelter, and hide amongst the rocks. With tired eyes, I read for a while, until the relentless rhythm of crashing waves lulls me to sleep. Hours later, I awake, shivering and hungry, but I've still got three more hours to kill. I wish I'd brought a flask and nibbles. A normal person would go to a café or shop, but I make do.

Bubble Bath

As agreed, I return home at five, ready for Barbara's update. Sitting at the kitchen table, she puts her hand on mine. "You're cold and you look a little glazed," she says. "Are you coming down with something?"

"I'm okay. Cleaning the house has worn me out."

"Maybe you should get something from the pharmacy."

"I'm fine, thank you."

With excitement, she tells me, "There's been a lot of interest. I'm certain we'll receive a serious offer next week."

I wait for Barbara's engine before pouring a coffee. It's stewed, but at least it's hot and wet. I guess Barbara must've brewed it to entice potential buyers into imagining an idyllic life in their new home. Sitting in the family room, gazing into space, I'm brought back to reality by noise from above—Butch, no doubt, jumping from a high perch and scampering around. After several minutes I conclude he's tormenting a bird.

From the hallway I yell, "Butch, whatever you're doing up there, cut it out!" Like he'll understand.

I open the back door and gaze at the flowers, but can't find any pleasure or beauty in anything today. I consider how I must appear to others. I sit on the grass and weep. The phone rings, but I've no inclination to answer it.

Back indoors, I sit at the kitchen table and smell roses—my mother's come back to haunt me. More likely, Barbara's been active with the air freshener, her sensitive nose detecting the aroma of kitty food or cat shit. The smell gets stronger and I glance around, expecting an encounter with my mother's leering ghost. I'm going crazy.

Upstairs, a floorboard creaks followed by the distinctive whine of the bathroom cabinet door. Butch is stomping around, probably investigating new territory and examining the contents of cupboards left open by visitors. I pick up his box of *Kitty Bisk-Witz*, stand in the hallway and rattle the contents.

"Butch get down here, now."

Cats, though, aren't like dogs, they don't ever come when you call them. They're single-minded and selfish.

So, I go upstairs to see what's captured his interest. Holding his fishy cat treats, I wander into the spare bedroom I use as a study and watch the sun dip behind a cloud. Movement in the garden catches my eye. How did Butch manage to sneak downstairs and escape through his cat flap without me noticing—the cat flap I locked earlier to prevent him coming into the house. My heart pounds, fear erupts, and my skin prickles. What exactly is that noise, coming from the adjacent room… my bedroom?

I leave the biscuits on my desk and creep onto the landing. I poke my bedroom door with a cautious finger, like the paint's red-hot. All is quiet, and daylight deadens the possibility of ghosts. On my dresser, a vase I've never seen before displays a bouquet of white roses, rose-infused steam escapes my bathroom door, and a hideous red dress is laid out on my bed. The obvious assumption is Kaleb, but these trappings are not his style, nor mine. He'd never choose such a dress, he prefers sheer cotton, lace-up blouses—he likes to unbutton, unzip, and undo me. He also knows how the musky bluebell bath essence affects me—he'd never choose rose.

I can't imagine Barbara staged all this for the open house, it's beyond tacky. I tiptoe towards my bathroom and prod the door. Inside, I find foggy mirrors and a steaming bubble bath surrounded by dancing rose scented candles. This is creeping me out and I don't like it. I want to run, but can't.

"Kaleb?" I whisper, afraid to say his name.

My bedroom door closes. I'm terrified. My chest heaves and my lungs fill with steamy rose-infused air. A champagne bottle pops and fires a cork bullet. Instinctively, I press my back to the wall. I'm under attack.

A presence looms behind me, but I'm frozen in place and unable to turn. Ken Hunter's distinctive greying hair materializes in the steamy mirror.

"Raychelle, I've run you a bath."

He puts a hand on my shoulder, slides it down my arm and squeezes. With his other hand he offers me a glass of champagne. "To us."

I stand stone still. Noticing my reluctance to take what's on offer, he says "I know you enjoy champagne. This will help you relax, drink up." He raises the glass to my lips. "Don't spoil the moment, darling. I've gone to so much trouble to create this perfect scene."

I take the glass and raise it to my lips. He nudges the base. The liquid spills and fizzes down my chin. I gag and choke on what manages to go down.

"You're shaking. I heard Barbara ask if you were unwell. What you need is a nice hot bath. Let me undress you."

"No," I say feebly, and sink to my knees. Ken kneels behind me and puts his hands on my shoulders. I lean forward and curl into a ball, straining to escape his touch. He gropes his way to my breasts. I struggle to sit upright. Instantly, he yanks my shirt, exposes my shoulders, and converts my top into a restraint. His thin mean lips press against my neck. He stands, pours more champagne, and swishes the glass. He crouches before me. "Open up." My lips remain sealed. He pinches my nose, my lips part, and he drains the contents of the glass into my mouth. Fearing I might drown, my eyes bulge, and I rapidly swallow the liquid. The bubbles make me cough.

He leans forward, grabs my arms, and drags me up. Fight, fight, my mind tells me, but I can't, I'm too woozy. Whatever he's forced me to drink takes rapid effect on an empty stomach.

Awkwardly, he tugs at my clothes. He issues instructions, but my limbs are asleep. He pushes and pulls me into my bedroom and lets me flop onto the bed. He rolls me onto my back. He unfastens my belt, and orders me to remove my jeans—just like last time. Remembering the rape alarm is in my pocket, my hands twitch, but they're useless. The bed is uncomfortable. Lumpy things stick in my back. Kaleb's clothes are stuffed under the comforter.

I smell roses. I smell my mother… she's back from the dead. Seeking the light, my head rolls towards the window. Red floods my eyes. My eyelids are sleeping. Clammy hands paw my body. My skin's smarting… probably a rope burn from my bra. He's ripping my underwear. I don't want him to see me naked, but I have no choice. He's dragging me. My shoulders hurt. My heels are burning.

I sit in my bath, and let this man lather his hands and wash me like a baby in a bath tub. He kneads and squeezes my body, and washes my breasts over and over again—they must be very dirty. My head lolls around. He ties my hair to the faucet to stop me keeling forward into the blue lagoon. Ingenious. But, my hair slips loose. Silky soft conditioner smooths the cuticle, and makes tying anything around your hair, impossible. They don't mention this detail on the bottle.

The phone rings, the doorbell rings. Lots of ringing. Ring, ring, ring. We both ignore it.

"Who the hell is that?" He's angry. "What *is* the matter with them? Don't they realize the open house event is over? Can't they see no one's home? Are you expecting anyone?"

Kal... I want to shout his name, but can't.

A weak hum escapes my lips. "Nnn." Why have I never given Kaleb a key? He has a key! Maybe he lost it. He sounds like he's completely lost it. He's banging on the door now and shouting, but I don't understand what he's saying. He's yelling. "Miss Carter, I've come for my money. If you don't come to your fucking door right now, and pay me what you fucking owe me, I'm going to shoot your fucking locks off."

"Is it that odd job man?" Ken asks. "That scruffy, low-down loser from Washington State. He looks like trouble. I could tell his sort the moment I laid eyes on him. You need to be more careful who you let into your home. Do you owe him money?"

"Yeah." I say.

"How much?" Ken asks.

"Hun... reds."

Ken brushes soap bubbles from his arms. They go up my nose. I have an urge to shake my head, but can't. Ken clips my head with the towel as he dries his hands. "Wait here," he tells me. Where might I go?

Kaleb's banging on the door. The whole house is rattling. Now, he's shouting, "I fucking mean it! Don't fuck with me, or you'll be fucking sorry!" I've never heard anyone so angry.

Ken leaves the room. I should stand and do something, but I'm at the beach, and diving into warm Pacific water is much more appealing. The weight of my head releases my hair yet again, leaving me free to escape into the turquoise ocean. Down, down I go, to Neptune's kingdom, to swim amongst the fish and mermaids.

Even with my head submerged, I register the bathroom door slamming quietly against the wall. My dead mother yells, "*Mind the paintwork!*" A great force yanks me from my underwater adventure. I'm heavy and cold and can't breathe. I'm gasping for air. I'm a floppy ragdoll. A drowsy floppy ragdoll. Someone's holding me tight. He smells smoky and I want to smile because I know its Kaleb. He carries me. His body is hard. His limbs are strong.

I think we're on the bed. He tosses his lumpy clothes onto the floor. I want to kiss him, but my lips won't work. My mouth hangs open like a fish. He's still holding me. He wraps us inside the quilt. Raindrops land on my face. There must be a hole in the roof. The raindrops splashing on my skin are tears, but they're not mine. My ear is pressed against Kaleb's chest. He places a hand against my other ear and seals me inside his body. I can hear the sea again and the rhythm of him. His heartbeat drums inside my head, and plays my favorite melody. He rocks me slowly and kisses my hair. I want to respond, but can't. Something awful has happened to me, but I'm okay with it. I'm content, cozy, and everything is peaceful, but Kaleb's upset. I want to comfort him, but can't move. I'm relaxed. Totally chilled.

Many hours later, I wake up with a burning headache, kicking and punching, and lashing out.

"Fucking, ow!" Kaleb says. He wraps himself around me to restrain my battling limbs. "It's okay, my love, it's okay. You're safe now. You're with me."

I want to scream, but a puzzled groan emerges.

"You're okay. You were drugged. You're waking up. Everything is fine. You're okay, my love."

I whimper like a frightened animal, because I am.

"Here, drink some water." He holds a plastic bottle to my lips.

After a restless night, I'm fully alert by midday. I've passed through my state of tranquility, through the agitated fog, and I'm a shaking paranoid mess. I'm on the sofa in the family room clutching my teddy bear, curled up tight with a blanket over me.

I want to ask Kaleb what Hunter said when he answered the door to him. Paradoxically, I don't want to talk about it either, but Kaleb does.

"What the fuck happened?"

"I can't remember," and I don't want to try. Earlier, Kaleb tore my room apart, and constructed his own version of events. He stamped on the roses, hurled the vase down into the garden and shredded the dress. He gathered my clothes from the bedroom floor and put them in the washer. He smashed the champagne glasses in the bathroom sink, dismantled the plumbing to remove the shards of broken crystal from the P-trap then reassembled the pipes. I wish he could fix me that easily.

Ken removed his wristwatch before he bathed me. Kaleb took the Rolex to the garage and whacked it with a hammer—several times. Now, it's an ex-Rolex. Kaleb unfurls his fingers and proudly displays the expensive designer trash sparkling in his palm.

My body flinches at every vivid flashback. Sudden dread releases a cascade of slow heat down each limb. What if…? Stomach acid burns my throat. I rub my chest.

Kaleb's hand brushes my face. "More water, my love?"

He hands me the bottle and the ice-cold liquid soothes my insides. Knowing not to ask the obvious question. Instead, I manage, "Did you lose your key?"

"No, I wanted to coax him away from you!"

"How did you know?"

"His Bimmer was parked around the corner. Seeing it, instantly triggered visions of an unpleasant scenario and I pelted to the front door. When he answered, drying his hands on your bathroom towel, I thought he'd fucking drowned you." Kaleb's eyes sparkle with stubborn tears. "I barged past him and dashed upstairs. The pain in my broken toe and ribs stimulated the adrenalin and made me even fucking angrier." Kaleb strokes my hair. "Lucky for him he'd scarpered by the time I'd got you settled, otherwise I would've pulverized his sad, sick ass and stomped him into the ground."

Reliving the scene induces another adrenalin rush. Kaleb stands, he's fired up, glistening with sweat, and incandescent with rage. He's gone from being a gentle tender man to Mr. Angry, to crazed psycho killer. Dragon breath escapes his lungs, his nostrils flare, and his eyes gleam with murderous intent. White knuckles blink as he flexes and curls his fingers—all the while, pumping oxygen-rich blood into his steely forearms, preparing for a fight. He's a man with a mission, and I get why Carl uses him for insurance.

I'm terrified of what Kaleb might do. "Please don't hurt him," I say.

"I'm not going to hurt him, my love," Kaleb says through clenched teeth. His right hand punches his left palm. His forceful fist smacking against flesh, makes me recoil. "I'm going to kill the fucking bastard."

I believe him. "Please don't. I don't want you getting in trouble for my sake."

"I'm not doing it for you, my love, I'm doing it for me."

"Kaleb, please don't kill him."

"Okay, I'll just maim the cunt. I'll cut his fucking hands off—stick one up his ass and one down his throat, and see how he likes it."

"Please don't. What if you get caught?"

"I won't."

"Please promise me you won't go near him."

"My word's no good. I lie when it suits me."

"Kaleb, please I'm begging you. Please don't do anything to jeopardize our future."

Silence. Mrs. Tracey's prophetic words echo in my mind, "He won't lie down and die for you, but he'll sure as hell kill anyone who tries to lay a finger on you." Ken's done more than try. It's only a matter of time and opportunity before Kaleb will strike. My eyes well up. Kaleb squeezes onto the end of the sofa and lifts my head onto his lap. He strokes my hair.

"I'm sorry, my love," he says.

I've won him over, but I want further reassurance he'll stay away from trouble. "What for?" I ask.

"My hard-on's sticking in your ear."

10. Blind Panic

I'm in a blind panic and can't think straight, because Sofie is expecting me at her house tomorrow morning at ten, and I need to create a monumental excuse to avoid her wedding. As if the event itself isn't stressful enough already, it's been made a hundred times worse by Sofie's mom inviting Ken Hunter and his wife to the evening celebration. To make matters worse still, Kaleb has casually volunteered to be my "and guest." The thought of Kaleb coming face to face with Ken Hunter has my head and stomach in turmoil, but I need to get past that and manufacture some believable lies.

Saturday is the biggest day of Sofie's life and, months ago, I promised I'd stay with her in the run-up to the momentous event. A necessary concession on my part after refusing to be her bridesmaid. Without uttering a word, we both know it's our last chance to share some time together before she embarks on her new life, far away in Italy.

Who said weddings are joyous occasions? Sofie's imminent nuptials are reminiscent of Pops' passing—waiting for the inevitable bereavement and knowing a period of mourning will follow.

Reasons for not wanting Ken Hunter at Sofie's wedding extend beyond me. Obviously, I don't want to be anywhere near this vile man. Plus, I hate the thought of his presence tarnishing Sofie's special day—of him wearing a cloak of respectability and hoodwinking the guests. Then there's Kaleb—an unknown quantity. I can't even mention my dilemma directly to him either, because I fear he might view the chance encounter with Ken as an ideal opportunity to do something we'll all regret. The problem with Kaleb is, you never know what he's thinking, and he freely admits to lying. Even if he promised to behave himself, I can't believe him. And I can't see any way out of this predicament, apart from lying.

I prepare dinner, using the largest, sharpest knife in the kitchen, and take my frustrations out on poor defenseless vegetables. With force, I dice the carrots.

Maybe I could slice off the end of my pinkie. A trip to the ER would be a suitable excuse. I'll just embellish the details, make out it's more serious than it is. An allergy to the meds...

I hold my left hand out and splay my fingers. I use the tip of the knife to hide the distal phalange, and to better imagine how my disfigured hand might appear. As well as losing the end of my finger, I'll also lose the chance of maybe one day showing-off a wedding ring without the viewer recoiling in horror at the unpleasant sight of my amputated digit.

"Hey, careful with that knife," Kaleb reminds me. "They're sharp as fuck. I sharpened them all the other day."

His unexpected reappearance in the kitchen startles me back to reality.

He's assembling new garden furniture for Mrs. Tracey. "I need the hex keys. I left them in your bathroom." He wanders upstairs, then back through the kitchen jangling the bunch of steel tools.

I stab the onion and cry, glad of an excuse. Guilt consumes me. How can I even think of letting Sofie down? This is Sofie's day, not mine. I'll endure Ken's presence for Sofie's sake. Maybe Ken won't come. Maybe he has other plans, he often golfs at the weekend. Maybe Kaleb won't show. Maybe the recording process will drag on.

I slice the peppers, red and green. Reasons for and against attending the wedding grapple inside my head. Maybe I could leave early before the nighttime celebrations get underway. Satisfied I've reached a suitable compromise, I sigh, and reach for the garlic.

The doorbell rings. I glance at the timer on the microwave. "*6:13?*" Who's this calling at dinnertime?

Ken Hunter or Carl come to mind. Knife in hand, I freeze and listen for the sound of them leaving, of a vehicle pulling away. The caller bangs on the door. I don't move. The phone starts ringing. I'm under siege. I walk to the kitchen door, scan Mrs. Tracey's garden and look for Kaleb. I don't want to shout, because I don't want to alert the caller, I want them to believe I'm out. Brandishing the ten-inch steel knife I step outside and spin around, unsure if I should hide inside the house or search for Kaleb. I step back indoors as the phone message ends. I've missed the caller.

Whoever's at the front door slaps the wood.

"Raych, it's me. Rick."

Why is Rick banging on my door? Knowing he's harmless, I put the knife down and reluctantly open the door. He rushes in, overnight bag in hand and, with the ferocity of a two-hundred-and-thirty-pound footballer, he holds me in a firm one-armed hug. With my face pressed against his chest, I'm unable to see or breathe.

"God, I've missed you." He drops his bag on the floor and fully embraces me.

Determined to create some distance between us, and struggling with shock, I press my hands against his chest and push back.

Before I can free myself, Rick asks, "Who are you?"

From behind me, Kaleb says, "I was just about to ask you the same question."

Rick loosens his grip and I wriggle free. Kaleb and Rick stand either side of me, eyes locked, sizing each other up. I throw my arms out and swiftly introduce them. "Kaleb, Rick. Rick, Kaleb."

Kaleb smirks and stands down. He leans against the staircase and folds his arms across his chest. Rick puffs his chest out and stands, hands on hips. Our heads collectively gyrate, each waiting for each other to speak first and supply some answers.

I turn to Rick. "What are you doing here?"

"I know we said seven," he says, "but I didn't think you'd mind if I showed up early."

Kaleb, steps up behind me.

Rick bristles. "Who is this guy, anyway?"

"Kaleb... I just introduced you."

"Yeah, but what is he to you?"

Good question.

Kaleb, possessively grips my shoulder. "I'm her lover. Got a problem with that?"

Rick's face ignites in a flash of anger, and I have no idea how or why this is happening.

"Raych, stop acting weird," Rick says. "You told me to come over at seven, I've got the rest of my gear in the car."

"What is going on?" I ask in a panicked voice.

"We agreed I was moving in tonight." Rick sniggers and nods, like he's suddenly twigged what's going on. "I get it," he says to me. "You want me to sort this dude out."

Kaleb's pumping his fists and breathing deeply, a sign I recognize.

"No!"

"It's okay, Raych," Rick says, "I understand. You can't let on in front of him, because he'll beat you, too."

"No! No!" I yell. "Stop it, both of you. There's been some misunderstanding."

Sounding increasingly exasperated, Rick says, "In your email, you said *tonight*, right?" He throws his hands up, like he's balancing invisible objects. "You said Wednesday, right? Well today is Wednesday."

"Rick, I promise you, I've not sent you any emails. The only email I've sent you, was when I responded to your baby pic. I said Junior was cute or something and looked like his dad."

"What about all the other emails? The ones you've been sending me these past two weeks. You said you still loved me." Kaleb snorts. Rick continues, "You said you missed me, that we should never have split, that you wished it was our baby."

Kaleb laughs. "You're deluded, dude."

Looking down the driveway, through the open door, I see a silver car pull up. My attention switches back to Rick.

"No, way," Rick says, shaking his head. "I'll show you. Where's your computer?"

"You lying cheating bastard!" yells the young woman holding a baby in a car-seat. "I've caught you red-handed, so don't think you can talk your way out of this." She deposits the baby by the bay tree and pummels Rick with her fists.

I intervene. "Stop it, both of you, stop it. There's been some kind of misunderstanding."

The aggrieved woman, who I assume is Rick's wife, turns her attention to me. "You! You selfish bitch!" She lunges at me, grabs my hair, and yanks my head forward.

"Hey!" Kaleb hollers. "Rick, get your woman off, Raych… or I will."

Rick steps forward, clamps the woman's arms and drags her off. "Tiff, leave Raych alone."

"Listen to me," I say to Rick's wife. "Rick wrongly thought I'd been sending him emails and trying to win him back. He came over here to tell me to stop it. We've cleared up the mistake now and everything is fine."

I believe I've said the right thing, saved face for all of us, and resolved this crazy mix-up.

"Liar!" The woman yells and spits in my face.

"Nasty." Kaleb steps forward to pull me away. "That's really fucking rude."

"Tiffany, what the hell?" Rick yells, and starts shaking her. "Don't ever do that again."

"She's a liar, she's a liar!" Tiffany screeches at me, baring her teeth.

"No," I say. "Rick, doesn't want to leave you and the baby. This is just some crazy mix-up."

All the time, I'm questioning why she won't believe my simple lie, and why she won't just take her husband and her baby and clear off home.

"You're both liars and I hate you!" In between sobbing and convulsing, she admits. "I sent the emails. I knew Rick still loved you and I wanted to test how far he'd go."

The baby cries. Kaleb reaches for the carrier and places the boy out of harm's way.

I wipe my face on my shirtsleeve and hold my arms out to keep everyone at bay. "Can we all just calm down." I glance down the driveway. "Oh, god," I say to myself. I turn to Kaleb. "I need emergency back-up. Go and fetch Mrs. Tracey *now*, please."

"I know you," Tiffany yells at Kaleb. "You were on the news. You're that singer."

"Oh, yeah?" Kaleb says. "I think you're confusing me with someone else."

"You killed your bandmate with bad drugs."

Kaleb laughs. "I'm a mechanic. You off your meds or what?"

"Go. Now!" I remind Kaleb.

Stella, Rick's mom, barges through the open door and like a fencer with an epee, drives me into a corner with her accusatory finger. "Homewrecker. Selfish little bitch. Prostitute. You had your chance, young lady, and you threw it away. I never liked you. Selfish to the core. More concerned about a career than creating a loving family. You've brought shame and embarrassment on my family once already, and now you're back to your evil ways, trying to ruin Rick's marriage before it's even started."

Rick steps forward. "Mom." He tries to knock Stella's arm away from me. She deflects his feeble attempt to stop her. "Don't!" she yells. "Someone needs to confront this brazen little slut with the truth, especially now she has no parents to keep her in check."

"Mom!" Still no reaction. "Dad?"

I hadn't noticed Dick, Rick's father. The whole family are here to vilify me.

"You should be ashamed of yourself carrying on with a married man!" Stella yells.

Smarmy Dick looks at me like he thinks he's still in with a chance. I hitch up my low-cut vest and wrap my shirt tightly across my body.

"Look," I say, "I have no idea what is going on here."

"We've heard that excuse before!" Stella shouts. "Last year we also heard your father allude to your mental health issues as well. I'm calling the police."

I shake with sheer terror. "Why? What's this got to do with the police?"

"You're clearly insane. You're causing trouble between a man and his wife. You need locking up."

"And she's living with a heroin dealer," Tiffany accuses.

I glance at Rick struggling with his hysterical wife. "Rick, help me? You know this has nothing to do with me."

"Leave Rick out of this," Stella says. "You're dealing with me now."

I press my palm against my forehead. Noise from the kitchen assures me the cavalry has arrived.

Mrs. Tracey steps forward, hand out ready to greet Rick's mom. She cocks her head. "Doreen Tracey, pleased to meet you. And you are?"

"Stella Martyn, and *who* are you?"

"Raychelle's neighbor and confidante."

And fairy godmother.

Mrs. Tracey greets each person in turn. "Now, let's all be civil, and let's get to the crux of the matter."

Tiffany jabs her finger at Kaleb. "He's the drug dealer on the TV. He's in that grunge band from Seattle."

Mrs. Tracey scrunches her face in puzzlement. "*Him?* I think you're mistaken, young lady. I've heard his sad attempt at warbling and I can assure you he can't sing to save his life."

"It's him," Tiffany insists, but the Martyns ignore her. Kaleb won't register in their narrow view of the world.

Several people talk at once. Mrs. Tracey points a crooked finger. "Rick, I believe you were first on the scene, if you would care to elaborate."

Mrs. Tracey smiles sweetly at Stella, and flashes her palm, signaling for her to remain silent while Rick finishes speaking. Stella's fuming. Tiffany continues throwing out accusations.

Along the way, Kaleb's managed to grab himself a beer. He stands nonchalantly against the wall, sipping his Blue Moon and observing the farce in the foyer. I usually call it the hall because it annoyed my mother, but she always referred to this space as a foyer or reception area.

As we're winding up, and getting the facts straight, the phone rings. I step forward to adjust the volume and silence the caller, but Stella's arm comes down and blocks me. All eyes focus on the machine as it clicks on.

"Raych, Sofie here. Raych, I know you're there." She sighs. "Raych, come to the bloody phone now!" she shouts, "I have juicy gossip." There's a pause and I will the tape to run out of space. "Be like that. I'm going to tell you anyway, and then I'm coming over to collect you. I'm just finishing up in a bar down the road, I'm about ten minutes away.

"I was in the nail salon today and I bumped into that girl who's dating Rick's best friend."

I close my eyes, my throat grows thick and my blood slowly drains away. Once Sofie starts there's no stopping her.

"Anyway, she told me that you and Rick with the silent P are getting back together, and that he's moving in with you."

I said, 'not bloody likely. You need to lay off the mushrooms, you crazy bitch.'" Sofie laughs.

Tiffany kicks off again, and scuffles with Rick.

"Be quiet," scolds Stella.

"But she was really insistent," Sofie confirms. "Said her man's helping Rick move some of his furniture over this weekend. I said, 'I don't think so, I'm getting married on Saturday and Raych will be at the wedding.' Then her boyfriend shows up to collect her and he tells me the exact same story. Raych, what the fuck…"

The machine clicks and whirs. It is now full with unanswered messages, and Sofie is on her way over. Everyone stands quietly in the hall looking at the machine. Tiffany and Ricky Junior are both crying. Butch walks through the door, and prowls amongst the forest of legs. His body convulses, he wretches, and pukes up a grassy fur-ball.

"Show's over," Kaleb announces. Bottle in hand, he points at the vomit. "That was the finale."

Stella looks at him, dumbstruck for once.

Kaleb steps forward and holds his arms out straight to funnel the Martyns towards the open door. "Thanks for coming. Happy trails, until next time."

Stella stands her ground and confronts Kaleb. "Who… exactly… are you?"

Kaleb leans forward and puts his face close to Stella's so she can get a closer look. "Every mother's worst fucking nightmare." He pulls back and reaches for the baby carrier. "Don't forget your grandson, Grandma."

Stella purses her lips, her nostrils flare.

Dick grabs her elbow. "Come on, dear, let's be off."

Stella shrugs him away and swings the carrier towards him. "Take this." She wheels back around to Kaleb. "How dare you speak to me like this?"

"Fuck you, lady." Kaleb tips his head back and finishes his beer.

Rick releases distraught Tiffany, and puts his arm around his mother. "Mom, let's go."

"Not until I've had my say."

"Raychelle, just look at you," she sneers. "Shacking up with this scruffy foul-mouthed drug addict. Your parents would be utterly disgusted and ashamed of you."

"That is quite enough from you, Stella," says Mrs. Tracey. "All of you, please leave." Mrs. Tracey stands with a hand on the door and waves the family away, like she's shooing a dog out into the backyard. "Out you go."

Kaleb grabs Rick's bag and throws it at his feet. As he bends to grip the handles, Kaleb slaps him on the back. "Word of advice, frat-boy. She's way out of your league, buddy. Stick to college football and shagging cheerleaders." Rick swivels and launches a fist at Kaleb, but he's not quick enough. Kaleb intercepts the punch and holds Rick's wrist in a steely vise. "I don't think so."

Tiffany has the last say. "It *is* him."

Mrs. Tracey closes the front door and takes a deep breath. "Well, that was a rum do." She heads for the kitchen. "We all need a nice cup of tea. I'll put the kettle on."

We follow and Kaleb grabs his whiskey bottle from the kitchen table. "I need something a little stronger after all the excitement. That was really quite intense."

Clasping my head and still reeling, I say, "Sofie's coming over. I don't want to see her. I need time to recover." Kaleb sidles over, slips an arm around my shoulders, and points the bottle at my mouth. I take it and swallow the burning liquor.

"Don't worry, my dear," says Mrs. Tracey. "I'll deal with, Sofie."

We hear her Audi pull into the driveway. With perfect timing, Mrs. Tracey steps onto the porch and closes the front door.

"Hi, Mrs. Tracey," Sofie says, excitement evident in her voice. "Love your outfit, girlfriend. Is that Dior?"

"Burberry, dear."

"Nice. Is Raychelle home?"

"No, my dear. You've had a wasted journey. I've just been in to feed the cat, she's working late."

"Who does the truck belong to?"

"One of the workmen left it here... a few repairs to satisfy the Realtor. It's your wedding this Saturday, isn't it?"

"Sure is, you should come to the party in the evening. Mom's gone mad inviting everyone. Better idea… Raych's got a guest invite. You can come as her guest."

"That's very kind, Sofie, but I've got a date with my gentleman friend on Saturday."

"Bring him, too."

"We'll see. So, is your visit something last minute to do with the wedding?"

"Not exactly. I heard some *crazy* gossip about Raych—she won't even believe me."

"Ooh, there's nothing worse is there, when you're bursting to tell. Would you like to come next door for a cup of tea, my dear?"

"Oh sure, love to."

Mrs. Tracey's heels click down the steps.

"Do you remember that guy, Rick?" Sofie asks. "The one she nearly married last year."

"Oh yes, I remember him."

Their voices fade away. Kaleb sniggers. I put my finger to his lips, "Shh. We need to be very quiet and not put any lights on until Sofie leaves. I wish we could just run away."

Kaleb kisses my head, "Soon, my love. Let's go to your bedroom and misbehave quietly."

As we climb the stairs he says. "That showdown—you can't make that kind of shit up. The barflies at The Last Chance Saloon love this kind of stuff. Maybe I should reopen the saloon doors. What d'you think?"

11. Hibiscus, Darling

Kaleb's cooking breakfast burritos downstairs, so I jump out of bed with time enough for a quick shower. On the way to bathroom, I unfasten Kaleb's necklace for the first time since attaching it around my neck and place the tooth in a small dish on my dresser by the window. I shan't be wearing it for the next few days, it won't match with my outfits and might draw unwanted questions.

I'm in a trance, I hardly slept last night—too busy processing the foyer fiasco and worrying my way down my list of pending anxieties. The water hits my face and I rush through my ablutions. Kaleb and I will be apart for almost three days, so every minute is precious.

He's back to working long hours at the recording studio. Carl's exerting pressure, he wants the album wrapped up by Saturday, but they're struggling with the new guitarist. I don't recall the full story, I have selective hearing whenever Carl's name is mentioned. I did, however, use the recording deadline to generate a "get out" excuse for Kaleb.

"Don't worry if you miss Sofie's wedding," I said. "I won't be mad, finishing your album is much more important."

"Sounds like you don't want me there."

"No, no," I said. "Of course I want you there."

"I'll be there, don't you worry." Then he kissed me.

My attempt at putting him off backfired and reinforced his commitment to attend the event.

Hibiscus, Darling

I grab my bathrobe, drop my nail polish and hairbrush in the pockets, and race downstairs, stumbling as I go. I appear in the kitchen as Kaleb's assembling his culinary creations.

"Great timing," he says. "We're eating outside. Grab the mugs and coffee jug."

I wander across the patio and sink onto a lounger. Kaleb follows with a burrito in each hand, and two forks and a bottle of hot sauce stuffed in his shirt pockets. He hands me a plate, fork, and Tabasco, and takes a seat on the adjacent lounger. We devour the delicious concoction in silence, while the hot chili rush makes my eyes water. Fresh air, warm sun—another beautiful day in paradise. Remembering what today promises, though, unleashes an unrelenting tide of worries, along with the threat of heartburn.

I preview the next few days and stop when an image of Kaleb's broad fist connecting with Ken Hunter's soft face plays out. My stomach clenches and I toy with my food.

"On Saturday, if you're running late, I really won't mind if you can't make it."

"So you keep saying, but don't worry, I'll be there."

I stab at a green pepper. "I might try to leave early."

"Don't you want to be seen with me? Dating some 'scruffy foul-mouthed drug addict.'" He laughs. "Raych, stop worrying." He loads his fork and sprinkles more hot sauce. "Are you going to tell Sofie about last night's drama?"

"No way. The less people know, the better."

"You'd better get your story straight, and you'll need to act surprised when she divulges her 'juicy gossip.'"

Halfway through the mega-tortilla, I lie back, defeated.

"What's up?" Kaleb asks. "Not a fan of my cooking?"

I rub my stomach. "I'm bursting."

Kaleb extends his arm and I hand over what's left. He scrapes my leftovers onto his plate and adds more hot sauce. I sip my coffee, and confess my most immediate anxiety out loud. "I don't want to go the wedding."

Kaleb looks at me with hamster cheeks and continues munching, followed by a loud swallow. "Well, don't go. Problem solved."

"You're not meant to agree with me, you're meant to offer support and encouragement, and assuage my doubts. Or better still, create a monumental, but plausible, excuse."

He crosses to my lounger, takes my coffee from my hand, and opens my robe. "You have an incredible body." He takes a swig and places my mug on the ground.

I laugh. "What's my body got to do with anything?"

"The whole time I was eating I was thinking you resemble a giant burrito I want to unwrap to devour the filling."

My nail polish falls to the ground. "I need to paint my toes."

He reaches for the bottle and, plays toss and catch. "You're going to make me late for work."

He straddles my lounger, grips my ankles, and places my feet between his legs. Slowly, he massages my feet, and watches my reaction. He raises my foot to his mouth, and weaves his tongue between each toe. My cheeks burn. Although embarrassed, I love every sensual moment.

He twists the lid and opens the bottle of Vampyre Claret. Meticulously he applies the blood-red varnish. When he's done, he brings my feet to rest on his crotch. The warm soft ground beneath my toes firms up and develops a pulse. I blush some more, but he sits there—legs spread, leaning on arms locked behind him, and smirks.

"Let me paint your toes," I say.

"If you wish."

We swap places.

৪০ ♈ ৫৪

Kaleb left me with his pewter hip flask and a final piece of advice. "Wear your dress with a smile. Take this, and take a sneaky-wee shot. Pretend everything's fine, and it will be."

Ignoring the dress, maybe it's a mantra he recites before a reluctant performance. Resigned to fate, I leave the wedding invite propped against the toaster, along with a map and detailed directions so he won't get lost. Still, I'm anxious about him joining me on the actual day, about the curiosity he'll provoke, and the revenge he might reap.

Hibiscus, Darling

Kaleb's been at the recording studio all week, and I've been under the watchful eye of Mrs. Tracey. She's only next door, but I'm too scared to stay alone in this house for any length of time. My mind subconsciously sends a message to my fingers every few minutes, to check that the high-pitched alarm is still tucked inside my jeans' pocket. This, in turn, prompts an automatic scan of the kitchen counter to check the pepper spray still nests amongst the condiments. A glance down the hallway confirms the baseball bat is lurking behind the bay tree.

Mrs. Tracey sits on guard duty in her front window, keeping watch, while I load my car with wedding paraphernalia. Ready to set off, I massage the mounting dread rumbling around my stomach and wave goodbye.

෨ ♈ ଓ

Pulling into the Ventura's driveway, the security gates are open. A uniformed security officer checks my license plate against a list and beckons me on. Approaching, *Casa Ventura*, I look between the Italian cypress trees and I'm distracted by all the activity, resulting in me almost rear-ending a large white van. Several more are parked by the French doors leading into the Summer Room. Tables and chairs are being unloaded, and Trevor's frenetic pointy finger directs the crew on where to place each item of furniture. I park beside Fabian's black Porsche Spyder, as far away from the chaos as possible.

Sofie's mother, Abrianna reminds the lackeys, "Please avoid walking on the lawn—that is what the *pathway* is for." She authoritatively instructs the lighting crew, comments on the drapes, and questions the florist's credentials. I hoick my bag from the trunk and, despite giving the preparations her full attention, Mrs. Ventura still notices me sneaking between the cars, and flutters her talons at me.

An area of lawn on the other side of the driveway has been commandeered for parking, and cordoned off with shiny chrome posts strung with thick golden ropes and dark red tassels. Nothing escapes Trevor's eye for detail.

Trevor, as well as being Fabian's lover, is an event organizer for Hollywood's glitterati and comes with extensive contacts. Knowing this, Sofie exploited his relationship with Fabian and cajoled Trevor into organizing her wedding.

Since our teens, Sofie's been busy compiling a substantial scrapbook of grand ideas for her big day. Within the hefty tome are hundreds of magazine cuttings and her exhaustive list of expectations. At a meeting I attended during the early planning stages, Trevor felt the weight and employed his usual sarcasm, "You don't want much do you, love?"

His initial reluctance soon disappeared once he realized he could exploit the occasion for his own benefit. He'd unashamedly declared, "What a marvelous platform to showcase my talents, not to mention all the free publicity."

After flicking through her collection of images, Trevor concluded, "I sense a princess fantasy, and therefore recommend a medieval castle theme. *Casa Ventura*, your Tuscan-style family home, will serve as the perfect stage."

Sofie had beamed with delight.

Burgundy, amber, and aubergine were chosen for the core color scheme, with jewel-encrusted accents for emphasis.

The groom had always been the unknown factor, but Sofie resolved this small outstanding issue two years ago when she was introduced to Fabian's business partner Paolo, over dinner in New York.

Paolo worked as a restoration technician at The Metropolitan Museum of Art, and Fabian, a fine art student, met him while attending a college course. An instant kinship sparked, a shared ambition was realized, and they established their business—importing art and antiquities from Europe—before Fabian had even graduated.

With his killer looks and assassin's stare, Sofie instantly succumbed to Paolo's charm. He stole her heart and brain, and left her dead on her feet. No, I'm not a fan. He scares me to death.

Strolling towards the house, I notice through the open double-doors to the Summer Room another team arranging table linen, fastidiously aligning burgundy runners to match exactly with each neighboring table, even using a ruler to measure where centerpiece decorations will be placed. *What a strange world this is*. New pool furniture is being delivered, the cushions conforming to the overall color scheme—gold and blood red.

"It will hide the stains and cover the crime," Fabian had quipped during our planning session.

I crunch along the gravel driveway until I'm face-to-face with the familiar snarling stone lions that flank the grey stone steps and guard the house. As a child, these fearsome beasts, with enormous paws and vicious mouths, once scared me. I imagined them alive and roaming free within the grounds.

A podium decorated with a fringed, gold satin banner bearing red velvet letters, announces, *"Valet,"* and stands before the lion to my left. I peer into the other big kitty's cavernous roaring mouth, and see Fabian's gum depository has been cleaned for this auspicious occasion.

At the top of the steps, the heavy studded wooden door stands ajar, and I accept the open invitation.

"Sofie?" She doesn't respond, but laughter echoes down the hallway and pinpoints her and Fabian's whereabouts. Kaleb's words come to mind: "Get your story straight."

I mentally prepare myself for a volley of questions. Fabian is no one's fool, and I fear he'll see right through me. With his accusatory voice, devastating good looks, and flamboyant dress sense, he has the power to arrest most folks and stop them dead in their tracks. Add to this his cool confidence, outrageous antics, and tongue as sharp a sushi knife—no one is safe.

The moment I appear under the ornate stone archway leading into the kitchen, Fabian squeals my nickname. "Vicky, darling! We were just talking about you." I flush with fear. "Sofie's been telling me all about the crazy Rick shit." He leaps from his barstool and bounds towards me like an excited puppy. He sweeps me into the air, twirls me around, and teases me with slobbery kisses. "We were wondering when you'd show up, Tricky. Thought maybe you'd been delayed... helping Rick move in!"

Sofie and Fabian howl with laughter, and I join in because I have to.

"We've opened the champagne," Fabian says, "We couldn't wait any longer."

Fabian releases me from his clutches and fixes me in place with his irresistible, devilish grin.

"So, what's all this Rick shit nonsense?"

"I've no idea, I'm as stunned as you are."

Fabian reaches for the bottle. "Time for serious trouble," he announces. He grabs a glass and pours, while I walk over to Sofie and greet her with a guilt-laden hug and kiss.

"Where were you last night?" she asks.

"I... er..."

Fabian hands me a glass of champagne, a timely distraction. I force a smile, take the glass and we collectively clink crystal. I knew this would happen, that I would be expected to drink champagne. When I'm with Sofie and Fabian, it's our default drink. Kaleb's been plying me with bubbly all week and trying his best to rid me of my nightmarish associations. He's tried various tricks: refusing kisses unless I first drink a glass of champagne; laying me on a lounger, stripping me naked, spraying me with foam and licking it off—fizzy fun, he calls it; disallowing doughnuts unless consumed with champers. All part of my positive reinforcement therapy.

As I pull the flute from my lips, I spy a large red soggy tissue lurking at the bottom of my drink. I bring the glass to eye level and closely examine the foreign body. "What the hell..."

"Wild hibiscus flower, darling." Fabian informs me.

"And, what does that do?"

"It's like me, darling," Fabian says, with a shriek and a twirl. "It's enticing, exciting, erotic, and exotic."

I seek Sofie's reassurance. Her perfect eyebrows shoot towards the ceiling, and she shakes her head. "He's been like this all morning. I hoped a drink might calm him, but it's made him worse."

"To the sibling twin of the bride," Fabian toasts, and pours himself another glass.

"I'm so glad you're here," says Sofie.

"You're incredibly calm, considering all the commotion going on around us. I thought you'd be frantic by now. Is everything under control?"

"After two glasses of this, I don't care. Trevor's in charge and Mom's his second in command. She's in her element ordering the minions around. Together, they have a promising future, overthrowing small nations. Anyway, enough about me. So, what the fuck is going down with, Rick? I couldn't believe what I was hearing. It's just totally fucking crazy."

"I've no idea what it's about. D'you think she got me mixed up with someone else? Did she say my name, or did she say Rick's ex-girlfriend?"

"Hmmm, I'm sure she said, Raychelle, but you've got me thinking now." Sofie places a perfectly manicured red-nailed finger against her lip. "I bet he only married that cheerleader because she was pregnant. You had a lucky escape there."

"Tell me about it."

"Let's talk about something else," Fabian says. "Rick with the silent P is so, yesterday."

Thank you-thank you-thank you!

Fabian pops cork number two and refills our glasses. He cranks the volume and demonstrates his latest dance moves, but stops abruptly when Abrianna storms in and censors the music. She scolds us like naughty children, and we listen in silence, heads bowed as she runs through our misdemeanors. I can't understand a word, but know it's serious because she's ranting in her native Italian.

Fortunately, the florist saves us. "Excuse me, Mrs. Ventura. We're intertwining the white roses around the gazebo and we need to harness your vision."

Fabian snorts, grabs the bottle, and yells, "Yee-ha!" and dashes out of the kitchen.

Sofie and I follow, chasing him upstairs into Sofie's bedroom where the laughter and silliness continues. We smoke some grass and argue over who is brave, or foolish enough to face the wrath of Abrianna and raid the fridge. Sofie and I gang up against Fabian. "I can't go because I'm the bride," says Sofie.

"And, I'm a guest," I say.

"It's all your fault anyway," Sofie reminds Fabian. "Trust you to crank the volume just as the guy's singing 'screw your mind, I want to fuck your body.'" I nod in agreement.

"Fuck you, too," says Fabian.

We fall about laughing until we're stunned into silence by a booming male baritone, singing bad opera in a foreign language. The only word I recognize is "Sofia." The noise emanates from the grand hallway. We look at each other and, in unison, conclude, "Big Tex."

Sofie and Fabian's dad is performing with gusto and, in a bid to summon an audience, is getting louder by the second.

"Follow me," says Fabian. And we blindly do, because we always regress to five-year-olds after drinking champagne.

We crawl along the landing, giggling as we go, and peer through the stone balustrade at Big Tex making a big fool of himself as he sings to the gallery. Despite our sniggers, he has no idea we're watching. A small group of amused wedding helpers congregate and share the spectacle. Big Tex plucks a bright orange flower from the arrangement on the console table and sings passionately to the wilting bloom.

"He's singing to a gerbera," I say.

"A *gerbil*?" Fabian shrieks loudly, giving us away.

We stick our heads above the parapet and join in with the applause.

Big Tex takes a bow and raises his voice to Sofie. "Have you seen how many people are flouncing around the garden? How much is this costing me? I've only got two kidneys and I need to keep one of them."

Abrianna strides briskly towards Big Tex. He presents her with the wilted orange bloom. Her loud fast Italian response—still unintelligible to me—sends a clear signal, and we retreat with stealth back to Sofie's room.

We smoke another spliff, burn patchouli joss sticks to hide the smell, and torture ourselves by describing our immediate mouthwatering food fantasies. None of us are capable of driving, so Fabian makes a call.

"Hi, Big Tex Taxis? We're in Sofie's room, we're out of it, and we're starving. Will you take us out for dinner, Daddy? Pretty please."

Minutes later there's a knock at the door. Big Tex jangles his car keys.

"Come on, kiddos, let's get outta here. Your mother's gone power crazy, and the 'time-out' corner is getting mighty crowded."

ʘ ϒ ʘ

At the time, dessert was a fantastic decision. Now sober and in bed, though, my cannabis-fueled appetite has disappeared, and the ice cream sundae sits like concrete in my stomach.

Unable to sleep, I reflect on today's antics. For a while, I forgot about my hoard of woes but, in the darkness, my fears emerge with vivid clarity and reveal themselves. The comforting nightlight glow from the en suite bathroom creates the terrifying possibility Ken Hunter is lurking behind the door. I toss and turn, until I stop and watch a graphic replay of Kaleb's deadly fight. So, I lie on my back, and stare at the ceiling—Raychelle's death certificate materializes. My heart should slow in readiness for sleep, but instead, it races.

I rest my hand on my ready-to-explode, rock-hard stomach, and rub slowly in gentle circles, the way I've seen Kaleb massage his own belly when he overeats. He always knows how to make himself feel better.

I miss him dreadfully, imagine the worst, and picture him with a new lover. Or using my absence as the perfect opportunity to pack up and clear out without a word. Being apart from him is torment and misery.

12. That Hat Thing

Mother Nature is party to Trevor's fastidious planning, and expertly blends her elements to create the perfect atmospheric conditions for Sofie's idyllic day. Sunshine, fair-weather clouds, and a gentle ocean breeze ripple the drapes festooned around the garden, and breathe life into the romantic setting. The delicious scent of damask roses and lily of the valley, circulate on warm air currents, and my nose drags my eyes to the source of the exquisite smell. The voluptuous floral displays around the garden suggest more than romance.

Luxurious chairs and loungers strung with gold tassels, and strewn with sumptuous pillows, transform the outdoor space into a stunning lounge. Around the grounds, heraldic amber tapestries, adorned with red faceted gems and silhouettes of ominous black birds, flap like sails in the breeze. Above our heads, the Ravenna and Ventura family crests hang from trees and poles, and display an "unkindness," or group, of ravens tempered with jeweled good fortune.

Trevor patrols his creation with a critical eye, and fluffs up everything within reach, including the guests.

Last night, Trevor had insisted Fabian and I join him for a final inspection of the house and gardens. Along the way, he relived each tortuous moment, describing in detail the extensive planning and logistics required for staging such an event. He spoke of confronting crisis and chaos at every corner and how, with his skill and great pains, he overcame obstacles and averted mayhem and disaster at every turn. Clearly delighted with the outcome, he sought praise and adoration. So, Fabian and I gushed enthusiastically, issued expressions of disbelief, and showered him in praise until he stood completely drenched.

The preview left me knowing exactly where to hide once the wedding ceremony is over. A glance at my watch confirms the nuptials will start within the hour.

The location I have in mind is a perfectly secluded, small, circular tent situated in the far corner of the lawn on a slightly raised embankment.

To my horror, I've been cajoled into wearing some heavily pruned, hideous feather monstrosity on my head.

"*Bellissima*," says Sofie's sister-in-law-to-be, as she assesses my appearance, and everyone agrees.

But, I can't see it myself. I look ridiculous, like an extinct bird—a dodo. Apparently, it's called a fascinator, and it's certainly grabbed my attention now that I realize I'll be wearing it on my head. Furthermore, it flew in from Italy—not on its own accord—in a black-and-white stripy box, and cost five hundred dollars. Paolo's sister insists I accept the gift.

I argue, "I'm not worthy of such a beautiful and expensive 'head thing,'" but my protestations fall on deaf ears, or ears incapable of understanding English.

So, here I am lurking by the shrubbery, attempting to blend in with tall ornamental grasses and hoping I don't get attacked by a hungry cat. With my shawl pulled tight to hold myself together, I remove Kaleb's flask from my handbag and take a "sneaky-wee shot" of whiskey to neutralize my discomfort while I await the call to arms.

In my numb condition, I observe the social interaction amongst the other guests, and decipher the hidden narrative in their actions. Young women balancing on high heels thrust their heads back in exaggerated laughter, expose their necks, and offer their surgically enhanced cleavage. Fake laughter issued from wide-open mouths permits a full dental inspection, and their perfect molars and evenly white teeth pay tribute to modern dentistry. They flex their Botox-enhanced fish lips, hoping to avoid lipstick smears on their ultra-white expensive veneers. Some touch their ears and throat—a chance to show off their manicured talons and check their jewels are still in place.

I can't imagine ever fitting in. How come I'm not like everyone else? I recognize a few faces from high school, but their eyes skim right past me as if I don't exist. I reach into my bag and bring the flask to my lips for another swig. *Damn, it's almost empty.*

My attention shifts to the men, who display a wide range of awkward poses in their bid to appear casual. But it's early days, the alcohol's not taken effect, yet. Those holding cigarettes or drinks fare better, they're less fidgety. The straight men are unsure where to rest their eyes and hands, although it's clear, female breasts are the preferred option for both.

All are guilty of feigning interest in the conversation. They rake fingers through their hair, grin, and nod, but their roving eyes give them away. They scan the crowd, check out their competition, and seek out new targets. Those bold enough look for escape routes, break free, and move onto fresh prey. Those who remain suffer the stilted interaction. Both sexes are guilty of contrived behavior, except, maybe Fabian. He confronts his lover head on, grabs Trevor's crotch, and they part, laughing.

A lull in conversation and activity amongst the ushers, indicates it's time for us to take our designated places.

Abrianna casts her eye along the front-row guests and points a finger at me.

"There are too many men wearing drab suits. We need more color and sparkle. Make yourself useful, go and stand between Sebastian and Fabian."

I follow orders.

"Your green and lilac clashes with Fabian's sanguine tie." She wants me to change into something else, though I'd prefer to change into someone else.

It seems my wish might come true, this time.

We reshuffle into place, and sadness creeps in as Kaleb's medicinal whiskey wears off. The buglers' shrill blare signals Sofie's slow commencement down the aisle, and has a sobering effect. Tears sting, my stomach lurches, and my throat swells. Nervous laughter threatens. I bite my lip and suck on greasy lipstick. Fabian and Trevor's quiet bickering grounds me.

Sebastian, Sofie's eldest brother, takes my hand and squeezes. He leans into me with a reassuring smile. "See the yellow bird on the pergola?" he asks. "Bullock's Oriole, and it's got the hots for your feathery hat thing."

His statement catches Fabian and Trevor's attention. Sniggering breaks out amongst the three of us. Directed by Sebastian's demonstrative eyes, our heads turn to observe the fat yellow bird. It chirps, turns around, raises its tail feathers, shits on the dark red drapery, and flies away. Sebastian releases my hand and returns his solemn gaze to the altar within the gazebo. Laughter and panic bubble up. Desperate to staunch my reaction, I clench my lips—an extremely difficult feat, given the slippery gloss coating my mouth—and swallow. My brain scrabbles for mental distraction. I recite tax-form codes in my head, because *now* is a hugely inappropriate moment for uncontrollable giggles.

Fabian presses his arm against my side and shares his quivering body. Trevor snorts loudly and makes matters worse by attempting to disguise the noise with a cough. I shake. Fabian trembles even more, and explodes with a loud shriek just as Sofie appears before us on Big Tex's arm.

Abrianna regards us with a scathing look. "*Behave* children!"

ஐ ϒ ଔ

En route to my hideaway, a waiter presents a salver of champagne. Eager to reach my lair before someone else steals the spot, I swipe two glasses from his tray on passing and rush up the slope towards the fabric-swathed turret. A dozen curtained conical structures stand dotted around the garden, but mine is the most remote with the added bonus of best panoramic view. An inviting archway of intertwined ivy and white roses decorates the entrance. Inside, a swirl of roses and heart-shaped evergreen leaves coil around the interior and reach up inside the turret. Occupying most of the space, are four sumptuous loungers angled around a circular hand-carved wooden table. On the tabletop sits rusty wrought-iron candelabras bound with ivy, white roses, and one burgundy rose.

"Nothing is perfect," Trevor had commented last night.

Chunky scented candles adorned with gold leaf rest on nests of claret glass discs inside large etched hurricane lamps—by day offering a subtle flicker, at night a mirage of shimmering jewels. They shine on vases of dark-red roses, lily of the valley, and maidenhair ferns, which complete the abundant display.

During last night's tour, Trevor also pointed out, "The turrets readily convert into private and intimate enclosures. Should anyone feel frisky later on, one simply pulls the restraining sash to release the tent flaps."

"Don't judge people by your own standards," Fabian retorted.

Whatever Trevor's creative intentions are, he's created the perfect hiding place for me. If Ken Hunter shows up with his wife, I shall release the sash and block them from view.

Knowing the worst is over, I relax and knock back the champagne, eager for the bubbles to work their magic. Instantly tipsy, I recall one of Kaleb's "therapy" sessions, and smile. I kick off my sandals. Next to go is the shaved feathery monstrosity perched on my head, which I secrete behind the lounger, with the vague notion some cleaner might delight at their find.

A passing waiter replenishes my empty glass and, after checking my allergy status, leaves behind a small bowl of mixed nuts. If only Kaleb were here to release the sash and close the tent. I tingle as I imagine him peeling my dress away and pouring champagne over the length of my body. A satisfied "mmm," escapes as the fantasy continues, but it's replaced by a sobering thought. I mustn't get too comfortable, I need to leave soon. I check my watch and it's just turned six. I'll go to the bathroom, shortly, and phone Kaleb from inside the house to let him know I'm heading home. I'll leave at seven and will be back at Oak Tree Place within twenty minutes.

I sip some more champagne. The air, thick with the scent of trampled rose petals, conjures an image of the downstairs bathroom back home, and I picture Kaleb showering and dressing. I smile and my skin glows with nervous anticipation. The thrill of him appearing, coupled with the dread of introducing him, is an antagonizing dilemma, but not one I need face now that I've decided to leave. Once I've mustered the courage to deliver my excuses, I will depart. I raise my glass to my lips and toast my resolution, but immediately regret my actions. I'm not really in a fit state to drive. I shouldn't be consuming more alcohol, but it's not far. My mother's accident comes to mind. Did she have the exact same thought?

I cannot drive—I'll ask the valet to call a cab.

Kaleb's band is working on their new album's final song, "Vengeance." He mentioned progress was slow, and warned me he might be late, so I'm not surprised he skipped the ceremony. I'm greatly relieved he never witnessed me wearing the dodo head thing.

I glance at my watch again. Maybe he's already on his way, or maybe he'll find an excuse. Maybe I should leave… now. I know it's rude, but I could easily sneak away. After all, I'll probably never see these people ever again, once today is over. I drown my emotions with what's left in my glass and sigh. I lean back into the sumptuous cushions, close my eyes for a minute, and relax. I'm aching to be with Kaleb, but his absence prevents some awkward explanations. The thoughtful waiter takes good care of me and replenishes my glass. The champagne is cold, crisp and refreshing. I sip and savor each exploding bubble. Background, music, laughter, and chatter merge into a jumble of sound, and slowly I drift away.

I wake up confused, unsure how long I've been napping. The sun has shifted, and guests are arriving for this evening's party. As consciousness returns, I overhear conversations and the latecomers complain about an accident on Copper Canyon Pass. "We were stuck for hours… so frustrating."

"It must've been serious."

"They closed the road. The air ambulance landed on the highway."

It's too late to leave, Kaleb's probably on his way. Mild panic has me formulating plans. Once he arrives, I'll keep him inside the tent and permanently distracted to ensure there's no possibility of him coming into contact with Ken, if he's here.

With no sign of Kaleb, I create a road accident inside my head. Niggling worries worm around my brain and make me think the worst. Realizing I'm reacting in the same manner as my mother, I annoy myself.

I stand, peer out from behind the safety of the tent flap, and scan the crowd of heads for Ken Hunter's distinctive sweeping grey hair. I venture outside to use the bathroom, and move furtively amongst the guests, all the time looking out for him and his wife Janine. I ought to seek out Sofie and congratulate her. It takes a moment to locate her, standing by her mother and surrounded by Paolo's adoring family.

Now is not the moment to approach. My head tells me she's gone, my heart grieves. I use the bathroom and rush back to my sanctuary.

I plump the cushions and settle myself back down.

"Ah, Miss Vicky," Fabian announces, as he appears in the doorway. "I thought it was you. I saw you from afar. All on your lonesome? Are we sad, or is this your usual melancholy self, displaying a reluctance to participate?"

"I'm fine." I lift my glass and discover it's empty. Without thinking, I blurt out, "My boss might be here."

"Oh, is that why you're hiding."

"Well, no... and yes. Have you seen him on your travels?"

"I don't know what he looks like, honey."

"You've met his wife, though? Your mom's redesigning their house, and she said you supplied some paintings."

"Oh, her. No I've not seen her wandering around."

Comforted by this news, I reach for Fabian's glass and pinch his drink.

Because I can't ask Sofie, I ask her twin instead. "Is Sofie pleased with how the ceremony went?"

"I guess so. I've not had chance to speak with her. She's constantly surrounded by Paolo's coven of sisters—the witches of Ravenna."

We snort at Fabian's analogy. As usual his acute observations are never far from the truth.

"They're an ugly bunch," he says. "Being a guy, Paolo gets away with the big nose, large appendages, and bushy black eyebrows, but his sisters don't carry it off quite so well." I giggle. "They constantly chatter and cackle, and look for husbands—if I wasn't gay already, a night with them would surely send me over the fence. At least Sofie will inject some much-needed beauty into the Ravenna gene pool. I can just imagine her with a tribe of cute and adorable little boys, who all look exactly like me."

Fabian leaves me laughing. He reappears minutes later clutching a bottle of champagne.

"Dr. Fabian knows best," he proclaims as he sets down the bottle and ice bucket on the table. "Sure you're okay, Tricky?"

"Sure, but I can't wait to get out of these clothes."

Fabian uncages and pops the cork with a suggestive groan. "I bet you say that to all the boys."

"No, what I mean is, I'm uncomfortable in this stupid dress."

He angles the glasses and expertly pours so as not to waste a drop. "Have another glass of this."

I do. We chink glasses and raise elbows.

Fabian removes the crystal from his lips, lifts the hem of my dress and gasps. "Oh my god, Miss Vicky! What the fuck is going on with you?"

He's discovered my hairy legs. He takes my hand and yanks my arm up. "Oh no, you're a mama bear. What's going on, have you crossed over to my side?" I snatch my arm back and rearrange my dress.

"Are you a lipstick lesbian?"

I don't know what to say.

"A feminist?"

I bite my lip.

"It's because of a man isn't it? Does he shave you on a full moon? Or, is it to deter you from going with other guys?"

"Fabian, shut it."

"Oh, I get it, you've hooked up with a pervy control freak."

Fabian plies me with drink, determined to get answers, but he's already discovered the truth. Realizing he's getting no further, we pass the time gossiping about other guests. The more we drink, the more salacious our conversation becomes, and concern about Ken Hunter appearing dissipates, too.

Thoughts of Kaleb surface, and turn morbid when I associate him with the canyon accident. I banish the anxiety with more champagne. Earlier this afternoon, I felt sure he'd turn up but, as time progresses, I'm convinced he's backed out—the recording delay merely a convenient excuse. He's probably exhausted, plus I assured him more than once it wasn't a problem if he couldn't make it, and not to worry. I glance at Fabian's watch—almost eight o'clock. I conclude that, despite Kaleb's strong assurances, he's had a change of heart. But that's okay because Fabian and I are having our own private party, and the champagne is producing the desired effect.

Trevor's deserted Fabian, he's busy promoting his talents, handing out business cards, and discussing the minutiae of the wedding with anyone who cares to listen. He's even taking credit for the weather.

"You seem a little pensive, Miss Vicky."

"Just tired. Drinking in the afternoon makes me drowsy."

"Well, foxy lady, the evening is well underway and we need another bottle."

I close my eyes, press my head against the cushion and breathe deeply to, once again, inhale the smell of new cotton fabric and freshly cut flowers. The general hubbub blurs and I float away.

That Hat Thing

13. Petals & Pearls

"In here," the wine waiter says, and I'm brought back from my slumber by a shower of rose petals falling gently on my face and neck. Fabian and Trevor giggle. I smile as consciousness returns.

"Fabian, what *are* you doing?"

"Wake up, sleeping beauty."

Kaleb's voice startles me. "Oh god!" My eyes spring open and I sit bolt upright.

"I wouldn't elevate him to that level," Trevor says, "but he's very cute in a Clint Eastwood kind of way."

Kaleb holds a clenched fist of petals to his face and inhales the heady perfume. In his other hand, he grasps the skeletal remains of a rose plucked from the table decoration.

He leans over and kisses me. "Sorry, I didn't mean to scare you."

As he pulls away I'm taken aback by his clean-shaven appearance and gelled-back hair. He's trimmed his good eyebrow to match the regrowth on the other. He's wearing a crisp white shirt, black waistcoat with gold brocade lining, and a golden diamante-rose bolo tie. The black jeans look fairly new, but the transformation ends there—the scuffed boots are still present.

Trevor says to Fabian. "How stunningly romantic. How come you never wake me with a shower of rose petals?"

"Because you'd gag on them and choke," replies Fabian.

"*I do not* sleep with my mouth open," insists Trevor.

Fabian stares at me with wide eyes and pursed lips, looking as though he may burst from the building pressure of pertinent questions

Petals & Pearls

contained within. His raised eyebrows imply I have much explaining to do. "I'll just get another glass, shall I, Miss Vicky?"

"Yes, if you don't mind, thanks Fabby."

Kaleb slowly brushes the petals away, using the clean-up as an excuse to stroke my skin. "Having used your rose-decorated bathroom for several weeks now, I associate roses with shitting," he remarks.

"How *utterly* romantic," Trevor says. "I find letters from the IRS have that effect on me."

Trevor's face takes on the expression of the Cheshire Cat and he laps up Kaleb like a saucer of cream. He lifts the diamante-rose bolo from Kaleb's chest. "Ooh, that's nice, honey, not everyone's man enough to get away with that. I don't believe I've had you or had the pleasure? I'm Trevor and you are?"

"Kaleb. Pleased to meet you." He extends his hand.

"Nubuck, honey?" Trevor asks. He strokes the fleshy fingerless gloves Kaleb's wearing to hide the distinctive cleft in his hand caused by a childhood accident.

"Excuse me?"

"Your gloves, honey, are they nubuck?"

"No, I've had them a while."

"How delightful!" Trevor giggles. "So, Kaleb, what do you do for a living, honey?"

I tense, worried what he'll disclose. He's been reluctant to appear in public since the Seattle incident, but we decided he'd go unrecognized amongst Sofie's social circle. Now, with his altered appearance, if someone questions his identity he can acknowledge the resemblance, and explain his name is a freak coincidence.

"I restore old cars."

"Ooh, that's nice. You can pull up to my bumper anytime, honey."

Kaleb snorts and Trevor continues. "Do you wear overalls? Do they have buttons or poppers? Have you ever tried poppers? Ooh, I love poppers. Do you get covered in oil and grease? Do you get all dirty? How do you get the dirt off, honey?"

Kaleb sits on the edge of the lounger and smirks as Trevor enjoys his flirty reverie. "Yes, I get dirty. I use Swarfega."

"Ooh, Swarfega sounds sexy."

"Green gunk, you rub it into your skin."

"Like lubricant?"

"No, a cleanser for removing oil."

Trevor squeezes Kaleb's knee. "Sorry, I was just having a little fantasy interlude."

Kaleb laughs, amused by Trevor's blatant flirting. Fabian reappears with two more glasses, and another bottle of Veuve Clicquot.

"What's he saying about being lewd?" asks Fabian. "Have I missed something juicy?"

"Fantasy interlude, darling, I've just been having one."

Before I start on introductions, Fabian grasps Kaleb's hand.

"Well hello... I'm Fabby, short for, *Fabulous*." He talks whilst sustaining a hyena grin. "Are you Miss Vicky's *guest*?" he hisses. "She's managed to keep that quiet, haven't you, Miss Tricky Vicky?"

I sit, bewildered, unsure what to do next. Kaleb steers the conversation away from us, and redirects attention back to Trevor. "So, what do you do?"

"I do this, honey." Trevor looks skyward and raises his arms in supplication.

"What, you're a preacher?" Kaleb teases.

Fabian snorts loudly and sprays champagne into the midst. Kaleb tries again. "What? You carry stuff on your head?"

"No, fool, I created this."

"Oh, I see. *You* are God," Kaleb says, teasing him further.

"Finally, someone recognizes my creative genius. Here's my card, honey." Trevor presents Kaleb with his business details. The cards are attractive—midnight-blue background edged with pink and lime-green planets, and embossed with tiny hologram stars.

Kaleb studies the details for a moment, and smirks as he reads aloud, "'Cosmic Events. Organizer of Stars, Mover of Planets.' I see... you're an astrologer."

"The Sun's moving through Uranus," quips Fabian.

Trevor's peeved no one's taking him seriously, but Kaleb restores him. "You've done a fantastic job, this is most impressive."

Trevor flutters his eyelashes at Kaleb. "Why thank you, darling, how very kind. Most people don't appreciate the intense effort and strategic planning required to pull off an event such as this."

Kaleb continues reading the business card. "'Trevor Llewellyn.' Is your family from Wales?"

"Well, I'm from London, darling, but my mother was from Wales."

Fabian interrupts. "She wears black and white, and her name is Orca."

Trevor turns to Fabian, thumb and index finger pinched, and swipes his hand across his mouth. "Zip it, Moby. And my mother is not fat."

"Did you just call me a dick?"

Kaleb sniggers at their verbal sniping. It's difficult not to. It's highly entertaining, as long as they don't get too vicious. From the elevated position of our tent, I glance down at the open-air dancefloor and distract everyone by pointing out Big Tex. He's wearing his new Hawaiian shirt, and busting out his Austin Powers moves to "Beautiful Stranger." Paolo's patrician relatives look on with bemused fascination, while Abrianna attempts distraction by offering wine and canapés.

Trevor makes his farewells and resumes his mingling—there're still people out there who need impressing.

"So, Kaleb, were you inconvenienced by the catastrophic road accident everyone's talking about?" asks Fabian.

"No, it didn't affect me. My day went exactly as planned." Kaleb reaches into his waistcoat pocket and produces his battered tobacco tin. "I'm going for a smoke and a chat with the valet."

Fabian springs up. "I'll join you, darling."

Sofie's conniving brother winks at me, my stomach lurches, and they both disappear into the Summer Room. I envisage Fabian giving Kaleb the third degree in a bid to extrude information. My skin burns as my mind manufactures worst-case scenarios—one of which involves Kaleb confronting Ken Hunter.

Time passes slowly. I'm convinced Kaleb's either involved in an altercation, or he's left, and I wish I could, too. I'm staring directly at the doorway when Fabian reappears looking like mischief personified. He ripples his fingers at me and comes striding over wearing a broad grin. I'm relying on Kaleb's good sense and caution, but brace myself for a barrage of questions. Fabian notices me furtively scanning the entrance.

"Don't worry, honey, he's not done a runner, he's having a riveting conversation with the valet about car engines. I had to leave when they moved on to leaky brakes."

Knowing this small piece of information immediately calms me. Why do I always think the worst? Of course, Kaleb wouldn't just go off and leave me stranded... although he has in the past.

"So, Miss Vicky, is there anything you wish to share with Uncle Fabian?"

"Like what?" I ask, knowing full well he wants the dirt. Before I say anything, I'm anxious to know what Kaleb's disclosed.

"Like, where did you meet Timberland the timber wolf? How long has this been going on, and how come I didn't know about it?"

"I met him at a gig in Vegas, and I'm not sure what's going on. It's not like that."

"It's not like *what*? And, what were you doing at a gig in Vegas?"

"I was at an audit conference. Some of us went to this gig, and I bumped into him at the bar."

"Name the band?"

"I can't remember off the top of my head."

"Probably off your head! Pissed, I expect. So, are you shagging him?"

"*No*, I am not!"

"'The lady doth protest too much, methinks.' Are you sure you're not shagging him?"

"Well, once or twice, but we're just getting to know each other."

"How sweet. Well, I'm sure you'll be at it again very soon, he's salivating like a rabid dog." To demonstrate, Fabian sticks his tongue out and pants. "Here he comes now, Mr. Hungry Eyes, himself. Does he like it doggy *stylie*?"

Kaleb approaches and Fabian continues singing "Hungry Eyes." He stands, changes the refrain to a loud hum, and offers Kaleb his seat with a flamboyant flourish.

Flustered, I tentatively enquire, "Is everything okay?"

Kaleb nods.

Fabian produces a joint, "Shall we take a promenade around the garden?"

I decide against a walk, opting to stay in control of my already frayed faculties, and to lessen the possibility of bumping into Ken

Hunter. Although the alcohol has lowered my inhibitions, I've not completely lost it... yet. I envision Kaleb being frog-marched to the gazebo and held hostage until Fabian's satisfied he has the truth. Meanwhile, I'm left fretting over which probing questions he's inflicting on Kaleb. My mind races as I imagine Fabian asking Kaleb the exact same questions he asked me, and comparing answers.

To my relief, they return with Trevor in tow, glassy eyed and laughing.

Fabian tweaks my toe, "Vicky, you gotta hear this, Trevor's just told us this fucking hilarious story."

Kaleb looks directly at me and presses a sly vertical finger to his mouth—not a word, his lips are sealed.

"You tell her, Trevor," Fabian insists, "it's a classic."

Kaleb sits beside me and holds my hand. We face Trevor, and I mentally and physically brace for what I know will be an excruciatingly embarrassing tale, which at some point will involve nudity, a compromising situation, and too much detail. Trevor wriggles into position before his captive audience, rubs his hands together, and launches into the story.

"Last weekend I was organizing this charitable Fun Run at the children's hospital with a few minor celebrities in attendance. Anyway, after the race, I was mingling, as one does, when I spied this incredibly hunky sweaty specimen who'd just done the run. With perfect timing, I approached just as he's stripping off his T-shirt, and he had the most *fabulous* tats—that's tats not tits. Anyway, he starts wiping his body with his T-shirt, and I said to him, 'Oo, you're stimulating my appetite, honey, and making me seriously hungry.' His tats were like bits of torn flesh—slivers of raw meat hanging off his bones." Trevor draws his hands down his chest until his fingers point to his groin. "And I said to him, 'I'd love to squirt some relish on those and take a bite.'"

Kaleb's grip tightens, a signal to prepare myself. I don't look at him, but I understand where the story's leading. A fleeting image of Kaleb's bandmate flashes up.

Trevor continues, "He was called Ryder, and I said, 'You can ride me anytime, honey.' Anyway, turns out he's in some band called *Telsea* from Seattle, who I've never heard of."

Kaleb snorts—he can't help it. He presses his fingers against his injured cheekbone to staunch the pain. Trevor's misinterpretation of Torment Loves Company's abbreviation, TLC, is understandable and priceless.

"I've not got to the funny bit," Trevor chides.

"I know," Kaleb says. "This grass is wicked."

"Anyway, this is the funny part, his girlfriend's *vegan*."

The boys fall about laughing, and I join in, grateful to release some tension.

Trevor explains, "Apparently, the first month they were shagging she made them do it in the dark, and now she lets him keep the lights on, if he keeps his T-shirt on."

We're all crying with laughter. It's pretty funny, I have to admit, and I can picture exactly who and what he's referring to. Trevor continues, "I told him, 'For your next tat, you should get a big bowl of fruit and nuts inked across your groin in case she fancies a nibble.'"

Recovering his composure, Fabian announces, "All this talk of food is making me hungry, shall we go and check out the grub situation?" He stands and turns to Kaleb. "Are you coming?"

We head en masse to the buffet laid out in the banquet hall. Kaleb drapes an arm across my shoulders, and Fabian and Trevor tag along beside me, keeping me shielded from view. As they chatter I scan the crowd and focus on grey-haired men. Fortunately, there's no sign of Ken or Janine, but there must be several hundred guests here.

Inside the hall, the five-thousand-dollar cake takes center stage. It is truly breathtaking, but the price-tag still disturbs me. I perform a mental cost analysis—flour, sugar, butter, and eggs don't cost much, so the main element is profit followed by labor.

Trevor explains, "Each flower and jewel are individually handcrafted by artisans using icing sugar and marzipan, then hand painted, and some are gilded with twenty-four-karat gold leaf."

It's exquisite, but still obscene.

Kaleb's captivated by the design and Trevor describes the symbolism behind each intricate detail.

"The string of pearls is a nice touch," Kaleb says.

"Entirely for Paolo's benefit," Trevor replies. "I mean, who doesn't enjoy seeing their loved one wearing a pearl necklace?"

Trevor and Kaleb howl with laughter. Something registers in Fabian's mind, and his eyes and mouth fall, open. "Will you two keep it down, and quit talking about pearl necklaces."

"What's wrong with pearl necklaces?" I ask.

"Nothing Miss Vicky, some people laugh at anything, especially when they're stoned."

"I never know what Trevor's talking about half the time. Most of what he says goes right over my head."

My observation prompts another outburst from Kaleb and Trevor. They hang onto each other like a pair of schoolgirls.

"Calm down, you two," Fabian reprimands, "And, stop turning this beautiful day into a smut-fest."

We continue our tour of the tables, and view the food before making our selections.

Fabian points to plates of fruits and vegetables with dip. "Ooh, look at those Trevor, a magnificent display of crudités… your favorites."

"What are those things?" I ask. "Are they baby oranges?"

"Kumquats, darling," replies Trevor, which sparks another peal of hysterical laughter. We're attracting disapproving looks from other guests, so we load our plates and head back to our den in the corner of the garden.

Big Tex pokes his leonine head inside our cozy little tent. "So, kids, this is where you've been hiding out. They're playing our song in a minute."

"Hi, Big T, come on in and join us." Fabian pats his lounger.

His dad sits and drapes an arm across Fabian's shoulders. "One princess married off, one to go. What do you reckon, Trevor? I'll pay you to take him off my hands."

Trevor turns to Tex. "Love to, darling, but you can't afford me."

Big Tex sniffs the air. "What's that smell?"

"Scented candles," Fabian explains. "They're rather pungent."

"No it reminds me of something… it smells like… like a skunk."

Kaleb looks down to hide his amusement, and Fabian continues offering plausible explanations for the distinctive odor clinging to our clothes. "It might be those plants by the doorway, they're stood in pots of *real* earth. It must be the potting compost."

"No, I definitely think it might be a skunk. We've got one in the garden, I get a whiff of it by the gazebo, but I've not told your mother. Have you been standing near the trellis? You might've got it on your clothes."

Trevor joins in the speculation. "I didn't know you had urban skunks in Santa Monica?"

Fabian swallows a near laugh, and waves a hand at the newcomer. "Kaleb this is my dad, Big Tex. Biggy, this is Kaleb, Vicky's new *friend*."

The change of subject is an obvious ploy to minimize his agony over the pot topic.

"Pleased to meet you, Kaleb, and what do you do for a living?"

"Mechanic. I restore old cars."

"At last, someone with a proper job." He shakes Fabian's shoulder. "This one here buys ornaments in Italy for a living, and Trevor hangs curtains in folks' gardens, covers them in flowers and fairy lights, then charges a bloody fortune. Call that a job? And Raychelle here, engages in the dark art of alchemy, turning paper into gold." He faces Kaleb again. "So, what are you working on at the moment?"

"A '71 SS350 Camaro."

"*A Camaro.* My first love was a '67 convertible. I hung onto her as long as I could. It was fine when we just had Sebastian, but once the twins arrived I lost my case and lost my car. She was a classic, a rare beauty."

Fabian cuts in. "Oh, here we go, we're going for a drive down memory lane. We're going to hear about the big fairytale romance, how Saint Sebastian was conceived on the hood by the shores of the Indian River."

Big Tex looks away and shakes his head in mock indignation. "Well, Kaleb, I hope you're looking after Raychelle, she's had a rough time lately."

"Yes, sir."

Fabian shrieks. "Did you hear that, he called him *sir*?"

Tex turns to address Fabian, "Some folk have been raised properly, their parents instilling good manners and respect for their elders." Tex turns to Kaleb, "I often ask myself, 'Where did I go wrong?'"

I admire Kaleb's composure, no one would ever guess the truth about his horribly dysfunctional family and abusive upbringing.

Big Tex slaps his knee and stands. "Come on, it's our song." Saved by the DJ, Tex herds us to the dancefloor. Kaleb remains on the sidelines, looks on, and grins as we cavort to Sister Sledge confirming, "We Are Family." Sofie, Paolo, his sisters, and Sebastian join us, in what has become a Ventura family tradition at all their gatherings. Abrianna sits with her Italian relatives and looks on with mild disdain.

The end of the song signals Sofie and Paolo's departure. The witches break their circle and the newlyweds are granted permission to escape. During their long goodbye, they're smothered in hugs and kisses, showered with rose petals, and bestowed with best wishes and good luck. I bustle forward, tears in my eyes, and throw my arms around Sofie.

"I love you. I'm going to miss you so much."

"I love you, too. I'll phone or email once things settle down."

Arms bent, we hold hands. Sofie looks over my shoulder. "Who's your man? He's sexy as fuck."

I turn my head for a second and, before I can respond, one of the witches snatches Sofie away. I wander back to Kaleb, and through tear-filled eyes, watch my only friend being whisked away to her new life.

He envelopes me from behind, pulls me close, and presses his body against mine. I receive his firm, but silent message, and tingle with lust. I reach behind and squeeze his thigh to communicate my willingness. He licks my neck, kisses my ear, and whispers, "I've missed you. Is there somewhere we can go?"

While I think of somewhere secluded, I ask, "How did you find me earlier?"

"Asleep."

"You know what I mean."

"I apprehended a waiter touting champagne and asked where I might find a beautiful young woman sitting alone." Hidden from Kaleb's view, my smile is wide and tears trickle down my cheeks. "As he escorted me to your hideaway, he admitted to paying you frequent visits. My therapy sessions obviously worked." Kaleb hugs me close. "Then your friends showed up, too."

Enthusiastically, we wave through a haze of tears and rose petals as the newlyweds drive away in a white 1950s Cadillac. Kaleb follows me to a fenced-off section of garden, where compost bins lurk and garden waste decays in private.

A while later, we reconvene back at the tent to continue drinking. Trevor celebrates our return by ordering Fabian to, "Skin up." Fabian reaches for the cigarette papers and bag of grass.

We lie in a collective stoned stupor, and agree how fond we are of our tented turret.

"Let's sleep out here, tonight," Fabian suggests. "Pretend we're glamping."

This is the perfect solution to Abrianna's earlier ruling, when she made clear her family took priority, informing us, "They have come from Italy, if you need a bed, take a taxi... find a hotel." Fabian was, rightly, miffed at being evicted from his room, but I was unconcerned, because I anticipated sleeping in my own bed.

Fabian wanders off in search of a nightcap, while Kaleb and Trevor push the loungers together to form two double beds. Fabian reappears, brandishing a bottle of brandy, and wearing four big bubble glasses slotted between his fingers. We've already drunk too much, but inhaling the fumes and swishing the liquor around inside big glass bubbles, is fun.

At two in the morning, the DJ packs up.

"Most clubs I go to are just setting up at this time," Trevor remarks.

"So, do something," Fabian says, and pokes Trevor in the ribs.

Trevor departs. His footsteps scrunch along the gravel path. A car door opens and slams. Minutes later Trevor sets up his laptop and speakers, and we chill out and doze off to the ambient sounds of Enigma. Some of us take our clothes off, some of us don't.

"Hey Fabian," Kaleb says, as we're losing consciousness.

"Yeah, man."

"Thank you."

"For what?" asks Fabian, but he gets no answer.

My cheeks—still aching from earlier—burn.

Petals & Pearls

14. Razor Cut

Tweeting birds wake me, but gray light confirms I should be sleeping, even though the finches vociferously disagree. A cool breeze ripples our tent and plays with the candle inside the crystal-cut hurricane lamp. Fractals of light dance across the fabric walls to the sound of the distant ocean and create a tapestry of shimmering jewels. Kaleb with lily of the valley woven into his hair, completes this magical scene, and his unconscious state allows my finger to trace every contour of his face, without waking him. I wonder at his beauty, and rest my fingers on his lips. Still asleep, he kisses my fingertips and pulls me close. My heart swells. I peer across his chest at our fellow campers and smile at our disheveled state. Fabian's Lucky Brand lucky pants are on display and Trevor, mouth open, is naked except for Kaleb's diamante-rose bolo and a piece of black-forest gateaux sitting precariously atop his belly. I raise my arm and discover I'm wearing Fabian's shirt, and my dress is laid across my feet. How did that happen?

Despite my headache, relief floods my body. The wedding passed off without any hitches, Kaleb went unrecognized, and worrying about Ken Hunter was an unnecessary distraction as he never showed. Content, I will myself back to sleep.

Squeals and splashing wake me—people playing in the pool. A glance at Kaleb's watch indicates *"6:15 a.m."* At most, I've had four hours sleep. I raise my head to check on Fabian and Trevor and, as suspected, they're the culprits. Kaleb sleeps, but dehydration and mild nausea won't let me. I crave orange juice and carbohydrates. With the kitchen in my sights, I extricate myself from Kaleb. A glance at my hairy legs prompts me to use my shawl as a sarong. I cast my hand around searching for my bra, and visually check Kaleb's pockets. Easily defeated, I venture forth, braless and still wearing Fabian's shirt.

The house lies in silent disarray. I peel open the fridge doors, cast my eyes over the vast display of options, and settle for blueberry and pomegranate juice, a punnet of strawberries, and an apple Danish pastry left over from yesterday. Making coffee requires too much effort—I'll wait for someone else to do the honors. Sitting at the kitchen counter, I pop strawberries into my mouth, gaze across the garden, and recall the day the Northridge earthquake struck.

We were asleep for the big jolt. Minutes later, Big Tex came to Sofie's room and insisted we get out of bed and set-up camp in the garden. Later that afternoon came the second major aftershock. Sofie and I froze. Sebastian yelled "fucking hell" as waves sloshed up and down the pool. Fabian jumped in. And, Big Tex, braced on all fours, clung resolutely to his burger spatula.

Trevor runs past the window, squealing. Fabian's chasing him around the garden with a water gun. Lost in thought, I mourn the childhood I was denied, then despise myself when I consider Kaleb's harsh upbringing.

A hand clamps my shoulder. My arm jerks in response. I chuck purple juice across the counter. It drips onto the tiled floor.

"Oh my god, Kaleb, you startled me."

"So I see." He reaches for the kitchen towel.

Lily of the valley still adorns his hair. His crumpled shirt hangs loose over his jeans and, with the cufflinks gone, his shirtsleeve falls far enough to hide his disfigured hand from inquisitive eyes. I want to kiss him, but he's cleaning up my mess. I check the floor for stray spatters and notice he's barefoot. I focus on his big hairy toes and the Vampyre Claret nail polish. My delicate stomach somersaults and my temples throb.

"You should cover those up, you might frighten someone."

Fabian and Trevor come crashing through the French doors, dripping everywhere.

"Good morning, darlings," Fabian declares, as he creates puddles in his wake. He smiles at me. "Nice shirt, Tricky."

He raises his arms to eye level, pulls taught a length of lacy fabric and catapults my bra towards me. "Found near the compost bins. Explain that if you can!"

I blush and stare at my bra lying on the counter in front of me. "I can't understand how it got there."

Kaleb sniggers. "Those pesky skunks must've dragged it away." He strokes my hair.

The men all laugh.

Fabian opens the fridge and methodically transfers the contents to the table, clearing one shelf before starting on another. The unappetizing buffet he creates makes me queasy. Even more so, when he pairs Parma ham with apricot pastries, and garlic bread with peanut butter, and washes it down with chocolate milk spiked with a dash of caramel syrup. They're the type of exotic combinations enjoyed only after a close encounter with the skunk that hangs out by the gazebo.

Trevor opens champagne, but Kaleb and I decline. I'm still tipsy and Kaleb's more interested in coffee.

"You look rough, Miss Vicky," Fabian says. "A mimosa might help."

I never expected to find myself here this morning. I was convinced Kaleb wouldn't show, and anticipated going home early and waking up in my own bed. "I need a shower."

"Use the pool shower," Fabian suggests. "We won't look."

"My toiletry bag's in the car."

"I'll go," volunteers Kaleb.

Fabian catches sight of Kaleb's bare feet. "No, you can't. There's broken glass on the steps." Fabian's eyes remain fixed on Kaleb's feet, on the Vampyre Claret nail polish adorning his hairy fingerlike toes—the same seductive red as my toes.

I blush—more than blush—I resemble a tomato.

"Oh... kay." Fabian's eyes rise slowly and meet Kaleb's. "Do, dee-do, dee-do—do we enjoy taking a walk on the wild side, now and again?"

"No," says Kaleb. "But, I love getting into ladies' underwear."

"Ooh, we've got a cheeky one, here!" Fabian shrieks, loud enough to wake the whole house. "With those hobbit feet, it's just as well you're not into dressing up, they'd never fit into a pair of strappy sandals."

Trevor comes for a gander, and we all stare at Kaleb's prehensile toes.

"Oh, my god," says Trevor. "Another mystery solved—Sasquatch, lives!"

I want to defend Kaleb's beautiful feet, but can't muster any mitigating arguments.

Fabian puts a hand to his brow. "What was I doing?" he asks himself. He flicks his finger in the air. "Oh, yes, I was going to get Miss Vicky's toiletry bag from her car." He looks at me. "Keys?"

"It's not locked."

Fabian returns, and places my bag on the counter with a small plastic package. "Here's a *razor*... in case you need one."

Another rush of blood to my face—an even riper tomato.

Kaleb reaches for the razor. "Thanks," he says, "how thoughtful."

"It's for..."

"Shaving... I know."

Just after eight, the catering crew appear with their cleaners to clear away the debris and restore order to the house. A procession of strong young men carry chairs and tables to a discreetly parked truck, while Trevor checks and counts each piece of inventory. He watches closely as they load the items into the vehicle, ready for transportation to the next event.

The cleaners descend on the kitchen. "Would you care to move into the Summer Room?" the supervisor asks.

"Breakfast preparations," Trevor explains.

We relocate poolside and settle on the loungers, sheltered by umbrellas. Our cooperation is soon rewarded with several large tempting platters of smoked salmon and cream cheese bagels, fresh fruit, and a selection of pastries. Green smoothies and a large jug of coffee, also appear.

Conversation returns to the wedding. "I can promise you an equally lavish affair when the time comes," says Trevor. "Considering Kaleb's love of cars and your obsession with budgets, I'm thinking a 'drive-thru' in Vegas and, if you want to push the boat out, maybe an Elvis impersonator to conduct the ceremony. What d'you think?"

Kaleb looks at the ground, snorts, and shakes his head. He's more amused than embarrassed, but I'm mortified.

Fabian registers my discomfort. "Shut up, Trevor, you're making Miss Vicky blush. You're being a bit previous anyway, they're barely even shagging."

"You could've fooled me, honey." Trevor sticks his chin up and turns his head.

I redden so much I'm tempted to jump in the pool. Kaleb bites his lip. I can't take much more of their subtle and not so subtle jibes. It's time to leave.

I find Mrs. Ventura and Big Tex, thank them for their hospitality, and agree to drop by from time to time, although I know I won't. Big Tex, envelopes me in an asphyxiating bear hug. After releasing me, he transfers his attention to Kaleb, grips his shoulder and shakes his hand. "Promise me you'll look after her." A demand, not a request.

"I will, sir, I'll take good care of her."

Fabian and Trevor hold us captive with protracted goodbyes. Trevor's besotted with Kaleb and can't resist a final flirt. "I'll call you if my bodywork needs attention."

"You do that," says Kaleb. "I'll give you a thorough waxing, a good buffing, and a firm rubdown with a soft cloth."

"I'd prefer an oily rag."

Lost for words, and with a wry smile, Kaleb shakes his head. "Incorrigible."

Fabian and Trevor often communicate on a wavelength I'm not attuned to, and without Sofie here to translate, I'm lost. I could ask Kaleb to explain, but don't want to appear stupid.

We descend the stone steps, and Kaleb carries my bag to the few remaining vehicles parked on the lawn. Opening the trunk seems to activate a voice in the distance.

"Pardon me miss, you forgot something."

A short man rushes over, eager to present me with the feathery head creation I tried so hard to lose. Reluctantly, I take the monstrosity from the proud finder and lay it to rest inside the black-and-white striped Milano hat box. I thank him profusely, and Kaleb gives him twenty dollars for his trouble.

Kaleb looks at me. "Nice try. Don't worry I'll use it for fishing flies."

It's just one of those things, in life you always lose the things you love, but the things you hate always follow you around.

Razor Cut

15. Totally Wrecked

Midday Sunday finds us back at Oak Tree Place with burgeoning hangovers, and feeling totally wrecked from too little sleep, and too much partying. Elbows wedged against the kitchen table, I prop my chin in my hands and watch Kaleb actively seek a remedy.

After drinking gherkin juice straight from the jar, he announces, "Caffeine and sugar will revitalize us."

He brews extra strong coffee and revives a half-eaten box of doughnuts in the microwave. "If this fails," he says, "amphetamines and a cattle prod are the next best option."

Anchored in place with condiment bottles, the documents pertaining to Redfield Mine cover the table. Kaleb's created a long list of names, dates and numbers, and I'm curious. "Who *are* these people?"

"Previous claim owners. All dead... died prematurely. Only five alive."

"Should I be worried?"

"Please yourself... I'm not."

Kaleb hands me a large mug of black coffee, so strong the fumes make my nose tingle. He takes the doughnuts from the microwave. They've been zapped to within an inch of their lives, and the caramel icing is cracked and sliding off the dough, but sugar is sugar.

I take a bite, close my eyes, and the moment I open them I'm drawn to the numbers on Kaleb's lists. I scatter his scribblings in front of me, and while I chew, I study the figures and exercise my analytical accounting skills. I interrogate the data, look for patterns, and apply logic.

I summarize out loud. "The land was settled in 1849 by Jabez Gunn, and the mine and its location were originally listed as Red Bird Mine, Gunn's Camp. In 1882, claim ownership was transferred to Gregory McCavity, then Benjamin Turner in 1884. From thereon, it's referred to as Redfield Mine, Weeping Creek, with ownership passing to the next claimant in quick succession until the present day. Last named owner is Prescott Adams. So, the earrings you gave to Mrs. Tracey belonged to Mrs. Adams?"

"I guess so. Sounds about right."

"There must be more than a hundred names on this list. Is it normal for a claim to change hands so frequently?"

Kaleb bites into his jam doughnut. The red viscous filling oozes over his chin, making him appear as if he's sustained a violent injury to his mouth whilst eating, but he manages to say, "I don't know. It's interesting though."

I scan the names. "The majority of claim owners were men, but there are a few women on the list. Esmerelda Pine-Coffin—wow, you wouldn't forget her in a hurry."

Kaleb's long tongue performs a thorough clean-up and removes every last trace of raspberry jam. "I wonder what her family did for a living?"

I smile and look back at his scribblings. "Most people held the claim for less than a year. Why do you think the claim owners never held onto the mine?"

"Claim owners are liars. At best they exaggerate. Maybe Red Bird Mine was really a red herring. Maybe the promise of gold never materialized, so the owner sold it on as fast as possible."

"During the 1890s, there's a group of seven men and one woman with the same surname, and the title passes from one to the other in quick succession, some only holding the deed for a few months. How do you explain ownership passing through eight family members?"

Kaleb smirks. "Is this what you're like at work? Pinning unsuspecting folk with your pointed questions."

I play along. "Answer the question, please. If the mine was a dud, why would you sell it to your family?"

Kaleb sniggers. "Maybe they hated their relatives... but I shouldn't judge people by own warped standards."

I read Kaleb's notes. "So, according to your research, these columns represent the date the claim was purchased, date sold, and the date the claim owner died... and this column," I say pointing with my finger, "is the number of days they lived after selling the claim. Zero indicates they died whilst still owning the deed."

Kaleb slurps his coffee. "Sounds about right."

"And this column shows total days of ownership. Sean O'Sullivan... Ten days, and zero days after selling, so he died ten days after purchasing the claim."

"You got it."

I run my finger down the list and one name stands out. "So, the longest anyone survived after relinquishing ownership, was nine-hundred and thirteen days. Ramona Velasquez, who died in 1907, two years and six months after she sold the deed."

"Uh-huh."

"I see you've found cause of death for some of them, too; drowning, seizure, gunshot wound, trampled by horse, lightning, vehicular accident. According to your list of five alive, Rory Travers is close to beating Ramona's record, if he can stay alive for two more weeks."

"Yes, I'm keeping an eye on him. Age forty-two, works for a tech company in San Francisco, and appears to be fit and healthy by the look of his photo on the company website."

"Aren't you worried? Owning this deed is like a death sentence."

"I don't *actually* own it. I'm safeguarding the documents."

"You're splitting hairs. I think you should get rid of it. Hand it back to Carl so fate can do us all a favor."

Kaleb sniggers. "Meow, what a bitch."

"Well, someone should teach him a lesson, and maybe fate *is* that person."

"There's probably a logical explanation here. My money's on heavy metal. Arsenic was commonly used in gold mining."

I pull my hands away and grip my elbows. "Do you think the actual paper the claim is written on is contaminated?"

"If it is, we're both dead."

I get up, rush to the sink and wash my hands and up to my elbows with a generous measure of antibacterial soap. Outside, a raven viciously attacks a birdfeeder and sends it crashing to the ground. The contents scatter. "That bird's becoming a nuisance."

Kaleb leans back in his chair. "Ravens and their corvid kind are birds of great intelligence. Just something I observed from my time as a lumberjack hanging around in trees. I once dropped my knife from fifty feet and the raven I'd been feeding slices of apple to earlier that day, swooped down, grabbed it, and returned it to me before it hit the ground. I guess he figured—no more knife, no more apple."

Battling tiredness, but determined to stay awake, we retire to the sofa and support ourselves with pillows. Kaleb surfs the TV channels searching for intelligent lifeforms, and predictably lands on The Weather Channel. We watch Jim Cantore, all fired up in his blue cagoule, reporting live from an unfolding hurricane disaster. He clutches the microphone in one hand and wrestles against storm-force winds and rain with the other, while urging residents of southern Louisiana, "Hunker down... it's too late to evacuate."

Kaleb compares his hangover to transatlantic jet lag, and treats the symptoms with more coffee and a can of mixed nuts. Entwined, we fall asleep, only to be disturbed by the familiar sound of Butch destroying the kitchen. Guttural growls and frantic scurrying imply a bird is being batted across the tiles and tormented for sheer amusement. Disturbed by the poor creature's unnecessary suffering, I disentangle myself from Kaleb, but wake him in the process.

"Shall I deal with it?" he asks.

"You're okay. I need a pee."

The perpetrator has fled the crime scene, but minimal investigation locates the culprit hiding in the garden shrubbery, eyeing his next target. I apply my detective skills and make a stab at identifying the deceased victim. Purple and green psychedelic cat puke indicates an exotic subject and, although the plumage looks familiar, I don't recognize the species. The feathers appear too large and garish for a humming bird. I walk around eagle-eyed, searching for a body, until it suddenly dawns on me. A glance at the countertop confirms my suspicions. An empty black-and-white hat box rests on its side—its bird flown. Lying in the corner by the kitty litter tray are the chewed remains of the rare *Italiano* Milano fascinator bird. It will never fly again, nor perch on some unfortunate person's head.

"Cat with the Hat." This cat goes one step further, cat kills hat and eats it. I love Butch, but somedays, like today, I *really* love this cat. And, even though Kaleb paid twenty dollars for the feathery creation, I'm sure he can still salvage a few fishing flies from the mangled corpse.

While I'm waiting for more coffee to brew, I think about dinner and investigate the pantry's contents, but everything requires too much effort—unless it involves cereal. I check the fridge. Wilted vegetables and a piece of cracked cheese stare back at me.

The freezer holds potential. Kaleb's stocked up on my favorites—caramel choc-bomb blast—maybe we can have ice cream for dinner? Dark chocolate magnums provide another tempting option, but I make an adult decision and choose the goat cheese and roasted red pepper pizza, instead. The "artisanal" frozen creation receives a sprinkling of oregano before I bung it in the oven and set the timer. Time's marching on, evening is upon us, and I'm still suffering the hangover from hell. I can't remember the last time I felt so wasted—probably last time I went clubbing with Fabian.

Kaleb's snoozing with one leg on the sofa and one foot on the floor. He holds the remote like a kitten protectively cradled against his belly. With stealth, I seize the controls and switch to local news.

From the kitchen, I glance at the screen and catch the headlines. It's the usual stuff: car chase, house fire, three shootings, a child drowning in the family's pool, and a local council member under investigation for striking his girlfriend. Suddenly, the local news anchor's face instantly changes from false smile to false regret, an indicator she's about to deliver even sadder, *badder* news—a more gruesome death, in even more tragic circumstances.

"Now, for an update on Saturday's near-fatal accident in Copper Canyon Pass. This busy section of road was closed for several hours yesterday as rescue crews turned the highway into an operational staging area. The accident occurred on the perimeter road leading from the exclusive Pine Canyon residences. Yesterday's footage from our news chopper reveals the road's particularly steep drop off, and highlights the difficult task rescue teams faced as they endeavored to reach the scene. It took crews two hours to free the driver from the wreckage, after which he was airlifted to Canyon Medical Center."

I stop what I'm doing and stand, transfixed. Copper Canyon Pass is a stretch of road I know well, and this is the wreck responsible for delaying several wedding guests.

The presenter continues. "Today, we are learning the injured motorist is Kenneth Alexander Hunter, one of the founding partners at Hunter, Gomez & Smith. He had just left his home when the accident occurred. He has sustained serious life-threatening injuries, and yesterday underwent emergency surgery at Canyon Medical Center. We understand he is currently in a critical, but stable, condition."

I raise my head, take a deep breath and look outside at the stunning sunset. Moments like this make me believe in karma.

My eyes turn back to the screen. "Investigators continue to examine the site to establish cause, but we do know no other vehicles were involved in the accident. Impairment has been ruled out. It may simply be a case of driver error. We will of course keep you informed on Mr. Hunter's condition."

Scalp tingling, I walk to the sofa and nudge Kaleb. "Did you catch that?"

"What?" he says as he struggles to open his eyes.

"Yesterday's accident in Copper Canyon Pass. It was *Ken Hunter*."

The oven timer beeps and cancels out Kaleb's response. It sounds like, "Too bad... vengeance rides a slow horse."

"Sorry, what did you say?"

"I said, 'Too bad, the road's like a race course.'"

༄ ♈ ༅

Lying in bed, I run through the events of this past weekend, and after dreading the wedding for so long, I conclude the celebration was a great success, considering the potential for disaster. I admit, it wasn't so bad, even enjoyable at times, and learning of Ken's accident was the icing on the wedding cake.

Kaleb declared, "Best wedding I've been to."

Turns out, it's the only wedding either of us has attended. I'm glad Kaleb had the opportunity to meet Sofie's family—the people I hold most dear.

Fabian and Trevor are harsh judges when it comes to straight boyfriends, but Kaleb aced their rigorous test. Fabian employs subtle confrontational techniques to reveal a person's true nature, and expose their prejudices. He challenges their flawed logic and attacks their blind dogma. Rick, that previous bad habit of mine, was guilty of both, and studiously avoided Fabian.

Kaleb's cool response to awkward questions was also impressive. He displayed an aptitude for diverting attention, and skillfully steered the conversation around the mantraps laid down by Fabian. He's so adept at concealing the truth—or lying, as it's often referred to—and remained unfazed when Trevor told his story about Ryder's meaty tattoos. Fabian met his match. Snaring a skilled predator is difficult, they recognize the tricks and are aware of all the pitfalls.

Kaleb's sleeping downstairs. His cracked ribs still bother him and, after Saturday night's uncomfortable sleep on the loungers, I reluctantly agreed he's better off on the sofa. My hand goes to my heart and I stroke my breastbone. I picture Kaleb's pendant nesting in the dish on my dresser and a sudden urge compels me to throw back the comforter and reattach the good luck charm around my neck. He hasn't exactly given me the necklace, but knowing he allows me to wear something he holds most dear makes me feel special and a tiny big smug. Treading carefully, I wander across the room in semi-darkness and reach into the dish to retrieve Fang's precious tooth.

My fingers scrape around the trinket dish. My eyes open wide and my heart stops.

The necklace is gone.

My heart bangs into action and I cast my mind back. Even though my head was in a muddle last Thursday morning I'm one hundred percent sure I put the tooth in this dish... well maybe ninety-five percent sure. I switch the light on and shuffle things around: hair ties, earrings, random pieces of attractive rock, but the fang is nowhere in sight. I've got a missing tooth and it isn't funny. The tooth-fairy won't be leaving a reward under my pillow anytime soon. I get down on my hands and knees, and grope along the wall, where carpet meets baseboard.

Totally Wrecked

In my head, I create a plausible scene. Butch sitting on the window ledge. Butch being attracted to the animal relic, his curious paw swiping the object from the trinket dish... Then what? Chewing it? Swallowing it? Taking it outside?

That bloody cat.

Lying in bed staring at the overhead fan, I fret about the tooth. A comforting and more reasonable explanation manifests. Kaleb has probably reclaimed his treasure. He was never without it, and was likely missing the sensation of it resting against his chest. He's almost situated right below me and is probably toying with the tooth right now.

Satisfied with this plausible deduction, I relax, roll over, and close my eyes.

I'll sneak-a-peek at breakfast.

೫ ♈ ೞ

Monday morning, I deliver Kaleb's coffee to the kitchen table, press my lips against his neck, and slip my hand down his shirt. He isn't wearing the tooth. He still might've stashed it somewhere safe. Figuring out how to casually raise the topic is difficult. Maybe a throwaway question might work. *Did you find your necklace?* What if he says, *no*? My head aches with worry. There's always something new to fret about.

The phone rings in the hallway, I pause my spoonful of muesli midair, and listen.

"Raych, come to the phone, now!"

I drop the spoon back in the bowl. It's Sofie, yelling, all the way from Italy.

"I've no idea what the bloody time is over there. I think it's the morning, right? Answer the phone! Raych, you've gotta speak to me. Mom's been telling me all this crazy shit. She said that road accident that delayed the guests on my wedding day was Ken bloody Hunter... and he nearly died... and it's been all over the news."

My eyes flit around and I listen intently. Kaleb smears crunchy peanut butter across a sesame seed bagel.

"He'd just left his house and was going to pick his wife up from the hairdresser's. I found all this out because Janine Hunter just phoned Mom and cancelled her design consultation appointment. Anyway, she tells Mom that you and Ken Hunter are having a 'sordid affair.' I told Mom that was a bunch of crap, that you thought the guy was a creep, but Mom said Janine has proof. What the fuck is going on with you, girlfriend? First Rick, now Ken Hunter. God, it's like every guy you come across falls madly in love with you." Sofie laughs.

"So, I've hooked up with a heartbreaker," Kaleb says. "Are you going to break my heart, too?"

"Never," I vow.

Still giggling, Sofie says, "I bet it's that bloody book I bought you for your birthday last year: *Love Magic, Potions & Spells*. Knowing you, you've probably got the ingredients mixed up—you've probably been substituting dandelions for roses."

Sofie's infectious laughter encourages me to join in, even though she hasn't said anything funny.

Kaleb takes my trembling hand and raises it to his lips. "I'm the victim of witchcraft—bewitched, and hopelessly spellbound."

Sofie recovers enough to continue. "Then Janine tells Mom you've got a reputation for having affairs with older men, that you were 'involved' with Rick's dad, and that was why you split with your fiancé. I didn't tell Mom what really happened, I just said it was whole load of crap. And, guess what else I hear? Rick's split with his wife. We're going to be away for a few days on someone's yacht, but I'll phone again, maybe at the weekend. In the meantime I'll speak to Mom and see if I can dig up anymore gossip. That reminds me, that neighbor of yours, Doreen Tracey, she's wild. I've asked her to be godmother to my first kid. I'm not pregnant yet, but we're working on it."

Kaleb snorts.

"Love you, Raych. Miss you." Sofie smacks her lips together and makes kissing noises.

"Interesting," Kaleb says, and bites into his bagel.

Totally Wrecked

16. Identity Crisis

Monday, mid-afternoon, and I'm supposedly clearing Mom's room, but easily distracted. Resting on Mom's bed, I flick through celebrity tittle-tattle magazines. I wasn't aware my mother indulged in gossip porn, but she probably found the headline, irresistible: "Princess Diana, Murdered." But, I'm more interested in, "Twenty Years Later: Missing Girl Returns."

Sofie turned me onto reading this nonsense when I admitted being deficient in *shit* chat, but I've never bought one—too embarrassing. I'd pinch them from the office kitchen when others left them lying around. Reading excruciating details of celebrity downfalls provides comfort, knowing that, despite their wealth and circumstances, glamorous folk also lead tumultuous lives. At least my sad little life isn't being photographed, scrutinized, and analyzed every time I step outside.

Reading which celebs have gained twenty-five pounds during the last three months turns my thoughts to food. I conjure the contents of the fridge, and picture what's sitting where. A slice of apple pie on the second shelf comes into sharp focus, and beckons. Anticipating my reward, I bounce off the bed and skip downstairs. Minutes later the pie accompanies me to my computer. Emails from friends at Pottery Barn, Nordstrom, Macy's, and Last Call by NM fill the screen. Barbara's email comes flagged as important. *"Saturday, tasks requiring immediate action!!!"*

After scanning through flash sales and twenty-percent off, I open Barbara's email and succumb to her suggestions. I print the list, hoping the hard copy will encourage me to follow instructions, and derive some satisfaction by placing a tick beside each completed task.

A message pops up from Richard Martyn II, with the heading *"Sorry."* On the screen I make ponderous circles with the cursor. Should I or shouldn't I?

I shouldn't, but I do. Impulsively, I open the missive.

"Raych, really sorry about my family shouting at you. I should've realized it was a wind-up. No hard feelings? If you ever fancy going for a drink, I'm kind of single now.

Rick x"

I take a deep breath. So, I've opened it. What now? Do I respond? My fingers jitter across the keyboard. *"Apology accepted,"* I type and send. There's no point acting offended, I need to let this go and move on, and Rick's obviously having a hard time.

Another message pings, this time from Karen Lewis at Hunter, Gomez, & Smith, entitled, *"Collection for Ken."* My finger hovers over the delete button, but I'm curious to know if he's dead. Feeling buoyed by my mature handling of Rick's email, I open this message, too.

"Hi, Raychelle:

I expect you heard the awful news about Ken's accident. He'll be in hospital for weeks. It's so sad!! ☹ *We've started a collection and card. You must drop by the office and sign it. Thought you'd want to be included, and I know he misses you.*

Luv, Karen"

I stare at the screen until the words blur. Twice, he's come into my house with the specific intention of assaulting me. Instantly, I'm sucked back into the nightmare, bombarded with images of him pawing at my body. I sit in a trance until the phone rings and breaks my conscious nightmare. Finally, I crack. My chest heaves and tears erupt. I wipe my eyes with balled fists and read the email, again. How should I respond? I'm tempted to shock them with the truth.

Absolutely delighted Ken sustained such serious injuries. My guardian angel finally caught up with him.

Never again will I step inside that office.

I wish him prolonged pain and misery, and send many hateful thoughts his way.—Raychelle

Or maybe I should lie and write what's expected.

Such sad news. Please wish Ken a full and speedy recovery. I do hope he's not in too much pain. I'd love to contribute to his collection. I'll drop by later, can't wait to see you all.
Kind regards, Raychelle x x x

Karma bit his ass. He got what was coming to him—what goes around comes around.

I ignore the email. The truth isn't always wise, possible, believable, or appropriate. Sometimes secrets and lies are the best option.

After this morning's positive start, I'm back to square one. I reach for my coffee—it's cold, but I drink it, anyway. A fly lands on the apple pie. I watch it walk all over the pastry, not caring to shoo it away. I've lost my appetite.

Kaleb finds me leaning back in the desk chair, hand on my stomach, gazing into space.

"What's up?" he asks.

I shrug.

He casts his eyes over my body and notes the pie. "Do you need to tell me something?"

"Like what?"

"The tiredness, the eating."

"Time of the month. I'm hormonal, craving carbs."

Kaleb smirks, like he knows something I don't, but I know something he doesn't... I've lost his precious necklace and I don't have the courage to tell him. He walks away, back to the garage to install the camper's latest replacement part.

He reappears, and finds me exactly where he left me ten minutes ago—flopped in the computer chair staring at the ceiling fan, and pondering how I'm going to break the news about his missing pendant.

To counter my guilt, I flirt. "Missing me, already?"

He puts a finger to his lips. His stern expression kills my playful mood. The doorbell rings. I stand to attention and listen. Ken Hunter springs to mind, although it cannot be. Chatter from a walkie-talkie radio creates an equally fearful sensation, and mild terror washes over me. The doorbell chimes again. My lips part, but before I have the chance to ask, Kaleb's hand covers my mouth.

"Sshhh, be very quiet."

He grips my upper arm with his other hand, hustles me from the study, down the hallway, and into the pantry. With his hand still clamped over my mouth, he closes the door.

Standing in silence in the dark, I smell his sweat and the poison still leaking from his wounds. His deep exhalations on my neck confirm I'm perspiring, too. My head pounds, my chest heaves, and whooshing noises make me question if I'm about to faint. There's an urgent knock at the kitchen door, accompanied by more radio chatter.

An authoritative voice demands, "Is anyone home?"

Kaleb slides his hand from my mouth to my throat—one squeeze could choke me. Minutes pass. My ears prick at the distant sound of an engine starting and a vehicle pulling away. Kaleb opens the door to bright sunlight. I squint. There's no point asking what the visit was about. Kaleb reaches for the whiskey bottle and takes a swig.

I avoid the obvious question, and ask instead. "How did you see him coming?"

"Through the small windows in the garage door."

The phone rings. We both freeze and listen as the answering machine kicks in.

"Miss Carter, this is Officer Perez. I stopped by your house today. I have an item of yours. I must…" The message ends.

Kaleb's off the hook and celebrates with a hearty, but painful, laugh. He flattens his hands against his lower right ribs and presses.

My anxiety level shoots higher, and higher still when I reconfirm the absence of a wolf tooth hanging around his neck.

"Return the call. See what he wants," says Kaleb.

"I haven't lost anything." *Apart from your precious necklace.*

ಸ ♈ ಲ

After another long day of sorting and packing, we lie on the sofa, too exhausted to sleep, and I'm too tired to climb upstairs to bed. I fret in silence about the earlier phone call, and search for the right words to explain to Kaleb that I've lost his most treasured possession.

Kaleb announces, "I'm packing it in. This album is the last. I'm not signing the contract. Carl will be seriously pissed, but tough shit."

"You're exhausted. Is now the right time for such a momentous decision?"

He squeezes my thigh. "I know what I want. I've had it with this constant cycle of recording and touring. My heart's not in it. It was Jake's dream, not mine. Let's run away."

"Where to?"

"Wherever. We'll leave the past behind, and create our own history, instead of being part of someone else's."

God knows we both have so many reasons to run away.

ಸಂ ♈ ಚಿ

Fresh air streams in through my bedroom window and the linen curtains billow like sails. I imagine my bed's a boat in full sail and I'm steering a course through a blue jean sea. Cresting white waves break on the shoreline and deposit my underwear along the length of the rug.

The room is seriously untidy—"a pigsty" Mom would call it—clothes are strewn everywhere, flung over furniture and dropped on the floor. Overhead, I smile at the sight of yesterday's panties hanging off the ceiling fan, catapulted there by Kaleb. But, we're both to blame for the rest of the mess, our cast-off garments litter wherever they land.

Kaleb's first morning here, he tipped the contents of his bag onto my bedroom floor. His clothes provide comfort in his absence, add permanence to our arrangement, and reassure me he's staying. Before each open house event, I stuff his belongings under the comforter, and when the viewing is over, his clobber gets tossed back onto the floor. I like it this way, but I doubt Barbara will.

With her imminent house inspection in mind, I step out of bed and investigate the jumble with my toe. Unsure if the crumpled items are dirty, I scoop everything into my arms and stagger downstairs with a huge bundle of washing.

Passing through the kitchen towards the laundry room, I hear Kaleb clanging around in the garage. I dump our clothes on the floor by the washer, and set about sorting them into piles of light, dark, and extra dirty. With the necklace in mind, pockets are searched and garments shaken, but all I find are coins and tissues. I put his favorite jeans aside, unsure what to do with them until the stain is identified and named.

Identity Crisis

I've mastered a new spell and learned how to summon Kaleb without words. My simple hex requires the mixing of scalding water with one mystical ingredient. The coffee machine sputters and beeps, and Kaleb magically materializes, oblivious to my power. Seeing me, he smirks, but his body language reveals he's torn between kissing me and refilling his mug. I help out and assist with both.

"What's this mark on your jeans?" I ask. "Is it oil? I've got a bunch of stain removers, but I'm unsure which one to use."

"Oil... the truck's been acting up."

Over coffee, my identity comes into question. We construct and demolish theories until feasible scenarios emerge. My thoughts lead me down long, circuitous paths, and I rush towards the answer, only to find myself back at the beginning. My convoluted thought processes travel the infinite loop of a Möbius strip.

I'm done with logic, I treat the conundrum like a game of chance and cast the dice. Slowly, I ascend the rungs of a wobbly ladder, slotting the facts into place as I climb each tread. Another roll of the dice earns me a few more steps, but I land on the serpent's head and am instantly transported down the length of its slithery body back to the beginning.

Although difficult to believe, my parents must've faked my death for a reason, and collecting the insurance proceeds seems the most likely scenario. But, Kaleb's reluctant to accept this neat explanation and challenges me.

"Stop kidding yourself, Raych, you look nothing like your parents."

His blatant rejection of this theory leaves me stranded. "What are the alternatives?"

"Open your eyes to other options."

"Like what?"

"What was the name of your first bear?" Kaleb asks. "The one you lost."

Why is he asking, he already knows?

"Teddy."

"And, what's the name of the bear you're holding onto now?"

"Teddy." We exchange looks.

He's making a point and I'm not getting it. He offers no explanation. "Think about it."

Twice Dead

I do. I think about it for the rest of the day. I think about it until bedtime. I hold Teddy tight against my chest and think about it in the middle of the night and on into the wee hours, until it's almost dawn... until it dawns on me. Only when I'm drifting off, do I connect Kaleb's logic. Jolted by realization, I open my eyes and stare into the darkness.

You lose the thing you love the most. You get a replacement. You transfer the name and gradually your love to the replacement—assimilation occurs. I've forgotten Teddy number one, I'm now fully invested in Teddy number two, but the sense of loss still haunts me and makes me cling a little harder to number two. My new love is wary, tainted by the possibility of loss, and prevents me from fully engaging with the new subject. Behind the new love resides a dark shadow. The naive joy associated with number one transforms into a fear of losing number two. What was once infinite and unconditional becomes a controlling force.

Maybe my mother, Michelle, couldn't forget and failed to fully commit to number two—the replacement wasn't good enough. In fact, nothing or no one could ever replace the original. My head is bursting.

I reach for Kaleb, but he's gone. He must be downstairs on the sofa. His ribs are tender, and I don't help matters because I won't leave him alone.

"Don't touch," he says.

But I do, I can't resist. It's four a.m. and I want him. I scream.

The hallway light goes on. "Raych! You okay?"

I don't respond. Kaleb crashes up the stairs, slams the bedroom open, and rushes towards the bed. He pulls back the cover and urgently reaches out. His hand lands on my shoulder. I grab his wrist and haul him in.

"You okay?" he asks.

"Just testing the alarm system."

"The girl who cried wolf... and got one."

I stroke his golden fur, his eyes ignite. His long drooling tongue extends, and I smile, my fears momentarily forgotten.

ಖ ϒ ಐ

Contrary to Barbara's wishes, our focus shifts from clearing the house to proving where I came from, and we scour every nook and cranny searching for evidence. If adoption was my route into this family, I'm certain my parents would've kept the legal documents. Then again, they could've been destroyed by the fire. We turn the house upside down, first combing all the obvious places—Pops' study, Mom's lounge—but nothing gives. Other rooms seem unlikely harbors for important paperwork but, still, we search.

Our efforts turn to more obscure locations and, as I balance on a ladder looking for evidence in high places, Kaleb slaps the wall.

"This doesn't make sense. Your death certificate was in a box with all the other important documents, why hide your adoption papers?"

I can't fault his logic.

Kaleb's convinced I'm a changeling, but I'm certain I'm Raychelle. Why does the evidence point towards me being someone else? It's all subjective, but his arguments are so convincing he almost has me believing I'm not Raychelle. I find this difficult to accept, and the possibility keeps throwing me off balance, not a good thing when you're perched up a ladder and over-stretching.

Doubts unsettle me, paranoia sets in, and I question whether Kaleb possesses some hidden motives, but can't find any. The ladder wobbles and Kaleb steadies me.

It's difficult shedding your identity overnight, especially when you don't who you're meant to be.

17. Road to Nowhere

Another Saturday, another open house. Barbara's been working tirelessly all week enticing potential buyers with her fancy invitations and promises of fine wine and tempting canapés. She's made it clear she wants me off the premises, and Kaleb regards this weekend's forced exile as an ideal opportunity to revisit my previous home in San Diego to see if it sparks any memories.

Earlier this week, I took my death certificate from the folder on the shelf in the spare bedroom I use as an office, and questioned its validity. I remain skeptical, but Kaleb's convinced it's legitimate. To prove his theory, we scrutinized the document under a bright desk lamp with Pops' magnifying glass and, though neither of us are forgery experts, the certificate appears genuine. The trouble is, we don't have another authenticated record at hand to compare the original against. Seeing the document online is one thing, but holding it in your hand is another.

So, where does this leave me? At a dead end.

"You need to investigate," Kaleb urges. "You can't ignore something as serious as this."

But, I can—quite easily.

"Viewing the property in context might help," he says, "and it'll keep your mind from wandering back to what happened at the last open house event."

My throat tightens. Dead or alive, truth or lies, whatever the outcome... there will be serious consequences and unforeseen repercussions. For me, the trip represents replacing one acute anxiety with another.

༄ ♈ ༄

Kaleb's about to disappear, he's keen to leave a wide margin between *his* departure and Barbara's arrival. I'm meeting Kaleb later at Cravings on Ocean Park and, in the meantime, he'll eat his way through the menu. He'll take his truck, I'll drive up later, and we'll take my car from there. He's convinced the good folks of Coronado Trail might think we've come to rob the place if we turn up in his truck—my car arouses less suspicion.

"I'll drive," he says. "You seem a little distracted."

I can't argue, my head's a tumble dryer stuck on the fast spin cycle. Earlier, he caught me red-handed pouring orange juice into my coffee, and discovered a box of muesli in the fridge.

To say I'm experiencing great trepidation is an understatement. I'm shaky and fragile, my nerves in tatters, and tears threaten. I'm ill-equipped to deal with any more devastating news. I've cried so much recently, my eyes are constantly swollen, and the skin around my nose is dry from continual wiping with tissues. I have a ready excuse for comments on my appearance... Allergies.

"Hey, come here," Kaleb says. "You still fretting over the death certificate?" He gently rubs the tension in my shoulders, takes my hands in his, and guides my arms around his waist. He engulfs me in a hug and kisses my head. His shirt blots my tears.

"Don't you want to know the truth?" he asks.

That's rich, coming from a self-professed liar. I pull away and regard him. His cheek creases into a sneer, amused by his own irony.

"Whether you're dead, or alive?" he adds, to qualify his question.

I'm in a state of suspended animation, too scared to move. Kaleb raises his hand to my face, rests his palm on my cheek and brushes his thumb across my lips. "You feel very much alive to me."

"I'm frightened of digging—scared about what we might uncover."

"No stone unturned, my love. We must explore and exhaust all possibilities, until the unquestionable truth emerges."

I've grown up believing my family moved to Oak Tree Place as a consequence of the San Diego fire—a fresh start—because that's what Mom and Pops told me. Believing they might've lied to me and committed fraud on such a grand scale is too shocking, but I admit it's a feasible explanation. I desperately want to recognize my first home, to prove I *am* Raychelle, but Kaleb's looking for different proof. He's convinced I'm a cuckoo in the nest, intentionally abandoned by my natural parents, and raised by willing coconspirators. Whatever the truth, whether I'm misguided or a misfit, the uncertainty is tearing me apart and making me paranoid.

Familiar daydreams crowd my mind. I often wished I was someone else but, now that I might be, I crawl and hide inside Raychelle's skin, and cling desperately to her identity. I caution myself to be careful of what I wish for in the future. Today might provide answers. Whether I can handle the truth is another matter entirely.

Kaleb's unfazed by the conundrum. "It's natural to be afraid of the unknown." He taps my skull. "Give your brain a rest and stop imagining things."

He kisses my forehead. "I need to go." He extracts his keys from his pocket and jangles them impatiently. "See you soon, my love."

Barbara's due at nine. She'll conduct a brief inspection, flare her sensitive nostrils, decide we don't smell like top-dollar and spray the house with a more alluring aroma. She has some promising appointments lined up, and is already reckoning on her bonus. The Garcia's are due at ten along with their architect, followed by Arnold Thomas and his partner Hugo Alonso at midday, and representatives from the Markham Family Trust are scheduled for three-thirty. Barbara's confident one of these will be the *lucky* new owner of this property.

For our day trip, I've thrown a random assortment of food and drinks into a thermal bag, but the way my stomach's reacting right now, I can't imagine eating anytime soon.

Barbara arrives, punctual as ever. She snoops around, expecting perfection, but finds disappointment.

"You've still not addressed the doll situation," she accuses. She removes an aerosol from her handbag and squirts.

Kaleb sits on the terrace outside Cravings and the stack of dirty plates by his elbow implies *all* his cravings are satisfied. He's drinking coffee, tapping a pen against the table, and puzzling over a crossword. He looks up to ponder a clue and smirks at the sight of me heading towards him. I blush, still amazed how a man like Kaleb can react to me in this way. He anchors some dollars under a Tabasco sauce bottle and hurries over.

"I've missed you," he says.

Anyone witnessing our embrace would believe we've just reunited after a long separation. It's been less than an hour—I wallow in his desire.

Inside my car, I hand Pops' old bank statement to Kaleb, and he punches the Coronado Trail address into the satnav to ensure we arrive at the correct destination.

"Should be there in two hours, if the roads are clear."

Nerves and introspection render me speechless. Kaleb fills the void by detailing everything he's eaten, and finishes off with a bacon and pecan caramel doughnut. With nothing more to say, he tunes the radio into *Rock Hard*.

Traveling along Interstate 10, vehicles slow as we approach the I-405 intersection. There's no accident, just congestion, the result of erratic driving.

The *Rock Hard* DJ announces, "After the break, we're coming right back with a new song from Torment Loves Company. Prepare for 'Vengeance.'"

During the commercials I ask Kaleb in all seriousness, "What do you think when you hear yourself on the radio?"

He smirks. "Wow, this guy's got an incredible voice, and if he looks as good as he sounds, he must be a fucking handsome bastard."

Doe-eyed, I smile. "Well, I've seen him in the flesh, and I can tell you he looks even hotter than he sounds."

Kaleb chuckles and reaches over to squeeze my knee.

News on the hour, amongst other things, mentions, "Crash scene investigators conclude the recent near-fatal accident in Copper Canyon Pass was due to malfunctioning brakes. The driver, Kenneth Hunter, is expected to recover, despite suffering severe spinal injuries."

Kaleb slams the heel of his hand against the steering wheel. "Fuck!" He brakes hard. "What the fuck is this wanker in front doing?"

His mood has changed in an instant. His eyes dart between mirrors, and he twists his neck to see who's sitting on his left shoulder. *Probably the devil.* I turn my head, too, to assess the situation. With hair-breadth precision, Kaleb accelerates into a tight gap in the express lane. I close my eyes, press my back against the seat, and brace for impact. Realizing we haven't been hit, I dare to look. My downcast eyes rest on the stubborn stain still evident on his jeans. Kaleb's normally a calm driver, but not today. He mutters relentless obscenities at fellow motorists.

"What's this pig in lipstick up to? Putting her fucking mascara on… Un-fucking-believable!" He lowers the passenger window and yells across me, "Are you late for your next client?"

I wait for the DJ to come back and reconsider how weird it must be to hear yourself coming through the airwaves. I remove Kaleb's signed copy of their newly released CD from my glove compartment and study the cover. *Lost Vegas Rocks:* like so many of his statements, double meanings and hidden truths. I study the photo of the red rocks and recall the day he hijacked my car and took us to the Valley of Fire. I look at the California-shaped stain on his jeans. Pulling out the CD insert, I read the dedication. *"For Jake, Brother Black Crow—forever, flying high. Further credits thank, Lost Soul—inspiration for: 'Haunted Man,' 'Vivid Grey,' 'Hooker's Eyes,' and 'Vengeance.'"*

"Vengeance" fills the air, and I follow the lyrics.

"She gambled dreams on her tomorrows,
Wagered all her love, an' won back sorrows.
All or nothing on the Jack of Spades,
Won her bet, but the thrill soon fades.
She keeps on betting; she gets a stranger.
Thinks she's won, thinks she's out of danger,
But the odds aren't stacked in her favor.
She relies on luck, he's come to save her.
She picks a card from the Devil's hand,
Throws the dice, sees how they land.

Vengeance rides a slow horse.
She sends you on a crash course.
Vengeance best served cold,
She's got you in her hold.
Vengeance is a blinding force.
She's mean as nature, no remorse.
Vengeance best served old
Sweet Vengeance pure as gold.

I've tracked you down across this desert land.
You understand what guides my hand.
I cannot let this lie, I cannot let it go.
The time has come for you to reap what you did sow.
I ride a slow horse down a rocky trail to retribution.
You drive a fast KAH [car] down a black path to destruction.
I gave my word, promised her, justice will not escape you.
The gaping canyon takes you, the rocks will surely break you.
Spokane Words, revenge has spoken,
As you lie crushed and broken.

Remember what you did that hateful day,
You think you're going to walk away.
Think again, my twisted friend.
Press the brakes and meet your end.
It's only fair, you must crash and burn.
She's still hurting, time for you to take a turn.
I can't bear each day to see her suffer
For the simple reason, that I love her.
She thinks she cries alone each day,
But I see each tear and kiss each one away."

My brain toys with the initials KAH. The same answer keeps popping up. Kenneth Alexander Hunter. My eyes wander to the indelible stain on Kaleb's jeans. Vengeance not only rides a slow horse, but he drives a truck, and also my car. Am I fool enough to believe his words appear from the ether, or am I brave enough to acknowledge his confession?

We hear what we want to hear. We twist the words to suit our circumstances. We project our emotions onto songs, make it about us, and turn it into *our* song. Listeners interpret songs in ways the composer never intended. I glance at Kaleb, the one I love, and consider REM's misconstrued words.

I read Kaleb's lyrics again and point out, "There's a print error. They've spelt car K A H."

"No mistake," Kaleb says, "they're my initials."

"Oh… I didn't know you had a middle name."

"There're many things you don't know about me," he replies with another smirk.

"So, what does the A stand for?"

"Angel."

"Really? *Angel?*"

I can't hide my surprise, even though I know he enjoys winding me up and baiting my gullibility. But, recently, my views on life have shifted—moving away from green, through grey, and into darker shades.

"What's so shocking?" he asks.

"Angel… it's unusual. So… Heaven or Hell?"

"You tell me."

I hesitate and he volunteers more options.

"Angel of death, angel of destruction," he sings with amusement.

I look at the stain on his jeans. He could've chucked them, worn a different pair, but instead he chooses to wear the evidence with pride, a reminder to us both, how far he's willing to go. I don't bother asking—I know it's brake fluid. I love him so much, and glimpse the depth of his love, too. Any doubts regarding his motives evaporate.

In the wake of last night's storm, a beautiful warm day unfolds, sending candy floss clouds scooting across the sky. This morning the weather-lady promised another chance of showers later today, as this unsettled weather pattern persists. Right now though, the skies look picture perfect.

Unique homes, fashioned from glass and steel by wealthy aspirationalists, hug the coastline. Sunlight bounces off their expensive tinted windows and turns the ocean into a shimmering abstract painting.

Kaleb's laugh startles me. He winces and touches his cheek. He surprised himself, but can't hide his amusement.

"What's so funny?" I ask.

He points at the road sign indicating the next turnoff... Carlsbad.

"I must stop and get a T-shirt on the way back."

Conversation ceases. Kaleb massages his cheek and crunches painkillers, and I chew minty Mentos to stop myself from asking questions. Frightening scenarios, some too upsetting to contemplate, cartwheel through my head as I anticipate San Diego. Whatever we discover, it will be disturbing.

We're making good progress, there're no accidents or unexpected holdups today—there never are when you want one. To the outside world, we appear as regular day-trippers. No one would suspect I'm a young woman of questionable identity, sitting beside a man hiding a host of dark secrets.

The satnav's honing in on our target and my heart's banging. Kaleb turns the radio off. "You okay with this, Raych? We can go for a coffee first, if you want."

"Let's get it over with."

We turn into Coronado Trail and Kaleb drives slowly. "Let me know if you recognize anything, or if you want to stop."

I lean forward and jerk my head from side to side, anticipating a flash of recognition. I scan every house and tree, desperate to recognize something. Can somewhere change so much in seventeen years?

"Can we drive up and down the road first? I want to approach the house from both directions, and take in the general ambiance."

"Sure, whatever."

We curb crawl, and eventually park away from 15036. With unsteady legs, I step from the car and take a deep breath. Kaleb skirts the vehicle, grips my shoulder, and steers me towards the house... my first home.

Most of the properties along the street, although not identical, share a similar design. Well-established gardens and certain architectural features place them in the sixties. Our slow pace halts outside 15036. We stand and stare. After absorbing the view, I focus on specific details: front door, garage door, windows, house number. Nothing resonates. I cast my eyes over the garden, searching for a familiar tree or flower.

"Recognize anything?" Kaleb asks.

Slowly, I shake my head. "Not a single thing."

"Remember though, if it burned down, it might not look exactly as it did before. That said, it is in keeping with the other homes."

"Even if it was rebuilt to mimic the original, it doesn't help me."

"Why don't you walk up the driveway and look back towards the road? As a kid you probably spent more time looking out the window than at it."

"I don't know, what if someone's home? What if they see me?"

"Say you're looking for your puppy."

Kaleb releases his grip, and nudges me forward into the driveway. I take a few hesitant steps, but the next-door neighbor materializes from behind a hedge and frightens the life out of me. Kaleb reaches for my shoulder and reels me to his side.

The neighbor must've been spying on us, our odd behavior arousing his suspicions.

"Hello there, can I help you?" The old man raises his chin and marches towards us in his bright-white tennis shoes, ready for a confrontation.

A fringe of gray hair stretches from ear to ear, and through heavy-rimmed glasses, his doubtful eyes sum us up. The man's holding a can of polish in one hand, and a yellow cloth in the other, but it doesn't deter Kaleb from extending his hand to greet him. The vigilant neighbor tucks the duster under his arm and shakes Kaleb's hand. A wave of panic flushes through my body—what if he recognizes me, what if I recognize him? I bow my head.

"Hello, sir," Kaleb says. "I'm Scott Carter. Maybe you can help me, I'm looking for my aunt and uncle, and I think they might live here."

The old man's suspicious eyes examine the freshly healed wounds on Kaleb's arms. He nudges his glasses up his nose and stares into Kaleb's face, clearly unsettled by his beaten-up appearance.

Kaleb rolls his sleeves down. "Sorry... nasty climbing accident."

The man nods, instantly taken in by the casual lie. Kaleb continues the story. "My dad's not got much longer, and he wants to see his brother before he passes. I promised I'd track him down. I don't suppose you know them do you... Ray and Michelle Carter?"

"Sorry to hear about your father, son. I do remember Ray and Michelle, but it's been a good long while since they lived here."

Kaleb senses my legs wobble, and slips his hand under my armpit for support. An elderly lady totters towards us. I assume she is the wife. I grip Kaleb's arm and partially hide my face against his sleeve. My appearance must imply, a shy, possessive girlfriend—not far from the truth.

The lady, not wanting to miss out on this interesting sidewalk encounter, smiles as she approaches, and greets us.

"This is my wife, Betty," the man confirms.

"Hello, Betty, pleased to meet you." Kaleb extends his hand again.

I'm grateful I bear no resemblance to Mom or Pops, but am disappointed I don't recognize "the neighbors." I muster a feeble smile. They must think Scott's—Kaleb's—mute girlfriend is a little odd.

"Betty, this is Scott Carter... Ray and Michelle's nephew."

I'm overlooked, regarded as too strange and insignificant for introductions.

"Goodness me, how are they?"

"He's trying to find them, Betty. I was just saying it's been donkey's years since they moved."

"Well, it is." Betty closes her eyes for a moment. "It was seventeen this August, because we've been married for forty-two now, and I remember it because they disappeared the month before our silver anniversary. I thought it odd at the time because I'd been discussing party plans with Michelle, but you can't blame them."

Kaleb ignores Betty's afterthought. "Do you know where they moved to?"

"We heard they moved to LA after the accident," says the man.

Betty elbows her husband—he's said too much.

I'm impressed with Kaleb's quick reaction. He takes his cue. "Are you referring to the fire? My dad mentioned something about a house fire."

The man's brow furrows. "*Fire*? There was no fire."

"How well did you know the family, Scott?" Betty asks.

"I didn't. I believe I met them once when I was a kid, but I honestly don't remember."

"I don't know if we should say any more," says Betty, "it's not our business to tell."

Kaleb lays on the charm. "Forgive me, I don't mean to impose on you in any way."

"Betty, it's okay," her husband assures, "it happened a long time ago and the lad's looking for his uncle." The man turns to Kaleb and sighs. "I take it you don't know about their daughter, Raychelle... your cousin?"

Fortunately, the couple are engrossed in conversation, all I receive is a cursory glance, and they don't notice my grip tightening on Kaleb's arm. The sun sinks behind a cloud, a breeze picks up and my hair covers my face.

"I'm vaguely aware of a cousin, but I never met her."

"Well, I'm sorry to be the one to tell you this, son, but she died. Five years old. She drowned in the pool in their back yard. A godawful tragic accident, it upset the whole neighborhood. Anyway, a month or so later, Ray and Michelle went on vacation and never came back. Their Realtor said they'd settled up in LA. I guess they just couldn't face coming back and living here after the tragedy."

"Wow, what a shocker," says Kaleb. "But, it might explain why my dad lost touch with them—it kind of makes sense now. Looks like I should focus my efforts on LA. It's been great talking to you, er..."

"Ralph. Ralph Henderson," the man says. "If you do catch up with them, tell them Betty and I send our regards."

"I will. Ralph, Betty, it's been a pleasure meeting you both."

Kaleb shakes their hands and makes excuses for me. "Morning sickness. It's our first."

"Congratulations," says Betty, beaming at us.

My limbs are leaden, but Kaleb has strength enough for both of us and sweeps me back to the car. He opens the passenger door, and I collapse exhausted onto the seat. So, it's true—I'm dead. Raychelle *is* dead.

Kaleb climbs in beside me. I push back against the seat and weep. "Who am I?"

He takes my hand, raises it to his lips, and speaks to my knuckle. "The girl I love. Raychelle's just a name, we'll choose a new one."

I cover my hideous screwed-up red face and pink eyes with my hands.

He squeezes my thigh. "Raych, I'm driving away now, because Ralph and Betty are still looking at us."

As we pull away, Kaleb sends a smile and a wave, and I keel forward to hide myself from view. His hand comes to rest on my back. "It's okay, my love."

The outside world remains unchanged, but the space inside my head has undergone a massive distortion. Raychelle is dead. Assimilating this disturbing, independent third-party corroboration rocks me to my core. I have no idea who I am or where I came from. Reality is no longer a certainty.

I slump back in my seat. A violent tornado rips through me and scours my soul. Shocked and confused, I examine the damage, but cannot comprehend what has happened. One loud question emerges from the tangle of debris…

Who the hell am I?

18. Wiped Out

By the time Kaleb pulls into the beach parking lot I've located the tissues and regained composure. We look out across the grey ocean, something big and empty in contrast to my head but, within minutes, we're smothered by a blanket of fog, and our world shrinks. The cold front they spoke about on the weather forecast is coming in, and the warm descending air doesn't stand a chance.

Shrouded in sea fog, encapsulated inside our private bubble of gloom, we stroll along La Jolla Cove Beach. I breathe deep, hoping the salty air will clear my head, but briny sea spray stings my nose.

I remove my sandals. The sand between my toes provides cold gritty reassurance and proves I'm not dreaming.

"Don't go near the edge," my dead mother cautions. *"Stay away from the water. Water is very dangerous."*

Despite her warnings, I run now into the ocean, drop to my knees, scream, and beat the water with wild gesticulating arms. Kaleb hauls me out and drags me back onto the beach. Saltwater makes my tears sting even more.

A man emerges through the mist and throws driftwood for his dog. He makes a point of avoiding us—probably convinced we're high on something and acting crazy. But, whatever's running through my veins isn't going to wear off anytime soon.

I'm cold and shaking. Kaleb carries me to a rocky alcove to hide me from public view. He peels off my cold wet clothes and wraps me in his almost-dry shirt. Enveloped in his arms, he rocks and comforts me like a child. His large hands, tender kisses, and strong steady heartbeat soothes my raging fears.

Against a background of crashing waves, I replay snippets of Kaleb's conversation with Ralph and Betty. "She died... five years old... drowned in the pool... in their back yard." She died. I died. Are they certain? How do they know? Did they see the body? Did they attend Raychelle's funeral?

The fog begins to dissipate as the wind picks up.

I want to see Raychelle's headstone—I want conclusive proof. We can't take the word of elderly folk, they might have dementia.

I glimpse blue sky.

The incessant, timeless ocean pounds the shore. Surfers catch air and wipe out. I know how they feel. They rush back in, and get back on their boards, but I don't how to surf.

I claw at the sand and grab a fistful of powder. Slowly, the fine particles escape through gaps between my fingers, until nothing remains. I unfurl my hand and examine the remaining stubborn grains in my palm, but a sudden gust blows everything away, leaving nothing behind—no trace.

Just like the sand, my life has drizzled away. For years, I've been masquerading as someone else. Without costume and mask, I'm no one. I don't exist.

I'm thankful for Kaleb's silence. He lets me digest the information and assemble my thoughts. He doesn't steer my thinking or question my reactions. He's here and I don't want to imagine my life without him. I burrow my face into the space between his neck and shoulder. His arms tighten their hold. His hands stroke and soothe and reassure.

Kaleb's special. Given all my recent problems, most men would run or, after the latest revelations, insist the police get involved. Kaleb's supportive and undemanding. He reads my moods, and knows instinctively when to question and when to remain silent. It's scary to realize what he's capable of, but he's only ever shown me love. There's never any pressure or expectation, only pragmatic solutions without judgement—he lets me be. Who else would react this way?

The composure he displays must stem from his own extensive soul searching, as he struggled to reconcile his past. What was it he said to me earlier? He said he loved me, and I was so self-absorbed in my distress I ignored him. My finger traces the California-stain on his jeans. I want him... forever. I search his face, he pins me with his steely-grey eyes and strokes my shoulder.

"Thank you," I say.

He responds with a slow smirk. The crescent moon crease manifests on his cheek, but he admits nothing. We seal the secret with a kiss.

Letting go feels good—knowing he'll catch me feels even better. I open my mouth, about to admit I love him, too, but he speaks first.

"You did great back there, you handled it really well."

"I was worried they might recognize me."

"I think we both knew they wouldn't. So, what now?"

"Raychelle's dead... somebody's dead or there wouldn't be a death certificate. Even if they faked my death for insurance, there must've been a body. I'm too confused, I can't make sense of this. I can't imagine Mom and Pops doing something dishonest, they were so normal."

"Raych, I know you're finding this difficult to accept, but you're not the original Raychelle, you're someone else. They might've adopted you after the accident—legally or not—and given you Raychelle's identity." After a brief pause he says, "Abduction is another possibility."

His words punch me in the guts. "Abduction? Don't be ridiculous! If they adopted me, though, would they be allowed to give me a dead persons' identity? My whole life is a lie, I've been pretending to be someone else."

"You're not the pretender, Raych, it was your parents. *They* pretended you were someone else." Kaleb takes my hand and squeezes. "But, what we have is real."

Maybe so, but I'm locked inside a disturbing dream, and on the verge of tipping into a nightmare. I take a deep breath, shake my head, but don't wake up.

Kaleb plays with my fingers. "When I met you, you weren't too happy with your life. Now you're free to be whoever you want to be, you don't need to live Raychelle's life anymore. We'll get through this, it'll be okay."

He stands and offers me his hand. I take it. He drapes my damp clothes over his shoulder and stuffs my underwear in his pockets.

Wiped Out

With our arms entwined, we follow the trail of seaweed and small pebbles cast down by the breaking waves, and continue our saunter along the sand. Prompted by our surroundings, Kaleb hums a familiar tune. Quietly, he sings "Deadwood."

"Flotsam floating on an aimless swell,
Where I'll end up who can tell?
Throw a line, this boy is sinking,
Consumed by briny water I am drinking.

The tide comes crashing in,
Pebbles pound my skin.
The waves pull me apart,
Salt water fills my heart.
Take my body, pull me down,
Sweet release let me drown.

Jetsam cast aside to save the rest,
Thrown away and drifting west.
Swimming hard against the tide,
Cold, exposed, I cannot hide.

Lagan, weighted down, don't forget me,
Cut this chain and set me free.
The cold grey sea the endless churning,
This heavy shackle keeps me turning.

But, I am washed up on a distant shore,
Cold, exhausted, can't take no more.
Lying at the tide end, I am driftwood.
Nail me to your door, I am deadwood.

Screeching gulls and silent surfers plummet into the ocean. Each footprint in the sand represents a step away from Raychelle. I leave behind my mother's expectations and throwaway Pops' ambitions, too. Firmly holding Kaleb's hand, I enter an imaginary portal as Raychelle, and emerge, still holding on, as someone else. I'm light and free, inhabiting a strange place. I thread my fingers through Kaleb's hair and tug his lips to mine.

Going back to *that* house in Santa Monica fills me with dread. I hope its teeming with potential buyers. I want it sold, and rid of it.

I rack my brain for a happy memory, but nothing comes to mind. My happy times were spent with Sofie lounging around the Ventura's forbidden pool.

Raychelle's accident might explain Mom's meltdown when, at age ten, I suggested we had ample space to install a pool in the back yard. The drowning might also explain Mom's vehement refusal to allow me near any body of water, and her unwillingness to let me participate in anything offering a hint of danger. She was probably more concerned with discovery rather than my wellbeing. If I'd suffered a serious injury, doctors might test my blood, or scour my medical records and learn the truth. The situation would also explain why Mom lost touch with her sister, although I'm sure, after a few years, she could've reintroduced me—children change so much from year to year.

Did her sister even know of Raychelle's death? If she did, and they adopted me... why the secrecy? And, why foist a dead child's identity upon me? It occurs to me how little I know about my own parents. You grow up accepting, never questioning; never expecting to discover your life is a lie. Too much emphasis has been placed on belief and too little attention paid to reality. I want to believe they faked my death and embezzled the insurance proceeds, but I suspect something more sinister will emerge.

I cast my eyes across the ocean. "Kaleb, I don't want to go back to Oak Tree Place."

He squeezes my shoulder. "Where do you want to go, my love? We could find a hotel?"

"We could, but I didn't bring an overnight bag. I don't have anything with me, not even a toothbrush."

"That's what shops are for. We can buy whatever, find a cool hotel, raid the mini bar, and shag all night."

I blush and snigger, shocked and excited by Kaleb's forthright suggestion.

His finger traces my rosy cheek. "I've still got my room in West Hollywood."

"Great idea." It's an easy option, and I've no desire to stay in San Diego, I've seen and heard enough.

೯೦ ♈ ೧೩

Sitting in my car, seatbelts fastened and about to set off, Kaleb reaches over, takes my face in his hands and delivers the most delicious kiss. He pulls back and looks into my eyes, his own bursting with devilment.

Out of the blue, I confess, "I've lost your necklace."

"You've probably just mislaid it. Your room is usually a mess, and you keep stashing things in cupboards every time Barbara shows up."

"No really, I think I've lost it. I thought I left it in a dish on my dresser, but I can't find it anywhere."

"It'll turn up."

"What if it doesn't? I know how much it means to you. You wore it all the time. You told me it was your lucky talisman, a precious reminder of your dog, and how he died trying to protect you. You trusted me to keep it safe. I've let you down and I feel awful."

Kaleb transfers his hands to the steering wheel and looks ahead. "There are worse things to worry about."

"I'm so sorry."

He issues a resigned sigh, and turns to me with glassy eyes. "Maybe I've used up my quota of good luck. Maybe finding you was my ultimate prize." He squeezes my knee. "Don't dwell on it, my love, nothing is forever."

His statement stabs like a knife. I cannot imagine ever wanting to be apart from this man. I want *us* to be together forever. Sadness fills my heart and tears pool in my eyes.

Kaleb puts the key in the ignition and we drive away. In the wing mirror San Diego vanishes into the distance, but today's vivid memories replay on a loop inside my head. Anticipating what lies ahead in the next few hours is a pleasant distraction. A sumptuous hotel bed, wrapped up with Kaleb in a tangle of crisp white cotton sheets. My fingers caress my forearm, and I imagine Kaleb's strong hands running up my arms, massaging my shoulders, and…

"Are you cold?" he asks.

"No." I smile to myself. He's so attentive, even while driving. I'm impatient to reach our destination, but with no warning, memories crowd my mind of our last two hotel encounters—ending in disaster. First the Seattle fiasco, the result of his bandmate Jake's most shocking death. Second, the Spokane incident, where Kaleb left me high and dry after I brought the trip to a dramatic conclusion with, "Did you really kill your mother?"

He had walked out on me with hardly a word, and left me stranded at a hotel in Spokane. We'd just spent several awkward and intimate days together at his cabin in Wenatchee, and I was due to return home. As we traveled to the airport we made a short detour, and I had the misfortune of meeting his unpleasant family. Revelations about his harrowing childhood surfaced and I misinterpreted the facts. At the hotel, aware that time was running out and feeling uncharacteristically bold, I asked "the" question. Even now, the echo of my insensitive words makes me cringe.

I glance at Kaleb and silently vow to make tonight a night he'll remember for all the right reasons.

Still tuned to *Rock Hard* radio, a different DJ announces, "All you Rock Heads out there, let's remember Jake MacClintock. Here's 'Jack of Clubs,' the tale of a guy who played too hard and died too young."

Kaleb's familiar words are too close for comfort, and verge on prophetic.

"Split the deck, deal a card.
Bend the light, diamond shard.
Draw the knife, stab me hard.
Burn the dragon, chase the highs,
Twist the truth and spill the lies.
Twist her head until she cries.
Twist her neck until she dies.
Twisting, turning in your bed,
Twisted nightmares fuck your head,
Twist the odds and now you're dead.

King of spades, dig my grave,
A deep dark hole for a foolish knave.

Queen of hearts, lay me down.
Jack the lad lies 'neath this town.
Twist!"

Kaleb twists the steering wheel, taking a sudden and unexpected detour. We pull onto the hard shoulder, the tires screech and gravel crackles as we jerk to an abrupt halt. Kaleb exits the car and slams the door. I turn my head and follow his back. Maybe nature's calling. Or maybe he's angry with me about the necklace and doesn't want to say.

He perches against the trunk. Hesitantly, I climb out to investigate. Arms folded across his chest—with his fists, eyes, and jaw all clenched tight—he struggles to fight back tears. Seeing him so distressed, so vulnerable, disturbs me. I've been so wrapped inside my own misery, I've been oblivious to his, and I've neglected him.

My puny fingers pull at his steely forearms. I'm no match against his resistance, but he soon relents. I ease his T-shirt up, slide my arms around his body, and provide skin contact for reassurance. With my head pressed against his chest, I hear his pounding heart. His tears fall on my hair and seep through to my scalp. Pulling away, I clasp his face in my hands and say what I've been feeling ever since I met him.

"I love you, Bear."

Saying those words releases the floodgates. I laugh. I can't believe I've said it at last.

He grabs my wrists. "I love you bare, too."

He devours me with passionate kisses until he's sated. He releases me and we relax into a hug. A long moment passes until he buries his face in my hair, grips my shoulders, and pushes me away.

"I'm massively in love with you," he says. "I never realized love could be... so big."

"Nor, did I. It's bursting through your jeans."

I'm still wearing his shirt, he grabs my bare ass, and turns me away from passing motorists.

Our roadside passion provokes jeers and honks. "Get a room," someone shouts.

"Good thinking, Batman," Kaleb replies.

"Whore," someone yells.

"My whore," whispers Kaleb.

19. No Accident

We pull in at Kaleb's West Hollywood boutique hotel, both jumpy with anticipation. The moment we walk through the black glass doors, though, my mood plummets. Carl's holding court at the bar, sharing wine and wisdom with some sleazy-looking guys. He waves and, catching sight of me in Kaleb's shirt, sneers, and raises an eyebrow.

His mouth opens, but Kaleb orders him to, "Shut it."

Carl ignores Kaleb's rebuke. With sickly insincerity he smiles. "Greetings, my friend. Join me for a drink?"

I look the other way and trust Kaleb to make an excuse. He yanks my hand, leads me through the lobby towards the elevator. "Love to Carl, but something's come up—needs urgent attention."

"How about dinner?" Carl yells back.

Kaleb looks at me as Carl issues a final plea, "I'll pay."

"Too fucking true." Kaleb looks at me, awaiting my response. I shrug. "Okay, see you here at seven."

Kaleb's corner suite is located on the sixth floor at the end of the corridor. I'm undressed before the door closes behind us. The room is cool and dark, thanks to AC and blackout curtains, but it's not difficult to guess where the bed is.

Two hours isn't long enough for what I have in mind, and I wish Kaleb hadn't agreed to meet Carl.

Time flies. We cling to each other for as long as we can, but the digital clock indicates our time is up. Kaleb reaches for the sidelight and we squint as our eyes adjust. My fingers trace a crease in his skin left there by the rumpled sheet. He pulls my hand away, kisses my fingertips, and slips out of bed and into the shower. Eyes closed, blissed out, and basking in the afterglow, I prop myself against a stack of plumped-up feathery pillows. I imagine our idyllic future, how this scene will play out every day, becoming routine, but never old.

Kaleb interrupts my daydream. "Wake up, lovely."

I open my eyes. He stands in the bathroom doorway vigorously toweling his hair. Having shed Raychelle's identity, I cast aside her inhibitions, too. Emboldened, I roll my head a few degrees and wonder at the pleasure his hard naked body provides. It's powered by his wicked imagination, fluid athleticism, and the confidence of a choreographed performer. Satisfied he's mine, my eyes linger and savor every inch. Sinewy muscles wrap tight around his long, lean limbs, and his concave stomach hides his voracious appetite incredibly well. Green and yellow mottled bruises decorate his torso to create a camouflage of autumn leaves, and a resemblance to the folkloric Green Man. My attention slips to his slim hips that fit so perfectly between my thighs, and seeing him semi-hard makes me want him back in bed, now.

He tugs the curtain and examines the daylight status. The muscles in his shoulders ripple, and my fingers flex involuntarily as I imagine hanging onto their boney orbs. His chest looks especially bare without the crescent tooth dangling from its silver chain, and my reverie is halted by a stab of guilt.

I look away and my eyes flit to the mirror behind him, to the reflection of his broad back, bearing shiny old pink diagonal scars. I sit bolt upright and glare at the shocking image. Why have I not noticed them before?

Since his return, he's rarely shared my bed for the entire night. His recent injuries made sleeping downstairs a more comfortable option and, whenever we've participated in random lovemaking around the house, he's usually semi-clothed. I assumed his open shirt was either to protect or hide his injured forearms. Back at the cabin, it was dark, and every time he appeared half naked, modesty forced me to look away. When we're in bed we face each other, one of us on top... or he's behind. Most often, I lie beneath him and moan and sigh... with my eyes closed.

With my eyes closed.

Eyes closed and oblivious to almost everything around me.

They're wide open and unblinking now. His right shoulder's worse than the left. Lower down, livid red lines flare out from his right hip to his left buttock. Suddenly, he raises his head, registers my shocked expression, and twists his neck to see what's triggered my distress. He catches sight of his reflection.

High thread-count cotton sheets are not responsible for the creases in his skin.

"Was it an accident?" I hope he'll reply they are rope burns sustained while climbing rocks or trees.

"No accident."

I bite my lip to quell the tears, and study the horizontal pattern on the jacquard sheets. My skin burns as I envision his suffering. He's not been hiding his cruel scars—it's me—my eyes have been closed. The evidence is on full display, but I've not been seeing, or listening, until now. "Evoking Spokane Ghosts" plays in my head: *Read between the lines across my back, the whip, the whoosh, the hellfire crack.*

Anger rises, my face reddens. Uncle Joe, Maggie, and Granny—all complicit in the brutality dished out on an innocent young boy. I want them all to suffer. Teardrops turns the white sheet grey. The mattress sinks under Kaleb's weight. He brushes my hair aside and smooths my tears away with his thumbs. I kiss his palms. He holds my face and I stare back through a blur of tears.

"I thought you were being cool about it," he says. "How come you've only just noticed?"

I can't speak. I'm overwhelmed with love for this man, and enraged by the people who did this to him. His Uncle Joe did this, and the rest of his family turned a blind eye. How could they condone such abuse? Seeing him after the fight was bad enough, but this is worse.

"My eyes were closed."

"Ignore it, my love," he says. "Don't dwell on it, it's just a few marks. I can't see them, I forget they're there."

He's so dismissive of these awful scars. God knows what damage has been done? His flesh is marked, but what about his heart and soul—the damage I cannot see. He might be able to forget about these lines, but I'll see them every day now, a constant reminder of how a child was brutalized. I love him so deeply, that's why it hurts so much.

His hands rest on my shoulders. I latch onto his wrists. "How…"

He's smirks. "Believe me, you don't need to know. My scars are behind me now, I've turned my back on them."

"*Not* funny."

"I know, but it's the best I can do with the material. There's nothing to be gained or changed from telling the tale, so I'll hold onto my secret, and you know better than most we all have secrets.

"I know I promised you a lifetime of torment and misery, but not all the time. I want you to smile now and again, and this…" his hands move to my neck. His thumbs nudge my chin up, "is the only way I know how."

The taste of his minty fresh mouth sets my skin tingling and guarantees we'll be late for our dinner engagement. He pulls the sheet away from my body, and his damp hair flicks across my face as he nuzzles my neck. "Please don't cry, my love. Look at me, don't be shy. Kiss me with your eyes open."

His firm grip on my face, leaves me no choice. His lips on mine finish me off. He pulls back, inches from my face. "This is us and it's beautiful," he says. "Watch me, watching you, while I do *this* to your body." His hand moves south. "Your pleasure is my pleasure. Eyes. Open."

In between his traveling kisses, I remind him, "We're going to be late for dinner."

"Fuck dinner, I'm fucking my appetizer."

The phone rings but Kaleb's not answering… he's busy, very busy. Minutes pass. When the phone rings again, he raises his head and lifts the receiver.

"I'm still on it, Carl, give me ten."

so ♈ ℰ

When Carl extended his dinner invitation I wish, instead of shrugging, I'd uttered an emphatic "No." Kaleb must realize Carl's the last person I want to share a meal with. My intense dislike of Carl hasn't diminished, I loathe him for numerous reasons.

Kaleb stares at my frown as we descend to the lobby in the elevator. "What's up?"

"I'm not sure this is a good idea."

"Tired?" He cups my breast in his hand and smirks.

I look down and nod in agreement.

"It's payback for him crashing our meal the other week."

"I'd prefer to write it off, as an unavoidable loss."

He strokes my cheek. "Over-order the most expensive stuff on the menu, and I'll screw him for the wine."

In his black Jeep, Carl chauffeurs us to a Vietnamese restaurant located in an unfamiliar run-down part of town. After ordering the wine, and more food than we can eat, I sit quietly and leave the conversation to the guys. Carl complains about the wine, but guzzles it anyway.

When the food arrives, the wine is already gone.

Carl instructs Kaleb, "Get behind the bar and pick some decent shit."

The waitress smiles and Kaleb follows, leaving me with Carl. I play with my food. I spear a piece of chicken and dab it around my plate.

"So, how's the rich bitch from Santa-fucking-Monica?"

I don't respond.

"What's up? Am I not your type? He's just like me, you know… hides it well."

Carl's words land like punches. I look towards the bar. Kaleb's chatting and laughing with the attractive waitress. I will him to come back immediately and save me.

"He's getting her number so he can fuck her later," Carl says. "Him and Jake were quite an act, must've fucked hundreds of slags over the years… when they weren't smacked out their heads."

I press my lips together, and breathe deeply.

"He's probably got Hep C… and a host of other unpleasant diseases."

My eyes fill up. My skin burns.

Kaleb returns. *Thank God.* "Hey Carl, I hope this satisfies your discerning palate, it's their most expensive." Kaleb winks at me and pours the wine. He doesn't sit. He wanders back to the bar.

Carl slurps, swills the wine around his mouth like mouthwash, and swallows. "Why won't you talk? Fucking stuck-up bitch. Not much of a conversationalist are you? Mind you, I don't suppose he cares when he's got his dick rammed down your throat."

I'm blind with rage. I'm frozen with anger but, most of all, I'm inert.

"You look like you've been crying, honey. Have you had a row? Has he been telling you about past conquests and his litter of bastards?"

Carl noisily sucks up noodles and spatters sauce across my chest.

"We had to torch the place," he says, "incriminating evidence. The bodies were stinking, attracting vermin. Rats and flies."

Carl dips his fingers in each bowl picking at whatever he fancies. He licks his digits and dives back in, contaminating everything.

"He's after your money—thinks you're loaded. He's probably told you he's got plenty stashed away, but he's skint. Too much *high living*, if you know what I mean."

Carl pours more wine and slugs it back. "Apart from your tits, you've gotta ask yourself why he'd be attracted to someone like you? I mean you're okay, but he's had some real ballbusters after him. Anyway, I'm just saying, wouldn't want you getting hurt."

My head's spinning, I can hardly breathe. I stand, and the chair screeches against wooden boards as I push back. I spit out stupid threats and throw my wine in Carl's face, but stop short of smashing the glass into his mouth.

Kaleb's disappeared. I can't see him and I can't see her—the attentive waitress.

Carl wipes his chest with a napkin. "Fuckin' hostile bitch."

Fuming, I head for the door. Outside, I stand, shaking, expecting Kaleb to come racing after me—but he doesn't. I'm torn between running to him, and running away from him. I want to hide, but I want him to find me. Streetlights and headlamps become abstract shards of glass in my tear-filled eyes. Carl's harsh words have destroyed me, left me broken and humiliated. Hatred for Carl readily converts into anger at Kaleb for hanging around with such an asshole. Why hasn't he come to my rescue? *Because he's chatting-up the waitress*. My rage quickly escalates. I want to punish Kaleb for leaving me in the company of this vile monster.

Adrenalin and an urge to flee send me careening down a dark alleyway adjacent to the restaurant. I don't know where I am or where I'm going, I just want to get away from Carl, and teach Kaleb a lesson, too. Even if he comes looking for me now, he won't find me. I'll hide, I'll let him panic—let him suffer.

My energy's soon depleted, and running in these stupid flip flops hurts my feet. I slow and catch my breath. My vision's blurred and rubbing my eyes makes little difference. In the darkness, I stumble over an obstacle and reach down to steady myself. An arm bats my hand off a leg. Shocked, I gasp. A bottle rolls across the pavement. Another man emits a drunken yell—he's spilt his liquor. Terror forces my eyes wide open.

The ground becomes a morass of serpents—silhouettes of men squirming on cardboard beds line the alleyway. Movement in a doorway draws my attention—a man receiving a blowjob offers a toothless grin. Paralyzing fear and a horrible realization anchor me to the spot. I should run—but where? Men are closing in on me. From behind, a phantom hand grips my shoulder.

"Hey blondie, come here," instructs a deep voice. "I could use someone like you."

Horrific scenarios crowd my mind. I'm suffocating with terror, barely able to breathe. I lurch forward and scramble away. Hands grab me. Someone's laughing.

The flouncy skirt I wore to hide my hairy legs catches on a discarded broken bicycle. The flimsy material rips, exposes my legs and threatens to reveal much more. I'm especially vulnerable because, wanting to please Kaleb, I neglected underwear. I scrunch the torn fabric into a bundle, press the ragged skirt against my crotch, and run. One flip-flop rips, unbalancing me, and I crash to my knees. I save myself, but graze my hands. Quickly rising, I tread on my torn skirt and rip it farther. Again, I gather the rags about my body and run. My flip-flops are useless now, and without them I yelp with every painful footfall. My heel lands on a sharp stone, which topples me once more. Again, I use my arms to save my face.

A man steps out and offers a grimy hand. I refuse. He grips my wrist, hauls me up, and draws me towards him. He regards me with demonic eyes and a hideous decaying grin. I should strike with my free hand, but I'm holding onto my tattered skirt to hide my flesh. I close my eyes and instinctively turn away from his foul breath.

Kaleb taught me how to scream, and now's the time to exercise my lungs and demonstrate what I learned. I recall the night at his cabin, how he incited me to scream with his vicious words, coupled with the terror and intense excitement he provoked when he pressed the cold blade against my throat. For one long moment, I believed my life was over and issued a convincing scream. Evoking the memory, I scream my lungs out.

The guy twists my arm. "Shut it, bitch."

The silhouette of a running man stands out against distant streetlights.

"Raych! Where the *fuck* are you?"

Startled by the angry shout, my captor attempts to clamp his dirty hand across my mouth. I bite his finger and scream again… even louder. The guy lets go and melts into the night.

Kaleb finds me on my knees, crumpled and hysterical, shaking and sobbing. He scoops me up in his arms and jogs along the alleyway towards the busy street… to safety. He bundles me into Carl's awaiting Jeep.

As we speed away, Kaleb drags me onto his lap. "You okay?" I'm too traumatized to speak. "Don't *ever* run away from me again."

Chastised for my foolish behavior, I shake and whimper, and press my face against his chest. He picks at my shredded skirt and runs a hand along my legs. Discovering a wet patch, he puts a finger to his tongue, and concludes, "Blood."

I burrow in farther. I'd crawl inside his body if I could. His hand covers my head, and amplifies his pounding heart.

"What the fuck were you thinking?"

I won't utter a word in front of Carl. I hate him.

"This is down to you, Carl. Fucking apologize."

"Why the fuck would I want to do that, and break the habit of a lifetime?"

Kaleb strokes my hair. "Carl's a cunt of the first order, isn't that right, Carl?"

Carl accepts the accolade with honor. "A five-star cunt, that's me. Top of my game."

"Apologize you bastard," Kaleb insists.

"Sorry," Carl says, with insincerity. "Nothing personal."

But, his words were immensely personal, and deeply hurtful.

"Worth a try," he adds.

"He blames you for making me pack in the music," Kaleb explains. "Thinks if he scares you shitless I'll change my mind. But, he's wrong, as usual. The thing is, I love you more than music or money."

"You're making me want to vomit," Carl says. "Hey, honey, what you said earlier about where you work... you were mouthing off, right?"

I don't respond. I obviously hit a nerve.

Back at the hotel, the valet swipes open the black-glass door, giving Kaleb space enough to enter, carrying a bedraggled woman with bleeding feet. Inside, the receptionist doesn't bat an eyelid. My torn and dirty clothes are ignored, and Kaleb proceeds unchallenged. The night manager pays no attention to my disheveled state either. He's apparently seen it all before—and worse—this sight is nothing new.

"Fancy a nightcap?" Carl asks as we pass the bar.

"No, I fucking don't!" Kaleb whisks me towards the elevator.

Back in his room, he lays my bruised and battered body on the bed. Overloaded nerves send messages of physical and emotional trauma to my brain, and jostle for priority. Painful bleeding feet, humiliation, ripped fingernails, shame, grazed knees, and fear—the terrible dread Kaleb will no longer love someone as stupid as me.

I wish I could erase these past few hours and return to the post-coital bliss of earlier. Kaleb stands over me, his anger palpable. I close my eyes. He gently places his hand on my shin. My face crumples and I cry like a desperate child, too naive and dumb to contemplate a remedy.

Gushing water from the bathroom faucet fills the tub and drowns my sobbing. Kaleb pulls a chair up to the bottom of the bed, grabs my ankles and hauls me towards him. His rough handling alarms me, but I bite my lip. He grips my left ankle and lifts, forcing me to bend a smarting knee. He closely examines the damage, then switches feet. When he's done, he leaves my legs dangling over the edge of the bed while he shuts off the water.

He returns. "Raych, what the hell were you thinking?"

I'm loathe to admit my flawed logic, and less inclined to speak. I stare at the ceiling.

"Look at me," he demands. "I *want* an answer."

Kaleb's harsh tone upsets me. My lips tremble. He stands between my parted legs and leans forward. His hand darts towards my face, I flinch and turn my head.

My reaction shocks him. "Hey, Raych? I'm sorry, I'm not going to hurt you. I don't mean to sound aggressive, but I'm fucking upset seeing you like this, knowing I contributed to the situation. Please understand, you must never run away from me, you must always run *to* me."

I clench my lips and nod.

Kaleb lifts my hand, notes my broken nails, and kisses my knuckle. "What *exactly* did Carl say to make you run?"

With hindsight, Carl's words were an obvious wind-up. I'm stupid to imagine Kaleb would ever intentionally hurt me. I offer my pathetic explanation. "Carl made some vile and nasty accusations about you, and said you were getting the waitress's number..."

"Carl talks shit. He's a cunt. Her name's Kim, and I was asking after her brother, Lenny. He's a violinist—a session musician at the studio. He damaged his hand skate-boarding. She disappeared into the kitchen. I went for a piss."

"I'm sorry."

"No apology necessary. Believe me. You hurt yourself more than you hurt me." Kaleb gently places my arm by my side and sits between my knees. "No more running away from me, okay. Bad things happen when you do, you must stay close." Curiosity drives him to lift the rag that used to be my skirt. He smirks approvingly at my lack of underwear.

"For me?" he asks. I nod. His anger dissipates. He leans forward and plants an appreciative kiss on my crotch. "What did you say to Carl anyway? He's totally rattled."

"I told him I worked for the IRS." Wide-eyed and mouth agape, I wait for Kaleb's laughing to subside. "Are you going to tell him?"

"Hell no. It was great seeing Carl wearing wine and panicking about his dirty money. Best of all, he got fucked by a girl... my girl."

The fear of Kaleb leaving me diminishes.

"I need to undress you," he says.

"Go ahead."

He peels away what remains of my ripped clothing and tosses the remnants onto the floor. Fully naked, I raise my back and bend my knees, allowing Kaleb's arms to slide under my body. He carries me to the water, and dips my butt to test the temperature.

"Not too hot, is it, baby?"

"It's fine." He gently lowers me into the bath.

He kneels by the tub, reaches into the water and grabs an ankle. Closely, he examines the damage to each extremity.

"Bite on this." He puts the washcloth to my mouth, and I open wide allowing him to insert the gag.

Starting with my feet, he gently massages soap into the cuts, and carefully cleans the wounds. When he takes the nailbrush and scrubs with force to remove the embedded dirt, I chomp down hard on the damp cloth. I scream so loud, my eyes bulge, but no one can hear, because the washcloth serves it purpose to stifle my protestations. He removes the gag, reaches for his nail clippers on the counter, and precisely trims each finger and toenail. He picks up a file and carefully finishes the job.

"You'll need new clothes." He gets up and leaves the bathroom.

Moments later, the door to our room opens and closes. I'm left soaking in humiliation. A while later, I pull the plug and the evidence drains away with the dirty bathwater, leaving only an embarrassing ring of scum around the tub.

Wrapped in a towel, I hobble to the bed and sit and wait for Kaleb. The digital clock indicates *"23:37."* I'm shattered... so much has happened today. I doze for a while, but wake up cold. I discard the damp towel and crawl under the covers. Kaleb's absence bothers me, but I'm too exhausted to lie awake and worry.

The door opens. Through heavy eyelids I see *"3:13"* on the clock and watch Kaleb, laden with shopping bags, stumble into the room. He smells of booze and smoke, and I pretend to sleep. The bathroom light goes on. He pees and simultaneously brushes his teeth. He spits in the sink.

He stands at the foot of the bed and lifts the cover from my feet. "Don't wake up, my love." His gentle hands attend to the damage. He rubs antiseptic into my cuts and eases my feet into the softest socks ever. I love his touch and anticipate him crawling in bed beside me, but he doesn't.

Hours later, I wake up chilled and reach for the sheet, but it's vanished. I cast my arm around searching for something to cover myself with. Forced to open my eyes, I find Kaleb naked on the recliner. The sheet is balled up by his feet. He's staring at me, brooding. Fear grips me.

He stands and approaches the foot of the bed. "Only I get the pleasure of seeing you like this."

My eyes open wide and I struggle to breathe. He's looking at fear, but clearly sees arousal. With a confident sneer, he grips my ankles and gently separates my willing legs.

"Me. Only. Ever. Me. Only *I,* will have the pleasure. Only *I,* will give you pleasure."

He scares me sometimes… most of the time, if I'm honest.

20. Passport Control

Monday, late morning, we pull into the driveway at Oak Tree Place. Since leaving Saturday morning, and after such a strange weekend, it's difficult believing only forty-eight hours have elapsed.

Creeping around on bandaged feet, each step becomes a painful and constant reminder of Carl's cruel words. The niggling worm of doubt burrows into my mind and sets up home… was there a grain of truth in anything he said?

Listening to Barbara's phone message, I register her upbeat tone. "There are three offers on the table. A bidding war is underway." Her excitement escalates as she explains, "Something is always more desirable if you know someone else wants it, too."

I'm not in a celebratory mood, but it's good knowing my days in this house are numbered. Staying within these walls, knowingly surrounding myself with evidence, is not an option, but selling the house and disappearing will disrupt the trail of lies. The family who once occupied this space will vanish without trace and soon be forgotten.

Kaleb's out front cleaning windows, and I'm standing in Mom's bedroom with the window open, contemplating where to start. Kaleb's had several positive responses regarding the camper van, and test drives are scheduled, so I'm not surprised to hear him say, "Greetings."

But, then he says, "How can I help?"

Anything unusual makes me anxious, especially when the anonymous caller's response is cancelled out by a police radio. I momentarily freeze. I crane my neck, peek through the billowing lace curtain, and spy a Santa Monica police cruiser parked in the street. My heart races and a sudden fever produces cold sweats and trembling.

"The lady of the house is indoors," Kaleb says. "Come on in." *Is he mad?*

In the hallway, the officer comments, "Those are serious marks on your arms, sir, if you don't mind me saying."

Kaleb, ever ready with excuses, says, "Yeah, nasty climbing accident. The guy above me fell. I grabbed the ropes." He calls upstairs, "Hey, Raych, someone here to see you."

I can't move, I'm terrified.

"Wait in the kitchen, I'll fetch her," Kaleb instructs the officer.

He finds me standing, stone still. "Hey, there you are. What's up?"

Wide-eyed and sweating, it doesn't take a genius to work out I'm scared to death. "What's happening?"

"Something to do with Hunter, I think."

My eyes widen farther. Kaleb grips my upper arms and engages my eyes. "Listen to whatever the officer says. If you don't want to respond… cry and leave the talking to me."

"What if he asks awkward questions?"

"I'm a liar with no conscience. Let's go."

Slowly, I head downstairs in my giant fluffy slippers—the only suitable footwear available to hide the bandages.

The young officer stands. "Hello, miss, I'm Officer Perez. Can I ask your name?"

My lips tremble. I stammer, "Raychelle Carter."

Kaleb grips my neck and administers a deep-tissue massage, communicating a nonverbal message. His touch is mildly painful and my face reacts accordingly—tears well up.

"Her mother died recently," Kaleb explains. "She's taken it badly."

Officer Perez, tilts his head. "I'm sorry for your loss, Miss Carter. My mother passed last year. It's a terrible thing."

"Yes, indeed, it's a terrible thing to lose your mother," Kaleb agrees.

"Forgive me, but I'm here regarding a vehicular accident involving Mr. Kenneth Hunter. I left a message the other day."

Kaleb's fingers dig deep into skin and bone—the tears spill. He guides me into Butch's chair and applies more pressure, forcing me to sit. He explains to Officer Perez. "She lost her mother in a collision. Mentioning Hunter's accident and seeing an officer in the house is a harsh reminder."

"I'm so sorry, miss," says Officer Perez. "But, the reason I'm here is, we recovered a bag containing your possessions from the wreckage. Mrs. Hunter is insistent we return it to you in person."

I haven't a clue what he's talking about. "How do you know it's mine?" I ask.

"Your passport, miss."

I don't have a passport. I suck my lips and nod. From underneath the table Officer Perez produces a bag I don't recognize.

Kaleb explains, "Raychelle worked for Hunter. She must've left it at his office, I guess he was on his way to drop it off."

Officer Perez's startled look morphs into embarrassment. Abruptly he stands. "I'll be on my way," he says. "God bless you, miss. Losing your mother is hard."

Kaleb escorts him off the premises. My head is throbbing, about to explode. I raise my hands and grip my skull, determined to hold everything together.

"What have we here?" Kaleb drops the bag onto the kitchen table. He unzips with caution and delves inside. Black lace panties appear. He holds a black lace bra aloft and sniggers. He reads the label. "36D. Wow, you're quite the handful."

Kaleb carries on digging. Rope. Handcuffs. Blindfold. I feel sick. Kaleb laughs like he's heard the funniest joke ever.

I make a dash for the bathroom and puke.

Kaleb follows, lifts my hair aside, and offers a wet washcloth. "I'm sorry, I wasn't thinking."

We return to the kitchen table and sit. Kaleb presents me with *my* passport. My name is Raychelle Hunter. A note falls out.

"How dare you conduct a sordid affair with my husband after all our family has done for you! You ungrateful little bitch. Thank God your parents are not around to witness this aberration. Stay away from my family, you dirty little whore.
—Mrs. Janine Hunter"

"Why has Ken Hunter got a false passport containing my picture, inside a bag full of tricks?" I ask in a weak voice.

His wife is convinced we've been engaging in pervy sex, and Officer Perez—if he looked inside the bag, which he must've done—must think I'm banging my boss, and catering to his every tawdry desire. This must be the proof Sofie was referring to in her phone call last week. Janine Hunter has probably told Sofie's mother all about the bag, or maybe even shown her what's inside. I close my eyes and hide behind my hands.

Kaleb slams his hands hard against the table, and makes everything jump, including me. "Would you feel safer if I..."

"No. No!" I interject before Kaleb has chance to voice his intentions.

"I can make it appear like an accident," he assures me.

Just like last time... and the time before... and...

The doorbell rings. We both look up, Kaleb stuffs the contents back into the bag and throws it under the table. "That'll be Larry from Pasadena about the van. He phoned earlier and said he was in a cab, on his way over." He marches towards the door to greet him.

I wander into Pops' study and observe Larry through the window—a tubby, middle-aged guy who's come dressed for the occasion in baggy yellow shorts, a loud Aloha shirt and flip-flops. They walk over to the camper and Kaleb questions Larry's proficiency. "Have you driven something this big before?"

Minutes later, they set off on their test drive with Larry behind the wheel.

Larry's our favored buyer, he's offering cash and we're underselling—a mutually beneficial deal leaving no paper trail. Anything other than cash would delay handing over the keys. I admit I have trust issues and would insist on waiting for confirmation of cleared funds.

The van pulls into the driveway, prompting me to stand behind the front door and eavesdrop on their conversation. Through the spyhole, I watch Kaleb, in full control, interact with nervous Larry. Kaleb casually sweeps his hair back and moves at his own pace, while grinning Larry with the beer-belly nervously hops from foot to foot, and scratches at his arms.

Kaleb shakes Larry's hand. Larry thrusts a Macy's carrier bag at Kaleb.

"Aren't you going to count it?" asks Larry.

"No. I know what twenty-five grand looks like. Besides, you wouldn't want to rip *me* off, would you?" Kaleb nonchalantly pushes his sleeves back to reveal his recent battle scars.

Larry adopts the expression of someone facing a pointing gun. "No, sir."

Kaleb dangles the keys midair and Larry swipes them away. Minutes later, Larry from Pasadena drives away in the magic bus. I scurry into the kitchen and act surprised when Kaleb bursts through the door brandishing a red-starred shopping bag.

"Here you go." He dumps the bag on the kitchen table. "I'll collect my commission later—I'll accept payment in kind."

            ಬ ϒ ಙ

After a late lunch, I venture into Pops' study, fully intent on shredding any superfluous personal documents. The shredder has its own little cubby hole in the built-in shelf unit. Opening the cupboard door, the machine rolls out on rails—ready for business. Per their labeled files, IRS documents, pensions, and shares are set aside for tax purposes, but everything else—credit card statements, utility bills, and property tax demands—get fed to the hungry machine. Discovering old bank statements stalls my ruthless rhythm as, using my forensic accounting skills, I search for clues.

The documents are addressed to an unfamiliar apartment in San Diego—Ray and Michelle's first home—where they lived until moving to Coronado Trail.

Starting with the oldest statements, I scour the figures for any irregular or suspicious transactions. My finger glides slowly down each page, through the months and into each consecutive year. I follow a simple pattern of electronic salary deposits, along with regular spending and saving routines. My death year holds special interest, so I meticulously study each entry and look for any divergence in their predictable routine. August presents a clue—Pops' salary stops.

I scan the debits column looking for large inexplicable withdrawals amongst the gas and grocery payments. Finding nothing, I search the credits for substantive income which might indicate insurance fraud. It occurs to me insurance companies are slow to settle up, so I flick forward through five more years of records, but find nothing unusual.

Back to my death year—I notice Pops is on Webber's December payroll, where he worked until he retired. All subsequent transactions follow a regular cycle of deposits and withdrawals. It's possible there are other undiscovered accounts concealing vast fortunes, but our family's lifestyle never led me to believe we lived beyond our means, or were subsidized by fraudulent cash injections. On the contrary, we were careful, our only extravagance being our cars, and Mom's obsessive doll and figurine collection.

The savings account is a much slimmer volume. Within moments of flicking through statements, a transaction for twenty-seven thousand dollars leaps out—paid out the same month we moved into this house. My heart quickens. Is this how much I cost? No. A calculation in pencil on the adjacent statement provides an instant answer, and details the purchase price, deposit, and monthly mortgage payments for Oak Tree Place.

I conclude there are no large withdrawals to indicate I was bought, and no large cash deposits to indicate fraud. Financially, everything *appears* to be in order.

Why am I desperately hoping to prove I'm the subject of an elaborate insurance fraud, when the evidence unearthed so far clearly indicates the real Raychelle is dead? Because, I can't or won't accept I'm not Raychelle. But, who else can I possibly be? Where did I come from? I can't get my head around this. I rock back and forth, and hope I'll wake up.

This past weekend's brief flirtation with freedom and confidence has evaporated. I've slipped back inside cautious, timid Raychelle's skin because it's easy, comfortable and familiar. Being Raychelle is much less scary than not being her.

My attention shifts to the filing cabinet. Systematically, I examine each compartment, and scrutinize every scrap of paper for clues before assigning the contents to recycling or shredding. The top drawer contains receipts for furniture and household appliances along with user manuals, instructions, and warranties, most of which have now expired. The user manuals I put aside for the next owner. The bottom drawer holds maps, leaflets, and mementos from summer vacations. I spend an age reminiscing and hesitate before consigning these memories to the shredder, but it's where they belong. I remove the racks holding the dividers and find a Yosemite souvenir pen and a small cassette tape. I'm uncertain if it's video or audio. Whatever it is, it looks obsolete, but the date inscribed on the case *is* significant—August '86.

Kaleb's wearing earbuds and rocking out to Nirvana as he empties cupboards in the garage. His chore has become a performance, and now he's swearing he doesn't have a gun, although I know he does. Oblivious to my presence, he taps a screwdriver against Pops' workbench and shakes his head to emphasize his conviction.

Hoping I won't startle him, I rest my fingers on his arm. His eyes widen with mild surprise, and he smiles. His reaction indicates nerves of steel—I would've jumped a mile. He tugs his earplugs out.

"Great performance," I say. "Have you ever considered going professional?"

"Che-e-eky." He grips my wrist and playfully spanks my butt.

I wriggle free and produce the tape. "What's this?"

He examines the object between his fingers. "A mini digital video tape used in movie cameras."

"How can we see what's on it?"

"D'you have the camera?"

"No idea, I haven't come across one."

"I could take it down the studio. Steve, our sound engineer can convert anything into different media formats."

"What if there's something controversial on it?"

Kaleb eyes me, suspiciously. "Steve's cool. He won't say anything."

"What if there's something incriminating on it? What if he makes a copy and tries to blackmail me? It's a big risk. I don't want anyone viewing the content."

"Raych, there's nothing else you remember is there? Something you're not telling me?"

"What do you mean?"

"You know what I mean. Are you expecting to find disturbing images?"

"Only because of the date and the fact it was hidden."

"Okay, as long as that's all. How about, I ask Steve to show *me* how to copy it?"

"Hmm… might work. It won't automatically get saved anywhere, will it?"

Kaleb strokes my cheek. "You have a suspicious mind, young lady." *Is it any wonder?*

ఈ ♈ ಙ

I've made good progress in Pops' study. The desk and filing cabinet are empty, and a huge stack of magazines await recycling. I've wrapped and packed most of the objects and curios, and put aside the seafaring collection for Kaleb. Over dinner, we appraise the situation and prioritize the tasks still requiring attention. Barbara's expecting a "best and final" offer by the weekend, so I'm focused on emptying all the free-standing furniture, ready for donation to the family shelter project or disposal at the dump.

21. Evidently Not

This morning I'm in Mom's bedroom clearing out the bedside cabinets. Mrs. Tracey mentioned she'd like them for her guest bedroom. I've stripped the bed and put the quilt and pillows aside for the homeless shelter. The flowery rugs are rolled up and tied with string. One more rug to go, but the heavy ottoman on top of it won't budge. Weeks ago, I intended using the seat to stand on so I could reach into high cupboards, but tried and failed to move it. Instead, I dragged the unwieldy stepladder upstairs and broke a light fixture in the hallway.

Today though, I have a better option—I'll commandeer Kaleb. He's in the garage stacking cans of paint and other noxious substances ready for responsible disposal.

"The cabinets are ready to go," I announce. "And, can you help me move the ottoman when you're ready, please?"

"I'm always ready for you."

He chases me up the stairs and grabs at my ankles. I squeal because my feet are still sore and the terror of being pursued is still fresh in my mind.

Standing by the seat and poised to lift, Kaleb states the obvious. "Why don't you empty it first?"

"Can't find the key."

"It's locked?" He examines the mechanism. "No problem. I'll fetch some tools."

He returns with a small screwdriver and a thick piece of bendy wire. Eyes closed, he fiddles with the keyhole until the latch releases.

I reach for the lid, but Kaleb's hand darts out and grabs my arm. "It was locked for a reason… to deter trespassers or protect valuables."

We kneel and he lifts the lid. A waft of roses escapes. An innocuous pink baby blanket reveals itself, but Kaleb sees a red flag. "Take it easy Raych, that's a child's blanket."

His tone implies he's expecting something sinister to emerge from the chest. A body comes to mind, but I don't share my morbid thoughts.

Putting the blanket aside, I pull out a pink short-sleeved frilly dress—a typical example of the humiliating garments Mom forced me to wear. The sight of it summons uncomfortable memories of being teased at school. Also, of a party at Sofie's—all the other children wore shorts and T-shirts, apart from me, forced to wear a pink-and-green flowery dress with a scratchy white-lace collar, plus silly frilly white lacey socks. Sofie's mom took pity and allowed me to wear some of Sofie's clothes. Instant elation. I fit in with the others. That's all I ever wanted—to fit in.

"Is that your dress, Raych?" Kaleb asks, incredulous.

"I don't recognize it, but it resembles the dresses I was forced to wear. Don't smirk, it's not funny. It was traumatic—it still is. Look, I have the scars to prove it."

I point at the pink mark on my neck that I'm convinced was caused by stiff lacerating lace.

Delving deeper, I extract smaller dresses and baby clothes. Realization hits. "These are Raychelle's clothes, aren't they?"

"I would say so."

I inspect each garment before laying it on the carpet. A doll with curly blonde hair emerges. Her smug expression and moveable blue eyes with long lashes make me believe she knows something I don't. She's wearing an identical dress to one I've just laid out. I never played with dolls. I disliked the hard, cold, resistant plastic. Bears are my thing: cuddly, furry and comforting. I snuggle against Kaleb—my Bear. He grips my shoulder and delivers a reassuring squeeze.

I unwrap a lacey white handkerchief and a small christening bracelet bounces across the carpet. Kaleb springs forward and snatches the silver band. He reads the inscription. "Raychelle Sarah Carter, June 14th, 1981, christened, July 26th, 1981."

Twice Dead

To my knowledge the only time my parents stepped inside a church was the day of my father's funeral and he had to be carried in. God was never mentioned in our house.

Sadness turns to anger. "How could they do this to me?"

"Raych, this was never about *you*. It's about them and their loss. You were a consequence."

"You don't believe I'm the real Raychelle do you?"

If I'm honest, neither do I.

"No, my love, I don't."

His succinct reply is kind and without doubt. Solving this puzzle is impossible. Emotions get in the way and interrupt my logic. "Who the hell am I?"

"Who knows?"

"How could they leave all this evidence lying around for me to find?"

"Grief makes people do strange things. They held onto the past, unable or unwilling to let go."

"What if someone else had stumbled across it?"

"I don't expect they gave it much consideration."

"Why didn't they get rid of it?"

"The contents of this box represent a tangible connection to Raychelle. Not many people possess the discipline to tie up loose ends before they die, and your mom's death was completely unexpected."

"What happened to Raychelle?"

"She drowned, right?"

"Yeah, but what happened to her body? I don't expect there's a grave, they wouldn't be so stupid, would they?"

"Maybe she was cremated. Maybe they scattered her ashes somewhere."

I gaze at the remaining contents. "Considering everything else they've hung onto you don't think they might've…"

"Just go easy, Raych. We're not finished, yet."

There're no shocking surprises lurking at the bottom of the ottoman, but there are video tapes and the missing photo albums—the ones I'd ask to see, but was always told had been destroyed in the fire.

Gold embossed numbers stamped into the spine of each photo album indicate the year. Kaleb runs a finger down the chronological stack of albums and sings Bowie's "Golden Years."

Evidently Not

I sit cross-legged and stare unfocused at the tomes before me, but dare not open them. For years I mourned their loss, but now that they've materialized I'm too scared to look.

Kaleb senses my reluctance. "Are you ready?"

I nod. We reposition ourselves, backs against the bed. Kaleb drapes an arm across my shoulders and kisses my head. I take a deep breath, remove 1981 from the top of the pile, and balance history on our laps. With trepidation, I enter the portal to my past.

Relaxed and happy images of Mom and Pops holding a baby in their garden stare back at me. Methodically, I study each image. It's the house in San Diego. Mom's wearing a pink-and-white swimsuit, and oversize sunglasses. She's reclining on a lounger by an azure pool. An umbrella shades her from the sun. Mom and Pops are in the pool and hold Raychelle aloft like a trophy. Who took the picture? Maybe they had a time delay button on the camera. They appear joyous. I've never seen them look so happy. At *that* moment, they were happy, because they had no way of knowing their precious baby would drown in that pool several years later.

My hand goes to my chest.

"Breathe in," Kaleb reminds me. "Breathe out."

Who the hell am I?

We spend hours poring through the albums, scrutinizing each photo, picking out every detail, searching for clues. Clues about what, I don't know. Pops' neat handwriting identifies vacation locations, but nothing more. We make notes and discuss different scenarios at length, hoping something will jog my memory. Deep down, I know this is a futile exercise, but Kaleb patiently indulges me.

Kaleb's already cast me as a changeling, a concept I'm finding impossible to accept, because I don't remember ever being someone else. But, with each passing year, the photographic evidence makes his argument more apparent—I'm not the child in the photographs. I'm not the original Raychelle. I'm a replacement. Yet, I can't recall another life.

It's devastating to discover you're not who you thought you were, that you've been living the wrong life, and not the one originally intended for you. Something is very wrong and I'm impatient to know the truth.

Twice Dead

The 1986 album is a work in progress. The page is labeled, *"Raychelle, age 5 - Birthday Party,"* but the photos are loose; lodged between the pages, awaiting their corners.

Children with their mothers play in and around a swimming pool in a garden I presume is located behind 15036 Coronado Trail. The scene is unfamiliar, I don't recall it being *my* fifth birthday. I'm not there, I don't ever recall being there, and I don't ever remember meeting a little girl called Raychelle who looks like the girl in the pictures. I am clearly not Raychelle, but I believe I was five when we moved into this house.

"I never had a birthday party."

"Nor did I," replies Kaleb.

His words cut through me. I'm so self-absorbed I forget about his traumatic childhood. "I'm sorry... I don't mean to be so insensitive."

We speculate about every imaginable scenario, dispelling the most ludicrous and concentrate on the more likely. The secrecy and lack of formal adoption papers surrounding my insertion into this family makes us consider more unorthodox routes. Maybe I was unofficially adopted, the illegitimate offspring of a relative. Michelle would never speak of her sister, maybe I'm her niece, and her sister is my real mother. Maybe my birth mother was young and desperate, unable to care for me. Maybe she was in a bad or difficult situation like Kaleb's mother. Maybe she was too poor and decided this nice couple would give me a better life. Maybe Ray and Michelle took me in as an act of kindness, and not for their own selfish reasons. Maybe I'm maligning their good nature.

Did money exchange hands? Was I bought? Was I sold? Am I a missing person? Am I featured on a milk carton? Will I ever discover my true identity? Does it matter?

Maybe I belong to the group of thousands of adopted and laboratory conceived children who'll never know who their biological parents are. And, what about the countless children of dubious parentage who go through life calling the wrong man "Daddy."

Even though the photo albums provide visual prompts, I remember none of it. I can picture the photograph, but not original context. The real Raychelle died on June 16th, two days after her fifth birthday. I moved into this house three months later with her mom and dad, but where did I come from?

My life began in this house.

I'm an only child with no known living relatives, and unsure if the few fleeting memories I do have are real or imagined. There's no one around to substantiate my recall, the only people who've known me any length of time are Sofie's family and Mrs. Tracey. The only other inanimate witness, appearing in so many photos, is the camper van we just sold. Many secrets must reside within its metal frame—if only it could talk. The old van has far outlived its human family, and sentimentality accuses me of selling my grandmother.

Kaleb has no early photos, just a past he'd rather forget. Instead, he's cursed with vivid recall, and the scars on his body provide permanent reminders. Kaleb has memories but no photographs, I have photos but no memory. I try hard to remember, he tries harder to forget.

The phone interrupts my contemplation. We look towards the door, strain our ears, and listen to Barbara's rambling edict. "All three parties are still at the table, but want another look before submitting their best and final offers, so *please,* could you make a special effort to address *all* the issues on the list I sent you the other week. And, *please* do something about those dolls, they give me the willies. I honestly think those dolls are responsible for scaring Mr. Morgan away."

Kaleb sniggers.

"I'll speak to you later but, in the meantime, I'm resending the 'to do' list, in case you accidentally deleted it. I'm trying my very best to get you the best possible deal, Raychelle, but I need you to work with me to achieve our common goal. I know some of my requests might appear trivial, but they could translate into thousands of dollars. I'll drop by Friday to see how things are coming along. A fresh expert eye can make all the difference."

Kaleb does his usual job of cutting to the chase. "Barbara's fucked off with you. You need to pull your finger out and get rid of the voodoo collection coz it's freaking everyone out. You're screwing her commission chances and she's coming to check up on you, and make sure you're following orders."

Butch pops his head round the door and issues his most pathetic meow, implying the severity of my neglect—he's starving and near death. Kaleb reacts like Pavlov's dog and gets up to feed him.

"I need to attend to your feet," Kaleb says as he leaves the room.

He sets the bath running in the en suite connected to my study, and goes downstairs. We often use this room now, it's the only place in the house untainted and devoid of any disturbing associations. Five minutes later, the faucet shuts off and Kaleb shouts, "Hey Raych, get a load of this!"

I get to my feet and gingerly cross the landing—what's he discovered now? I find him lying naked on the bed.

He pats the mattress. "You owe me big time for selling the camper. Time to pay up and I need to negotiate favorable terms regarding the remaining vehicles."

"Do you mind if I pay in instalments?"

"Not at all, but my interest rates are exorbitant."

"How long will it take to repay you?"

"A lifetime."

"Sounds reasonable."

"I must also warn you, any missed payments come with stiff penalties."

"How stiff?"

"I'll show you."

"No need, I can already see." My fingers eagerly fumble with my shirt buttons.

"Come here," he says. "That's my job."

I kneel on the bed and let him undress me. I let him do anything he wants.

"What did I do to deserve such an obedient woman?" he asks as he draws me to him. It's nothing he did, it's me—I can't resist him.

He works his way down my body and stops to kiss my cocooned feet. "Safe sox," he says, and sniggers. "The ultimate protection. Maybe that's where we've been going wrong. But, your feet can wait a moment. First, I must attend to your body."

※ ♈ ☙

We're exhausted. There's no structure to our existence. Dark of night and light of day are irrelevant. We've slipped into our own time zone and reverted to our most base animal instincts. We make love often, we eat when we're hungry, and sleep when we can. We can't leave each other alone. He kisses my shoulder—I press my butt against his body. I caress his face—he gets on top of me. He touches my hip—I let him roll me one way or the other. His thumb strokes my breast—I reach for his head and draw his lips to my nipple.

"That's why it's called falling in love," Kaleb says. "You're either face down or flat on your back."

"Well, I'm flying, soaring high above, and standing tall."

"No, my love, we're still falling, plummeting to new and undiscovered depths of depravity. The only thing standing tall is my dick. They make out falling in love is a wonderful thing. In reality, it incapacitates you: fries your senses, puts Space Invaders in your brain, hooks in your heart, and a dynamo in your dick."

"You're so romantic." I stand up, he pulls me back.

"Lie down I want to fuck you again."

Thirty hours later and what happened to Tuesday? Kaleb's still attending to my body, and the bathwater is cold.

"So... I'm fucking a dead person," Kaleb announces. "I never fancied necrophilia, but it feels dead fucking good. Or, should that be good fucking dead."

The room resembles the epitome of debauchery. Two wasted bodies lying in a tangle of dirty sheets, surrounded by wine and whiskey bottles, empty glasses, discarded condoms, half-eaten food, and a brimming ashtray. Barbara's gonna love this—not.

"Oh my God, it's midday Wednesday. I need to take Mrs. Tracey shopping."

I spring out of bed. Kaleb reaches out and grabs my wrist. "Hey, slow down. Remember, Doreen said Dr. Daydream is taking her this week. Come back to bed."

22. Dead Roses

After spending days on the horizontal plane, I wake up groggy instead of refreshed. I'm inclined to lie here on the pretext of feeling unwell, but I'm unable to sleep because it's predawn Thursday, and Barbara's expectation of a "beautifully presented house," is buzzing around my brain. I slink away from the bed so as not to disturb Kaleb, and shower in another bathroom so I won't wake him. With my head tilted back, the spray hits my face and goes part way to clearing my mind.

The house is a bomb site. We trashed the place earlier this week in our bid to unearth god knows what, and now I'm faced with spritzing this place up in just *one* day.

Fueled by panic and coffee, I assemble flat-pack boxes in Mom's lounge, a room I especially hate after what happened here. But, I can't dwell on negative thoughts right now—the doll situation needs tackling. I look upon them with malice and they stare at me with startled eyes. They know something is afoot. My mother's "adorable little friends" with their "angelic little expressions" won't be so damn smug when they're tucked up and taped inside their cardboard coffins.

The Queen of England's portrait comes down first—I don't need royal approval for this task. I wonder if Mrs. Tracey might like HRH, but decide Trevor's a more suitable recipient. In fact, I'll offload all the English junk on him, he'll enjoy the joke. The royal family commemorative items from the china cabinet soon fill a box. I throw in lace doilies for good measure and label the goods—*"Queen/Trevor."*

Kaleb's appearance in the doorway startles me. "I've never seen you up and active so early," he comments.

I glance at the carriage clock—just past six in the morning. "Yeah, well there's a ton of crap to get rid of."

He wanders off, in search of coffee, no doubt. Without caffeine on board, he's grumpy and dysfunctional. He returns with two mugs and hands one over.

"You look happy," he observes. "Still thinking about last night?"

I blush. "Not until you mentioned it."

"So, why the smile?"

I wave an open hand at the empty china cabinet. "All packed... Trevor's in for a big surprise."

He reads the box label. "Too true! He's gonna love you."

Kaleb puts his mug down, ready to assist with packing dolls in boxes. He picks up Beulah, the big freaky doll, by the hair. "We're gonna need a casket for this one." He dangles her in midair and looks her in the eye. "Just *how* crazy was your mother?"

"Very. I need to hide that thing somewhere, I can't risk frightening anymore potential buyers. Poor Mr. Morgan, I hope he's okay."

Kaleb sidles over. "He needs a kiss." I oblige, and he continues assessing Beulah at arm's length. "This thing is fucking creepy. Does it remind you of someone?"

I take a closer look. "Oh, god! The child in the photos... Raychelle."

"What shall we do with it?"

"Put it in the garage, in one of the cars."

"The trunk."

"Yes, the trunk. Good thinking."

Having disposed of the body, Kaleb returns ready for his next task. He stands on a chair, unhooks the lacey curtains, and opens the windows. Ghosts and the sickly smell of synthetic rose gardens escape the room. Cool, invigorating, morning air floods in and displaces the stale atmosphere and, with the dolls and porcelain ladies packed away, the room already feels much brighter. Barbara's vision of a "neutral canvas for buyers to project their personality onto" has been achieved. She'll be impressed with our efforts.

Twice Dead

With a ruthless, unforgiving eye I survey the remaining clutter. "That stupid corner table can go." It serves no purpose, apart from displaying a grotesque crystal vase Mom kept perpetually filled with pink roses—the crispy dehydrated remains of the last bunch still litter the carpet. I scoop the latest windfall of brown petals into the trash.

Seeing the vase empty allows me to fully appreciate its hideous nature. With both hands, I pass the heavy object to Kaleb. He smothers it in bubble wrap, complete with its crusty green slime, and buries it in the charity box. The pink doily it stood on, I toss into Trevor's haul.

An ornately carved white box remains on the table. I swipe a finger across my engraved initials and am poised to lift the lid.

Kaleb grabs my wrist. "No!"

Realizing, *who* is in the box sets me shaking. Kaleb ushers me from the room, through the kitchen, and into the garden. Birds are chirping and Butch springs amongst the flowerbeds like a creature possessed.

Kaleb walks me around the garden and points at a flower—a scarlet trumpet. "What's that called?"

I rack my brain. "They wear them in Hawaii. They make tea... and soap... and Fabian drops them in champagne."

"Mmm, sounds good."

Mrs. Tracey and cookies spring to mind. "Biscuits... Hibiscus." His distraction technique is working.

Butch wiggles into position and primes his body for the first kill of the day. I intervene, but my bid to save a life leads to lacerations and blood. I blot the wounds with my T-shirt. Kaleb settles me on a lounger and goes back indoors.

Ten minutes later, he emerges bearing a tray laden with coffee and blueberry muffins. He places the tray on the table and squeezes beside me on the lounger.

"I've put her in the garage... in the trunk next to the doll," he says. "We'll decide what to do with her, later."

Kaleb's phone rings. He wanders towards the house and stands with his back to me. He presses a button and ends the call. "Fuck."

Anxiety spikes. I assume it's Carl but, of course, I don't ask.

"Someone's coming to look at the cars. I need to move the bodies. It won't look good if they peer inside the trunk." He disappears.

ꕤ ♈ ꕤ

Back in Mom's lounge, the corner is bare, with the box and table gone. Also gone is the slim possibility I might be Raychelle.

Like a sentry on duty, I press my hands against my thighs and stand, feet planted firmly together, within the four-dot boundary left by the table legs—the exact same spot where Raychelle has stood for seventeen years. Kaleb leans against the doorframe, arms folded, and observes my curious behavior, but says nothing. I want to feel something—a connection.

Undeniable and mounting evidence indicates I'm someone other than Raychelle. But who? I'm a character in a play, but can't remember who the actress is in real life. I'm lost to the world and lost inside myself. I'm the key witness and I *should* know the answer, but I'm unable to shed any light. My identity's such a fiercely guarded and shocking secret, I keep the truth from myself. Who am I *meant* to be?

I close my eyes.

"I can still see you," Kaleb says. I don't respond. He steps forward, grips my upper arms, and squeezes. "Now is not a good time to start acting all cosmic. We need to get this shit packed away."

Side-by-side, we kneel and roll up the rose-patterned rug. With all the pictures removed and only the mirror remaining, Barbara's neutral goal is realized.

Dolls and ornaments contained in their cardboard coffers line the hallway, and I'm grateful for Mrs. Tracey's offer to use her garage for storage. Kaleb lifts the boxes two and three at a time and marches them next door. With Beulah bound up in refuse sacks, I follow and imagine how a child killer disposing of a body must feel. If Mom wasn't dust she'd be turning in her grave at the prospect of Beulah being trussed up and locked inside a dark garage.

Mrs. Tracey's garage seems more spacious than usual. With lightning speed, a bolt of realization enters my head and exits my toes, and I drop Beulah onto the concrete floor. "Where's my car?"

Kaleb bends and dumps his stack of boxes against the wall. Standing, he turns and smirks. "I sold it."

I stare in disbelief, unsure if he's toying with me.

"It had to go. I was gonna tell you."

"I loved that car."

"I know. There'll be others."

My heart actually aches at my loss. "Who…"

He rubs the stubble on his chin. "Carl."

I recoil in disgust, but have no time to dwell on the fate of my poor car.

        ℘ ϒ ℘

With the hallway clear, I tackle Pops' study. Outside, Kaleb assembles the extendable ladder on the front lawn, ready to clean the windows. Instead of partaking in my own chores, I'm captivated by Kaleb's nonchalant ascent of the ladder whilst balancing a bucket. Moments later, using his knees, he slides down the outer rails, without using the rungs, and lands on the ground.

By the end of the day, we've polished and scoured every surface imaginable. My feet are sore. Every time I crouch, the cuts re-open and supply unwanted reminders of Carl's callous words, accompanied by images of him driving around LA in my beautiful car. I picture him using women for his personal gratification on the rear leather seats. Vigorously scrubbing the toilet bowl dulls the unpleasant image. My hands are red and throbbing, ruined by detergent and nasty chemicals. I'm guilt-laden as well, concerned about the damage these cleaning products have inflicted on the environment. To make amends and restore Earth's fragile balance, I reckon I must plant six new trees.

I'm exhausted, but still have all the bathrooms to clean. Kaleb's on kitchen duty. He raids the freezer—pepperoni pizza and caramel ice cream for dinner.

Kaleb sprinkles hot sauce on his pizza. "By the way, Rory Travers died two days ago. Drowned—swimming in San Francisco Bay."

My chewing slows. *Who is Rory Travers?*

"So, Ramona's still head of the league table," he adds.

Redfield Mine. Rory Travers was competing with Ramona Velasquez to become the longest surviving claim owner. "How do you know?"

"His company website posted a nice obituary."

Inside the pink powder room, I bend over the toilet and scrub. The food in my stomach curdles, and the sight of the bowl urges me to vomit. At least I'm in the right place.

Midnight passes, and Kaleb sits in Butch's chair, swigging beer, while I finish off and perform the final touches ready for Barbara's nine o'clock inspection tomorrow morning. I venture outside into the garden and cut some roses—my final feeble attempt to make this place look homey.

23. She Is Me

I wake up, dazed, to the sound of Kaleb's departing truck. Avoiding Barbara affords Kaleb the opportunity to deliver the recently discovered tapes and videos to Steve, the sound engineer. Relinquishing the tapes is a worry, and contemplating their content agitates me further—you read and hear such awful stories in the media. What if they contain shocking or incriminating images… surely, I'd remember if I was abused in any way. Kaleb's sworn to secrecy, but knowing his secrets far outweigh any of mine provides little comfort.

A glance at my clock confirms Barbara's due in fifty-three minutes, so I allow myself ten more minutes of Kaleb daydreams. His absence leaves me vulnerable, but Ken Hunter is no longer a threat. I picture the indelible stain on Kaleb's jeans and Ken's unfortunate accident, and smile. I close my eyes and relive what Kaleb did to me last night. *Mmmm.*

Time's up. I must turn my thoughts to more practical matters.

I quickly shower and dress. From Mom's bedroom window, I witness Barbara's arrival. She's two minutes early. She casts her eyes across the garden, proceeds to pinch off dead-heads I've missed, and secretes them in a bush. She assesses the house as she approaches, her every move reflected in her windshield. She swipes a finger down a window and raises an eyebrow—surprised to find them absolutely spotless. Big Ben chimes in the hallway, and Barbara's insistent finger has you believing it's high noon in London Town.

I bounce down the stairs, swing the door open, and muster a smile. "Good morning, Raychelle, and I'm sure it will be a good day, too."

Barbara makes a beeline for Mom's lounge. "This looks fabulous. You have been busy. The dolls are gone, *and* I see you've got rid of the unusual vase complete with its dried flowers."

Yes, and I know it wasn't on your list, but we also removed the remains of the previous owner's deceased daughter. And, yes, I have no idea who I am.

"This is what the buyer wants to see."

She storms off to the kitchen and I trail in her wake. Head raised, her nose twitches, sniffing for traces of kitty food, cat shit, and allergens. Butch stares through the window, and his wide eyes question what he's done to warrant exile. He only wants to come in, though, because he can't.

Barbara sweeps through each room meticulously flicking curtains, adjusting blinds, and rearranging ornaments. All the bathrooms are checked for function and cleanliness. She lifts each toilet lid, peers inside, and flushes. Two steps behind her, I feel like a chambermaid auditioning for a job.

"You've made excellent progress. Carry on with the good work. I'll see you tomorrow—nine sharp. I'm nervously optimistic about a sale."

Having passed Barbara's pre-show house inspection, I close the door on her, and continue my crusade. But first, a well-earned coffee and double-chocolate brownie.

☙ ♈ ❧

Most of the day I'm fine, I pretend all is normal, and nothing's changed. I promised Kaleb I wouldn't dig around too much while he's away, and I don't. I play it safe. His absence allows me to scour my bedroom and search high and low for his necklace, but it's definitely missing. Butch the cat burglar is the number one suspect, and I toy with the idea of taking him to the vet and getting him x-rayed. He appears perfectly well, so I don't expect the chain is tangled around his innards. I'm probably too late anyway, if he has swallowed the tooth he will have deposited it somewhere in the garden by now. Maybe I should go over the flowerbeds with a metal detector?

By lunchtime, I end up with a pile of dirty washing and an assortment of bird feathers, courtesy of Butch, but no mummified corpses, thank god.

Downstairs, I stick the trophy feathers in a shot glass on Pops' desk, and waste another ten minutes pointlessly arranging them before checking my emails.

With a sigh, I open Rick's latest communication. The first few words are warning, enough.

"Hi, Raych,

I've been thinking. That guy you're hanging around with. Is everything OK? Mom thinks he's going to turn you into a prostitute to pay for his drugs. Dad says you can stay in our cabin up at Tahoe (but don't tell Mom). Just say the word and I'll come and rescue you.

Rick x"

So, Stella thinks Kaleb's my pimp. Husband Dick thinks he's still in with a chance, and would like to keep me as his sex slave in the family's remote cabin. And dickless Rick, dense as ever, has no clue.

If I don't respond, Rick might pay me a welfare visit. If I do respond, it might encourage him.

"*Thank you for your concern. All is well.*"

ಖ ♈ ಐ

Clearing Pops' closet occupies the afternoon, even his old slippers are gone. I reward myself with another Sudoku challenge, and relish my achievement on successfully completing another *killer* puzzle.

I watch the early evening local news and I'm still okay but when the phone rings the specter of devastating tragedy rips through me. I postpone the moment and wait for the message to play.

"Hey, hot thing, I've found you out. I'm still working on the videos with Steve. I'll be home about nine."

By nine-forty, I'm frantic with worry. Kaleb's either been killed in a road accident or Carl's kidnapped him. I tell myself I'm irrational—it's highly unlikely he's come to any harm, because recently we've both experienced more than our fair share of bad luck.

I regret not answering the phone, for missing my chance to speak with Kaleb... one last time.

When his truck pulls up, I run to the door and stand there sobbing uncontrollably. Kaleb steps from his vehicle and adjusts his battered cowboy hat. He rushes over, envelopes me in his arms, and restores my sanity with hugs and kisses—sympathetic as ever.

Kaleb removes the memory stick from his pocket and places it in my palm. It weighs heavy in my hand, and more so in my head and heart. I'm certain there will be images I'd rather not see, and my imagination has already manufactured vivid recreations of the most terrible media stories.

In preparation for disturbing revelations, I ask Kaleb, "Did you notice anything?"

"I skimmed through for quality control... looks like old home movies. Nothing scary."

I sit at Pops' desk and Kaleb squats on the footstool beside me. "What's with the feather display? You dabbling in love magic again, putting some witchy hex on me?"

Mildly embarrassed, I say, "They were lying around my bedroom. Morbid reminders of Butch's past kills."

Kaleb reaches over, extracts the black iridescent feather from my collection and slots it into his hatband. He smirks. "The perfect adornment for a *raven* lunatic like me."

Done with the brief feathery distraction, I fumble with the memory stick and mouse, and my shaky hand sends the cursor flying off the screen. The files are ordered chronologically, and I want to open the last one first, but instead, start at the beginning. We find ourselves in San Diego—Mom's on the front porch of the house in Coronado Trail, and although the house is newer and neater than when we visited, it is essentially the same. The house was never destroyed by fire—the first lie is revealed. Mom shows off her precious pink bundle of joy—who *isn't* me—and beams with delight.

Our next encounter takes place in the backyard. Mom saunters poolside holding a slightly larger baby, and raises the child's small hand to wave at the camera. Pops' toes momentarily appear in the frame—he must be reclining on a lounger.

A year later, the bandy-legged baby, clad in pink frills, takes a few faltering steps. Mom bends forward and holds the infant's chubby arms aloft. The gleeful blonde-haired toddler staggers towards the camera, displaying scrunched up eyes, chubby cheeks, and a baby-tooth smile. I avidly search the child's face for my own facial features.

The next file shows a pretty young girl riding a tricycle along a garden path. She is delighted with her achievement and squeals, "Look at me, look at me." *It's not me.* I would never call out and invite attention—it's not who I am, it's not part of my psyche. The young child *is not* me, her hair is bright blonde, and she has Michelle's delicate bone structure.

"It's not you," Kaleb declares.

"What makes you say that?"

He flicks my earlobe with his finger. "Earlobes. Your earlobes hang free, hers are tapered and stuck to her head—like her parents'. Recessive gene."

I swallow and open the last file, the one from the filing cabinet—August 1986.

A soundtrack of bird chatter and the slow creep of someone wading through undergrowth accompanies a surreal landscape of brilliant red rocks surrounded by pine trees. Shafts of sunlight bore through the firs, the contrast enhanced by aquamarine skies. The photographer steps out onto a ledge, pans around the sculpted mountains, and zooms in on a small and unusual wedge-shaped church, perched upon a rocky outcrop. The next clip finds our videographer at the chapel, surveying the magnificent panorama from another perspective.

"I know this place," Kaleb announces. "I've always wanted to go there. It's between Phoenix and Flagstaff. Our tour bus drove past the turnoff earlier this year, but I didn't get chance to visit. What's it called?" Kaleb clicks his fingers. "*Seconda, Segona...* something like that." His fingers snap like synapses. "The Pixies did a song about it? You know the one that goes, 'Havalina...'" He hums the tune, but I'm none the wiser. "You don't know it, do you?" He taps his finger on the desk. "Sedona!"

The next shot follows a bird of prey gliding high on thermals above a densely forested canyon. Distance makes it unclear whether it's a vulture, an eagle, or a hawk. The bird descends and disappears against the backdrop as its plumage blends with the rock face. The zoom is deployed and a shaky image emerges until the bird is recaptured, soaring high above the treetops. The photographer, who I assume is Pops, zooms back out and scans the fiery horizon. "Sunrise or sunset?" I ask.

"Sunset."

More sweeping views of an emerald canyon follow, and tilting the lens downwards gives the audience a sense of depth—not for those with vertigo.

A change of scene sends us wandering amongst trees. Mom comes into view, sitting at a picnic table in front of the camper van. She flaps her hand to shoo Pops away. On the table, a blue cool box and two cups indicate they're about to eat, or have just eaten.

Mom stretches her arm, waves her finger, and points to something out of frame. To maintain a steady shot and preserve continuity, Pops turns slowly towards the direction she's indicating. Something stirs by the trash can—a shadow, a movement, possibly a critter raiding the rubbish for a meal. I anticipate a squirrel or raccoon. The shaky zoom hones in and reveals a small furtive creature—a child—checking its surroundings before pushing up onto the top of the bin and reaching inside. The camera jerks. From the left, Mom saunters into frame.

"Hello sweetheart, don't be scared. Where's your mommy?"

Frozen in fear at being caught by a grown-up, the stricken child stares at Mom with big, round, panicked eyes. The youngster slips from the top of the bin and walks backwards with small, almost imperceptible steps until a wall halts the retreat. Mom crouches and extends a slender arm. Fingers displaying pink manicured nails clamp around the petrified child's arm.

"It's okay, sweetheart. What's your name? Are you hungry? Would you like a cookie?"

The child remains unblinking and still as a statue. Suddenly, the sound of approaching footsteps on a gravelly path present a new threat, and the child's small head turns sharply. Startled round eyes peer directly into the lens. The child's mouth falls open—the look of a terrified animal ensnared in a trap. The youngster wears blue jeans, red Converse shoes, and a dark-red hoodie with a bear's head emblazoned on the front. The girl is grubby and disheveled.

She is me.

I gasp in shock and stop breathing. Kaleb rubs my back and clicks the mouse to pause the action. He squeezes my shoulder. "Breathe in… breathe out."

I follow the rhythm of his words, until my respiration moderates. Kaleb asks, "Okay to go on?"

I nod.

"Hello, sweetie, what's your name?" Pops' voice confirms he's the person behind the lens. He lowers the camera, mistakenly thinking he's turned it off. The world turns upside down, the sky is where the earth should be, and the earth is where the sky should be. We trudge along a gravel path. The camera bounces against Pops' back and records blurred images of trees hanging from the sky, and birds flying through a clear blue lake.

We're watching the actual moment when the intervention occurred, when my life was interrupted, and my world shifted on its axis. Grabbed by the shoulders, I was turned around and forced to proceed in the wrong direction. From that point forward I was lost.

A vehicle passes in the distance. The questions continue.

"Do you live here?"

"How did you get here?"

"Where do you sleep at night?"

"Are you alone?"

"How old are you?"

"Where's your mommy?"

"Where's your daddy?"

"Are you hungry?"

The gravel noises cease, we are walking on grass. The camera swings and pans from side to side. The trash can is upside down now, but nothing falls out. We stop, and sit at the picnic table. The scene is still, the horizon is a forty-five degree slope. Trees and scrub appear to grow from the ground at an impossible angle.

"Do you want a drink, sweetheart? We've got fizzy orange, lemonade, or cola."

There's a brief pause. The distinct sound of a metal tab being pulled breaks the silence—a small explosion, the release of gas, followed by the slow tear of aluminum peeling away from the body of the can before the final violent rip.

Mom pours the dark fizzy liquid into my pink Disney princess cup. She rustles a plastic wrapper. "Have a cookie, sweetheart. They're chocolate chip... your favorites." I reach out and take what's on offer. "Ooh, is that a cut on your hand? Show me your hand, sweetie. Does it hurt? What a nasty scrape. Ray, honey, fetch me the pink washcloth from the bathroom, please, and a bottle of water from the fridge."

Another lie, exposed. The mark on my hand has nothing to do with strawberries.

Pops rises from the bench, the camera jerks into action and images bob around. His footfalls count the steps—one, two three—as he enters the camper, and the video simultaneously records the visual interior of the van and the audible exterior.

Inside the sound of heavy breathing. Outside it's just heavy.

Inside the picture fades to grey, followed by a fast sweeping shot of the interior as Pops lifts the strap over his head, and places the camera on the draining board next to the sink. His breathing is labored. His inaudible mutterings make no sense. A gloomy mid-height view of the camper fills the screen. Pops opens the white Formica bathroom door and a pink washcloth appears. He opens the fridge door, and a shock of dark hair flops forward as he reaches inside for a bottle of water.

Meanwhile, the conversation continues outside. "You're a pretty little girl. Do you have a pretty name?" A brief pause. "Everyone needs a name and, seeing as you don't have one, I'm going to call you Raychelle. A pretty name for a pretty little girl. Do you want to know what my name is? My name is Mommy and the nice man is Pops."

More heavy breathing, followed by footsteps... one, two, three, and Pops is back outside.

"Thank you, dear," says Michelle. "Hold out your hand, sweetie. Let Mommy wash that nasty cut. There's a good girl."

A loud humming noise, the film spooling, a click... the end of the tape.

After a long pause, Kaleb asks, "Do you remember?"

Slowly, I shake my head. "No."

My mind and body are numb with disbelief.

So, this is how it happened. This is how Ray and Michelle acquired their replacement daughter. I wasn't bought or sold, nor was I handed over by a desperate parent. I was looking for food in a garbage can, dirty and alone, unable to speak. I wasn't kidnapped, there was no kicking and screaming. I was seduced by soda and a cookie.

I could've been abandoned. I could've been lost. I could've run away.

I could've run away again, but I stayed. I stayed with Ray and Michelle. There was no resistance. I surrendered. Did I realize at the time they were my best option?

The footage still doesn't answer the question of who I was, or who I am, or where I came from, or where the acquisition happened.

Every muscle in my body tenses, determined to resist the urge to shake. My ankles are crossed, my arms are rigid, and I clench my fists between my knees. Unrelenting tears land on my T-shirt and create dark expanding patches of moisture on each breast. Kaleb grabs the armrest and swivels the chair to face him. He pries me apart and draws me to him. I tumble forward onto my knees and land between his legs. I burrow my head into his belly, heedless of his recent injury. He massages my back, but his healing hands cannot erase this nightmare. He presses against my shoulders, forces me into an upright position, and cups my ugly face in his hands. His thumbs smooth away my tears and he kisses my forehead.

"So, you're a Black Bears fan."

Once the initial shock subsides, I insist on watching the footage again... and again. I can't cry anymore. My nose and eyes are raw—my sinuses bunged up. My tongue explores the scratchy skin above my lip, made dry from paper tissues—despite the manufacturer's aloe-infused claims.

I was never a crybaby, in fact, Mom accused me of being hard-faced with a cold heart, but everything's changed now. I'm a fragile emotional mess. Luckily, I have Kaleb to cling to, otherwise I'd drown.

We check maps of Arizona and images of Sedona. We identify the Church of the Holy Cross and deduce I was probably acquired somewhere in the vicinity of Sedona in August 1986.

It's late, but I make a fire in the fire pit outside. I toss the tapes into the flames, and listen to the hiss and sizzle as I watch the evidence disappear in a cloud of acrid black smoke. The memory stick will not leave my possession until I discover who I am—then I will destroy that, too.

She Is Me

24. China Sea

Questions roil, resentment simmers and, together, they generate an unpleasant heat within. Those I wish to confront are dead. Ray and Michelle have selfishly taken the answers to their graves. My temper flares at this blatant injustice. Anger sets my skin aglow with incandescent rage and I snort like a cartoon bull.

Michelle is at the center of all this. If only she weren't dead—I'd kill her.

Kaleb wanders into the kitchen, coffee mug in hand, seeking another top-up. "Everything going okay, my love?"

"Yes," I bark, although clearly it isn't.

Kaleb's wise not to take the bait. He fuels up and heads back to the garage.

I mindlessly remove pots from the kitchen cupboards, wrap them in newspaper and shove them in boxes. My mind is elsewhere, wrangling with irreconcilable questions. As I wrap the Royal Albert cake platter in newspaper, I read the headline—*"Local Woman, Intoxicated, and Unbelted..."*—and can't help, but snigger. Michelle ends up wrapped around her fucking precious Royal Albert. How fucking poetic.

God, I've never felt so angry. I have no one to vent my anger on either. My abductors are both dead.

The blame rests firmly with Michelle. She's the one who stole me and, without a second thought, stuck me with Raychelle's name. She sent Ray inside the camper in search of a washcloth and water, while she stayed outside and unilaterally decided I was hers for the taking. Ray had no say in the matter, he was busy following her instructions, per usual. By the time he reappeared, she'd already instructed me to call him Pops.

What the hell were they thinking? How could I possibly replace Raychelle? And, what a disappointing substitute I turned out to be, unable to act the part and fit the role she had in mind. *Who am I?* The question bangs continuously inside my head. Who was I meant to be? What was my destiny before it was so rudely interrupted?

My anger ratchets up as I count the ways she tried to control me—how she restricted my life and denied me opportunities I'll never get the chance to revisit.

Hatred flares as I recall how she almost cajoled me into marrying Rick, and made clear her expectation of grandchildren on a biannual basis. Naively, I assumed she was projecting her own regrets onto me, and her enthusiasm for the wedding and babies was driven by misguided love.

"You must have your children early, so you'll have a lifetime to love them." In her eyes, I expect she considered the marriage a convenient solution and ideal opportunity to off-load her big mistake.

Now, I see her true colors, I'm incensed by her selfish and manipulative behavior. Resentment and bitter thoughts consume me. Gnawing hatred struggles like a caged monster fighting to escape. Try as I might to shunt these grotesque feelings aside, they're stubborn and resistant, and stand their ground. How much longer can I hide my ugly, unattractive thoughts from Kaleb?

I work methodically along the row of kitchen cupboards until I'm as glazed as the china I'm wrapping. I reach for the sacred Royal Albert tea-set with its garish crimson and yellow roses. A fleck of lipstick on a cup sparks the memory of a hot Saturday afternoon last year, when Mom invited Rick's parents over to discuss my behavior and cast judgment on my future, like I was a commodity up for barter. I remember later the same afternoon, she slapped me as I scrubbed lipstick from the cups. Oh yes, she also said, "Whatever you were up to, it will come back to haunt you, you mark my words." The irony and hypocrisy of it all.

And, she had the gall to die before I had a chance to confront her with the truth. I'm so bloody angry.

The almighty rage within erupts. The newssheet in my hand becomes a red rag, an invitation to charge. How dare they force me into a life that isn't mine?

Royal *fucking* Albert.

I flick the stupid cup into the air. The sound of breaking china is delightful.

"Totally smashing," I say with a fake English accent.

I add up all the precious hours I've wasted, washing her fucking pretentious Royal Albert tea cups, trying my utmost not to scratch the precious 22-karat gold trim. Normal people have six cups, but my mother has a dozen. *Had* a dozen—they're rapidly disappearing. I reach for the teapot, hold it high above my head and make my offering to the gods.

"Have this!"

Arms outstretched for maximum reach, I let the pot slip from my grasp. A shattering of deep satisfaction sends bone china missiles across the tiles. The sugar bowl and creamer meet the same fate. Side plates and dinner plates follow suit. My sobbing rage intensifies with each explosion.

Kaleb rushes in from the garage to investigate the noise, and finds me distraught and drowning in a sea of broken china.

"What the *fuck*..."

He crunches his way through the hailstorm of fragments littering the floor and holds me so tight I can barely breathe. I squirm and wrestle in his arms and beat him away, but he tightens his suffocating embrace. He grabs my wrists, backs me into the battered old armchair that's become Butch's bed, and pins me there. He crouches between my legs.

"Look at me," he demands.

Butch appears through the cat flap, wide-eyed, and curious. He's come to check out the commotion.

Meow.

"Yes, *fucking* me-e-e-*ow*," Kaleb replies. He diverts his attention to Butch, whisks him off his feet to take him outside. "Your mom's not too happy right now. Why don't you be a good kitty and go get her a nice little birdie to cheer her up."

My tantrum diminishes into sporadic chest convulsions, and Kaleb sets about clearing away my mess.

"Dustpan?" he asks. "Don't tell me... under the sink."

He checks the cupboard where the tea-set lived. "What about the saucers, do you want to do those now before I start sweeping?" He makes light of my little tantrum and attempts to coax a smile.

"No," I say, pouting like a petulant child.

"Okay, I will. It's pretty fucking hideous. I see why it offends you."

I watch through swollen eyes as Kaleb crawls around the kitchen floor on hands and knees. He uses a dustpan imprinted with roses, and a brush with three realistic rubber roses on the handle that quiver every time he sweeps. He drags the pink plastic bucket alongside and fills it with shards of 22-karat gold bone china roses. He looks ridiculous. I laugh. He peers at me through a forest of chair and table legs. I become hysterical.

"Hey, what's so funny, crazy lady?"

"You, with that brush."

"Oh yeah? I've gone from rock star to fucking crock star. I hope you realize how lucky you are, some people would pay good money for this. Kinky services don't come cheap."

"What else do you do?"

"When I'm done with this, I'll put the rubber gloves on and show you. Then, we'll see who's laughing."

The cat flap swings open and Butch comes trotting over with a hummingbird.

Kaleb looks up. "Hey, it's Outlaw Butch. He's been out and killed a man—shows how much he loves you."

Once the debris is cleared away, Kaleb lowers his chin and raises his eyes at me. "Would you like a cup of tea?"

"No, I fucking wouldn't."

"Hey! No bad language." He yanks me up by the hand, sits in my place, and pulls me onto his lap. "What brought this on?"

I confess the reasons for my mounting rage.

"Let's go through this. The footage proves your abduction was a spontaneous act. No premeditation, no malice. Michelle made an impulsive, snap decision to keep you. Her innocent act of kindness instantly became a crime, and maybe Ray kept quiet out of deep concern for his wife's sanity. Ray left you the tape. He wanted you to know the truth. Why else would he hang onto such damning evidence? Why not destroy it? Why keep it?"

"Why keep me?"

"The deal was sealed within hours. They couldn't just hand you back, they didn't know where you came from and, if they did, there would be questions. You represented the solution to a deep and painful hole in their lives."

"It's mad."

"Imagine their grief. Escaping unbearable pain sometimes leads us into an alternative reality. Maybe Michelle was so deluded by grief she convinced herself you were the real Raychelle. They weren't bad people."

"They stole me. They stole my destiny."

Kaleb holds my chin in his hand and forces eye contact. "Right here, right now is where you're meant to be." He tightens his embrace and cocoons me with his body. Resentment ebbs. Without Michelle's selfish intervention, *this* would never have happened.

"Look at me," Kaleb says.

I find I can. I'm transfixed, overwhelmed with love. The crescent moon crease appears on his cheek, a sure sign of mischief.

"We're going to exorcise your demons. You can hate your mother if you want, but tea and roses? What have they ever done to you? I'm going to ask you again, would you like some tea?"

"Yes, please."

"Okay, go to my couch and wait."

Ten minutes later, Kaleb enters Pops' study carrying a tray, bearing a plain white teapot, cups, saucers, milk, and sugar... and rubber gloves. It's not the only thing he's baring—he's naked apart from a rose tucked behind his ear.

I laugh. Who wouldn't?

"Why are you laughing?" he asks. "It's time for another positive reinforcement session. You responded well last time, and quickly overcame your aversion to champagne. You *will* love tea and roses.

"Arms up," he orders. He steps forward and removes my T-shirt. "Bra off." I reach behind and undo the clasp.

He pours the tea, adds milk and hands me the cup.

"Don't spill any," he warns, "or there'll be consequences."

I grasp the saucer.

"Drink your tea," he instructs. He kneels before me and unzips my shorts. "Raise your hips and mind your tea."

Saucer in one hand, cup in the other, I press my shoulders into the sofa and lift my butt.

He slides my shorts to my knees. "Sit," he instructs. He removes my cut-offs. "Let me top you up," he says.

One false move and my belly will receive scalding liquid. He puts the teapot down. "Drink your tea," he orders. He removes the rose from his ear and lays it across my stomach. He parts my knees and lowers his head, inducing palpitations even before his tongue comes near me. Within seconds, I slop tea into the saucer and seriously worry about spilling it on his head.

He looks up briefly. "Pay no attention to me, young lady, just drink your tea."

When we're both finished he asks, "More tea, madam? There's plenty in the pot."

"Yes please, waiter. I'd *love* another cup."

After taking only a few sips, I find I'm moaning and gasping, and Kaleb's encouraging me. "Let it out."

"No more, please," I cry. "I can't take it." Big Ben chimes in the hallway.

Kaleb surfaces. "Fuck. Who's that? This is a private tea party."

"Leave it."

But, someone's insistent finger is stuck in place and the doorbell chimes like Big Ben heralding a royal birth announcement.

Kaleb rummages in his pile of clothes by the sofa and steps into his shorts. "I'll send them away." He pulls his *Straight Outta Compton*, N.W.A., F.T.P. T-shirt over his head.

I lie back all sweaty and floppy, and my skin sticks to the leather. My eyes remain closed, but my ears scan the airwaves.

"Now's not a good time," Kaleb says.

Footsteps in the hallway induce blind panic. I grab the wooly tartan throw and cover myself. Kaleb sticks his head around the door to check I'm decent. "We have visitors."

Already flushed, I sweat profusely under the one-hundred-percent pure wool blanket. Two men follow Kaleb into the room and my face turns beet red.

"Are you okay, miss?" asks the scary man with evil prying eyes.

"She's not well," Kaleb explains. "As you can see she's running a temperature."

The gnarly looking man turns to me and asks in an authoritative tone, "Do you need assistance, miss? We heard someone in distress."

"It's the fever," Kaleb says.

I'm utterly mortified. I have no clue who these men are, and no idea why Kaleb's let them in. "I'm fine. I have a virus."

"As long as you're okay, but we're here concerning another matter. I'm Detective Mendez, and this is my colleague Detective Reed, from the Serious Crimes Unit. We're here regarding a vehicle registered to this property."

My heart races and my eyes focus on my shorts in the middle of the rug, as do Detective Reed's. Detective Mendez's x-ray eyes run up and down the blanket, but never reach my face. I swallow involuntarily, and believe I'm going to be physically sick. Since I'm naked, though, I can't get up to leave the room. I massage my throat.

Kaleb reads the signs. "Excuse me," he says to Detective Mendez, and places the trash can by my legs.

"You haven't taken anything have you, miss?" asks officer Evil Eyes. "Prescription or otherwise?"

"Dodgy street taco," Kaleb explains. All three men nod, knowingly.

My body convulses. The guys look at me. I raise my hand and cover my mouth. The blanket slips from my shoulder. Detective Mendez's gaze lands on my chest, eagerly willing the blanket to fall.

I'm not going to puke. I'm not going to puke.

"We can talk about this when you're feeling better, Miss Carter," says Detective Letch.

Kaleb grips the door, a subtle signal for them to take their leave. They do, thank god, but why are they here?

Footsteps and muttering in the hallway. After a couple of hour-long minutes, a disembodied voice calls out, "Hope you feel better, soon, miss."

Their car pulls away. Feeling genuinely ill, I fling the blanket off and glug some tea.

Kaleb bursts into the room, howling with laughter.

"Fucking classic," he says. "Another good reason to reopen The Last Chance Saloon website—the barflies will love this one."

"I'm glad you're amused, but what the hell is going on?"

"Nothing much."

"*Nothing much?* Serious Crimes Unit... Nothing?"

"It's sorted. You look like you need a shower and a big glass of cold water."

"Tell me."

"Larry from Pasadena was caught smuggling shit-loads of drugs across the border... in your dad's camper van."

"Oh my god!"

"I told them it was stolen from the driveway, and you're so sick you haven't had a chance to report the crime."

"But, he paid for it... with cash."

"Whatever. We'll get the van back when they've collected all their evidence and I'll relist it."

"But, it's *his* van."

"Not anymore. He doesn't deserve it. I spent fucking hours, not to mention all the blood sweat and tears, restoring that heap of shit back to its former glory."

25. So Long, Raychelle

Tuesday morning, ten o'clock, and the phone rings. I'm expecting Barbara to call me with an update, and this is her favored time. I leave my coffee on the kitchen table, and walk down the hall to the phone. I lift the receiver.

"Fantastic news," Barbara announces.

Kaleb creeps up behind me, enfolds me in his arms, and tucks his head against mine to earwig the conversation.

"Arnold and Hugo have offered two hundred thousand over the asking price."

I'm speechless. Kaleb whispers in my ear and I repeat his words. "I accept."

"The boys," as she calls them, "want a quick close. Is three weeks okay with you?"

With my office background, I respond well to deadlines, and a fixed date provides the perfect incentive to finish clearing this house. We don't need three weeks, though, we'll be gone by the end of the week.

"Yes."

Kaleb removes the phone from my hand, brushes my hair aside and kisses my neck. "This is cause for celebration. Come with me, little girl. I have candy."

Still holding me from behind, he clamps his hands on my hips and hustles me into Pops' study. He falls back onto the sofa, drags me with him, and I straddle his hips. With one swift yank, he wrenches open the poppers on my shirt. Reaching behind my back, he slips his fingers beneath the strap and deftly unhitches my bra.

♈

Knowing the house has sold removes a great weight from my shoulders and I pray nothing goes wrong during the escrow process.

I dare to look ahead, and realize I have no idea what tomorrow will bring. My foresight is severely restricted and only allows me to second guess what might happen in the next hour.

I do know we're both anxious to leave this place, though. We have wheels in our eyes, and a carefree gypsy lifestyle beckons. I romanticize about following the sun, traveling on a whim, and going wherever the road takes us. Although I have an inkling the trail, at some point, will lead to Weeping Creek. Kaleb's obsession with the place hasn't gone unnoticed.

There's no reason to stay in Santa Monica, so arguments for leaving are compelling and mounting.

"No disaster is too big or complicated to run away from," Kaleb reminds me.

I can't fault his logic.

"We're outlaws now," he proclaims, "officially on the run. No one's chasing us, yet, but give it time."

These past six months, so much has changed. It's hard to believe our chance encounter in Vegas was so recent, it feels like a lifetime ago, as though I've known Kaleb for years—I use the term loosely, because I don't know him at all. Come to think of it, I don't know myself, either.

The girl who responded to Kaleb's ad in a Lonely Hearts column is so different from the one he's with now. Our lives have been transformed, all because a Haunted Man reached out to a Lost Soul.

When I stumbled into The Last Chance Saloon under the guise of Lost Soul, I never imagined I'd find love. I shared my worries with Absinthe the bartender, and took guidance from Luna the astrologer. I became captivated with the Haunted Man, and he with me. He emerged from cyberspace and entered the physical world, determined to track me down. His invitation to share a lifetime of torment and misery resonated deep inside, and I responded with little hesitation. Kaleb's still haunted and I'm still lost, that's just how it is.

I take Kaleb's hand. We exchange a complicit look—our eyes speak volumes. We're in this together, up to our necks, and in for the long haul.

♒ ♈ ♋

The house is empty. All evidence of the family who once lived here has been meticulously dismantled, dispersed, or destroyed. No trace.

We've shipped the carved oak bookcase and Chesterfield sofa up to Seattle, along with tools and books—all consigned to storage for now, with an optional pick-up date. Sometime in the future, we'll haul them back to Kaleb's cabin.

He's loading the last few items into his truck and it's time for final farewells. After we say goodbye to Mrs. Tracey, we plan to bid so long to Raychelle, too—by dropping her off at Pirate's Cove, north of Pismo Beach, to reunite her with her parents. Having scattered Pops' ashes and disposed of Mom there, too, it's where she belongs. I never understood Pops' connection to the area, and if Mom knew the reason she never let on. Raychelle waits patiently in the truck, in her box behind my seat, along with a bunch of hand-picked flowers from the garden.

I lift the phone's receiver and punch one-one-three followed by my number to cancel the landline service. The answer machine is flashing. I listen to the message but it's too late to return their call.

"Raych, where the bloody hell are you? You're never home. I know you're not at work—I called your office and they said you no longer worked there. What is going on, girlfriend? I bet you're in bed shagging that stranger you brought to the wedding? He looks fucking hot. Who the hell is he? How come I never met him? Fabian and Trevor love him. They said he's a classic car dealer or something, right? It's an improvement on weird lumberjacks." Sofie laughs. "And don't forget to tell me where you're moving to. I don't want to come home and find you've disappeared." Sofie laughs again. I weep. "Speak soon, sweetie. Love you."

Eyes shut tight to prevent the tears, the muscles in my neck strain, and my lips quiver.

"Goodbye, Sofie. I love you. Thank you for everything. I miss you more than you'll ever know, and I always will." I unclench my hands and press replay. This will be the last time I hear Sofie's voice. This is how it must be.

No trace.

Pressing the delete button releases my tears and I wail like a pitiful child.

In the pink powder room, I splash my face with water, take some deep breaths and stick my chin up.

Walking back into the hall, I spy Kaleb through the open front door. He's loading his truck. He catches my eye and winks, instantly restoring my strength and readies me for the next emotional challenge.

My heart-wrenching goodbye to Mrs. Tracey cannot be postponed any longer. I'll miss her terribly, she's been so supportive this past year, and I struggle to push aside the morbid thought I might never see her again.

"You go ahead," Kaleb says. "I'll follow when I've finished securing the load."

Overhead, the ravens flit between the branches. They've been quorking all morning, laughing long and hard with each other over some private joke. Butch, equally irritated by these gloating birds, wriggles into his kill position, and whines and growls. A bird swoops down to taunt him. Incensed, he pounces, but the cackling tormentor flies away and perches in the oak tree in Mrs. Tracey's garden.

Undeterred, Butch races across the lawn, sinks his claws into the bark, and grapples up the trunk. He melds to the tree, wedged in the crook of two large limbs. He extends a paw and reaches inside the hollow doughnut scar of a missing branch. The raven's fury scares me. Maybe the bird is protecting her chicks. Another bird appears and I fear for Butch's safety.

"Kaleb, do something, please?"

Kaleb lets go of the rope he's tightening. He reaches inside his pocket and removes the raven's flint stone. He hurls with accuracy and hits the tree. Butch and the bird are momentarily startled, but neither are willing to back down. Kaleb jogs over to the scene and retrieves his stone. He jumps, seizes a branch, and hauls himself up with the strength of a gymnast. The bird flaps away. Butch releases a guttural growl, annoyed that his moment of victory has been denied.

"Come here, bad kitty," Kaleb says. Butch lashes out. Kaleb grabs him by the scruff of his neck—not a wise move. Butch jerks free, scampers off along a branch, out of reach. Defeated, Kaleb throws his hands up and shakes his head.

"What's in the hole?" I ask. "Are there any baby birds?"

Kaleb cautiously looks into the dark recess and reaches inside. A violent shiver runs through my body, accompanied by an image of my long-lost teddy bear.

Kaleb flicks beer-bottle tops at me. "This bird has a drink problem."

Curiosity causes Butch to saunter back up the branch. He peers inside the hollow scar as Kaleb gropes around. He pulls his furry head back and looks with wide-eyed interest as Kaleb opens his hand. Together they examine the treasure displayed in his palm.

"I don't fucking believe it!" Kaleb yells.

Pinched between finger and thumb he dangles his missing necklace aloft. I jog over to the tree, excited to see the evidence up close.

Kaleb clamps his hand around Fang's precious tooth and brings his fist to rest against his heart. His eyes glisten. He jumps down from the branch, unfurls his fingers and offers me the talisman.

I shake my head. "No... thank you, but no. You must wear the tooth, it belongs with you."

He stares long and hard at the fang. He lifts his head and fastens the clasp around his neck. My scalp prickles, my body tingles with hope. The return of the missing necklace, even by bizarre chance, is indeed a good omen. Butch brushes up against my legs... for one last time. My throat tightens.

Everything I do today is preceded by the thought, *this will be the last time I...* and immediately followed by the threat of tears. I walk down Mrs. Tracey's driveway, her front door is already open.

"Only me," I announce, as I walk through the door for one last time.

Mrs. Tracey greets me with a smile. "Are you all packed, my dear?"

Eyes brimming with tears, too choked to speak, I nod. I fall into Mrs. Tracey open arms. She lets me cry on her shoulder and strokes my hair with her gnarly hand.

"You've started me off now, my dear." She pulls away and wipes her eyes. "We're a right pair aren't we?"

"I'm sorry."

She kisses my head. "While I can, my dear, I want to say what a great comfort it's been seeing you grow into such a beautiful young woman. I spend many hours wondering how my Jessica might've turned out, and I like to imagine she would've been just like you."

"You're so kind, Mrs. Tracey, your words mean the world to me."

"I'll make us a nice pot of tea, my dear, and I've baked a date and walnut cake."

I sit in my usual place on her sofa and gaze around at the familiar objects. My eyes fix on the photo of Mrs. Tracey's daughter, Jessica, with her poodle. Life is so unfair, and death even more so.

Mrs. Tracey wheels her tea trolley in—for one last time. I know it is the final time, because I can't and won't return to Oak Tree Place. In silence, we exchange sad resigned smiles, drink our tea, and swallow our tears. The delicious cake sticks in my constricted throat.

Mrs. Tracey reaches into her handbag and hands me a small black leather jewelry box. "This is for you, my dear. I would've passed it to Jessica, but I want you to have it, now."

Nestled inside is a beautiful ring, a twisted Celtic rope of tiny diamonds set between two bands of small green stones.

"Emeralds symbolize love, rebirth, and the start of new life," she explains.

A shadow crosses my grave—Raychelle, I presume, or maybe, Jessica.

My hands shake as I remove the ring from its velvet pillow and slide it onto my finger. I kneel and hug her.

"Kaleb loves you very much and he'll keep you safe. He's as cool as a cucumber that one, but hot as hell on the inside. Heed my advice, my dear, remember not to ask questions if you already know the answer, some things are best left unsaid."

As I pull away, Kaleb appears in the doorway holding Butch.

Twice Dead

"Speak of the devil," Mrs. Tracey says, "and he's sure to appear." They lock eyes and Kaleb delivers a menacing smirk. "I've got your number, Mr. Hausser."

"You surely have, Doreen. I don't doubt that for a moment. You're a very shrewd lady."

I rise from my knees. Mrs. Tracey puts her hand on the small of my back and nudges me towards Kaleb. "I love this girl like my own daughter. She's precious and I wouldn't let her go off with just anyone. You look after her, Kaleb Hausser, or you'll have me to answer to."

His arm extends to receive me. He draws me to his side and clamps me in place. "I will, Doreen, I *promise*." He laughs. "And, don't let this moggy get the better of you."

Kaleb leans forward and pours Butch onto the carpet—the hostage exchange now complete.

"You remind me of my Frankie," says Mrs. Tracey. "He'd do anything for me. I was just saying to Raychelle, on the news this morning, they showed her old boss coming out of hospital in a wheelchair. He's a nasty piece of work that one. If anyone deserved to be in a car wreck, it was him. He got what was coming to him."

"Indeed," says Kaleb. "Karma kicked his ass."

"I didn't know your middle name was karma."

Kaleb smirks, but admits nothing. What passes between them is more like a reckoning than their usual flirtatious banter. I fade into the background, a superfluous guest intruding on a private conversation. I'm well practiced at presenting a deaf ear, I spent years listening to Mom and Pops exchanging cryptic comments in their own private code.

"Talking of rodents," Kaleb say, "I almost forgot the love rat." He yanks his T-shirt up and Mr. Ratty falls to the ground.

಄ ♈ ಆ

Mrs. Tracey waves goodbye from the bottom of her driveway. I wave back with one hand and wipe tears away with the other, until I'm no longer able to see her. I twist around in my seat, face forward, and catch her diminishing image in the wing mirror. As we round the corner she disappears completely, along with Oak Tree Place.

Kaleb, in his eagerness to leave, hits the gas, and slaps the steering wheel. "We're outta here. Let's head for the open road."

Can leaving the past behind us be this easy? Only time will tell.

Tears spill down my cheeks.

Kaleb gives me a sideways glance and laughs. "Sorry, Raych, but I'm so fucking happy."

He reaches for my hand, kisses my fingers, and brings them to rest on his hairy thigh.

Within the confines of the truck, cut flowers provide a sweet and sickly reminder there's one lingering task we must attend to before we're completely free. We must dispose of the real Raychelle. She's destined to join her parents at Pirate's Cove. Having driven this route twice already this past year, I direct Kaleb. "Turn left at the lights."

"Yes, my love." He sniggers. "I don't normally follow orders, but I get a warm sensation in my groin when you boss me around."

I squeeze his thigh.

"Hey, careful. You'll get me pulled over for distracted driving."

We take the Pacific Coast Highway northbound and follow the coastline to Avila Hot Springs. From there, it's a short trek to the beach. The route is straightforward, and we make frequent stops along the way to admire the ocean views.

༄ ༡ ༃

Sunset fades to dusk and moonrise creates a shimmering path across the water, making this the perfect time of day to perform our solemn task. Our procession of two must look quite odd as we wade into the ocean. The wind whips my hair into a nest of wild writhing snakes and turns me into a modern-day Medusa. In my hands, I ceremoniously bear a small white box engraved with my initials. Directly behind me, Kaleb carries a bunch of flowers and, with a hand on my shoulder, he steers my body. Thigh-high warm water laps our legs. My sundress absorbs water like blotting paper and the fabric becomes heavy and clings to my body.

There's no need to venture any farther. I lift the lid of the keepsake box and respectfully pour the contents into the vast Pacific Ocean. Particles of Raychelle go airborne. Against the indigo backdrop, she sparkles like fairy dust in the moonlight. Fortunately, the breeze is offshore, and the rest of her floats and sinks. I submerge the casket and let the outgoing tide carry the container away.

Kaleb moves to my side and offers up the flowers. I select a sweet-smelling pink rose, toss the bloom into the air, and watch as the ocean swell gently rocks the flower like a baby in a cradle and steals it away. I imagine the trauma surrounding this poor innocent child's premature death. Her potential so brutally arrested, all her hopes and dreams destroyed. Ray and Michelle, left shattered and plagued with regret, and their daily lives a constant torment.

"I wonder what role Ray and Michelle played in Raychelle's accident?" I muse aloud. "Whether they were responsible in any way?"

"She was obviously left unsupervised for however long it takes to drown."

"Maybe they shared the burdens of guilt and sorrow in equal measure."

Kaleb's hand clamps my shoulder. "Who knows?" A moment later he dismissively adds, "Who cares? Time to move on."

Easy for him to say, but I'm the one walking around with a dead-girl's identity.

One-by-one we cast the flowers onto the water and watch them form a floral trail across the glistening swell. A pathway for Raychelle to follow.

"Goodbye, Raychelle, I wish you well." I fling the final flower. "Your mom and dad are waiting for you at the other end. Your family will finally be reunited now, and I hope you all find peace."

I step in front of Kaleb, drawn by an urge to follow the snaking flowery serpent. From behind, he grabs my wrist and pulls me back. He folds his arms across my chest, and rests his chin on my head.

"I love you most in all the world."

My wet hands latch onto his forearms. "I love you, more." I stroke his hairy arm, trail my fingertip along the track left by a grazing bullet, and imagine I'm impregnating the scar with my healing love.

Entranced by the sparkling water, we sway with the rhythmic ebb and flow. Unfocused, I stare at the horizon and look back at my past, knowing there is something hiding in my subconscious that refuses to show itself. I try to imagine the future and draw a blank. I don't even know where I'll be sleeping tonight. I look down at the glistening water and feel the moon's reflection on my face. Here and now is where I am.

I lift my head. "This is a significant moment for me, too. This is where I forsake my old life, and my new life with you begins." Kaleb kisses my hair. "Whether I'll ever discover my true identity I don't know, and it doesn't really matter. I'm curious but, on balance, my life is working out just fine. I'm just grateful I've made it this far... not everyone does."

The waves lick our thighs and dampness creeps farther up my dress. A seagull dives into the water, plucks a white flower from the surface and flies away, probably confused.

"For years, I wanted to change, but never suspected I was, in fact, someone else. I'm a stranger to myself. I feel weird."

Kaleb's hands travel down my body and settle on my hips. "I like the feel of weird. Weird feels good."

"I'm being serious."

"I'm not." I turn in his arms and look at him with questioning eyes.

"Lighten up, Raych. View the situation as liberating. How many people get the opportunity to reinvent their self, to scrub out their mistakes and start afresh?"

"You're right. I'm no longer trapped inside my parents' expectations. I'm free of Mom's criticism, her opinion no longer matters. I'm slowly metamorphosing into the person I'm meant to be."

"Who I want you to be."

"Who's that?"

"You'll find out soon enough, my love," he says with a mischievous smirk.

I shake my head. "Kaleb Hausser... Michelle would wholeheartedly disapprove of you. She'd hate everything about you, which makes you even more attractive."

"And, knowing I'm *so* unsuitable incites me to corrupt you further." He leans in to kiss me, a bit too enthusiastically, and his bodyweight tips us over. We go down with a splash and tumble through the water, drowning in love. Seconds later we come up laughing and gasping.

"The sand shifted beneath my feet," Kaleb says. "I lost my balance."

I'm skeptical, but ultimately believe him.

Soaked, we locate the towels and climb into the truck. Kaleb spreads the map across the dashboard.

"Where next, my love?" Kaleb asks.

"I haven't a clue. Right now, I fancy a coffee."

So Long, Raychelle

26. Raychelle's Reflection

Sitting on the terrace of an oceanfront coffee bar, I knock back countless top-ups. Scalp tingling, nerve endings alive, and fired up on caffeine, I make a rash decision. "Can we go to Sedona?"

Kaleb's eyes shift from the distant horizon and he turns his head to look at me. He takes a mouthful of coffee and swallows. "If that is where you wish to go, my love, we will go there."

There's no need to vocalize my reasons. Earlier, I had no immediate desire to unravel the past. I'd convinced myself disposing of Raychelle's ashes would be the end of the story. I realize, though, saying goodbye to Raychelle was a line in the sand for her, but it's not the end of *my* story. Not knowing who I am leaves me adrift on a vast ocean, unsure if I'll ever find land. Kaleb reaches over and takes my hand. He anchors me in safe waters. He stops me drifting out to sea and prevents me from straying onto hazardous rocks. I smile, sad but amused by my topical analogy.

"Let's stay here tonight," Kaleb suggests. "We can make plans for tomorrow. I don't know about you, but this feels like a long day, already, and I'd love a beer, or three."

A few miles down the coast at Pismo Beach, we find a secluded oceanfront hotel with balcony rooms and the promise of spectacular sunsets, although we're a bit late for that.

Inside our room, the first thing we do is head for the shower. My hair's like straw, and sand from our ocean plunge sticks to every crease in my skin. Still wet, Kaleb grabs a beer from the fridge, takes a towel outside, and dries off naturally on an over-sized lounger.

Raychelle's Reflection

I dress, sit on the bed, and wrangle with my tangled hair. My eyes land on my driver's license I use for ID, and just flashed at the hotel receptionist.

Raychelle Sarah Carter.

For now, I'll use Raychelle's name because, until I know who I am, I can't decide who I want to be. Even if I discover my true self, will I want to reclaim the identity of someone lost to the world so long ago?

Kaleb advises, "See how you feel when the time comes."

I can guess though—the mere thought of some huge sentimental reunion with "the lost girl" documented by intrusive reporters leaves me squirming and recoiling inside.

I picture the inevitable media hysteria as every thread of my life unravels and is dangled in front of the baying public, only to provoke their unsolicited opinions. I foresee lengthy legal proceedings, dragging on for years.

Right now, Kaleb's love for isolation appeals. A world of two is what I crave, with Kaleb at the center, providing all the love, security and protection I could ever want. I trust him implicitly with my secret. He's the perfect gatekeeper, experienced at guarding his own dark secrets—a master of illusion, using smoke and mirrors to deflect and reflect the truth he wants the audience to see.

I'm no longer sure if I should refer to my parents as Mom and Pops, maybe Ray and Michelle is more appropriate. For all their faults they treated me kindly. Did they regret their rash decision? I scroll back through the years, and sift through a jumble of vague recollections. The problem being, when you go looking for trouble, you usually find it.

I once believed in Santa Claus, in faeries, that I was Raychelle Sarah Carter. If you want to believe in something enough, it's easy to twist the words to suit your theory. Songs and horoscopes for instance, you believe the oblique statements and obtuse sentiments are personal and meaningful, and aimed at you. You form false connections and interpret the words in ways to fit your circumstances. Even Luna, the astrologer from Kaleb's The Last Chance Saloon site, fooled me for a while, until Kaleb shone moonlight on her true identity.

My capacity for belief has gone. Believing is not enough. Believing is not reality. The more I believe, the less I know; the more

I know, the less I believe. I must focus on facts. All my points of reference have dissolved and what I thought was true is disappearing... fast. I'm transitioning into someone else and have no clue who will emerge from the chrysalis.

I cling to Kaleb mentally and physically. We share more than love, we share dark secrets. He loves my secret and calls me his phantom lover, but the situation leaves me on a knife edge. I want to revert back to being boring Raychelle—the girl who never questions, and who follows the advice of friends and family... most of the time.

I drag the brush through my hair until it feels smooth and I'm satisfied the conditioner has worked. A flash of memory conjures Sofie's face and her laughter as we styled each other's hair into crazy designs. She's in Italy now, oblivious to my predicament and always will be. I doubt I'll ever see her again, but I have no choice. It must be this way. Tears emerge, I hug my knees and rock myself, but find no comfort. Where's Kaleb?

Wandering out onto our private balcony, I find him sprawled across the lounger with his head in a book. Seeing Fang's tooth resting on his sternum is a comforting sight. He tosses the novel aside and invites me to crawl into his arms.

Unexpected trivial questions crowd my mind. Where was I born? When was I born? When is my real birthday? I've been using Raychelle's birthday for the past seventeen years. What are the chances I'm also Gemini? One in twelve. 8.33 percent, recurring.

"Tell me, Luna, am I a typical Gemini?"

Kaleb sweeps my hair from my face. "No way. Given all the tears, you must be a wishy-washy water sign."

I hope we're still compatible.

My fingers trace a scar on Kaleb's body. "Am I twenty-two years old?"

"Must be close, otherwise you would've stood out against the other kids in school."

I rest my palm on his belly and cover the knife scar. "I was small and slow at first, but soon caught up."

"How old when your periods started?"

I blush. He laughs.

"Fourteen."

Kaleb retrieves his book and continues reading.

Raychelle's Reflection

My mind assimilates these new factors.

After viewing the home movies and discovering Raychelle's ashes, any notion I might be her has evaporated. Hard facts tell me I arrived soon after Raychelle died and became their substitute daughter. The brief conversation Kaleb had with Ralph and Betty, Ray and Michelle's old neighbors, corroborated Raychelle's drowning and also my family's disappearance. Unable to return home with a strange child, they chose to settle in Santa Monica and commence their new life.

They acquired me during the summer of '86—from where? The possibilities seem endless, but they're not. The video tape of me rummaging in the trash is compelling evidence. There's no explicit reference to time and location, but it *is* a record of when and where. And, if the short film is to be believed, my absorption into their lives appears to have been a spontaneous event rather than a premeditated act. Still, the circumstances surrounding this random event seem too bizarre to fathom. However, the crystal-clear images record the pivotal moment my life changed, forever—when my true identity was ignored and Raychelle's name was foisted upon me. It happened to *me*, and I cannot remember a single thing about it.

Raucous gulls replace the mocking ravens of Oak Tree Place. They screech and dive, fly close, and look to steal any tidbits of food left out by foolish visitors.

Now and again, I interrupt Kaleb with random questions. "Why can't I remember what happened?"

"Maybe you were traumatized."

But, what makes you forget who you are? Why would I allow myself to be kidnapped by two adult strangers? Every time I attempt to recall the incident, the video plays in my mind and clouds the actual event. I've watched the clip so many times now, it's become part of me—a memory spun from a planted suggestion. What circumstances led a small child to rummage for food in the trash is anyone's guess. Was I lost or abandoned? Am I a runaway? Was I escaping from someone or something? The red Converse shoes and the Maine Black Bears sweatshirt—was I wearing them because I like bears, or because I'm connected to the area? Am I an East Coast girl?

Some days I drive myself crazy, but Kaleb's always ready to listen to my latest wild theory and help rationalize the situation. He cuddles me and kisses my head.

"I love you, Bear."

He tosses his book to the floor. "I love you bare, let me undress you."

Kaleb successfully distracts me for an hour, and leaves my body exhausted and relaxed, but my mind won't rest. There are so many puzzles to solve.

When? Where? Why? The questions won't stop and the answers don't come. Whatever the circumstances surrounding my abduction, my fate was sealed by Mom's spur-of-the-moment decision to keep me. They could've changed their minds a few days later and left me somewhere safe, like a hospital or library for someone to find. Then again, even though I was only five, I might've remembered incriminating details and led authorities back to my kidnappers.

I came with a no-refund policy—all sales are final. I might've been an impulse buy, but they couldn't return me. I was purchased "as is"—no refunds.

I roll onto my side and my eyes pool with emotion as I gaze at Kaleb sleeping. The initial anger I felt for Ray and Michelle diminishes considerably and I know, in time, I will forgive them for the simple fact that, without their rude intervention, I never would have met Kaleb.

Forgiving Ray is easy, but recalling what Michelle put me through still riles me. It plucks at the strand of residual anger stretching back to my childhood.

I don't remember my birth family, but I do remember the pain of losing my teddy bear. Unable to express my childish grief, I built a bonfire of hate and stuck Michelle on top. I'd hidden my bear and, according to "Mom," we couldn't look for him because it was dark and dangerous outside, and wild animals lay in wait behind every tree, ready to attack. We couldn't wait until morning either, because overnight parking wasn't permitted, and the park ranger would lock us up in jail if we didn't leave immediately.

Mom thrust a horrid plastic doll into my hands. I cried.

If Raychelle were alive, they never would've taken me. Their irrational and impulsive actions with no regard for the consequences were a direct result of the insurmountable grief and suffering brought on by the loss of their only child.

What if it wasn't them who'd found me? What if it had been a child molester? I could've been murdered or worse. I was never abused, and the only time Mom ever struck me was when I accidently reminded her of what she'd done. I recall the times Pops peered at me over the top of his glasses—was he considering the repercussions of discovery. Was he harboring regrets or was he proud of the way everything turned out?

Pops provided me with the financial support required for an excellent education, and left me debt free. Now, after the sale of Oak Tree Place and their other assets, I'm considered wealthy and have no necessity to work for the foreseeable future.

Our family's daily existence was perpetually overshadowed by the unspoken fear of discovery. My parents' paranoid concern for my safety and wellbeing now makes sense, as does our reclusive lifestyle and long periods of silence. In hindsight, I realize my parents' apathy stemmed from their relentless burden of profound sadness. I hope I wasn't too much of a disappointment. If I'd known I was meant to ease their loss, maybe I would've behaved better and been a little kinder.

I roll onto my back and look at the sky. What about me, though? Children don't just appear out of thin air? Why was nobody looking for me? Maybe they'd given up and assumed I was one of the hundreds—thousands—who go missing every year without a trace.

What about my birth mother? I rub my belly. This is what disturbs me most—is my natural mother still looking? Still hoping to find me? Is there a distraught and broken woman out there, who's trapped in time by an event that happened so long ago? Her life in limbo, yearning for the truth surrounding the disappearance of her daughter. She might've given up hope or might relive the day I disappeared on a perpetual loop, enduring the daily torture of not knowing what befell her child. As I carry on with my new life, I need reassurance my selfish secret isn't causing someone—my mother—unnecessary suffering. I never think about a father, but I must have one of those, too. I might have brothers, sisters, and grandparents, but my thoughts always focus on my birth mother.

Tears leak out. Kaleb's hand appears from nowhere to smooth them away.

"Whatever you're worrying about, my love, leave it be, let it rest."

But, I can't. I scratch the scab, tear it off, and reopen the wound. I refuse to let it heal.

Raychelle's Reflection

27. Mystery Tour

Over breakfast in the hotel restaurant, Kaleb produces a dog-eared roadmap.

"We can take The Lost Highway 58 to Bakersfield." His finger traverses the route. "Then onto Barstow. I need to swing by Vegas at some point, I've got some business to attend to, but I don't mind if we do it before or after Sedona."

I stab a potato and circle my plate while I decide what's worse; getting the visit over and done with, or prolonging the agony. "Can we do Sedona first?"

"Sure. Okay, from Barstow we'll pick up the forty all the way to Flagstaff, and Sedona's about thirty miles south of there. Sound good?"

I stick the potato in my mouth. Yesterday's caffeine-fueled enthusiasm is dwindling. Today, a fog of dread clouds my mind and makes me question whether unraveling my past is such a good idea. My stomach knots and I put my fork down.

Kaleb's gaze shifts from my face to my country fried potatoes and back. "So, are you going to finish those, or are you done?"

"You can have the omelet, too." I shunt the plate in his direction. He picks up the hot sauce and smothers everything in chili. I rub my belly and he smirks. "Potatoes good?" I ask, and he nods his approval.

Bombarded by all these new experiences, Santa Monica feels like a lifetime away, until sudden flashbacks strike like remnants from a nightmare. My skin emits an anxious glow and I catch my breath, but knowing I need never return to my former life releases a sigh.

Having previously concluded Sedona is the most likely abduction site, we collate the evidence, prepare notes, and vow to steer clear of the authorities. Examining the possibilities and anticipating the outcome leaves me exhausted.

"One more cup of coffee for the road," Kaleb says.

I bite my lip. His hand clamps my knee. "Everything will be okay, my love."

I wish I shared his optimism. I swallow the coffee and look out to sea, into the vast nothingness. I wonder how Raychelle's getting along, and whether she's met up with her parents yet.

A few miles into our journey, fear and trepidation take hold and my imagination conjures distressing scenarios. Remembering the San Diego trip and the disturbing evidence we unearthed produces the unpleasant sensation of invisible hands gouging my insides.

Kaleb talks in-depth about the geology along the way. "We're crossing the White Wolf fault, the epicenter of a 7.7 magnitude earthquake in 1952."

"Let's hope we aren't about to have another."

He laughs. "We should be coming up to the Tehachapi Loop pretty soon."

"The what?"

"Tehachapi Loop—a three-quarter-mile railroad track with a two-percent grade, rises seventy-seven feet and crosses over itself. The tunnel was constructed in the 1870s and the track loops around a granite hill to overcome the steep terrain. A train over four-thousand feet long can pass over itself."

"How do you know all this?"

"Books."

We pull off the road and take a short detour to admire this incredible feat of engineering that proves no obstacle is insurmountable.

After lunch in Tehachapi, we carry on to Barstow, where we will spend the night.

Kaleb's choice of lodgings is driven by the Bluebird Motel's close proximity to a seedy looking bar called Raven Mad Stoned Crow. Their tacos are surprisingly good and their margaritas incredibly strong. Fortunately, our bed is within a short staggering distance.

"Can I persuade you to go to Las Vegas first?" Kaleb asks.

"Is it important?"

"Yes and no," he says with a smirk. "No, it doesn't matter, Vegas can wait. I'm just being selfish."

ಬ ♈ ಬ

Feeling slightly hungover, we set off for Lake Havasu City—another minor detour to see London's famous bridge, transported all the way to the Arizona desert from London, England.

Strolling across the historic structure, I can't help but think of Michelle, and wonder why she was so obsessed with all things English. I guess I'll never know.

By the waterfront, we enjoy traditional English fish and chips, served up with some strange green delicacy called mushy peas that look like guacamole. They get a thumbs up from Kaleb, but I'm not so sure.

The next stop is Flagstaff, and I'm aware I'm becoming increasingly tense as our ultimate destination approaches. Tomorrow, we'll be in Sedona.

ಬ ♈ ಬ

Time is strange when you travel. It seems to stretch. What happened a few days ago seems like a lifetime ago. One day, I was Raychelle Carter living in Santa Monica, and now I'm a homeless girl-on-the-road traveling with her man. Where we'll end up who can tell.

After breakfast, we fuel up in Flagstaff. Kaleb's itching to visit Walnut Canyon and the ruined cliff dwellings built by the *Sinagua* people, but I'm too anxious to suffer any more delays. "It's really close," Kaleb says. "It won't take long."

I take a deep breath. "Okay, if you insist."

He's right, it's not far, and the setting is beautiful. Descending the steep steps at this moderately high altitude, I can't help but think the climb back up will be quite a challenge. The visit is a thrilling distraction, and we both agree living in these sheltered cliff dwellings would afford beautiful views all year round.

However, we cannot put off visiting Sedona any longer. We drive back towards Flagstaff, find road signs for 89A, and locate the highway entrance.

Kaleb reaches for my hand and brings it to his lips. "Okay, my love?"

Up ahead, I notice a Coconino County Sheriff's cruiser blocking the highway to halt our progress. A flash of panic has me believing it's a roadblock set up to apprehend us.

Kaleb doesn't share my paranoia. He lowers his window and asks the sheriff's deputy, "What's up?"

"A minor rock fall has temporarily closed the road."

"For how long?"

"Can't say. Where you heading?"

"Sedona."

The deputy pokes the brim of his hat and scratches his forehead. "If you want an alternative, get on the I-17 South and look out for State Route 179. It'll probably put another thirty miles on your journey, but clearing this might take a while."

I construe the hold-up as a sign, a warning that we should venture no farther. My anxiety ratchets up another notch.

Kaleb seems oblivious. "I love these pine forests."

He follows the officer's directions and connects with the I-17 southbound. Thirty minutes later, Kaleb turns onto highway 179, and follows the road's seductive curves through stunning scenery to the heart of Sedona's sinister allure. With her rocky red body, she appears irresistible in the blazing sun, and it's easy to understand why folk are captivated by her mystical beauty. Her welcome maybe as friendly as a homecoming fire, but don't be fooled, fire is a destructive and dangerous element.

Kaleb, with his eyes focused on the road, rummages in the door's side pocket. He produces *Sedona: Vortex City*, and hands me Pops' old book. Inside are wild accounts of alien visitors attracted to the place by electromagnetic energy emanating from living rocks.

Restaurants, galleries, and hotels line the highway and, as the sun goes down, fairy lights magically appear to illuminate the trees and buildings.

Driving through town, Kaleb tells me, "Look out for Howling Wolf Lodge." He made the reservation yesterday, enticed by the name, rustic décor, and promise of spectacular sunrises and sunsets from every cabin.

Kaleb pulls into *"Registration Only"* parking and dashes inside to collect our key—we don't want to miss the sunset. We took longer than expected at Walnut Canyon and the rock fall caused further delay.

Moonstone Cabin. Kaleb immediately flings open the French doors and we admire the incredible view. The low-angled sun sets the rock face ablaze, and the moon peeks over the mountain, ready to show its face once the sun has disappeared.

Kaleb joins me on the bed just in time to witness the setting sun turn the red rocks black. He goes down with the sun taking my mind and body with him.

৩ ϒ ৪

After breakfast, we follow the trail along Oak Creek and climb to the top of Lookout Mountain—the obvious place to begin our search. Kaleb sits atop a giant red rock, still and silent. I sit on my own solitary boulder, scan the landscape, and take a deep breath and a hard look. Nothing about this place appears or feels familiar though. I lie on the rock with a palm and cheek pressed against warm sandstone, desperate to sense a connection with the place, but nothing gives. Maybe I'll stumble across a vortex and discover a passage leading back to my previous existence.

We rule out contacting the local police in case our overt enquiries arouse suspicion. We decide, instead, to commence our research at the local library.

If the date on Pops' film is to be believed, Raychelle's reincarnation occurred in or around Sedona at the end of August 1986. We use this as our start date and trawl through the local archives—a missing child would surely make headline news. Kaleb changes tack and scours the Internet for child abductions and missing person databases. Because I'm paranoid, I demonstrate how to delete the search history. For all I know, Sedona might be my home town, and the woman reading in the corner might be my mother.

No reports of missing children in the area come to light.

We take a lunch break on the grass outside, and eat smoked salmon and avocado sandwiches purchased from the café close by. As I munch, my eyes roam back and forth across the stunning scenery.

"How could I forget living here? There's nothing subtle about these incredible views, they'd surely leave an indelible image on a child's mind... even if I was only five years old." Kaleb stares at me with a frown. "What are you thinking?"

"You don't want to know."

"Tell me."

He takes a deep breath and shifts his gaze to the landscape.

"You must understand, I often see things through my own childhood prism, and the view is often dark and distorted." He pauses. "Maybe you were held captive, and escaped."

I put my sandwich down, unable to eat until the lump in my throat disappears. Kaleb takes my hand and gently turns it over. He reexamines the mark on the heel of my palm. "What are you thinking?"

"Shackles."

I pull my hand away, hold it against my belly, and cover the scar with my other hand.

Back inside the library, we widen our search area to include Flagstaff, the large town to the north of us, and broaden our criteria to include the whole of July, August, and September. We know Raychelle died June 16th, and I don't remember another little girl, so we reason my abduction must've occurred after this date, but prior to moving into Oak Tree Place in early September.

Still, no sign.

"It must've happened here," Kaleb insists. "The footage of *you* is the final scene in a sequence of places situated in this locale."

I can't fault his logic, but there are no reports of any young girls disappearing during the summer of '86. We read accounts of strange occurrences in the area—naked folk dancing around and performing pagan rituals, spaceship sightings, an alien abduction, and a hiker found safe after wandering lost for three days. I don't know what we're expecting to find, but our search is fruitless. Frustration brings me to bang a fist on the table, and immediately regretting the attention I receive from other library patrons. The answer feels close enough to touch, but still eludes us.

Exhausted and bug-eyed after our unproductive search, we dine out on burritos and margaritas at a Mexican restaurant near Howling Wolf. We forego dessert and arrive back at our lodgings in time to catch another spectacular sunset. Kaleb reaches for the whiskey, but I abstain.

Kaleb swishes the amber liquid around his glass. "Flagstaff might be a better option. A town that size will keep more extensive records—more local, old newspaper clippings."

Over breakfast, we run through our current theories, always hoping a new angle might come to light. At nine we set off for Flagstaff, and take the twisty picturesque route through Oak Creek Canyon. We round another treacherous hairpin bend and pass a number of roadside crosses, memorializing loved ones lost in tragic accidents.

I massage my throat. "I feel sick."

"Is it my driving?"

With each sharp bend my queasiness increases, and I break into a cold sweat. I picture fruit salad curdling with yogurt and coffee inside my stomach, and use my hand to massage the image away. Kaleb glances at me.

"Don't look at me!" I snap. "Keep your eyes on the road!"

He stares all the more.

"Sorry, I didn't mean to yell." Guilt and self-loathing add to my heightened emotional state. I take slow deep breaths and regain my composure. Finally, we reach the summit and Kaleb, sensing I need a rest, follows the sign indicating "Scenic Overlook Parking."

We pull in and park. Kaleb rubs my thigh. "You'll be fine, my love." He unfastens his seatbelt and reaches over. "Come here. You're stressed, there's a lot going on at the moment."

Ten minutes later, we exit the truck and stroll along a row of stalls displaying American Indian crafts. I stop and admire the jewelry on display. A pair of silver feather earrings inlaid with turquoise and spiny oyster catch my eye. At the end of the row we find the scenic view—a far-reaching vista sweeping deep into a tree-lined canyon.

Visible between the pine-trees are sections of the winding road we just traversed. Overcome by dizziness, I grab the wall.

"Vertigo?" Kaleb asks.

"No, I feel a bit weird."

"I love feeling weird," he says, and puts his hands under my shirt and strokes my skin. He kisses my ear. "Let me buy you those earrings."

We stroll back towards the stalls and discover coach-loads of tourists have descended upon the scene. I can't face battling through the crowd, and I'm not certain I can remember the exact stall either, so we continue on our way to Flagstaff.

When we arrive at the library I let Kaleb do the talking. He has a talent for charming people with his manufactured, but plausible stories. The librarian on the reception desk smiles and recommends we look at the *Arizona Daily Sun*. She escorts us to the microfiche storage unit, explains the index system, and gives a brief demonstration on how to operate the equipment.

"If you need me, you know where to find me."

We vow to remain open-minded regarding the circumstances surrounding my acquisition, but it's difficult viewing the event as anything other than abduction. We use August 29th, the date on Pops' film, as our starting point. After scrolling back through the papers to the 1st, we find no reports of any missing children or abductions, no indication a mass search was organized to look for a missing child, and no pleas from distraught parents imploring the public to help find their missing daughter. No one missed me, or no one cared enough to miss me. Kaleb's sinister suggestion from yesterday looms large. With a finger I trace the scar on my palm and try to imagine what might've caused it. Consumed with self-pity, my bottom lip quivers. I'm about to plummet, until I glance at Kaleb sitting beside me. He never complains or appeals for sympathy, even though I know his past still haunts him.

I'm disappointed with our lack of progress. All I want is a glimmer of hope, a tiny hint, but nothing. Hunger drives us to a local deli.

Between a mouthful of pastrami and gherkin, Kaleb reminds me, "We *must* be impartial. Despite Sedona's reputation for being a vortex site and a popular destination for intergalactic travelers, small children don't just materialize. The chances that you arrived by spaceship are slim. There *must* be a clue in the papers."

ೞ ♈ ಞ

On our third trip to the library in as many days, and after hours spent scanning old newspapers, I am *so* bored.

"Let's take a hike, I'm fed up with this."

"Where d'you wanna go? Here or Sedona?"

"Sedona."

We take our familiar route along highway 89A and, as we approach the scenic overlook, we see the parking lot is empty.

"Let's stop for a minute," Kaleb says, "and see if we can find those silver feather earrings."

The place is void of tourists, some stall holders are packing away their wares and folding up their tables. We find *the* stall, and I'm pleased to see my earrings are waiting for me. An elderly lady places the feathers in my lobes and smiles as she holds a mirror up for my inspection. I turn my head from side to side, and admire the intricate craftsmanship. She speaks little English, so we smile and laugh and nod.

Kaleb hands over a bunch of dollars.

"Beautiful," the lady says.

"She is," Kaleb replies, "and the earrings are pretty special, too."

We continue walking arm-in-arm along the path towards a wooden picnic table. Kaleb sits astride the bench, and I snuggle in close with my back against his chest. He draws my hair back, kisses my neck, and my body tingles. He rests his chin on my shoulder, and we share a view of the vendors packing up for the day. A rush of emotion overwhelms me, my skin prickles.

From his pocket, Kaleb produces *Sedona: Vortex City*. He reads aloud tales of strange and outrageous alien encounters. We dissect each claim, examine the facts, and dismiss most as pure fantasy.

Something in the undergrowth catches Kaleb's eye. "I spy a snake."

Kaleb disentangles himself from me and sets off to investigate. I draw my knees up and rest my feet on the bench. He moves cautiously through the long grass and reaches down. I envision him grabbing a slippery viper, and flinch. He strides back towards me, laughing, wearing a child's pink plastic princess tiara complete with fake jewels. I remove my phone from my pocket and attempt to take a photo, but I'm unsuccessful. I'm quaking too much with laughter. Kaleb snatches the camera, but I squirm and resist. He tickles me. I squeal. In my feeble state, he wrestles me into submission with one hand.

"For my beautiful princess." He crowns me with the tiara.

He stands back, and I dutifully pout and pose for my picture. I'm weak with laughter, a sensation that's eluded me for quite some time. Side-by-side we giggle at the images on the screen, until I notice something missing.

I pinch my earlobes and realize I've lost an earring in the tussle. Luckily, I spot it lying under the picnic bench, but my arms aren't long enough to reach, so I go head first through the gap and end up on all fours under the table. Kaleb's howling now, and clicks away, taking shots of me stuck inside my little doggy kennel. I reattach my jewelry and search for the easiest way out. Looking through the inverted V of the table legs, my eyes lock onto the truncated tree directly ahead. I'm transfixed by the stump.

Invisible hands clamp my ears and muffle Kaleb's laughter. His mirth is replaced by blood pounding against my eardrums. I'm Alice falling down the rabbit hole, disappearing down the vortex. Head swirling, I clamber out from under the table and crawl on hands and knees through the dirt, towards the faerie door hidden in the tree stump.

I reach the bole and claw at dry vegetation accumulated around the base. I stick my hand through the portal and my fingers rake through grass and small stones. Frantically, I tear at the plant matter inside the cavity.

Where's Teddy, I know I left him here!

Kaleb's voice breaks the spell, "What the *fuck* are you doing? Have you totally lost it?"

Still dragging rotting leaves from the stump, I turn and sob. "This is where I left Teddy. I put Teddy in the tree to keep him safe."

I claw through the pile of vegetation, desperately searching for a scrap of evidence… and unearth a glimmer of hope. Amongst the debris, a beady brown-and-black glass eye twinkles. I drop the precious jewel, more valuable than a diamond, into my palm. Kaleb, sinks to his knees beside me, and the evidence stares him straight in the eye.

"I believe you, my love."

He places a hand behind my neck, draws me to him, and kisses my head. Kaleb attempts to hold my hand, but my fist is firmly clamped around my precious treasure.

Mystery Tour

28. Dead End

Following a restless night's sleep, today's journey into Flagstaff is no different than any other day. The skies are clear, but ominous clouds are billowing inside my head. As we pass the scenic overlook at the top of Oak Creek Canyon, Kaleb reaches over, runs his hand down my inner thigh, and squeezes my knee. I clench my fist and the glass button digs into my flesh.

"Now we know when and where the abduction happened," Kaleb says, "and we've a good idea why it happened, so the only remaining question is—what happened? What led up to this bizarre event? What were you doing here, alone?"

How will this end? I know it won't be happy, and at best it will be disappointing. My finger traces the mark on my palm, an injury I now know I sustained close to the time Michelle and Ray took me. The wound was fresh. In the video we saw Michelle clean it with water and a washcloth. Did I escape captivity? I hope Kaleb's words are not prophetic.

Inside the library, with a heightened sense of dread, we draw our chairs up to the microfiche machine and recommence our search for clues. We start from August 25th and work forward.

On Wednesday, August 27th, details of a horrific road accident near the top of Oak Creek Canyon, dominate the front page. The incident occurred about 8:20 p.m. Saturday, August 23rd, but information is slow to emerge. An SUV had left the road during a heavy monsoon storm and tumbled 200 feet into the canyon before bursting into flames.

Dead End

A credible eye witness, an off-duty firefighter, passed the vehicle minutes before the SUV slid over the edge. Both vehicles had slowed to negotiate a small landslide in the road and, even though the witness had right of way, he allowed the SUV and trailer to pass. As he waved at the passing motorist, he observed the vehicle's other occupants: two adults in the front—male and female—and three children in the back, one of whom appeared to be unrestrained and clambering over the backseat. Staring in his rearview mirror, he watched the vehicle swerve as it struggled to align behind him. At that point, the small trailer begin to fishtail. Seconds later, the trailer skidded over the edge, pulling the SUV with it.

The shocked firefighter pulled over and, exited his vehicle, ran to the broken guardrail, and peered into the canyon. For several seconds, he watched helplessly as the SUV teetered on a ledge. The earth beneath the trailer crumbled and a violent gust sent the vehicle plummeting farther. An explosion occurred, trees ignited, and the witness felt sure there would be no survivors. In the awful weather conditions, with no way down the steep cliff and through the fire, and unable to get a phone signal in the canyon, he drove several miles along treacherous roads to alert emergency services.

By the time rescue workers arrived on scene, already hampered by atrocious weather and darkness, they realized there was little they could do until daylight. The road was closed all day Sunday, causing major disruption, while crash-scene investigators examined the area and began the grim task of identifying those who had perished. Road safety engineers assessed the damage to the guardrail and geological surveyors examined the canyon walls for potential signs of further landslides.

Access to the burned-out vehicle was gained by abseiling. On the ground, the search party located and recovered the bodies of two adults. The rugged terrain added complexity to the task of removing the bodies. A more extensive search of the area was conducted to locate the missing children.

Subsequent days report on surveillance footage obtained from a gas station in Flagstaff one hour prior to the accident.

A white male of interest was seen at the pumps, filling up a gold-ash metallic Ford Escape. Inside the minimarket, a woman and three young children were recorded selecting items from the shelves.

From the gas station footage, and vehicle serial numbers retrieved from the wreckage, authorities reported their confidence in knowing who the victims were, but the bodies were badly burned. They stressed caution as they awaited positive identification by the medical examiner's office.

However, relatives of the deceased family had come forward and confirmed the Carlyon family from Portland, Maine, perished in the tragedy.

Friday's paper announces a memorial service for the Carlyon family to be held locally that Sunday at two in the afternoon at Red Rock Chapel. Each family member is described in detail:

Colin Edgar: Solar Engineer, BSc. Mechanical Engineering.
Erin Siobhan: Artist, BFA, Visual Arts.
Ryan Edgar: Student, Oaks Elementary School.
Bradley Colin: Student, Oaks Elementary School.
Taylar Louisa: Student, Acorn Kindergarten.

Embedded within the article is a professional group-photo of the family. Below the image, names and ages are ascribed to each individual: Colin, 42; Erin, 37; Ryan, 8; Bradley, 8; and Taylar, 4.

The photograph is described as recent, taken three months prior to the accident. I stare wide-eyed at the group of strangers, and focus on the only face I recognize—Teddy—my little brown bear, whose loss I still mourn. My hand tightens around the small glass bead and my fingernails cut into my palm.

I drag my eyes across the group of strangers and there *I* am, sitting between my twin brothers, wearing a benign smile and holding Teddy. The radiant adults, Colin and Erin, must be my parents.

Is it normal not to recognize your parents, to forget what they look like? I massage my tight throat, lean forward, and lower my head in case I faint. Kaleb, aware of my past physical reactions to shocking news, wedges a trash can between my knees as a precautionary measure and rubs my back.

The library assistant sneaks up and asks, "Everything, okay?" She's checking on us, alerted by my odd behavior.

"She's pregnant," Kaleb says.

Clearly lying, his false statement has the dual effect of sending the librarian away, and making the blood rush back to my head. I come up with my eyes wide open, and look at the little girl in the photo. So, *she* is the real me—Taylar Louisa Carlyon—and she is also dead. I am doubly dead. How many people die twice, but still live to tell the tale?

Taylar—*she* is who Pops addressed the night he passed away. He knew who I was. He spoke to Taylar. I thought he said Taylor but, in fact, it was Taylar. He was speaking to *me*, asking for *my* forgiveness. I assumed his request was the drug-induced ramblings of a dying man. But, he was making peace with himself and his god.

Weeks later, I asked Mom, "Who is Taylor?"

Mom, visibly agitated, claimed Taylor was her estranged sister. Liar.

The vigilant librarian stretches her neck, points her nose in the air, and views us with suspicion. "I'm not asking her for copies of this stuff," Kaleb says. "She's giving us the evil eye. I'll make notes."

He hurriedly scratches away in my notebook recording names, dates, locations, and the circumstances leading up to the accident. In his hurry to transcribe the facts, he abbreviates my real name, using only my initials. He shakes his head and sniggers as he writes *"TLC."*

"Coincidence," he declares, "but we all know darker forces are at play."

I now understand what drew me to him, why Truth, Lies, and Consequences resonated on his website, why The Last Chance Saloon felt familiar, and why any mention of Torment Loves Company sets my scalp tingling.

With his scribbling complete and our search history deleted, we stand, ready to leave. My head swims and, unsteady on my feet, I stumble. Kaleb slides his hand under my armpit and grips my breast to provide support. He steers us past the reception desk and winks at the librarian.

"Thanks for your help," he says.

She blushes and turns away, and Kaleb escorts me from the building.

Shockwaves reverberate throughout my body. My mind is a maelstrom, churning with snippets of information and fragmented memories. Everything is racing by in a confused muddle. I stagger towards a bench.

"You okay, my love?"

Clearly I'm not.

We crash down hard on the seat. I bury my face in Kaleb's chest. I'd crawl inside his shirt if I could. I'm so sick and tired of crying.

"You got your answer," Kaleb says. "Maybe not the one you wanted, or expected, but now you know the truth."

He leads me to the truck in a state of altered consciousness. The rapid chaotic traffic inside my brain is speeding, braking, driving on the wrong side of the road, jumping red lights, mowing down pedestrians, and hitting brick walls. I've reached a dead end. My dead end. I need a quiet parking lot, a place for contemplation where I can consider the implications of these latest revelations.

Should I come forward, declare my true identity, and face unimaginable intrusion into our lives. Or, should I keep quiet and carry on living the lie. I'd worried there might be a grieving mother somewhere holding onto a grain of hope her long-lost daughter might return one day. My conscience need not face this trial. My mother is dead. My father, too. And, my two brothers.

I wish I had a photo of them. I want to stare at their images until I recognize them.

"I was four when it happened, why can't I remember my early years?"

"You survived a traumatic accident, my love. You were young, alone in the elements for several days, and you may've suffered a brain injury."

I want to know when and where I was born, and where I used to live.

Back at the hotel, we use the computer in their business center, and I constantly check my back because I'm insanely paranoid about my true identity coming to light. Stepping forward would be hugely disruptive. My life would be minutely examined by intrusive police and news reporters, delivering untold misery, even though I've done nothing wrong. But, living the lie comes with an abundance of worries and legal implications. Will inheriting Mom's and Pops' estate be deemed unlawful? Will Mom's sister, whatever her name is, although I doubt it's Taylor, step forward and challenge my right to inherit? Are my qualifications valid? Is my driving license legal?

Whichever option I choose, both come with complications and serious consequences. Nor can I draw attention to Kaleb, not after what he's done.

We trawl the Internet for Colin Carlyon, and discover articles relating to the accident. My father was a solar power engineer, and the family was in the process of relocating from Portland, Maine, to Phoenix, Arizona. The cause of the accident was attributed to extreme weather conditions, resulting in slick roads and poor visibility. Additional speculation questions whether the small, but heavy, trailer in tow may have left the road and dragged the vehicle with it. The SUV was carrying a full tank of gas, and fuel for their camping stove, which also contributed to the intense fire.

The recovery team, hampered by inaccessible terrain and adverse weather conditions were unable to reach the site until the following day. Searchers located two badly burned adult bodies at the crash site, but there was no sign of the children. Wounds on those bodies provided clear evidence the site had been disturbed by wild animals, and investigators broadened their search area from the immediate vicinity. Over the next three days, the team recovered partial remains scattered over a wide area.

Dental records conclusively identified the two adults, but the coroner was unable to definitively identify all five individuals. Based on the garage surveillance footage, and reliable eye witness report moments before the incident, the authorities concluded all five members of the Carlyon family had perished in a tragic traffic accident.

Except one.

One, was flung from the vehicle and escaped the fiery inferno. She survived several days alone in a hostile environment, until a grief stricken couple—Ray and Michelle Carter from San Diego, California—discovered her rummaging for food in a trash can, at a "point of outstanding scenic beauty."

෴ ♈ ☙

Kaleb's right, I'm a water sign—Pisces, born March 7th, 1982. And I'm only twenty-one—a year younger than I believed.

We sit in bed, propped against sumptuous pillows, and Kaleb sweeps my hair from my face. His lips brush my ear. "You and me baby… we truly are, outlaws."

His take on my disturbing truth.

He strokes my skin and, even though I'm utterly exhausted, I want him.

He cups my face in his hands and kisses with hunger. He wants me. He pulls away, and I lose myself in his eyes.

"There's something I need to tell you." His words land like bombs. Dread courses through my veins. Dire situations flood my mind. I assume another Redfield claim owner has died.

His hand glides down my body and strokes my belly.

"Not now, Kaleb." I close my eyes. "Let it wait."

Dead End

29. Halloween Ball

I'm wasted and utterly exhausted. After the months of mental and physical strain, my body succumbs to fatigue.

"Where next, my love?" Kaleb asks.

"Somewhere dark and quiet. I want to rest and I want to hide."

"Las Vegas it is, then."

"Are you serious?"

"I've got some business I need to attend to, and it's not as crazy as it sounds. The massive hotels with enormous beds and mini-bars guarantee a good night's sleep and, with thousands of people milling around, it's the perfect place to hide."

☙ ♈ ❧

Today is Halloween, Kaleb's birthday.

These past few days, I've been promising him the world—whatever he wants. He needs little encouragement. He takes my words literally and introduces me to increasingly adventurous bedroom antics. By way of demonstration, he teaches me things I never knew existed, and adds new words to my vocabulary.

Yesterday, he left me crashed-out and sleeping, while he disappeared for a few hours to "sort stuff out." I didn't ask, but assumed it was band related.

While he was gone, I took the opportunity to arrange a birthday surprise, a champagne breakfast and, judging by the digital clock, it's due to arrive any moment now. I gently push Kaleb's hand from my belly and slide his arm away. A tiny pinprick of light visible through

Halloween Ball

the spyhole in the door guides me through the darkness as I tiptoe across the floor.

With my cheek pressed against the door, I position my eye over the concave lens, and get a wide-angle view of all the activity in the corridor outside. From the left, a porter approaches wheeling a trolley. *A tip*. Anticipating this moment, I left a ten dollar bill on the bathroom counter last night. Looking down, I discover I'm naked. I put the bathroom light on, grab a robe and the cash. I step back into our room as the man knocks on the door. I glance at Kaleb and witness his fugitive reflexes kick in as he springs upright in bed. I was hoping to receive the delivery without disturbing him, and add to the surprise. "It's okay, Bear, only room service."

Kaleb, grabs the sheet and conceals his immediate need. I open the door, tip the guy, and take possession of our breakfast. Instead of flowers, I opted for a carved pumpkin. It seemed appropriate since it is Halloween, and I specified a crow design, because they seem forever present in our lives at the moment. We have champagne on ice, a fruit platter, smoked salmon and scrambled eggs, and croissants.

"Wow, this is really special," Kaleb says. "Thank you, my love." He throws the sheet back. "Come here, I'm ready for my first gift of the day. I require urgent attention."

"I can see that, birthday boy, but you need to wait a moment."

I wheel the display bedside, lean towards him and deliver a kiss. "Happy birthday, Bear."

My robe falls open and he reaches between my legs.

"And I want you bare and on top of me right now."

"I wanted to surprise you."

"Oh yeah. Well, I've got a little surprise lined up for you, later on today."

"But it's not my birthday. What is it?"

"It won't be a surprise if I tell you."

I hoick the Moët & Chandon from the bucket and plant the ice cold bottle in Kaleb's lap. "Here, you open this while I fix your cake."

"Thank you, my love, that's positively chilled my ardor."

He fiddles with the foil and muselet, and I stick a solitary candle into a giant white-chocolate strawberry muffin. I reach for his Zippo, and make a clumsy attempt at rotating the wheel. Kaleb laughs as I light the candle, and even more so at my tuneless rendition of "Happy Birthday." He laughs so much, he struggles to snuff out the candle.

"Quick!" I say. "Close your eyes, blow it out, and make a wish. I'm worried about the smoke detector going off."

"Quick, blow on this," he says, and points south. "Make my wish come true."

"You haven't got the hang of this, have you? You're not meant to divulge your wish, *and* your eyes aren't closed."

Dutifully, he follows orders and blows the candle out. "My eyes are still closed," he announces. He clutches the neck of the champagne bottle with both hands, and shakes. His thumbs push against the cork. "How soon before my wish comes true?"

I don't respond—my mouth is full—his birthday wish, instantly granted. With perfect timing, the champagne stopper fires off the exact same moment he does. The second I raise my head I'm sprayed with champagne. Kaleb fills our glasses with what's left, and reaches for the fruit bowl.

He feeds me a chocolate dipped strawberry. He balances a large blueberry in the hollow at the base of my throat.

He peels a banana. "Let me demonstrate fun with fruit."

"Is there a name for this?"

"Sitophilia... lie down."

We surface an hour later.

Kaleb surveys the sheets. "The bed's a trifle messy."

I flush with embarrassment. Who would've guessed fruit and chocolate could create such shocking stains. Some stranger will come into our room now and be expected to clean up after us. Worse still, they'll probably share the details with other staff.

Acutely aware of the mess we've created and with panic evident in my voice. "What are we going to do?"

Kaleb howls with laughter. "You're priceless." He shakes his head. "What is the worst thing that can happen? They're going to charge us for additional cleaning, and possibly new sheets." He lifts the lid from the now-cold scrambled eggs and loads his plate with salmon. "Come and eat your breakfast."

Cold eggs don't appeal and I've just consumed a large amount of fruit. I eat a croissant and pick at the smoked salmon.

Halloween Ball

During our rest and refueling period, I suggest, "We should go out and celebrate."

Kaleb gets up and wanders over to the window. "I have something in mind."

"And, what might that be?"

He turns and gives me a mischievous look. "I told you… you're in for a big surprise."

He approaches, leans in for a kiss, and picks me up. He carries me to the shower, which further delays our departure.

℘ ♈ ℘

On our way to the elevator, Kaleb asks, "So, I can have anything I want?"

"Yes, *anything*."

Inside the confines of the elevator, he asks, "Have you got your driver's license with you?"

"Yes. What for?"

"ID. You look underage."

"For what?"

"Lots of things."

From his shirt pocket he brandishes a piece of paper. "Complimentary tickets. Our luxury suite entitles us to free entry to the hotel's Halloween Ball."

I'm puzzled, surprised he's interested in something like this, especially on his birthday. He usually avoids parties and opts for solitude.

"It'll be good," he says, "I promise. The freebie includes full-service costume hire, including hair and make-up."

My face morphs from skepticism to incredulity. "Are you serious?"

The lift door opens. "Let's get a cab and find out."

I'm convinced he's winding me up. "Where are we going?"

"Old-town Vegas. I've already reserved the werewolf outfit, and I envisage you as a red-hot Little Red Riding Hood."

I laugh uncontrollably. "You had me going for a moment, I thought you were serious."

We pull up outside Costa's Costumes and I sober up.

He squeezes my knee. "You're gonna love this." He holds my chin and kisses me.

He pays the cab driver and we step onto the sidewalk. Taking my hand, he leads me into the store, and uncertainty accompanies me all the way.

"Mr. Hausser," the assistant says. "Please, both of you, come this way."

We're escorted into different rooms and the transformation begins. I do exactly as the lady instructs. I: sit, stand, get undressed, close my eyes, get dressed, breathe in, and look in the mirror. With the transformation complete, I'm reminded of the time I dressed like a hooker and flirted with Rick's dad. I quickly banish the thought.

I emerge from the dressing room and I'm met with a howl of approval.

"Arrroooo," howls Mr. Wolf. Kaleb, barely recognizable in his lupine make-up steps forward, tongue dangling. "My perfect fairytale fetish fantasy. You're exactly what I envisioned, except you look even hotter in the flesh."

It takes a moment to fully appreciate Kaleb's metamorphosis, but his wolfish eyes are instantly recognizable—eager and hungry. He's extra hairy, his open shirt reveals a chest wig, and yellow-clawed furry hands protrude from big white billowy sleeves.

"You're very hairy."

He laughs. Tail between his legs, he looks very sexy in his wolf attire. He flicks a big furry ear with a big hairy paw—irresistible.

I step out into the shop and stand before a full-length gilt mirror to fully inspect myself. The too-small, white blouse is laced tightly across my cleavage, and a red satin corset worn over a red satin miniskirt, cinches my waist and holds everything in place. Kaleb stands behind and inserts his fingers down the back of the corset. "Not too tight, is it?"

Touched by his concern, I sit to test my limitations, and stand back up, a few inches taller than usual in my stiletto heels.

A red cloak, a small wicker basket, and black knee-high lace-up boots worn over white fishnet stockings completes my slutty outfit.

Kaleb's hands squeeze my laced-in waist. "My birthday. My fantasy. Whatever I want. Arrroooo."

I tweak his ear, poking out through his hair. "I love your furry ears."

He issues a warning growl.

Our street clothes get stuffed inside the rucksack he brought along. Fully kitted out, we parade down Fremont Street and turn some heads.

"Can I take your picture?" someone asks.

"Fuck off," Kaleb growls.

I flick his ear. "I adore your ears, Mr. Wolf. They're ever so cute."

"Don't call me cute." He bares his teeth and growls. "I'm going to eat you later."

"Promises, promises." I pull his tail. "You don't scare me, Mr. Wolf."

"Don't pull my tail, Miss Hood, it gets me very excited."

I hang on his arm and stroke his fur. "It's difficult, knowing where the man ends and the wolf begins."

"And I can't wait to show you."

"Where are we going?"

He sniggers but gives nothing away. "You'll find out soon enough." He leads me down side streets to an anonymous building and we stand on stone steps. "I've come up with the perfect name for you."

"Will I like it?"

"I hope so. I'll be upset if you don't and we don't want that do we? Not on my birthday. And, you did promise whatever, whenever, wherever, I wanted."

"Okay, let's hear it." I playfully cup my ears with my hands.

"Mrs. Hausser."

Eyes wide, I gasp in shock.

He grips my face in his big hairy hands. "I know you didn't mention whoever, but there's a wolf at your door, Miss Red, and he wants to come in. Tell me, do you like your new name?" He kisses my lips and, with his thumbs resting snugly against the curve of my throat, he applies gentle persuasion. "If you don't approve, I'll break your neck and suck the flesh from your bones. One way or another, I'll have you, either for dinner or for my wife. You decide."

I succumb to his threat. "I love it." My eyes, pool with emotion—with love for him. "And, I love you."

He holds my head. "I want to fuck you so bad. But, first, we must get married."

He's unwittingly lured me to Clark County Marriage License Bureau. Entering the foyer, we mill around with other couples and search for an empty wooden cubicle in which to complete our questionnaires. We squeeze into the tight space and reach for the pencils attached by string—loss-prevention precaution—and scribble our vital details onto the license application.

I pause before writing my name.

"Whoever you are," he reassures me, "I want you."

"I love you so much."

He kisses me. "I'm impatient for you to prove it."

With our license in his paw, we take a taxi back to our hotel. He drags me willingly to the wedding chapel, where Dracula's expecting us.

The Vampire greets us at the entrance with gleaming bloodstained teeth. "The perfect night for a bite." His arms rise up to reveal the cape's scarlet lining and, with a dramatic sweeping gesture, he points. "Let us proceed to the sacrificial altar."

"One moment," Kaleb says. "Everything's been pre-arranged, apart from witnesses." Morticia and Gomez stroll by on their way to the ball and Kaleb requests the pleasure of their company. "It won't take a moment," he promises.

We walk up the aisle, past empty pews draped in black satin fabric and decorated with blood-red roses. "So this is what you were planning. How did you know I'd agree?"

"I know you better than you know yourself, Miss Red. I know something else about you too... I'll tell you later."

Standing at the altar, surrounded by bats and candles and scarlet roses, Count Dracula performs the rites. "I now pronounce you... wolf and victim. The wolf may now bite his bride." He does, he ravishes my neck and paws my body. The Addams Family members whistle and applaud, and wave goodbye as they head to the Halloween Ball.

"I love you so much, I'm so fucking happy."

"*Language,* Miss Hood!"

"I'm Mrs. Hausser now."

"That's no excuse to cuss like your husband. We need to make this official. We must go to our room *now* and perform indecent acts."

Halloween Ball

"What about the party?"

"What about it? I never intended going, it was merely a ploy to get you into your wedding gown."

We rush to the elevator. The doors close. "What big hands you have, Mr. Wolf."

"All the better to maul you with."

Ping. We exit on the twenty-seventh floor. "What big teeth you have, Mr. Wolf."

He nips my neck. "All the better to eat you with."

"What big feet you have, Mr. Wolf." I playfully escape his clutches.

"All the better to chase you with."

I squeal as he pins me against our hotel door. I reach between his legs. "What a big cock you have, Mr. Wolf."

"All the better to fuck you with."

He inserts the key, and we topple into the room. The door emphatically slams behind us. He pulls his boots and breeches off, frantic with lust.

I reach to untie my boots. "Keep them on," he orders.

"I'll wreck the mattress."

He pulls the padded bench away from the foot of our bed, positions it by the window and sits.

"I'm ravenous, Miss Red. What's in your basket?"

"Nothing."

"What are you hiding in your blouse, Miss Red?" I approach and he pulls the inviting tie. My breasts spill out, allowing him access to both nipples.

"Show me what you're hiding under your little red skirt, Miss Red?" With one dexterous finger he peels away my panties, and I step out of them.

"Love, honor, and obey," he reminds me. "Stand over me." He lies back on the bench, reaches for my hands and guides me into place. I straddle him. The flesh of my thighs brushes the stubble on his cheeks. He clenches my buttocks, lowers me down and releases his tongue. Very soon, I'm breathless and weak and about to collapse on his face.

"You can sit, now," he tells me.

I stagger a few steps backwards and sink down slowly onto my favorite perch. His wicked eyes never leave mine. "You're the best porn star, ever, my love."

"You inspire me."

I buck up and down, adjust my position, and settle into my comfort zone and perfect rhythm.

"You're much better at riding at wolves than horses, Miss Red."

Halloween Ball

30. Las Vegas, Baby

Half asleep, I roll my head on the pillow and discover my smirking husband, lying beside me. Gently, he peels my hand from his chest, rests my palm across his mouth, and inhales the combined scent of "us." I respond and stroke his beard. He needs little encouragement. In a flash, he grabs my wrists and straddles my body.

"You want some more?" he asks.

"Mmm." Barely conscious, I agree I want more of him.

He trails slow kisses down my body and his hands glide over my swollen stomach. "Please ignore my Vegas buffet belly," I say. "I've been over indulging—too many desserts."

"Cheesecake and chocolate ice cream are innocent."

"Are you blaming the breakfast doughnuts?"

He kisses the gentle dome and presses an ear against the bulge.

"What *are* you doing?"

"Listening."

"To what?"

"To our little puppy."

I jerk up so quickly we crack heads, and I swear I see stars. "What are you saying?"

He rubs his forehead. "Raych, you're so out of touch with your body, and I'm so in touch with it."

"What?" I stare down at my middle. Realization begins to dawn. "How long have you known?"

"A few weeks."

"Why didn't you tell me?"

"I've been trying, but you've not been listening."

"When?"

"I've mentioned it a few times. I was expecting you to take the hint. It is *your* body, you're meant to make the surprise announcement. But, I'm impatient... I can't wait any longer. I want to be involved right from the start."

I wriggle free, leap out of bed, and adopt various poses in the full-length mirror. "I can't believe you didn't tell me."

"I can't believe you didn't realize."

"How did it happen?"

"Come back to bed and I'll demonstrate."

"We took precautions."

"We did, my love, but there's no accounting for lust, especially on my part. Trusting me to do the "right thing" was your big mistake—you ought to know better. All those moments of unguarded passion have paid off. Whether a ruptured condom is to blame or careless withdrawal on my part I can't say, but who cares, I got what I came for." He lies back and smirks.

"You did this on purpose?"

"*We* were careless, but I'm very happy with the outcome. You'll come around, my love, once you get over the shock."

ഗ ϒ ର

"I don't know anything about raising children," I say.

"Luckily, I'm an expert on the subject."

I look at him, doe-eyed and hopeful. He laughs. "You're so innocent, my love. I *love* your gullibility."

Watching me deal with my new reality amuses him—married and expectant mother, in less than a day. I wander around, wide-eyed, and check my profile in every reflective surface. I look at him and he grins. I'm tired and fidgety. He offers me a glass of champagne.

"I can't drink. I'm pregnant."

"The kid has my genes, he'll thank you."

I pause before accepting the crystal. "How do you know... it's a boy?"

"I just do."

I look at myself in the bathroom mirror—pregnant and terrified. To make matters worse, Kaleb's ecstatic about the imminent birth of our *"first* son." He's transformed, lifted, and outrageously optimistic about the future.

I don't have the heart or courage to air my hideous doubts and crush Kaleb's dreams. Instead, I weep alone and blame my blues on hormones. Less than a day into our marriage, he's forced me to acknowledge I'm carrying a baby—a boy he insists.

"How do you know it's a boy?" I'd asked, but what I really wanted to ask was, "How do you know the child is yours?"

I've suppressed any memories from the day Ken Hunter ambushed me, stripped me, and forced me into the bath tub. I don't believe he went that far—I stroke my belly—but I can't be sure. I stress about my stress hormones doing untold harm to my unborn child. My anxiety escalates and explodes into a pitiful wail. Kaleb pushes the door open and barges into the bathroom.

"Hey, come here, my love. You mustn't cry alone." He drops to his knees, caresses my belly, and kisses my forehead. "Once junior arrives, your hormones will regulate."

I pull in a giant jagged breath and spew out my terrifying fear. "What if it's not yours?"

Kaleb grips my shoulders and holds me at arms-length. His nostrils flare. With heavy breath and a face like thunder, he demands, *"Why* wouldn't it be mine?" With less control he yells, "Of course the baby is fucking mine!"

His temper leaves no room for doubt and his fury incites more tears. I bury my face in my hands.

Gently, he pries my fingers away. "I'm sorry, my love, I didn't mean to shout."

"I can't remember what *he* did to me," I stammer.

It takes a moment for Kaleb to register the source of my doubt.

"Raych, stop torturing yourself, he didn't go there. When I found you, I thoroughly examined every inch of your body. Believe me, if I'd detected the slightest evidence of rape, he'd be dead. And, his end would've been excruciatingly painful, extremely slow, and shockingly nasty.

"He's lucky to find himself in a wheelchair. I wasn't banking on the sudden appearance of a dedicated rescue team and expert

Las Vegas, Baby

surgeons. At least he's paralyzed from the waist down, so there's no chance he'll come near you again."

Kaleb's confession is mildly reassuring, and his firm belief the child is ours, more so. I mustn't let doubt cast a shadow over my pregnancy. My hands investigate my belly, and I still can't believe what's going on underneath my skin, inside my body— outside of my control.

I take a deep breath, push aside my immediate worry, and scan the horizon for a brighter future. My mind races, I envisage a curious child enquiring about their grandparents. What will I say? How will I explain? Having no ready answer, will I lie to my child? No. My life is built on a foundation of painful lies. But, how can I explain my existence? I will cross that bridge when I come to it, but not alone, with Kaleb by my side.

"We need a proper home. I need to register with a doctor. We need to be settled. I shouldn't be drinking."

"Raych, I've never witnessed anyone manufacture worries on such a grand scale. Relax."

His terms of reassurance play on a perpetual loop. "Relax, chill, calm down, and fuck it." He has answers for all my woes.

"Where will we live?"

"Where do you want to live, my love?"

"I don't know, but wherever we end up, I want a new name for my new life."

A simple and understandable request. I strain against invisible ropes that tether me to the past, to Raychelle and Taylar both dead to the world, and who no longer exist. I want to cut all ties with the past, shed my old skin and start anew. I want to be free and alive, discover who I really am, without the weight of the past dragging me down.

"Okay, Mrs. Hausser, what shall I call you? Wife, Wifey, Waif?"

I smile and shake my head. "You're not taking me seriously."

"My Love. I will call you My Love, because you are. You've given me a life I never imagined or ever thought possible, and for a fleeting moment, you make me forget I'm a cynical bastard."

"You'll need to come up with something better than that. I can't have everyone calling me, My Love. Why are you smiling?"

"Maybe, I'll call you Red. The image of Little Red Riding Hood riding me like a porn star is seared into my mind forever."

Red, is now the call sign he uses to alert me to his urgent and all-consuming desire.

"Red." He pats the bed. "My scarlet woman, my scarlet harlot, my Red."

I respond, using my name for him. "Bear." The force of our attraction draws me to him.

"Bare, that's how I want you." He takes my hands and drags me onto his body.

ഔ ♈ ☙

Hours later, while listening to Las Vegas Soft Rock radio, I take a shower. Carly Simon intones "You're So Vain," and I sing my heart out, too. I rinse shampoo from my hair and Kaleb steps under the spray to assist.

He sings along and teases. "Hey Carly, you're not thinking about me are you, while you're singing those words?"

The name sticks for a while, and I find I quite like it. Until he says, "I love you, Carl," and suddenly Carly is hugely inappropriate.

"It's a shame Carly didn't work out, I like the sound." He taps his fingers and mutters under his breath. "Come to bed, my love, and inspire me."

"Harley," he gasps, as we share an orgasm.

Minutes later when I've recovered, I ask, "What did you just call me?"

"Harley."

"Should I be offended?"

"No, my love. It just came to me as I was enjoying the ride of my life. I've always wanted a Harley. Iconic Americana, superb handling, exceptional performance, magnificent bodywork, excellent traction, guaranteed satisfaction, envy of most dudes, and every time I get my leg over, I know I'm in for an exhilarating ride."

"I'm not sure I like the connotations of being compared with a motorcycle, but I guess it's better than being stuck with the name of a drowning victim, or someone burned to death in a car wreck and dismembered by wild animals."

He smirks. "May I introduce Harley Hausser, hot housewife, special limited-edition classic, custom built, and designed with one skilled rider in mind?"

We lie in bed watching The Weather Channel and I'm still thinking about where the new me—where Harley—would like to live. Colorado seems nice, but an early winter storm scooting west to east through the northern states has dropped a ton of snow across the Rockies and removes several options from my consideration. "I want to be warm."

Kaleb wraps his arms around me. "Are you cold?"

"No, I was thinking about where to live and I want to be somewhere warm."

"Unfortunately, California is out of bounds, my love—close proximity to various crime scenes."

"Florida?"

He laughs. "You gotta be kidding."

"Texas?"

"No, but you're getting warmer."

"New Mexico?"

He scratches his chin, before declaring, "Harsh winters."

"Arizona?"

His lip curls. "It's a possibility. We should check it out, it's relatively close. North Scottsdale is trendy—might make your transition from California less painful."

He hasn't mentioned Weeping Creek for a while, but if the search history on my computer is anything to go by, he remains fascinated with the place and its apparent deadly curse. I catch sight of the deeds for Redfield Mine sitting on his nightstand. I'm curious to know if anyone else on the list of past claim owners has died, recently, but I'm loathe to ask.

The End...
for now.

"Wow... unbelievable."

"Without facts, there is no fiction."—*Kaleb Angel Hausser*

If you enjoyed this book,
please consider posting a review on
Cheryl Cocroft's book page
on Amazon.com, or Amazon.co.uk.

Acknowledgments

Thank you to Ann Narcisian Videan. Her dedication and insight are invaluable and, through her skills and experience, she coaxes the best possible story.

About the Author

Cheryl Cocroft, born and educated in Altrincham, England, lived and worked in London for twenty-five years until she moved to Cave Creek, Arizona. Usually steeped in numbers, she debuted *Spokane Words*, her first novel in the Twisted Tales from Luna's Attic series, in 2017. When she's not writing, you can find her hiking trails and taking photos of the landscape, the weather, and wildlife.

Future Works in the Luna's Attic Series

Weeping Creek, Book 3

Pregnant with their first child, Harley and Kaleb settle down in Weeping Creek, a small town north of Phoenix, Arizona. They are drawn there initially by Kaleb's curiosity after he finds himself in possession of the deeds for Redfield Mine. The property they choose to call home is the subject of a bitter family feud, and comes with a covenant, a bloody history, and a curse. Some of the locals make it clear they are not welcome.

When Harley finds herself in a terrible predicament, she can't share her fears with Kaleb, because she's scared of what he might do. Another secret to add to family's stockpile.

Will the Haussers satisfy the covenant and avoid the curse as this tale continues to twist?

Monsoon Love, Book 4

The Haussers' two boys, Declan and Cavon, are now teenagers, advanced for their years, and both exhibiting different, but enhanced, versions of their father's characteristics.

Lila Blue blows into town, bringing with her all the mayhem associated with a monsoon storm. Tornado survivor, and granddaughter of local saloon owner Claude Blue, she leaves her mark on many hearts.

When Cavon, the wildly eccentric second son, disappears amid shocking circumstances, the family stays silent. Unfinished business from California and buried secrets surface. The covenant threatens the loss of their home and, steeped in personal crises, the curse may well destroy their family.

Will unconventional solutions resolve the Haussers' problems in this latest twisted tale?